HEALING THE VISCOUNT'S HEART

Book 3 of The Hope Clinic

TRISHA MESSMER

Copyright © 2021 Trisha Messmer
All rights reserved.
ISBN-13: 979-8498130095
Cover design by: J.X. Duran
Cover image by: Period Images

All rights reserved by author. This story may not be transmitted, stored, or performed without written consent from the author. This includes, but not limited to, physical publications, electronic formats, audio books, and dramatic readings.

This is a work of fiction. Names, characters, places, and incidents are either the product of the author's imagination or are used fictitiously. Any resemblance to actual persons, living or dead, events, or locales is entirely coincidental.

Like free stuff? Check the back of the book to find out how to get a free book!

DEDICATION

To all the nerdy girls looking for their nerdy guy.

CONTENTS

ACKNOWLEDGMENTS

Where to begin? As always, to my family for their love and encouragement (not to mention their listening ears during the endless times I waxed poetic about a particular scene I either loved or struggled with). Their patience is boundless (or maybe they simply tuned me out).

To my intrepid critique partners at Critique Circle: Jessica, Brad, Stacey, Ellie, Vanessa, Clarissa, Michelle, and Lisa. You guys have become my second family. Also a shout out to Lisa's electrical engineer husband, Tim, who she kindly consulted about my crazy lightning idea. Your support, feedback, corrections, slaps alongside my head have meant the world to me. If I ever become rich and famous, I'll pay for your premium subscriptions. Thanks for pointing out plot holes, missing (or misplaced) commas, crazy long sentences where you got hopelessly lost, and times when my characters did something, well, out of character. A special thank you for loving these characters and supporting Bea.

To Jo for her amazing talent in creating the artwork for the cover.

To me, for (not so patiently) going down rabbit holes during my research into scientific topics I was not the least bit equipped to write about. Luckily, I still have all my hair, although my sanity is questionable.

And lastly, to my mother, who left this mortal coil long ago. Writing this book was a bit painful at times for me, but cathartic. We had our differences, but I know you loved me and wanted what was best for me. You were a woman of your times. We simply viewed "what was best" differently. I hope wherever you are, I've made you proud.

CHAPTER 1—THERE ARE NONE SO BLIND …

It is a truth universally acknowledged that a bespectacled woman with an interest in science is oft overlooked by eligible and marriageable men.

LONDON, ENGLAND, FEBRUARY 1824

As she did on all other social occasions such as this, Beatrix Marbry gazed in wonder at Laurence Townsend, Viscount Montgomery.

Was there ever a man so handsome, so genteel, and yet so virile?

She sighed, her brain so addled she remained stationary. For surely if she moved, she would stumble into another unsuspecting person.

His chestnut brown hair brushed the collar of his tailcoat enough to make him look enticingly disheveled. And most certainly, if he turned his deep brown eyes her way, she'd fall directly into the potted aspidistra that edged the wall of the Duke of Ashton's ballroom—whether she remained stationary or not.

One look from Lord Montgomery never failed to undo her. She ducked behind several of the taller plants, grateful their height hid her small stature.

Adjusting her spectacles, she sighed again. She had loved him since her come-out when he'd rescued her from utter embarrassment at Lord and Lady Cartwright's ball. The night had been a portent of what lay ahead for her. While handsome gentlemen whisked other girls across the dance floor, whispers of Bea's oddness left her waiting alone at the side of the ballroom in futile hope for a partner.

She'd fully understood the meaning of the term wallflower that evening, for she truly wished to fade into the patterned paper covering the ballroom walls. Until Laurence graciously offered his hand for the dance. Of course she'd made a complete and utter ninny of herself as she stumbled against him and trod upon his boots. Yet he smiled and bowed gallantly while he thanked her for the honor of the dance. Her heart left her that night—seemingly never to return.

Now, seven years later, at the age of five and twenty, she sat resolutely upon the shelf, condemned to spinsterhood.

Hidden behind the palm, Bea studied Laurence's every movement, a prickle of fear creeping up her spine as he chatted animatedly to a woman dressed in red she suspected was Lady Denby. Did he pursue the young widow as a marriageable prospect?

Not that she held any real hope he might search her way, but a tiny spark had ignited in her heart when Margaret, the Duchess of Ashton—and the object of Laurence's affection for years—had married the duke.

In truth, the fact that—despite his feelings—Laurence had come to the duke's assistance in securing the duke's union with the duchess made Bea love him even more. Lord Montgomery could be counted on to do the right thing at any cost, a virtue Beatrix valued highly.

She bit her lip, struggling for an actionable and achievable plan of attack.

For better or worse, her one confidant in discussing romantic pursuits had been her brother Timothy, a military officer, although she'd never actually revealed the object of her affection. As her beloved's closest friend, he would be unable to keep such

2

confidences to himself, and Bea would die of mortification if Lord Montgomery knew how much she mooned over him.

Still, Timothy counseled her, respecting her privacy as a good brother ought. His use of war terminology had taken root in her vocabulary. But love was not a war. Was it?

"You must learn your target's point of weakness, Bea," Timothy had said. "Once you do, plan carefully how best to take advantage. Then when his defenses are down and he's unsuspecting, you charge."

Oh, dear! It was precisely that strategy that had sabotaged every attempt she'd ever made to gain her beloved's attention. There had been falls into rose bushes, tumbles down staircases, and horrendous collisions on the dance floor, all due to her eagerness to capture Laurence's notice. She began to doubt Timothy's advice.

"Who are you hiding from, Miss Marbry?" The deep voice jolted her from her musings, and she peeked through the leaves of the palm. Although a half mask partially hid his face, there was no mistaking the duke, as his height set him apart from most other men —that and his kind smile. "And why aren't you wearing your mask? Aren't you enjoying the anonymity?"

"I'm not hiding, Your Grace, and I needed to remove the mask for my spectacles." She made a show of focusing her attention on the leaves of the plant. "Were you aware this particular variety of aspidistra is prone to infestation by spider mites? Especially in winter. Most often from being over-watered."

A slow smile crept across the duke's face. "I wasn't aware of that, no. I'll advise the staff to water less often. And please, Miss Marbry, since you've recognized me, call me Harry."

He held out his hand. "Now if you would, put on your mask and join me on the dance floor."

She removed her spectacles, tucking them into the reticule that hung from her wrist. Then she slipped on the mask her hosts had provided. It was actually quite lovely, decorated with tiny emerald-colored cut glass around the eyes.

Although its purpose was, as the duke said, to provide anonymity, Beatrix could identify almost everyone in attendance.

Years of being a wallflower had honed her skill of observation, learning people's mannerisms, how they moved, the tilt of their heads when they spoke. Why, she could even tell when someone prevaricated. Timothy had called them tells, stating they were extremely useful when playing cards.

She laid her hand on the duke's offered arm. "I suppose it's providential you're a physician, as I'm sure to injure either your feet or shins."

His low chuckle eased the building nervousness of being on display once again, especially since Lord Montgomery glanced up and over her way as the duke led her to the dance floor. She only stumbled a fraction, and Harry righted her immediately.

"I did warn you, Your Grace."

"That you did, Miss Marbry."

❧❦❧

LAURENCE HAD DREADED COMING TO THE BALL AND SEEING Margaret and the duke so happy. It didn't help that he had grown to like Harry. How could one not, when the man insisted on being called by his Christian name? They had formed a sort of understanding, a camaraderie of sorts, when they had joined forces and rescued Margaret from her kidnapper less than a year ago.

Still, it hurt to know they had found love while he remained a hopeless bachelor. Flirtatious laughter drifted from a couple next to him, only serving to magnify the dull ache in his chest. He yearned for a home, for a wife and children for as long as he could remember. He'd never been like many of his peers, chasing women, living wild until it came time to inherit. No, he'd always been deadly serious—intent on doing everything exactly right—of following the rules to the letter. And where had it left him?

Alone.

He sighed and looked up from his conversation with the lady in red, catching sight of a man leading a petite redhead to the dance floor. Her mask hid her face, but her emerald green gown showed off her figure to advantage. Who was she? A sensation stirred in

4

him, as if a heavy weight lay upon his chest, making it difficult to breathe.

Another gentleman approached, asking the lady in red next to him to dance, leaving Laurence alone to ponder the petite lady in green. Like the laws of magnetism he'd been discussing with the other lady, an unseen force pulled his attention toward the mysterious woman. He studied her as she moved around the dance floor with the man he suspected was the duke himself.

When the dance ended and the man bowed, she curtsied and moved to the side of the room. Her gaze drifted toward Laurence, and her feet stumbled. An odd niggling familiarity tickled the recesses of his mind. Quelling the urge to rush to her side and assist, he remained rooted in position as she disappeared from his view.

So as not to appear too anxious, he waited until another set had ended before seeking out the intriguing lady. Unfortunately, his plan proved faulty, and she had vanished from the ballroom altogether.

Instead, he performed his duty, dancing with a few other women and making idle conversation, enough to satisfy his mother's insistence that he mingle and be an appreciative guest. He realized navigating these gatherings was the most direct path to securing a wife, but truth be told, they tried his nerves.

In fact, any more time spent in the noisy room and he'd want to pull out his hair. The constant chatter from vapid debutantes irritated his sensibilities. The cloying scent of heavily applied rose water assaulted his nostrils. His cheeks began to throb from his forced smile to their endless comments about the weather and the latest fashion. He needed a quiet place to recoup and recharge before finishing the evening.

Ashton—he couldn't quite bring himself to call the man Harry, although the duke insisted upon it—had mentioned a book on Cow Pox he recently acquired, offering to loan it to Laurence if he was interested. Keen to do precisely that, Laurence scanned the ballroom one last time for the woman in green, then wandered down the hall toward the library.

Passing one of the parlors, sounds of muted conversation drifted out. He peeked in and smiled. The lady in red he'd spoken to earlier was ensconced in conversation with a dark-haired gentleman. As any true gentleman would, he proceeded on, leaving them to their tryst.

A faint light shone through the entrance to the library. Perhaps Ashton had anticipated his guests' need to escape to a sanctuary. He placed a hand against the slightly ajar door and pushed it open.

From the shadows of the dimly lit room, a gasp sounded, bringing him to a halt. The woman in green held a book in her hands, closer to her nose to be exact—so close he couldn't see her face.

His stomach gave an odd little jig. He took a step back. "I beg your pardon. I didn't mean to intrude."

Without lowering the book, she said, "It's no intrusion. A library should be open to all with inquisitive minds."

What an intriguing statement. So unlike the banal conversation from most of the women he'd spoken to that evening. "I agree. However, since you are unchaperoned, I should take my leave. I merely came seeking a particular book His Grace mentioned." He couldn't help but chuckle. "That and a moment of solitude."

A delightful giggle sounded from behind the book. "A perfect place to find both. Please don't leave on my account. However, I'm afraid I've removed my mask. If you wouldn't mind turning around." She released one hand from the book and made a circular motion with her finger.

"Ah. Of course." He dutifully turned his back. "Very well, you may don your mask." The natural curiosity running through his veins taunted him to take a peek, but his overwhelming belief in his responsibility as a gentleman convinced him to resist temptation.

When the rustling ceased, she said, "You may turn around. I have returned to my state of anonymity."

His breath hitched in his throat at the sight of her mere feet away. The nagging familiarity edged the corner of his mind again. "Have we met? I'm La—"

"No names." She held up a delicate hand. "We must abide by our hosts' rules."

"Of course, I beg your pardon."

"But to answer your question, I would wager that we've previously met the majority of people in attendance this evening. So odds are in our favor that we have indeed met before, wouldn't you say?"

"A most ingenious way of answering, and yet, not answering my question." Intrigued was too inadequate of a word for what he was experiencing. Fascination—or no, puzzlement seemed more appropriate. And he adored puzzles.

She pulled him from his musings. "You said you came seeking a book."

"Yes. His Grace recently acquired a book by Edward Jenner on experiments with Cow Pox. I'd hoped to borrow it."

"Do you mean *An Inquiry into the Causes and Effects of the Variolæ Vaccinæ?*"

Had someone removed all the air from the room? "Why, y-yes. You've heard of it?"

"I was reading it when you came in." She held up the slim book.

Good Lord, he'd died and gone to heaven. A woman with an interest in science. Here. In Ashton's library. "I'd hoped he had a copy of *The Discovery of Electromagnetism* by Hans Christian Ørsted, and he mentioned I might be interested in Jenner's book instead."

"Oh, I would love to read *Experimenta circa effectum conflictus electrici in acum magneticam.*"

Every intention of keeping a respectable distance left. The mention of the book's Latin title propelled him as if pulled by the magnetic force of said book. Unbidden, he took several steps forward. "You read Latin?"

"Yes, although not particularly fluently. Perhaps reading it would not only improve my mind on the subject, but allow me to work on my understanding of the language."

He couldn't help but smile. "You like challenges? I do as well. I once accepted a dare from a friend at school to commit one of Shakespeare's sonnets to memory."

He waved a hand in dismissal. "Not much of a challenge, I grant, but I was ten and testing the bounds of my memory."

Perhaps it was the masks they wore, but he found conversing with her easy—comfortable.

Light notes of orange blossom and vanilla teased the air. Unlike the overpowering rose water, he found her fresh fragrance most enticing. With difficulty, and for propriety's sake, he prepared to tear himself away. "Our discussion has been most enjoyable, but I should go and leave you to finish your reading. If you would be so kind as to leave the book on the table when you've finished, I shall return later and retrieve it."

"As you wish. I too have enjoyed our conversation immensely. I do hope you secure a copy of Ørsted's article. I understand there's to be a lecture on the subject at the Royal Society. For maximum enjoyment, if you plan to attend, it would be beneficial to be informed."

"Quite so." Regret pressed in on his chest that he didn't know her identity. He reminded himself of his own admission of enjoying a challenge. Turning to leave, he allowed himself one final look, searing it into his memory and vowing to discover who she was.

⚜

BEATRIX GRABBED ONTO THE EDGE OF THE SMALL TABLE IN FRONT OF her, hoping her knees wouldn't give out. How she'd managed to carry on a lucid conversation with Lord Montgomery amazed her. She attributed it to the anonymity of her mask. A momentary impulse to run after him and request a dance vanished. It was best not to press one's luck too far.

After a few deep breaths, her limbs steadied, and she opened the book to continue reading. But instead of words, only the smiling lips of Laurence Townsend, Lord Montgomery, appeared on the pages.

CHAPTER 2—AN UNWELCOME PROPOSAL

LONDON, ENGLAND, MAY 1825

Beatrix lifted her gaze from the parchment before her as she gathered her thoughts, pleased with what she had written so far. This would be her best submission yet. With stained fingers, she dipped her steel point pen into the inkpot when another thought sparked in her mind. She wished there was a way to retain the ink for longer periods.

Warm rays of sun streamed into her room, adding to her elevated spirits. Her cat stretched, elongating his black body on the soft cushion of the window seat. He yawned, his pink tongue curling at the tip. A glorious day, indeed.

Pushing her spectacles up the bridge of her nose, Bea sighed. If only she could sign her real name. What a coup that would be.

A knock on the door startled her from her daydreaming.

Her mother looked positively giddy as she entered the room. If possible, the woman would float right off of the floor. "Beatrix, make yourself presentable. You have a caller."

Blink, blink, blink. "A caller?" No one called on Beatrix—ever.

"Are you deaf as well as blind, girl? Yes. A caller." Her mother

9

gave her a simpering smile. An actual simper. "A *gentleman* caller." She practically cooed the words.

Had the world come to an untimely end? "You must be mistaken, Mother."

With a huff, her mother's smile changed into a deadly glare. "Hurry, don't keep him waiting."

Reluctantly, Bea set the pen down on the blotter and rose from her chair.

"Oh, dear," her mother muttered, her hand waving over Beatrix's form. "Your gown."

A quick glance down was all she needed. A large black splotch the shape of an unsightly insect marred her lavender day dress. She'd ruined more gowns by patting her stained fingers on the fabric as she struggled for the perfect words to convey her ideas.

"And your nose," her mother exclaimed as she pulled a handkerchief from the bodice of her gown.

"Please don't . . ." Beatrix started. But it was too late. With a spit to the cloth, her mother rubbed furiously on the bridge of Bea's nose in an attempt to remove the ink marring it.

The hope in her mother's eyes seemed to fade in an instant. "Stand away from the light. Perhaps he won't notice." She pulled Bea out of the room.

Remembering the reason for her mother's sudden intrusion, Bea asked, "Who is it?"

Her mother's nervous gaze darted toward her, making Bea increasingly uncomfortable. "You'll find out soon enough. Now, be on your best behavior. None of that silly science talk. Let him do all the speaking. Listen and smile. Agree with everything he says."

Bea rolled her eyes. She'd always been her mother's greatest disappointment. Today would be no exception. With each step, Bea's anxiety increased. *What if it's Laurence?* Would the gods of science truly be kind to her today, rewarding her for her faithful obedience and devotion?

She'd waited over a year, hoping he would use that glorious brain of his and deduce it was she he'd spoken to at the masquerade. However, at each subsequent social event, she'd displayed her typical clumsiness in his presence, literally falling out of his view each time he passed by.

Her mother gave her another nervous smile and pushed her toward the parlor door. "You're not coming in with me?" Bea asked, an oily unease rising to her mouth.

With a shake of her head, her mother vanished as quickly as water vapor from a boiling pot, leaving Bea to the mercy of what waited behind the door.

She took a deep breath and entered.

Apparently, the gods of science had nothing to do with this particular arrangement. They would not be so cruel. The portly form of Lord Middlebury rose from the settee and executed a bow. That's if it could be called such. The jerky movement of his awkward attempt was much like a mechanical toy she'd once witnessed in demonstration at a vendor's booth in Vauxhall Gardens.

"Miss Marbry. Such a delight to see you. I trust you are well?"

"Why are you here, Lord Middlebury?" Bea asked, cutting through the pleasantries. She had more important matters to attend to than listen to Lord Middlebury wax poetic about beans. Her last interaction with him had entailed a thirty minute discourse of their value to one's diet. As if he needed to expound on his fondness for the legume. His flatulence alone had attested to his own proclivity for their consumption.

He blinked, shaking his balding head, apparently perplexed at her directness, but recovered quickly. "To call upon you, of course." His high-pitched voice created an unpleasant shivering sensation up her spine, as if someone scraped their nails against slate.

She almost refrained from rolling her eyes—almost, but not quite. "Obviously, but why?"

Blotches of red dotted his face, much like the ink stains upon her gown. She waited as he pulled out a handkerchief and blew his nose, the sound reminding her of a swan during mating season.

After a peek into the handkerchief, which he stuck back into his pocket, he cleared his throat. "I'm here to offer for you. Your father has already agreed."

As if proving Copernicus's theory regarding planetary motion, Bea's world spun. However, Lord Middlebury was not at the center of her orbit. "Is it not customary to ask the woman first before approaching her father?"

It was common knowledge Middlebury experienced difficulty finding a bride. Even the majority of matchmaking mamas scuttled off in the opposite direction when he approached. Did he believe her spinstered state had made her so desperate?

"You'd be wise to accept me, my dear. You would be welcomed in the highest circles of society. Why, I have the ear of the Marquess of Edgerton. A most influential man. I was telling him the other day—"

"I don't care a fig about the Marquess of Edgerton." Bea had no time to listen to the man's obsequious kowtowing over the marquess when she had little respect for Edgerton herself. The man's cruelty and supercilious attitude could chill a room faster than a sudden storm on an autumn day.

"You would be wise to curb that tongue of yours. I will not tolerate such disrespect. Women should be lovely ornaments on a man's arm. Much like children, seen but not heard. I have no patience for a woman who speaks her mind."

Wise? He wouldn't know wise if it came up and bit him in the—

Possibly sensing his mistress's distress, the Polish priest's namesake raced into the room and launched himself onto Lord Middlebury's trouser leg.

"Catpurrnicus, no!"

"Get this *thing* off of me." Lord Middlebury was not pleased. He tried to shake the cat off as it hissed loudly at him.

"I beg your pardon, sir," Bea said, attempting to pull the demon cat from the man's leg. Catpurrnicus's claws dug in tightly, ripping eighteen miniature holes in the fabric.

With one final hiss, the cat released his grip and Bea cuddled him in her arms. "There, there, poor baby."

Lord Middlebury stared, aghast. "Does that creature belong to you?"

"He does." She petted the now purring cat with soothing strokes.

The man took the handkerchief from his pocket, the very one in which he'd blown his nose, and wiped his liver-spotted forehead.

Bea fought back the gag.

"Well, that won't do. No, it won't do at all. I won't have that beast in my home."

The spinning of Bea's mind returned. "Beg pardon?"

"Once we're wed. You'll have to find that *thing*"—he pointed the soiled handkerchief at Catpurrnicus—"another home."

Bea's world now ceased spinning and imploded. "I haven't agreed to marry you."

"You will." His icy tone sent shivers up Bea's spine. "Speak to your father. He'll explain everything. You have two weeks to accept my offer." With that, he stomped from the room, shaking the crystal vases and chandelier bobs in his wake.

Bea stumbled to the nearby settee, allowing her numb body to drop to its softness. "Good Galileo! What has happened?"

Her well-ordered, albeit lonely, world came to a screeching halt. Married to Lord Middlebury? It was not to be borne. Surely, her father would not agree to such a match. Would he? In a perfect demonstration of a vacuum, all the air was sucked from the room, and she struggled to breathe.

"Beatrix?" For the second time of the morning, her mother's figure appeared at the doorway. In direct opposition to her earlier giddy state, she appeared positively livid. "What did you say to Lord Middlebury? He left in a dither."

Yes, a more bitter disappointment had never existed. Bea swallowed the lump in her throat. "I . . . nothing. Catpurrnicus . . ."

With a decisive roll of her eyes, her mother sighed. "That cat shall be the ruin of us all."

Catpurrnicus hissed.

"Did you at least give Middlebury an answer?"

A sickly taste filled Bea's mouth. Unable to speak, she shook her head.

"Why ever not? The man's a viscount, Beatrix. You would be titled."

She sent a pleading look toward her mother, hoping to appeal to the sliver of compassion buried somewhere in her shriveled heart. "Mother, he's . . . ancient. And Catpurrnicus doesn't like him." *Nor do I.* To avoid angering her mother further, she kept that bit to herself.

"That cat doesn't like anyone but you. I do believe he's possessed by Satan." Her mother entered, taking a seat next to her. Catpurrnicus reached out with a paw, claws extended. Bea pulled it back in the nick of time.

"Bea," her mother said, using the nickname as a weapon. Her voice softened, adding to the effect of a sneak attack. "Marriage is a woman's duty. It's what you were born for, to marry and bear children."

"To a man I don't love?"

The façade fell away, and her mother's eyes flashed. "I don't see a line of gentlemen waiting outside our door, fighting for your affections. Love is overrated. Stability, that's what you need. And a firm hand to rid you of those silly notions of yours."

Bea's back stiffened at her mother's words, both for calling her love for science silly notions as much as the implication that a good swat would eradicate her of intelligent thought.

Her mother reached out to take her hand, jerking quickly back as Catpurrnicus hissed. "I'm at the end of my rope, Beatrix. Once, I'd hoped perhaps Mr. Weatherby would offer for you. But he had to go off after that Miss Galbraith."

Although a profoundly logical woman, Bea had to admit that the notion of Andrew traveling halfway around the world to India in search of the woman he loved was one of the most romantic things she'd ever heard. *If a man loved me like that . . .*

"And of course there was the duke," her mother continued, drawing Bea's attention back. "That would have been a coup. Sometimes I think Lady Cartwright had the right idea."

"Mother!" The idea her mother would even consider a staged compromise was unthinkable, especially against such a kind man as the Duke of Ashton. Thank goodness her mother didn't know she'd effectively told the duke she wasn't interested in a marriage to him, a pronouncement that had greatly relieved him and allowed them to slide into a comfortable friendship.

It seemed the whole of London had found their hearts—everyone except her. "But to be saddled with Lord Middlebury? I'd prefer to remain a spinster. Surely Papa will understand."

For once, her mother looked upon her with eyes of genuine compassion, and Bea's blood chilled. Something was afoot. Her mother reached over and patted Bea's hand. Catpurrnicus stared at the appendage with devious intent. "Go speak with your father. He's in his study."

Without another word, her mother rose and quit the room.

The gloomy foreboding settled deep within Bea as she forced herself from the settee and made her way to her father's study. Middlebury said her father had already agreed to the match. But why? Her papa loved her, had encouraged her intellectual pursuits. There must be some misunderstanding.

Any remaining doubt she had dissipated the moment she gazed upon her father's face. With a weak smile, he beckoned her in and motioned to the overstuffed Louis XVI armchair in front of his large mahogany desk. If forced to choose one word to describe him, it would have been contrite.

"Bea, please sit."

"Papa, tell me you didn't agree to Lord Middlebury's offer."

He lowered his gaze and fussed with some papers in front of him. "You must understand, my dear. It has nothing to do with what we want, but what we need."

"What *we* need? How is it that I need to be married to Lord Middlebury?"

He flinched at the sharpness of her tone, then ran a shaky hand through his thinning hair. "You need to be married, Bea. And as you've received no other offers . . ."

So her father was disappointed in her as well? "Why do I suspect there is more to this than my ongoing unmarried state? I've been on the shelf for several years now. Why the sudden urgency to marry me off?"

Although she'd never thought of her father as old, as his body fell back against the leather wingback, the word ancient crossed her mind. His complexion, usually ruddy and healthy, appeared sallow, his eyes sunken as if he hadn't slept in days.

A chill of concern inched up her spine, and she leaned forward. "Papa, are you ill? Should we consult your physician? Or better, His Grace?" Bea never cared much for her father's physician. The man still relied on leeches for every ailment. Bea shuddered at the thought of the slimy creatures attached to her father's skin.

He pulled in a deep breath. "Not in the way you think." He rose and strode over to the small credenza against the wall, then poured two glasses of brandy.

When he handed her one, it did nothing to ease her worry. "Go ahead. You deserve it."

The sweet liquor burned her throat, but she drank dutifully. Something in his tone warned her she should fortify herself for what he was about to say.

"I'm dished up, Bea. A rather large gambling debt of mine has been called in. I've tried putting it off in hopes of winning back enough to appease the holder of my vowels."

A sinking feeling formed in her stomach as she braced for his next words.

He raked a hand through his hair again. When had it become so streaked with gray? "Middlebury has agreed to make good on my debt in exchange for your hand."

Every muscle in her body stiffened. She blinked, struggling to comprehend the horrific words. "You're selling me? How could you?"

Color drained from his face. "You make it sound criminal. I'm asking for your help, Bea."

Her logical mind scrambled for a solution. The one hundred twenty-five pounds she'd acquired from her articles was no great fortune, but perhaps she could demand more for the recent masterpiece she'd been penning. "Surely there is some other way.

We can economize. Sell something to obtain the funds. How much do you owe?"

She strained to hear his mumbled response. "Approximately twenty thousand pounds."

"Good Galileo, Father! That's a small fortune. What on earth were you thinking? Surely you couldn't lose that much on whist or vingt-et-un?" Her pittance of savings would barely make a nick in the amount.

"You'd be surprised. But does it matter how?" He drained his brandy, then stared at the empty glass as if it would magically refill itself. "Middlebury is as rich as Croesus, Bea. You would want for nothing."

As if to remind her of what she would be losing, Catpurrnicus jumped on her lap and curled himself into a tight ball. "My cat. Middlebury doesn't like him. And what about love, not to mention the freedom to be myself?"

"You might grow to love him. It happens."

That confirmed it. Her father had officially lost his mind.

Before she could protest further, her father dismissed her. "At least consider it, Bea. I have two weeks to acquire the funds. I'm counting on you to save this family."

On leaden limbs, she pulled herself from the overstuffed chair, clutching Catpurrnicus to her chest. Two weeks, the precise time Middlebury had given her. Surely she'd been graced with her brain for more than embroidery and planning social gatherings. There had to be a solution.

With a final question, she turned. "Father, to whom do you owe the debt?"

"Lord Nash."

Like a strong wind against a candle flame, the name extinguished the flicker of hope in her heart.

CHAPTER 3—WHEN A MAN MUST FIND A WIFE

"**D**o put down that scandalous newspaper. Are you even listening to me?"

I'm trying not to. Laurence inhaled a fortifying breath and lowered his copy of *The Times*, preparing to meet his mother's disappointed glare. He questioned his decision to take breakfast at his parents' townhouse. "I'm sorry, Mother."

He loved his mother, truly he did, except when it came to the unwelcome topic currently at hand.

His mother, the countess Lady Clara Easton, straightened her shoulders as if readying for battle, then slathered a thin piece of toast with butter and jam. "We should have the doctor examine your hearing. Must I repeat myself?"

God forbid. All he needed was to have his mother reiterate her tirade regarding his unmarried state at an increased volume. He swore the footman standing by the sideboard swayed from the sheer force of her words.

"That won't be necessary. I'm simply formulating a response. Hopefully, one you will accept."

"Hmmpf. Unless it's to inform me you've already selected a bride, proposed, and obtained a license, I doubt it." She nibbled her toast, eyeing him, most likely expecting him to pull a fiancée from behind his coattails. "Must I remind you of your duty to produce an heir? Your father won't live forever."

"Father is in excellent health, and I'm barely thirty. Hardly ancient, Mother. There will be plenty of time to sire an heir."

"Life is precarious, my dear. Why, a carriage or runaway horses could run over your father at a moment's notice."

It took every ounce of his restraint not to roll his eyes. "Mother, please. Stop being melodramatic."

"I'm serious, Laurence. Why, think about poor Miss Marbry. It's a wonder that young lady has survived to adulthood. Just the other day when we passed her while strolling through Hyde Park, she fell into the rose bushes. She could well have been trampled to death."

"By what? Horses? Off the path?" Of course he had sympathy for the poor woman. Her proclivity for tripping and falling had become something of an art form. Perhaps she had some type of affliction.

"Don't be obtuse. You can't moon over the duchess forever."

Ah, there it is, the final nail. He pushed down the anger at his mother's precision attack on his Achilles' heel. "I am not *mooning* over Her Grace. I know very well she is happily married. I simply haven't found a suitable prospect."

"Because you are not looking, dearest." She directed her plea to his father, happily reading *The Morning Post*. "Nigel, do assist me and convince our son of his duty."

"Find a bride, Laurence, so we all may have some peace." His father's words traveled through the newsprint in front of his face.

"If you will excuse me"—Laurence tossed down his linen napkin on the still full plate before him—"I believe a walk is in order." With the newspaper in hand, he rose and strode from the room, seeking the peaceful solitude of the terrace.

Once seated in a cushioned wicker chair outside, he closed his eyes, regaining his composure. Birds tittered in the trees, and a gentle breeze teased his nose with a light fragrance of lilac. *Perfect.*

He'd been in the middle of a fascinating article by the intriguing O.B. when his mother had begun her attack. Truth be told, the mere sight of the man's initials counteracted all negative components of the day. The man's insight, intelligence, and clarity in expounding on scientific theory was nothing short of brilliance. How Laurence wished he knew the man's identity so he could correspond with him directly—or better yet, meet with him in person. He'd not only written the newspaper, but pleaded with them in person for information on the mysterious O.B., unfortunately, to no avail.

The latest offering in *The Times* delved into the wonders of electromagnetism, and Laurence's thoughts drifted back to the satisfying encounter with the lady in green over a year ago. As promised, she left Jenner's treatise on the experiments with Cow Pox on the table in the library, but when he searched for her in the crowd at the ball, she'd all but evaporated into the night. He often wondered if she was a figment of his overactive imagination.

Unsure how he would recognize her, except for her red hair, for the past year, he still scanned the ballrooms, music halls, garden parties, crowds in Vauxhall Gardens and Hyde Park, even lectures at the Royal Society.

Admittedly, chances of finding her in a venue for men only was a ridiculous notion. However, there had been a moment when he'd gotten a strange sense of her presence. When he turned, his gaze landed on Timothy Marbry and a young lad seated at the very back of the hall. Curious, as Timothy had no younger brothers. A cousin visiting London, perhaps?

At the end of the lecture, Laurence hurried to greet them. The boy darted a glance toward him, then stumbled against Timothy. Before Laurence could reach them, they disappeared into a waiting carriage. He questioned Timothy later, but his friend remained elusive, stating the lad was a relative interested in the sciences.

As time passed, memory of the intriguing lady with the forest green eyes, although ever present in the back of his mind, faded, and he began to accept she was elusive as the love he sought.

And now, his mother reminded him—yet again—he must find a bride. With the Season in full swing, he had no excuse. Yet the empty-headed chits who flirted and simpered held no interest for him. Was he doomed to live a life like so many others in the aristocracy? Married to a woman he barely knew and simply tolerated enough to sire the requisite heir and spare? A marriage much like the one of his own parents?

Deep in his maudlin thoughts, he stared at the newsprint without registering the words. A hand touched his shoulder.

"So they've run you off again?"

He lifted his gaze to his younger sister's empathetic face and placed his hand over hers. "Miranda. I didn't hear you approach."

"Obviously." She nodded to the empty chair next to his. "May I join you, or are you also avoiding me?"

"Never you, dear one. Please sit. Perhaps you will be able to distract me from my darkness."

Compassion shone in her dark brown eyes. "What can I do to help?"

He forced a smile. "Find me a bride?"

She rolled her eyes, the gesture alone enough to lift his spirits. "If I had the gift of matchmaking, I would focus such talents on finding my own spouse." She darted an apologetic glance toward him. "Forgive my callous remark."

He waved her off. "Nothing to forgive. I often forget I'm not the only object of Mother's obsession to be a grandmother. Any prospects?"

She gave a solemn shake to her pretty brunette head. "No. None that you would approve of."

"Oh? But someone I wouldn't?" He kept his tone light, but concern churned in his stomach.

"A simple flirtation, nothing serious. Besides, we were discussing your courting woes, not mine. What about Miss Pratt?"

"After what she did to His Grace? I'd rather remain a bachelor and face both mother's *and* grandmother's wrath."

"I do see your point. Although she seems quite contrite over that whole debacle. The *ton* has effectively blackballed the poor dear."

"There are always consequences to actions, my dear sister. Something to bear in mind if you're keeping company with a gentleman of whom I wouldn't approve."

She stiffened before him, the twitching muscle in her jaw the only discernible movement. "It must be difficult."

"What?"

"To be perfect all the time—the paragon of virtue." She rose in a huff.

"Miranda, forgive me. I didn't mean . . ."

But it was too late. She marched off, slamming the terrace door behind her. He drew a hand down his face. No wonder he couldn't find a bride when every time he spoke to a woman, he offended her. He picked up his newspaper again, focusing on the wonderful article by O.B. Yes, that's what he needed—the perfect remedy to woman problems, an intelligent, logical article by a man.

CHAPTER 4—THE PLAN

B ea's room—her sanctuary—always so welcoming, now closed in on her, suffocating her like the choice that lay ahead. She needed an actionable plan. Her hope that the man holding her family's future—indeed her very happiness—in his hands would be someone to whom she could appeal seemed futile. Lord Nash wasn't known for his compassion. At the very least, she could beg for time to repay the debt.

If there were only something she could sell or offer in exchange.

Her brother's voice followed a soft knock at her door. "Bea? May I come in?"

She raced to the door, throwing it open and herself into his arms. "Oh, Timothy, what am I to do?" Four years older than she, he'd always been her rock in times of trouble.

"Shush." He patted her back. "Chin up. Be a good soldier."

Horrified, she pulled back and stared into his moss green eyes, trying desperately to hold back her sobs. "Y-you w-want me to m-marry Lord M-M-Middlebury?"

"Of course not. But every good soldier must face the battle with a clear head . . . and a plan."

She sniffled, and Timothy pulled out his handkerchief. "You

never seem to have one of these when needed. Now blow your nose like a good girl."

The handkerchief only brought her mind back to Lord Middlebury and the disgusting handkerchief with which he wiped his forehead. She shuddered. "I've been racking my brain for a solution. The most logical would be to acquire the money to pay Father's debt. But it's so large. Whatever could we sell?"

Tea curdled in her stomach at the doleful expression on her dear brother's face.

"I'm afraid that's only part of the problem." He motioned to the chaise longue.

The unease plaguing her stomach transformed into icy dread, and her body dropped to the soft cushions. Timothy sat next to her and took her hands in his.

"What is it?" Her words, no more than a whisper, seemed to fill the space of her room.

"It would seem Mother is desperate to marry you off. She's tired of waiting, and since Lord Middlebury has been your only offer . . ."

"So even if we obtain the funds, they will insist I marry him?"

He nodded, his expression growing even more solemn.

"Can they . . . force me?"

"Legally, no. But Bea, as much as I love Mother, we both know she would make your life miserable."

"It might be preferable to life with Lord Fat Middle."

A smile played at the corner of his lips. "Bea, shame on you calling him names.

"I'm sorry, Timothy, but the man is a toady, expounding on his *connections* to the Marquess of Edgerton—another snake, I might add. It's more than the noxious odor following him wherever he goes. He has no interest in the sciences, and in no uncertain terms he stated I would be wise to keep my mouth shut." She puffed up her cheeks, offering an imitation of his proclamation on women. "'Women should be a lovely ornamentation on a man's arm.' Indeed! Can you imagine? It would be prison. Worse even."

"Although what you say might be true"—he held up a hand to

silence her objection—"Fine, *is* true. In Mother's eyes, refusing an offer—your *only* offer—would be an insult to our entire family."

She jerked her hands away, his touch no longer comforting. "I thought you supported me."

"Of course I do. I'm merely presenting the facts as I see them. The only way I could see Mother forsaking this fiasco is if you were deemed unmarriageable."

She sniffled again. "But I am. Six and twenty without even a hint of a suitor."

"But now there's Lord Middlebury. You're no longer unmarriageable in Mother's eyes."

Ugly clarity flooded her sharp mind. Timothy had a point. As long as Middlebury wanted *her*, she had no hope. A kernel of a plan took shape. She must become undesirable to *him*.

Timothy's eyes widened. "Oh, Bea, I'm not comfortable with that look in your eyes. What are you planning?"

"Nothing yet. Think of ways we can obtain the money for Father, and I'll work on the rest. Will you assist me? Together, we can do anything." She grasped his hands like they did as children. The unstoppable Marbry siblings. "Now leave me," she said, ushering him out of the room. "I have much to think about."

⁂

WITH EACH OPTION EXAMINED, EACH ARGUMENT COUNTERED, SHE formulated—what she believed to be—her foolproof plan. Of course, not being able to test and retest left the possibility things might go horribly awry. However, to paraphrase Hippocrates, "Desperate times called for desperate measures." And no better word could describe her than desperate. Thirteen days had passed, and time was running out. Lord Middlebury would expect an answer.

She'd been fortunate to sell her latest article to *The Times* for two pounds, hardly a dent, but they promised an equal amount for future articles of the same quality. Timothy had managed to accumulate fifty additional pounds through his luck at the card table. Bea had scolded him soundly, considering gambling had precipitated her dire situation.

Only nineteen thousand, eight hundred twenty-three pounds short. With a heavy sigh, she fell back against the chair at her escritoire. What else did she have of value? Naught but herself. Wasn't Middlebury valuing her as such? Unthinkable as the idea of marriage to the old fool, she pushed the thought back into the recesses of her mind, hoping she wouldn't have to pull it out.

She penned the letter, choosing every word carefully. It would not suffice to give too much away, but rather entice him to at least meet with her. Like fishing, she baited her hook with care. But how to deliver it? If her plan was to succeed, secrecy was paramount.

Using one of the precious pounds she'd saved, she bribed a footman. His eyebrows rose at the name upon the missive. "Miss, are you certain?"

"Yes. It's a matter of urgent business. Please deliver it posthaste and wait for an answer."

Wound tighter than the clock on the mantle, she paced the floor in her room, gazing out the window every few moments for the footman to return. When he approached at last, she ran down the steps to intercept him. Her hands shook as she took the response from him. Step one of her plan had been executed, but all else depended on the contents of his reply.

Her heart beat an erratic rhythm, matching her pounding feet as she raced back up to her room to read the response in private. With shaky fingers, she broke the wax seal, then closed her eyes and said a prayer before opening it to read.

My dear Miss Marbry,

Intrigued is too weak a word for my reaction to your letter. If only for my own amusement, I will meet you in Hyde Park at the designated place and time.

~N

Thank gods! All had been set in motion. And apparently none too soon. Sounds of horses' hooves drifted in from the open window, the carriage coming to rest in front of her home. The compartment of the vehicle shifted as the ungainly form of Lord Middlebury descended.

With a deep breath, she prepared herself, waiting to be summoned to meet with him. After one sharp rap against the door, her mother entered. Solemnness befitting the occasion replaced the giddiness her mother had exhibited two short weeks ago. "He is here for your answer, Beatrix. Do not disappoint us yet again."

Struck by the similarity of her her plan to her father's own wager, she girded herself and entered the parlor to meet her fate.

Lord Middlebury heaved his aging body from the settee, the simple action leaving him out of breath. He tipped his head in substitute of a bow. "Miss Marbry. I trust you're well. I've come for your answer."

The self-satisfied look on his face turned her stomach. He obviously knew she had no choice. She motioned to the settee. "Please rest, Lord Middlebury, you seem to have over-exerted yourself."

His body dropped to the cushions, and Bea swore his joints groaned in protest. She settled herself in a chair in front of him. "I have given great thought to your . . . generous proposal, sir." That much was true. "I do have one request before I agree."

He leaned forward, his wrinkled hand clutching the side of the settee. "What might that be? It's not to keep that infernal beast of yours?"

She bit back the retort forming on her tongue in defense of her dear Catpurrnicus and proceeded as planned. "If you would be so kind as to settle my father's debt prior to the ceremony, I would be most grateful. With the time necessary for the banns to be read before the wedding, his time will have run out."

Bea held her breath. Everything about her plan depended on Middlebury agreeing to pay off the debt first. Her logic was sound. He could hardly fault her there, yet a flicker of mistrust crossed his doughy face.

"Is this a trick? What assurances will you give me you will not retract your acceptance?"

"I give you my word, sir. I will not be the one to break our engagement." The bait dangled before him, and she figuratively saw his jaws open to swallow it whole.

"Very well, then. I shall settle the debt at our engagement party." His watery blue eyes studied her. The indecency in their depths sent an icy shiver up her spine. "I trust your parents will arrange everything quickly? I'm most anxious to begin our wedded bliss."

"Of course." She forced out the words, the idea of bliss in conjunction with a life with him as foreign as the Latin she'd been studying.

He hoisted himself from the tortured piece of furniture, and she rose as well. "Now that we are engaged, perhaps a kiss?"

Oh dear gods! "On the cheek, my lord. Let us leave some things for our marriage."

"Ah, a modest woman. I knew I had chosen well. I should have no fear of indecent behavior from you, my girl." He lumbered toward her, his lips smacking in anticipation. The distinct odor of camphor drifted forward with each step.

If she could only refrain from gagging. Wet, slobbery lips grazed her cheek, then slid quickly to her mouth. She stifled a scream.

"Forgive me, my dear, I'm overcome by your beauty."

"Perhaps we should say our goodbyes now before things become . . ."

"Yes, yes. Of course. I shall speak with your papa to tell him of your decision and request."

Once he had quit the room, Bea scrubbed at her mouth to remove the foul taste, more determined than ever for her plan to succeed. With step one completed, she prepared for step two, an even riskier proposition.

⚜

AFTER SECURING THE RIBBONS OF HER BONNET UNDER HER CHIN, Bea studied herself in the mirror. She must present the appropriate appearance. The lacy fichu draped around her shoulders and tucked into her bodice had to go, but not before she left the house. It was paramount she not raise suspicion.

Fortunately, Fanny, her abigail, proved a sympathetic partner in crime. Well, that and a bribe of her other odd pound secured the woman's promise of silence. Of course, Bea didn't confide in Fanny as to the nature of the meeting, but once the woman saw the other party, her protective nature would engage. Preparation of some sort became necessary.

"This meeting is of utmost importance to my family, Fanny," she said as they strode toward Hyde Park. "Not to mention my own happiness. I rely on your discretion."

"If I may say so, Miss Beatrix, what you're doing for your family is a great sacrifice." Fanny's words came in short pants as she struggled to keep pace with Bea's determined steps. "The staff talks, miss. We know about your father's predicament and your engagement to Lord Middlebury." The woman shuddered.

Since Bea had few friends, male or female, the two had formed a bond that went beyond lady and maid. Bea trusted her. "One does what one must. Which is the reason for this meeting. Don't be alarmed regarding the other party. I know what I'm doing." Bea tugged the fichu from her bodice, stuffing it into her reticule and hoping that her last statement was true. A goodly portion of Bea's bosom was now on display during the daylight hours.

Fanny's eyes widened. "Miss Beatrix!"

Bea ignored her and continued on, rounding a curve on the path not far from the Serpentine toward the assigned meeting place. *Let him be there.*

Lord Nash leaned against a tree off the path, his legs crossed at the ankles and a cheroot dangling casually between his fingers.

Bea swallowed down the lump in her throat. "Wait here," she instructed Fanny, and marched forward, summoning her courage.

Nash straightened at her approach, his eyes widening, then dipping to her exposed bosom. His lips twitched as he made a graceful bow. "Miss Marbry." His gaze remained fixed upon her chest.

She gave a delicate cough. "My eyes are up here, Lord Nash."

He chuckled. "Forgive me, Miss Marbry." He did not appear the least bit contrite. "You mentioned the debt owed to me in your message. Have you come to pay?"

"Not precisely. I've come to ask for mercy."

A flicker of annoyance flashed in his eyes. "You're wasting my time," he said through clenched teeth. "If you expect me to forgive the debt, you're sadly mistaken."

"Oh, no, you misunderstand. You will be paid in full. I require your assistance in another matter."

With a lazy gesture, he flicked the ashes from his cigar. "Go on."

Oh, how to phrase it? She'd rehearsed it countless times. However, under his licentious gaze, the words jumbled. "I'm in a terrible position. You see, Lord Middlebury has offered to settle my father's debt to you in exchange for my hand in marriage, and I do not wish to marry him."

"Although I sympathize with your position, Miss Marbry, I fail to see how I can assist. Such an arrangement is to my advantage, after all."

The words tumbled out. "I'd like you to compromise me."

He laughed, apparently thinking it a joke. "Here? In the middle of Hyde Park in front of your maid?"

Unable to restrain herself, she rolled her eyes. Were all rakes this dense? Perhaps blood didn't circulate well in their brains, being too often diverted to their—appendage. "Of course not. What good would that do? We would arrange it that Lord Middlebury will find us and break the engagement."

Her seriousness registering in his feeble brain, Nash held his hands up and backed away. "Oh, no. I have no wish to be leg-shackled to anyone. And if you think to trap me into marriage to expunge your father's debt because he would be my father-in-law, you'd best think again . . . on all counts."

She waved it away. "I quite understand. I have no desire to marry you either. It's precisely why I've chosen you. I only wish to break the engagement, and I know you wouldn't make a gentlemanly offer of marriage to save my reputation."

For a brief moment, he jerked back as if she'd slapped him. "I fail to see how this benefits me. In fact, the entire scheme is to my disadvantage. If Middlebury catches us in a compromising position, wouldn't he refuse to pay the debt?"

"I've made Middlebury promise to settle the debt prior to the wedding. In turn, I promised that *I* would not break our engagement. You'll have your money."

"So you intend to force his hand by being cuckolded?"

She straightened her shoulders. "Yes. It would brand me completely ruined to be found with a rake such as yourself."

Something flashed in his eyes, and she swore he cringed.

"Although I commend the . . . ingenuity of your proposal, what if he challenges me? Would you have me shoot him dead?"

"He won't. Dueling is illegal."

He laughed. "That's never stopped anyone. Although when it comes to Middlebury, you do have a point. But what if your father defends your honor? If I have my money, why should I spare his life?"

A greasy taste rose in her mouth. Step two was not progressing as planned. With two remaining cards to play, she pulled out the first from her reticule. "Here is one hundred twenty-five pounds in addition to the debt my father owes. It's yours if you promise to walk away from any challenge."

"You think I have no pride? I'd be branded a coward."

Closing her eyes and taking a deep breath, she played her ace in the hole. "I could be your mistress." Good Galileo, what had she become? But Lord Nash was preferable to Lord Middlebury.

Nash blinked, but his expression remained unreadable. He trailed a lazy finger up her arm. "My touch wouldn't disgust you?"

"Not as much as Middlebury's."

Her cheeks warmed at his raucous laugh. "Go home, Miss Marbry. I have no need for a mistress, and you're mad to think I'd agree to such a scheme."

"Please Lord Nash. I'd rather die than marry Lord Middlebury. Not when——"

Nash's gaze drifted off, his expression darkening.

Bea's heart raced at the one curt word.

"Montgomery."

"Nash. Miss Marbry." Laurence tipped his hat and strolled past, his sister, Miranda, on his arm.

Bea's knees buckled, and she collapsed against Lord Nash.

"Not when what, Miss Marbry?"

"Not when I love another. I know I cannot have him, but . . ."

A beat passed.

"Would this man be Laurence Townsend, Viscount Montgomery?"

Heat flooded her face, the late-May sun becoming unbearable.

Something in Nash's demeanor shifted. "Very well, Miss Marbry. I'll consider your proposal. But you must let me handle it my way."

"Lord Middlebury agreed to pay the debt at our engagement party. Perhaps once you receive the funds, it would be the ideal time and place?"

He nodded. "Make sure I'm on the guest list. I'm not always invited."

"Of course," she whispered, relief flooding every particle of her being. "Papa will want to repay you immediately."

He tipped his hat. "Then we are in agreement. Until we meet again, Miss Marbry."

As he strode away, his long legs taking him up the path away from where her beloved Laurence had gone, Bea wondered if she was doing the right thing.

CHAPTER 5—THE SETUP AT WHITE'S

Laurence's peaceful morning stroll through Hyde Park with Miranda had taken a strange turn. The sight they'd passed piqued his natural curiosity, and he puzzled over the possibilities. So much so that his sister squeezed his arm.

"Where is your mind off to now?" she asked, concern shining in her brown eyes.

"My apologies. What in the world is Nash doing with Miss Marbry? The pairing seems most unlikely."

"She could be inquiring about his sister. I understand Lady Charlotte took a tumble from her horse while riding along Rotten Row last week."

He couldn't resist chuckling. Not that he wished ill on any woman, even Nash's sister, but the word tumble in conjunction with Miss Marbry in any manner seemed à propos.

Miranda delivered a sound slap to his arm. "Stop laughing. It isn't funny."

"I merely wondered if Miss Marbry's affliction had become contagious."

"Oh, you're incorrigible. The poor dear can't help it if she doesn't see well. And honestly, I've had numerous conversations with her, and she's remained perfectly upright. Both you and mother judge her too harshly." Miranda paused as if considering her next words. "Although I will admit, once she begins her discourse of scientific subjects, my mind drifts."

His sister had proceeded a solid four steps ahead of him before Laurence realized he'd stopped dead on the path.

Miranda glanced back. "What is it? Are you ill? You're positively pale." She hurried back to his side. "Should we call the physician?"

With a dismissive wave of his hand, he silenced her. "No. I'm fine . . . physically. Would you repeat what you said?"

"I asked about your health."

"No, no. Not that. About Miss Marbry." Surely he'd misheard her.

"What? That she only seems to fall around you and Mother?"

He bit back an impatient retort, consciously keeping his voice calm. "No, the other thing."

"About her preoccupation with science? Seriously, Laurence, I get enough of that from you. Why would I wish to listen to a woman's musing on the boring subject?"

Good God. Could it be possible? He swallowed hard. Had she been under his nose the whole time?

He stared into space as if the all important fact had just occurred to him. "Miss Marbry has red hair."

He darted his attention back to Miranda, catching an obvious roll of her eyes. "Yes. What are you getting at?"

Desperate to know, he resisted the urge to give her a shake. "What color are her eyes?"

"Why are you obsessing about Miss Marbry? I refuse to provide any further ammunition to your unending supply of jabs regarding the poor woman's clumsiness."

His usually even temperament stretched to the breaking point. "Answer the question, Miranda."

She huffed and turned on her heel, proceeding down the path.

The beating of his heart matched the pounding of the horses' hooves in the distance. He raced after his sister, grabbing her arm when he reached her. "Please, Miranda. It is of the utmost importance."

"How in the world should I know? Her spectacles are so smudged most of the time, I can't imagine how she sees out of them, much less allow anyone to determine the color of her eyes."

"Who else has red hair? Women," he clarified, wishing for once in his life he'd paid more attention to the throngs of debutantes.

"Are you certain you're not ill? This conversation is bizarre."

He shot her a stern look.

"I don't know. Beatrix's mother, Lady Saxton. I suppose."

"Young women only, please."

Something shifted in his sister's demeanor, as if successfully connecting two pieces of copper wire, allowing current to pass through. "I'd completely forgotten. You'd mentioned a woman you met at the masquerade ball over a year ago. Then, nothing ever came of it, so I'd pushed it aside. Do you think Miss Marbry is the woman?"

"Possibly. Who else has red hair?"

"Let me think. Anne Weatherby?"

He shook his head. "I don't think it's her. I danced with Miss Weatherby at her come-out, and she seemed more preoccupied with the latest fashion and flirting with every man in the room. Although I can't remember the color of her eyes."

"Blue, I think, but I'm not certain." Miranda's gaze narrowed. "You should know these things. What happened to your renowned memory?"

"I have to make a conscious effort to memorize things.

She snorted an unladylike laugh. "That speaks volumes."

He waved her insult away. "Who else?" He cringed at the pleading tone in his voice.

Pinching the bridge of her nose, Miranda grew silent. The waiting became interminable, and he wanted to shake her and tell her to hurry.

She snapped her fingers. "There's Lady Honoria Bell. She's one and twenty, red hair and green eyes."

He plunged deep within the recesses of his neatly organized

mind regarding Honoria, figuratively thumbing through the files to find the necessary information. Ah, there. The daughter of the Marquess of Stratford, quiet, reserved. She'd been ill for a time, and he remembered the detail she'd gone into regarding her ailment. What he didn't remember was experiencing any attraction to her.

"Is she married?" he asked.

"No. However, gossip has it she's enamored with a commoner. Of course her father is opposed to such a union. But now that she's of age——"

He interrupted his sister's tangential exposition of Lady Honoria's romantic woes and grasped at a final straw. "Anyone else?"

"No one I can think of at the moment. Are you opposed to the idea that it might be Miss Marbry?"

He opened his mouth to refute Miranda's accusation, but snapped it shut. Was he? And if so, why? "I fear I cannot give a truthful answer, as I'm uncertain of it myself. She is . . . different from most women."

"Different from Her Grace, you mean."

He sighed. "Not you, too? Don't I receive enough badgering from Mother? I am no longer harboring a tendre for the duchess."

With tightening lips, she *graced* him with her famous castigatory look. "I cannot help you if you continue to be dishonest with yourself."

"Perhaps you have a point. Miss Marbry is quite different from Her Grace, both in appearance and demeanor. Margaret is beautiful, poised, elegant—kind." He added the last in an effort to avoid appearing superficial to his judgmental sister.

"But have you given Miss Marbry a chance? How much time have you spent with her?"

"None that I recall."

"Well, there you have it," she said, as if it provided the solution to all of life's problems.

"Would you mind terribly if we cut our walk short?"

"Are you going to return and speak with Miss Marbry if she's still there?"

Miranda was nothing if she wasn't persistent. "No. I need to clear my head. Time at the tables at White's seems in order."

"You and your cards." She executed the eye-roll to perfection. "Very well. Escort me home before you waste the time away with the other nodcocks at the gaming tables."

Stifling the chuckle, he offered his arm and did just that.

ﭏﬠﭏ

WHITE'S FAMILIAR SOUNDS OF SHUFFLING CARDS AND CLINKING crystal glasses settled around Laurence like a comforting blanket. Scents of leather, brandy, and cigar smoke attested to his masculine surroundings. Nothing like being in the calm presence of men to clear his head.

He'd barely settled into his seat at a table when Andrew Weatherby approached. It seemed the perfect opportunity to narrow down the suspects—err, prospects. He nodded in greeting to the amiable man with shocking red hair.

"Afternoon, Weatherby. How is life treating you?"

"Excellent, Montgomery, excellent. The girls are growing so quickly, they'll be out of leading strings before you know it." The contented smile on the man's face was testament to the love he felt for his twin daughters.

A pang of jealousy twisted Laurence's heart. He coughed, clearing his throat and hoping his next question would seem nonchalant. "How is your sister? Anne, isn't it?"

Andrew's hand poised mid-air as he prepared to drop his marker on the table. His eyebrows raised in question. "Willing to take her off my hands, Montgomery? The girl will be the death of me. My mother says if I don't find her a husband soon, we'll have scandal to pay."

The seriousness in Andrew's eyes sent an unwelcome itching around Laurence's collar, and he quickly clarified. "Simply inquiring about your family."

Andrew guffawed and slapped Laurence on the back. "Just bamming you, old man. But the expression on your face was worth thousands. Besides, you two wouldn't be a good match. Anne's much too young and flighty."

"She has no interest in the sciences?" It seemed a safe question to further eliminate the chit.

Andrew shook his head, his laughter continuing to ring throughout the card room, drawing annoyed glares from the other members. "Not unless there's a science to flirting." He stopped momentarily, as if considering. "However, I suppose there is. Or possibly an art."

For once, Laurence wished he were a master of small talk, but he pressed forward. "What do you know of Lady Honoria Bell?"

"Now I'm convinced there's something else to your questions," Andrew said. "Why the sudden interest in red-headed women?"

Although many accused Andrew Weatherby of being a dolt, the man's intellect was razor sharp. The speed with which he pieced together the commonality between the two women was nothing short of astounding. Laurence considered lying, but opted for the truth. "I'm trying to locate a particular young lady with red hair and green eyes."

"And an interest in science?"

"Yes."

"I've only a passing acquaintance with Lady Honoria. She seems intelligent and well educated and matches the description."

Laurence leaned forward, every nerve in his body on high alert.

"However, the woman most closely matching your description is Miss Beatrix Marbry."

Before Laurence had time to process the information, Nash strode up to the table, taking a seat. "Did I hear you mention Miss Marbry?"

Laurence wanted to plant him a facer and wipe the smirk off the man's face. His gut churned, remembering the scene he'd witnessed in the park. Especially with confirmation that Miss Marbry might very well be his lady in green. The idea she might be involved with Nash was unthinkable.

"It's a shame about her, wouldn't you say?" Nash continued, his eyes never leaving Laurence.

"What about her?"

Nash's smirk grew. "Haven't you heard? Lord Middlebury has offered for her. Can you imagine the poor woman? Underneath the weight of that disgusting excuse for a man? I doubt she'll be screaming 'Oh, Mervyn' in ecstasy." Nash raised his voice in falsetto, mimicking a woman's cry of passion.

No! Not now when he'd possibly found her. Why had he not thought to inquire like this before?

Andrew scoffed. "Really, Nash, must you be so crude? Why would her father agree to such a union? The man loves her."

"Money, my dear fellow. Owed to me. Middlebury has agreed to pay off his debt."

The scene in the park Laurence had witnessed now made sense. Miss Marbry most likely had gone to plead with Nash, asking him to show mercy. "I should have known you'd be involved. Can't you give the man time to pay?"

"Why should I be concerned where the money is coming from as long as I get it sooner rather than later?"

"Because it's the decent thing to do," Laurence mumbled.

"What's that, Montgomery?"

Laurence held his tongue. It would serve no purpose to allow Nash to be aware he now had a vested interest in the situation.

Andrew dealt the cards, sending Nash a glare and a sympathetic look toward Laurence.

Nash took a languorous sip of his tea. "Perhaps I should do the poor woman a favor and break her in for the old fool. Give her something to remember while she's buried beneath all that heaving flesh for years on end."

He threw a marker in the center of the table. "Yes, I think a seduction is in order. Perhaps it might even become a long standing association. The amount of time Middlebury spends toadying up to my brother could provide me easy access. She might prove an interesting diversion. While her husband entertains my brother, she could entertain me."

Laurence's urge to throw his cards down and launch himself at Nash grew. At the moment, nothing would feel better than having his hands around Nash's neck. Nothing except possibly having the lady in green in his arms.

He tamped down his anger. Could Miss Marbry actually harbor affection for old Middlebury? It seemed unlikely, but he hardly knew the woman. Hell, in truth, he didn't know her at all.

Yet, scouring the recesses of his memories, he recalled dancing with her years ago. Was it during her first Season? Something about Timothy objecting tickled the corner of his mind, but he was unable to pull it forth.

Could she be his lady in green? He needed time—proof—a plan. As casually as he could, he asked, "When and how are you planning this seduction?"

"Now why would I confide in you only to have you spoil it? Suffice to say it will be the most unexpected of times."

Laurence folded his hand, a certain winner, and rose from the table, unable to endure any more of the conversation. After marching from the room, he poured himself a large glass of brandy and swallowed it in one gulp. The burn of the alcohol did little to assuage his anger.

Someone touched his arm. He turned to find Andrew's kind face. After removing the glass from Laurence's hand, he said, "It's too early for that. Care to talk about it?"

What could he say that would make any sense? He couldn't even sort out his own feelings. "What he plans is vile. To take advantage of the poor woman."

Andrew tugged on his arm, pulling him into an empty room. "There's more to this than you're saying. The questions about a red-headed woman interested in science, now your reaction to Nash's news and plans. Although I agree with you, Nash might be all bluster. He seemed keen to elicit a reaction from you. There's more to this with him. He's baiting you, Montgomery. Don't fall for it."

"Am I that obvious?"

"I'm afraid so. Is the woman you seek Miss Marbry?"

"She might be. Regardless, she doesn't deserve either Middlebury or Nash."

"On that much, we agree. Miss Marbry and I have a friendship of sorts. Why don't I speak with her and see what I can find out?"

Relief flooded Laurence. "A logical step. Will you keep me apprised?"

"Of course." Andrew patted his back and left him alone with his thoughts.

Never had they been so jumbled.

CHAPTER 6—DOUBTS

Bea pondered Lord Nash's statement. *You must let me handle it my way.* What on earth did that mean? How many ways could you compromise someone? On second thought, perhaps she didn't want to know.

As much as she disliked it, Lord Nash controlled step three of her plan.

When she and Fanny returned home, rather than retreating to her room as usual, she sought out her mother. Poised at her escritoire, Matilda Marbry, Lady Saxton, was in her element, penning invitations to the engagement ball to be held within a week. A brief twinge of shame twisted in Bea's stomach that she would so soon disappoint her mother yet again. At least she would secure the funds for her father's debt, so perhaps in time her mother would forgive her.

She tapped lightly on the open door. Her mother lifted her gaze from the parchment before her. With a wide smile, she motioned Bea forward, the excited energy emanating from her practically palpable. "Beatrix. Come, darling. I've about finished with the invitations. I do hope the Duke and Duchess of Ashton will attend. Lady Cartwright said they are away from London at the moment."

Careful to control the tone of her voice, Bea asked, "Is Lord Nash invited?"

Her mother's hazel eyes narrowed. "I've invited his brother, the Marquess of Edgerton. Did you know Lord Middlebury has the marquess's ear? You'll be marrying a man of influence."

Bea had her doubts how much Lord Middlebury influenced anyone, especially the Marquess of Edgerton. "Lord Middlebury has mentioned it." *Ad nauseam.*

"An invitation to the marquess's household should be sufficient."

No, it wouldn't. "Has father spoken to you about his . . ." How could she phrase it? "His association with Lord Nash?"

The blank expression on her mother's face answered her question. It would seem her father had kept her mother in the dark.

"I believe Father would be most appreciative if you sent an invitation directly to Lord Nash. From what I understand, he doesn't reside with his brother."

With a huff, her mother plucked another piece of parchment from the stack on the escritoire. "Very well. But I certainly hope he doesn't make a scene if Ashton and the duchess are able to attend. There's no love lost between those two."

Guilt swarmed in her stomach like buzzing bees. Unfortunately, there *would* be a scene, but not the type her mother anticipated. "Thank you, Mother." Bea hurried off to speak with her father to prepare him should her mother question him about the request to invite Nash.

Pausing at the entrance of her father's study, she drew in a deep breath. If only he'd controlled himself at the tables. She knocked twice and waited for his permission before entering. His appearance had improved over the course of the last few days since she'd accepted Lord Middlebury's proposal. Color had returned to his face, and the worry lines around his eyes seemed smoother.

"Bea, Bea, come in." He rose to greet her and pulled out the very same chair where he'd delivered the horrific news two weeks prior. "And what may I do for my favorite daughter?"

"I'm your only daughter, Father."

"Yes, yes. Well, even if you weren't. Middlebury told me he

plans to provide the funds at the engagement ball. Lord Nash has yet to demand payment, so at the moment, things remain positive."

"About that, Father."

His countenance fell as if preparing for a death blow. "You haven't backed out?"

"No. I promised Middlebury I wouldn't break the engagement if he agreed to settle the debt before our wedding."

"As I said, my favorite daughter."

"However, it might be beneficial to ensure Lord Nash is in attendance so you may transfer the funds immediately. I've asked Mother to ensure he's invited." She cast a glance toward her hands, folded neatly on her lap. "I may have implied it was per your request. That you and Lord Nash had an . . . association."

One of his wiry eyebrows quirked. "I see."

Bea held her breath.

"You didn't mention what *type* of association to your mother, did you?"

"No."

He exhaled a heavy sigh, wiping at his forehead with two fingers. "Thank God. Very well, then. I appreciate your clever thinking. Don't mention anything to your mother. We wouldn't want to upset her. She's been flitting about the house like a new woman these past two days, planning an elaborate affair. I don't think I've seen her this happy since Timothy mustered out of the military and returned home."

Bea forced a smile and rose. "I didn't mean to interrupt. I should leave you."

"No interruption, dear girl, not at all. And Bea, I appreciate what you're doing for this family. For me. Truly."

She nodded and left, closing the door quietly behind her. The guilt transformed into a full-fledged pain, poking at her insides.

❃

BEA STARED AT THE BLANK PIECE OF PARCHMENT BEFORE HER. Preoccupied with worry about the possible failure of her plan, she'd been unable to formulate one coherent sentence for the article she attempted to write.

She refused to entertain the possibility of marriage to Lord Middlebury. She must succeed, she must! Failure was not an option.

But if she did succeed, at what cost? Timothy had a point. Her mother would at best refuse to speak with her for who knows how long, at worst, out of humiliation her mother might disown her. Bea would be ruined, her reputation left in tatters, removing any chance of a respectable marriage—not that she had much of a chance to begin with.

With easy grace, Catpurrnicus hopped on her lap and curled himself into a tight ball. "At least I would still have you, my little furball," she said, her throat tightening around the words. *And Timothy.* Surely he would understand and stand by her.

But if she failed? She shuddered at the thought of being trapped in a marriage to Lord Middlebury. Perhaps, given his weight and age, he might do her a favor and depart the mortal coil soon? She made a mental note to ask Ashton what might predispose a person to heart attacks.

The thought gave her pause. When had she become so blood thirsty to desire the demise of another living creature? *Desperation creates strange bedfellows.* The last word conjured unwanted images in her mind, and an oily liquid rose in her mouth, gagging her.

At least with the ball less than a week away, the outcome would soon be decided. Steady pounding resonated in her skull, growing stronger by the moment.

"Beatrix! Why is your door locked?" her mother's irate voice called from outside her room.

She rose to answer the increasingly persistent knocking. "I'm coming," she said, maintaining a calmness in her voice she didn't feel. *What now?*

"Really, Beatrix," her mother said, storming into her room. "I don't understand all this secrecy of yours." Her mother cast a quick glance toward the windows, presumably checking for bed sheets strung out of the window for an escape.

"Is it wrong to want a few moments of tranquility when I'm so soon to be sold off to the highest bidder?"

She waited and there it was—the roll of the eyes Bea knew all too well. "Secretive and melodramatic. Where do you get such notions? You should be grateful Lord Middlebury is willing to overlook such faults."

Bea bit her tongue so not to expound on the myriad of Lord Middlebury's faults. "What did you want, Mother?"

"Oh, yes," she said, waving a handkerchief about like a fan and sending the overbearing scent of rose water in Bea's direction. "You have callers."

Well, that is . . . unexpected.

"Now, hurry. Don't keep them waiting. You must learn these niceties to assume your place as Lady Middlebury."

Of course. As lady of the house, she would be expected to entertain, to play the devoted wife—the *lovely ornament*, agreeing with everything her husband said, keeping her opinions locked inside. However would she manage?

And what if they had children? There would be no happy romping in the dirt, digging for insects, chasing their favorite pet. Not with Middlebury as their father. Could she inflict his pompous and obsequious manner on another human being? The horror of what lay in wait should she truly have to marry Middlebury made her skin crawl. An icy shudder ran up her spine.

Relief flooded her as she entered the parlor after her mother. Andrew and Alice Weatherby smiled warmly in greeting. Andrew rose and executed a graceful bow. "Miss Marbry, I trust you're well."

Something in Andrew's face, a wariness in his eyes as he cast a quick glance toward her mother, piqued her curiosity. *Have they come to offer their condolences?* Surely not. The engagement had yet to be announced.

"Lady Saxton, my wife and I wouldn't want to detain you from your many important duties. I'm certain we would bore you to distraction with our idle conversation."

And people said Andrew Weatherby wasn't clever.

Her mother straightened, her eyes narrowing in suspicion at Andrew. "Very well."

She turned toward Beatrix. "I'll have Preston bring some tea."

As her mother left, Bea motioned for the Weatherbys to resume their seats, then settled on a sofa across from them. Andrew's gaze remained fixed on the doorway, as if expecting her mother to pop back into the room like one of those children's toys. The expression on Mrs. Weatherby's face confirmed it. They *had* heard something.

"Miss Marbry," Andrew said. "We've heard some . . . news. I trust our friendship permits me to enquire if it's true."

"If you're asking if Lord Middlebury has offered for me, yes, it's true."

Alice and Andrew exchanged a glance. Andrew lowered his voice to a hushed whisper. "Miss Marbry, you may speak freely with us, without fear of reprisal. But is this . . . welcome news to you? Are you happy about it?"

Tears were a waste of the precious resource of water. However, at the moment, Bea verged on wasting an ocean's worth. Without warning, the dam burst. Alice rushed to her side, pulling her into her arms. "Oh, Miss Marbry." She stroked Bea's back, a gesture Bea's own mother had rarely performed. Bea molded herself to the woman's comforting embrace.

Footsteps echoed in the hall, and Bea straightened, wiping the tears from her face moments before Preston entered the room with tea. Thankfully, the man seldom looked at her. He placed the tray on the table and asked, "Anything else, miss?"

"No, thank you." She managed to croak out the words and cringed at the emotion in her voice.

Alice Weatherby proved as clever as her husband. "The tea should help with that hoarseness, Miss Marbry."

Preston bowed and exited, closing the door behind him.

With shaking hands, Bea lifted the teapot to pour. What a horrible hostess she would make. No wonder she disappointed her mother. She failed utterly at all the social graces.

Alice placed a calming hand on Bea's. "Allow me, Miss Marbry." The ease at which Alice poured and handed her husband the cup and saucer established the bar Bea had never even striven to reach. Such niceties were of little importance to her. It shouldn't surprise her she had no suitors—except for Lord Middlebury.

After settling her emotions to a manageable degree, Bea's natural curiosity took over. "How did you hear? Mother is only now preparing the invitations to a ball where it will be announced."

Andrew sent her an apologetic look. "I'd hoped it was bluster since my source was Lord Nash."

Nash! The rogue. Terror gripped her that he'd revealed her plan. "What precisely did he say?"

Andrew shifted in his seat, his lips tightening as he cast a glance at his wife. "I don't wish to offend, but Nash said Middlebury has offered to settle a gambling debt owed to him by your father in exchange for your hand in marriage."

The weight of what Andrew might know lifted as if defying gravity itself. It wouldn't serve if anyone knew of her plan with Nash. "I'm afraid it's true. Papa needs me to marry to expunge the debt and Mama needs me to marry to redeem herself as a mother."

The compassion in Alice's face threatened to open the floodgates of Bea's tears once again, but she took a deep breath and fought the urge.

"Forgive me for saying so," Andrew said, "but he's been seeking a wife for years, and no woman has deemed him worthy. The fact that he's willing to buy a wife does not paint him in a favorable light. And to use your father's misfortune . . ." Andrew shook his head in disgust.

Alice nodded. "I narrowly escaped myself when my Great-Aunt Gertrude suggested a match with him. Thank goodness I met Andrew."

The love shining in Andrew's eyes as he gazed upon his wife warmed Bea's heart even in her moment of despair. "Indeed, Miss Marbry, we have you to thank."

"Me?" Confused, Bea choked out the word.

"Why, yes. Don't you remember?" Andrew asked. "A fortuitous stumble directly into the path of my beloved."

Of course! Bea thought back to the night. She had been dancing with Andrew, and Laurence had passed, precipitating the usual clumsiness and propelling Andrew into the Dowager Countess Brakefeld and her great-niece Alice.

"We shall be eternally grateful, Miss Marbry," Alice said.

"Is there no other way to obtain the money?" Andrew asked. "Perhaps I could loan—"

"It's twenty thousand pounds," Bea blurted, and Andrew's eyes widened. "But I have resigned myself to my fate. You need not worry about me, my dear friends. One must do what one must. Is that not so?" There, not a lie. She indeed had resigned herself to being ruined and unsuitable for the remainder of her days after Nash compromised her.

"Very well," Andrew said. "But if there's anything at all Alice or I can do, please don't hesitate to ask."

"Will you visit me often?" she asked, her voice hopeful that there might be some bright spots in her bleak future.

"Of course," Alice said.

"Now, shall we move on to a more pleasant topic? How are those dear twins of yours?"

As Alice spoke of her twin girls, Bea wondered what it would be like to have children by a man she loved. No matter what happened with her plan, she'd never know. She'd either be a spinster or married to Lord Middlebury.

One must do what one must.

CHAPTER 7—THE ENGAGEMENT BALL

The next few days passed in a haze for Bea. Her mother, at least, had been preoccupied with ordering the servants in preparation for the ball. After fussing at Bea for her lack of appropriate, ink-free gowns, they settled on the lovely emerald green gown she'd worn at the Duke of Ashton's masquerade ball over a year ago.

Bittersweet memories flooded Bea's mind as the seamstress pinned it to make slight adjustments. The brief interlude with Lord Montgomery in the duke's library had been something she'd called forward only late at night while she had lain alone in her bed, concocting a fairytale ending in which he'd taken her in his arms and declared his undying love. Those memories and fantasies would be tainted when the association of the gown forever became linked to her betrothal to Lord Middlebury and her ultimate ruination by Lord Nash.

The seamstress scowled, placing a pin in the bodice of the gown. "Hold still, Miss Marbry, unless you wish to be poked."

Her mother had asked for the neckline to be lowered per the latest fashion. Why go to such measures when she'd effectively already secured a husband—at least in her mother's eyes—Bea was unsure. Yet she did her best to be the submissive and obedient daughter. There would be enough hell to pay after the ball.

Lord Middlebury had called every day since she'd accepted his proposal. She had to remind herself not to call him Lord Fat Middle to his face. Catpurrnicus was relegated to a locked room during Middlebury's calls, and the caterwauling mercifully cut her time in his presence short. The idea of leaving her beloved pet or finding him another home—which in itself would be a challenge—set her more on edge than the idea of becoming Beatrix Thistlewhite, Lady Middlebury. That morning, he'd actually had the nerve to pinch her bottom, and she had an intense desire to release Catpurrnicus from his prison.

With the seamstress finally finished, Bea slipped off the dress, touching the fine satin and remembering Lord Montgomery's handsome face one last time in connection to the garment. She redressed in her peach-colored muslin day gown *decorated* with black spots of ink. Middlebury had commented that it appeared as if ants crawled upon the fabric, then muttered something about having to pay for a new wardrobe upon their marriage.

He'd already provided funds for her wedding gown. The seamstress had presented a rendering before her fitting, a lovely pale green the color of mint and embroidered with daisies around the bodice and sleeves. A sunny yellow ribbon under the bodice would complete it to perfection.

She would have loved the gown under any other circumstance. However, if things went as planned, and Middlebury ended their engagement, he would assuredly cancel the commission, and she'd never wear it. Or worse, her plan would fail and the dress would forever remind her of the day her life effectively ended.

Lost in her maudlin thoughts, she gazed out the window of her room. Catpurrnicus rubbed his body against her legs, purring contentedly. Her spirits lifted at the sight of Timothy alighting from a carriage. He halted, glancing up and giving her a wave, then bounded up the steps to their townhouse. Since he'd moved to his own residence, she missed him terribly, but she envied his independence.

Hoping to have a moment alone with him, she hurried downstairs to greet him. Certainly, as soon as Preston announced his arrival, their mother would monopolize his time. Timothy smiled in greeting upon seeing her, the gesture not quite reaching his moss green eyes.

"Bea, how are you holding up?" he asked, careful to wait until Preston had left.

"I need to speak with you in private." No sense in wasting time with polite exchanges.

His eyes widened. "What's happened?"

The excited voice of their mother sounded from the upstairs hallway, and Bea shook her head. "Nothing. Yet. But I need your assistance, and I can't discuss it in front of Mother."

"Very well." He nodded.

For the next hour and forty-three minutes Bea sat in relative silence as their mother fawned over Timothy. As usual, Bea had become virtually invisible, her presence hardly acknowledged. Although she loved her family, and especially her brother, she learned to block out most of their conversation, as it rarely involved her. However, her mother's protest at the latest thing Timothy had said recaptured her attention.

"But Timothy, why? You'll inherit someday. Why pursue an occupation?"

Occupation? Whatever does she mean?

"I developed quite an interest in medicine during my time in the military, Mother. I assisted the surgeons, and they agreed I have a gift for healing. My focus at university in Edinburgh these past two years has been medicine. I only have to return to finish my studies and take the exams. Perhaps I might obtain a position at Ashton's clinic."

"The ridiculous notions of the Duke of Ashton seem to be contagious," her mother said, then laughed at her own clever play on words.

Bea straightened, heartily approving of her brother's wish to be productive. "I think it's wonderful."

Her mother startled as if she'd just realized Bea was in the room, then waved her off with a dismissive hand. "Well, of course you would. It's a wonder you haven't considered it for yourself."

Obviously, her mother meant the last as a jest, but it ignited a spark in Bea's depressed state. "I would if they would permit women an occupation other than governess, maid, cook, seamstress, or wh—"

"Bea," Timothy interjected, quickly saving her from throwing their mother into a state of apoplexy.

Her mother squared her shoulders and faced Bea with an icy stare. "Well, be grateful that you won't have to worry about such trivialities once you become Lady Middlebury."

Grateful? Trivialities? Indeed! She gripped the arms of her chair with such ferocity her knuckles turned white.

Like a warning shot over the bow of a ship, Timothy sent a quelling glance her way. She bit her tongue, the metallic tang of blood and accompanying pain refocusing her pent up frustration.

Precisely seventeen minutes later, at the allotted two-hour limit her mother had placed on social calls—even with her own children —her mother dashed off to deliver more instructions to the servants, who no doubt had failed miserably in some task.

Alone with Timothy, Bea chose her words carefully, unable to be completely truthful regarding her plans with Lord Nash. "I have a task for you at the engagement ball."

"Bea, about that. I'm sorry I couldn't acquire the funds to settle the debt."

"It was hopeless from the onset. Twenty thousand pounds. What on earth had Father been thinking?"

"So you're resigned to marry Middlebury?" he asked, his voice cracking with emotion.

"If I must. However, I have a plan that may yet save us all."

He straightened, his bright eyes glimmering with hope. "Oh?"

"But you must trust me and ask me no questions."

"Bea?"

Guilt churned in her stomach at the warning in his voice. "During the engagement ball, I have a surprise planned. When I alert you, bring Lord Middlebury with you to a place I shall designate."

"What type of surprise?"

"No questions."

"I don't like the sound of this."

"If you love me, you'll help me."

He drew a hand down his face. "You're going to play that card, 'eh? Can you promise me that whatever you're planning won't hurt you?"

No, she couldn't promise that. "I can promise it will be the best for everyone involved."

With Timothy's reluctant agreement, the only unpredictable piece was Nash.

Bea prayed he'd deliver.

⚜

WHEN THE ANNOUNCEMENT FOR MISS MARBRY'S ENGAGEMENT arrived, an odd pressure constricted Laurence's chest. Not that he hadn't been prepared. He'd spoken to Andrew Weatherby, who confirmed both the news of the betrothal and the debt Lord Saxton owed Lord Nash. Three times Laurence set out for Lord Saxton's residence to call upon Miss Marbry, and three times he'd instructed his driver to turn the carriage around and return.

Andrew had mentioned that Miss Marbry, although not pleased with her situation, seemed resolute in her decision to marry Middlebury. Who was Laurence to interfere? Rules of etiquette dictated that he refrain from making a call upon an engaged woman for purposes of seeking an attachment.

However, try as he might to put her out of his mind, the chance she might be his lady in green tormented him. The ball itself might provide an opportunity to confirm his suspicions. The question remained, what would he do if those suspicions proved true? And even if they did, it didn't mean she'd felt the unique connection between them that he did the night of the masquerade.

He could hardly ask her to break an engagement based on a

connection only he might have experienced, could he? And of course there was the matter of the debt. As unfortunate as Miss Marbry's situation appeared, Laurence couldn't help but admire her sacrifice to ensure her family's well-being. Which only made him more drawn to her.

Damnation!

As his valet fussed with his cravat, Laurence's mind contemplated numerous scenarios. If Miss Marbry was indeed his mysterious lady, he would confront Nash regarding the debt. Although Andrew had informed him of the staggering amount, Laurence held Nash's vowels in the amount of three thousand, which would reduce the amount somewhat.

"Hold still, sir, or I'll have fashioned a noose more than a neckcloth," Stevens said, his brow furrowing in annoyance.

Had he been fidgeting?

It was as if his whole life hung on the unanswered question. Was Miss Beatrix Marbry his mysterious lady? Straightening his tailcoat and gauging his appearance in the mirror, he supposed he would soon find out.

⚜

BEA HAD NEVER BEEN COMFORTABLE ATTENDING BALLS OR PARTIES, but having one held in her honor elevated her discomfort to a whole new level. She much preferred blending into the woodwork as a wallflower, or at the very least, the anonymity of a masked ball, where she could observe the other party goers from afar and avoid judgmental eyes gathering gossip to share over their morning tea.

On full display, she had no doubt she would provide endless fodder for the next morning's scandal sheets. Of course, if her plan went accordingly, the last was a given, taking precedence over mere mention of any other minor mishap such as spilling a glass of ratafia or stumbling and treading on her dance partner's feet. Her "compromise" would surely be headline worthy.

Lord Middlebury arrived early, expounding on the virtues of punctuality to her parents. If his pompous pronouncement of never having been late for anything in his life hadn't been enough to make Bea gag, his obsequious praise of her mother's beauty would have done the trick.

Her mother flirted and blushed as if she were the one to be betrothed to the old fool. Her father merely stood stoically by, his mouth set in a tight line.

When her betrothed finally turned his gaze on her, his eyes widened, then dipped to the *now* low-cut bodice. She swore he licked his lips, and an oily queasiness churned in her stomach.

"My dear." He tipped his head in the facsimile of a bow, his tailcoat buttons straining against his corpulent body. She feared one of them would pop and soar forward, putting out someone's eye. Mercifully, her glasses provided some protection against such a fiasco.

Her mother surreptitiously elbowed her in the ribs, leaning over to whisper, "Offer him your hand."

Thank goodness gloves provided a barrier between her skin and his lips as he placed a slobbering kiss upon her fingers. She forced a smile, certain it appeared more like the grimace she tried to suppress. "You're looking . . ." She struggled for a flattering yet truthful word. "Well-fed."

Her father emitted a subdued groan, and although Lord Middlebury seemed unaffected, the icy glare from her mother proved sufficient to make Bea cringe with ignominy. But her current shame would pale in comparison to the ire she would face from her mother if her plan succeeded.

Bea amended the thought. *When my plan succeeds.* She cast a quick glance at Lord Middlebury. *For it must, or I am doomed.*

As guests began to arrive, her unease grew, her skin itching as if she contracted Cow Pox the venerable Mr. Jenner had so thoroughly discussed in his treatise. The thought itself exacerbated her anxiety as it led to the image of the warm brown eyes of Lord Montgomery and the night in the Duke of Ashton's library.

The tension in her neck lessened upon catching sight of Lord Nash as he strode into the ballroom with his brother, Roland, the Marquess of Edgerton, and their sister, Lady Charlotte. Thank the gods he'd come. All hinged upon his cooperation. His lips curved in a smile as he approached, and he bowed over her offered hand.

"My felicitations upon your engagement, Miss Marbry. If Lord Middlebury does not object, I hope you will grace me with a dance this evening." His dark eyes met hers, and he gave a discreet and conspiratorial wink.

"I would be honored, Lord Nash."

He moved to Lord Middlebury. "Congratulations, sir. Your good fortune has bereft the rest of us of Miss Marbry's charms."

Middlebury cleared his throat as if dislodging one of Catpurrnicus's hairballs, the sound wet and disgusting. "Indeed. She honors me." He moved closer to Bea as if he were a dog protecting his bone.

After Nash had moved on, Middlebury fawned over Nash's brother, Lord Edgerton, his ingratiating tone enough to turn Bea's stomach as if it hadn't already been roiling. When they moved on to join the rest of the guests, Middlebury leaned in, his foul breath torturing her nostrils. "One dance with Nash, since you've already agreed. But I don't approve of him, my dear. I demand you avoid him after this evening. On the other hand, his brother is a man of significant influence, and I expect you to maintain the decorum necessary to remain in his good graces."

Demand? How dare he? Only the sight of Lord Montgomery entering the ballroom suppressed the urge to stomp on Lord Middlebury's fat foot and tell him to go to the devil.

Lord and Lady Easton and Lady Miranda accompanied Lord Montgomery. As if sensing Bea's interest, his gaze met hers, and her heart tumbled in her chest. Even across the expanse of the room, he affected her, her knees weakening. Thankfully, she fell more into her father on her left than Lord Middlebury, who stood on her right.

Her father grasped her arm to steady her. "Are you ill, my dear? Perhaps the excitement of it all?" The touching concern in his voice eased the pain from the knowledge that he had used her as a solution to his problems.

The excitement? As if being betrothed to Lord Middlebury would make anyone giddy. The ludicrous thought elicited a giggle.

The arch of her father's brows indicated his confusion. He leaned closer. "Perhaps not ill. Have you fortified yourself for this evening with my whisky?"

She shook her head, trying desperately to compose herself. Lord Montgomery came closer, his eyes still trained on her in a most unnerving manner. Were there remnants of her light supper on her face? Surely Fanny would have said so when she'd helped Bea dress for the evening.

After greeting her parents, he stood before her, staring into her eyes. A flicker of something she couldn't name passed across his face.

Heat rushed up her neck, and her cheeks flamed at Lord Montgomery's direct gaze. Her insides had suddenly turned into the gooey substance she'd once concocted as a child in Cook's kitchen. Her hand shook as she extended it and placed it in his.

He bowed, as Nash had done. "May I offer my felicitations, Miss Marbry?" Although similar to Nash's words, the tone in which he'd delivered them didn't contain the teasing tone Nash's had. He sounded—sad. No, not sad—regretful.

But why?

He gave her no time to ponder the puzzlement. He turned toward Lord Middlebury. "Sir, with your permission, perhaps your lady would honor me with a dance this evening."

She gulped. Literally gulped, certain everyone around her heard the liquid being forced down her throat. The urge to scream *I'm not his lady* rose and grew dangerously close to finding voice.

"Of course, sir," Middlebury said, then turned toward her. "If you wish it, my dear."

Lord Montgomery's eyes were back on her in a flash, as if he had no other wish in the world but for her to agree.

"The honor would be mine, sir." How she managed the words, she'd never know.

His smile seemed bittersweet. "I shall look forward to it most eagerly."

At that moment, everything about her plan seemed horribly wrong.

FROM THE MOMENT LAURENCE WALKED INTO THE BALLROOM, ONE glimpse of the green gown Miss Marbry wore confirmed his suspicions. Had she worn it on purpose? Was it a message to him? A distress signal?

If that weren't enough, when he stood before her, he allowed himself to really study her, finally *see* her—past the smudged spectacles to those incredible forest green eyes. It had taken every measure of his strength to remain a gentleman and not utter a loud protest at the farce of the pairing before him.

His lady and Lord Middlebury! Except she wasn't his. When the music commenced and Middlebury lead her onto the dance floor, the memories of the masquerade ball surfaced as clear as if it were happening in that very moment. The petite redhead led in dance by the duke. The encounter in the library, how she hid behind the book. All became crystal clear. He'd been such a fool not to pursue it further, to inquire in more depth.

A moment of dizziness caught him off guard, and he wondered if the room had suddenly become warmer.

"Laurence." He turned, finding Miranda's concerned gaze. "What is it? You appear positively . . . lost."

An apt word, the irony of it all hitting him in the gut. He opened his mouth, but snapped it shut. What good would it do to confide in Miranda when there was nothing to be done about his dreadful situation? He had no fear she'd laugh at him, but neither did he wish her pity. A gentleman was *not* to be pitied.

"Is it the duchess?" she asked, nodding toward where Margaret stood next to Harry, the Duke of Ashton. Of course Miranda would attribute his melancholic state to his long-suffering tendre for Her Grace. He'd harbored it for so long it had become a part of him.

However, when he watched her affectionately touch her husband's arm as they spoke with Lord and Lady Saxton, a sense of peace filled him, and he realized he was grateful for the happiness she'd found with Harry. "No," he answered truthfully.

"Then what?"

He shook his head. "Nothing which to concern yourself. I'm merely feeling the sting of being a resigned bachelor, I suppose."

A delicate brown eyebrow lifted. "Resigned? Don't let mother hear you say that, or the pleasant evening I'd hoped for will vanish as quickly as my pin money on a new bonnet."

She perused the crowded ballroom. "However, should you wish to rectify that state, there are a number of eligible ladies here."

He coaxed a smile forward, reluctant to think of any other lady except Miss Marbry. Must he forever long for a woman who could not be his?

Mercifully, Miranda wandered off when she caught sight of Anne Weatherby. No doubt the two would spend time predicting what would appear in the next morning's gossip sheets. He lifted a glass of sherry off a tray from a passing footman, the sweetness of the liquor sending his mind back to Miss Marbry, wondering if her lips would be as sweet. Lord, he was hopeless.

Something vile churned in his gut as Middlebury led her around the dance floor, his enormous body blocking Laurence's view of Miss Marbry. He felt positively ill. Perhaps he had come down with something. Glancing at the small glass in his hand, he resisted the temptation to drink more and placed it on a nearby table.

"Lord Montgomery."

He turned toward the feminine voice and bowed toward Nash's sister. "Good evening, Lady Charlotte." Although he had nothing against Charlotte, her mere relationship to Nash set Laurence's teeth on edge when he remembered Nash's boast at the card table about seducing Miss Marbry. A quick scan of the room indicated Nash had partnered with Lady Honoria Bell on the dance floor.

"I must admit the announcement of Miss Marbry's engagement to Lord Middlebury came as a surprise. I believed she had remained resolutely on the shelf."

Laurence searched Lady Charlotte's face for expected signs of malice, but found none. What he did find was far more disgusting. *Pity.*

"I suppose," she said, "there is truth to the expression beggars can't be choosers. But I should think spinsterhood would be preferable to marriage to Mervyn Thistlewhite. Nash has found it quite amusing."

"I'm sure he has," Laurence said through clenched teeth.

With a delicate flick of her wrist, Lady Charlotte snapped open her fan and leaned in conspiratorially. "He believes Miss Marbry has only agreed to marry Lord Middlebury in order to hide her affair with another man. Although I find it difficult to believe, I shall remain alert for any suspicious activity."

Laurence's gaze shot to Nash, who happened to catch his eye as he maneuvered the dance. He swore Nash smirked, as if able to hear the sordid suspicions his sister had shared.

"This is hardly appropriate conversation during the lady's engagement ball, Lady Charlotte. I'm surprised you countenance such aspersions." Laurence had quite enough of the exchange and sought an excuse to remove himself from the situation.

The perfect opportunity arose as he discovered Timothy Marbry speaking with Miranda. "If you will forgive me, I must speak with my sister."

Lady Charlotte mumbled something. Probably affronted by Laurence's curt dismissal, but he didn't care. He needed some answers, and Timothy Marbry might be just the man to provide them. However, as he approached, the light in his sister's smile as she spoke with Timothy nearly stopped him in his tracks. Miranda had hinted about a man of whom he wouldn't approve. Surely not Timothy? He and Laurence were the best of friends. Why would she think he wouldn't approve?

"You two appear thick as thieves," he said, forcing a teasing tone to his voice.

Miranda jerked toward him, her cheeks darkening. "Must you sneak up on a person?"

Laurence made a show of gazing around the ballroom. "In a crowded room? What did I interrupt?"

Timothy remained silent, his gaze shifting to the left toward the dance floor.

"Nothing," Miranda said. "We were discussing the latest

fashions. Timothy believes waistlines in women's gowns will continue to lower."

"He does, does he?" As if his sister's ridiculous assertion wasn't enough to raise suspicion, Laurence studied his friend's face for the telltale signs of deceit. "Since when have you become a cognoscente of ladies garments, Marbry?"

Miranda rolled her eyes. "Perhaps if you devoted more time to pursuing women instead of those dreadfully dry science books, you might be more in tune to the latest styles, dear brother." She leaned toward Timothy. "Two years in Italy and all he has to show for it is increased vocabulary. You would have at least thought he would have picked up a seduction trick or two."

"Really, Miranda. Mother would be appalled," Laurence scolded.

His sister waved him off. "I have no desire to be censured by you. If you would excuse me, Mr. Marbry." She curtsied toward Timothy, then sent a glare over her shoulder at Laurence before wandering off toward the refreshment table.

"Is there something you wish to tell me, Marbry?" Laurence asked, doing his best to maintain coolness to his tone. "Is there something between you and my sister?"

Timothy snorted a laugh. "Heavens, no. I like Miranda, but I've abided by our silent agreement not to pursue a romantic entanglement with each other's sister."

Good Lord. So tucked away in the recesses of his mind, he'd forgotten about the pledge they'd taken at Eton when they were boys. At thirteen, they'd developed a keen interest in girls, but Timothy had become like a brother, so the idea of him kissing Miranda had been off-putting. As for himself, it was no hardship. When he'd visited Lowell Manor, Timothy's country home in Wiltshire, Beatrix had often been covered in dirt from her preoccupation with garden insects. At nine, she was far removed from the powdered, sweet-smelling girls whose budding figures captured his attention.

Could the promise, buried so deep, have unknowingly dissuaded him from considering Miss Marbry as a possible marriage prospect?

Laurence cast a sweeping glance across the room, landing squarely on Miss Marbry. "That was ages ago."

Timothy's head turned in the direction of Laurence's gaze. "If you're reconsidering, it's a bit too late."

Without warning, Laurence's neckcloth became unbearably tight, but he resisted the impulse to run a finger around his collar to loosen it. "Pardon?"

"It's a pity, too. She would have been much happier with you."

"I didn't say I—"

Timothy slapped him on the back. "Relax, old friend. I was bamming you. Although what I said is true."

"She's not happy about her engagement to Middlebury?"

The snort from Timothy would have been answer enough, but he grew serious. "Would you be if you were a woman? God, look at him. It pains me that there is nothing I can do to rescue her from this intolerable situation."

A spark of hope ignited in Laurence's chest. If Miss Marbry didn't wish for the match, perhaps it wasn't too late for him. He did his best to maintain a casual tone to his question. "What if she had another suitor?"

Timothy gave a sad shake to his head. "Not unless he were willing to offer a small fortune to settle my father's debt."

"So the rumor's true?"

"I'm afraid so," Timothy answered, his face glum. He jerked his chin, drawing Laurence's attention. "Speak of the devil."

As if sensing the conversation involved him, Nash approached from across the ballroom like a lion stalking his prey.

"Marbry, Montgomery," Nash said as if they were old friends.

Only the rules of decorum prevented Laurence from smashing a fist into the man's smug face.

"Excuse me, Montgomery, I'm suddenly feeling ill," Timothy said. With a disdainful glance at Nash over his shoulder, Timothy strode away, leaving Laurence alone with the reprobate of a man.

"My, he's touchy." Nash at least appeared to be in excellent humor.

"It's bad form to gloat, Nash. Especially at others' expense."

"I'm merely enjoying the evening. Unlike you. What's gotten under your skin? Surely not concern over the sacrificial lamb, Miss Marbry?"

"If you had a heart . . ."

Nash's laugh sent a chill up Laurence's spine. "I believe we've established I don't. But if I did"—his eyes darted toward the dance floor—"I might provide said lamb a moment's pleasure before she fell on her sword."

Had the temperature in the room risen? It had become unbearably warm.

"I shudder to think what *help* you would provide." A vile taste flooded Laurence's mouth at the thought.

"You might lengthen your life if, for once, you decided to forgo all your structure and rules of decorum and *live* a little, Montgomery. There's nothing at all wrong with enjoying the pleasures of a lovely woman."

"There is when it comes to seducing that lovely woman against her will."

Nash laughed again and gave a wink. "No one said she wouldn't be willing."

"Miss Marbry wouldn't . . ."

Nash's dark brows lifted. "Wouldn't she? There will come a day, Montgomery, when you'll be knocked off that white steed of yours, and I, for one, will be eager to witness it. Now, if you'll excuse me, I believe Miss Marbry owes me a dance."

CHAPTER 8—THE TRAP

Bea needed a clear head, and the presence of Lord Montgomery, in all his glorious manliness, did nothing to assist her pursuit. As she cast a quick glance in his direction, she stumbled yet again. This time against Lord Middlebury. Of course he himself proved as clumsy, stepping on her foot in return. She bit back the scream forming in her throat from the pain shooting up her leg.

Her task of inquiring about his intention to settle her father's debt grew more difficult as she navigated the steps of the country dance. With only mere snippets of time to speak to him, she chose her words carefully.

"Are we still in agreement, my lord?"

"Agreement regarding what, dear lady?" His question matched the clueless expression on his dim-witted face.

"My father's debt." *Blast.* The next few steps had her moving toward Lord Nash, positioned next to them in the line of dancers. She would need to wait for his answer.

Not one to waste an opportunity of his own, Lord Nash whispered. "Do you have my blunt?"

"Not yet. I'm in the process of securing it now."

He nodded, moving back to his own partner, Lady Honoria.

If only these infernal dances allowed partners to remain together. Her thoughts immediately turned to the waltz. She supposed, unless her plan progressed much sooner than she anticipated, she would be forced to partner that particular dance with her *betrothed*. The word stuck in her throat, but she forced a smile as she faced him once again. "Sir? My question."

"I'm ready to settle at the end of the evening," he said.

Not what she wanted to hear. She batted her eyes. Her mother had once informed her that was a useful tactic for flirting. "Is there nothing I can do to entice you to settle it sooner?"

She waited for the next pass to further her plea and ran a hand up his arm. "It would ease my mind considerably, my lord."

She surprised herself that she'd been able to deliver the performance with such aplomb. Perhaps once her reputation was in tatters, she could find employment as an actress.

The widening of Middlebury's eyes confirmed she'd struck her intended target, yet he remained silent. Two more passes and the dance would end. She must be bold. Gathering all the courage she could muster, she leaned close in the next pass, whispering, "I would be happy to express my gratitude *privately*, my lord."

And, bullseye. No one, not even the most naïve, could miss the lustful gleam in Lord Middlebury's eyes. She feigned innocence and at the last pass of the dance said, "It's only that Lord Nash is in attendance. It would make things so much easier."

The dance ended, and Middlebury made his pitiful excuse of a bow, saying, "Of course, my dear. I shall settle with your father forthwith." He leaned closer. "Alert me when and where I should meet you to receive your . . . gratitude."

As she curtsied, she caught Nash's eye and gave a discreet nod. She congratulated herself on the stroke of genius in suggesting Middlebury meet her alone, only to find her in the arms of Lord Nash. Perhaps her plan had righted itself.

She needed to finalize the plan with Nash, but Middlebury hovered by her side. "Perhaps a dance with my mother, my lord? I'm sure she would be most flattered. You will soon become family after all."

As if the thought hadn't occurred to him, his face turned a ghastly shade of puce, and he made a disgusting wet noise as he cleared his throat. "I should be delighted."

With Middlebury and her mother both occupied on the dance floor, Bea managed to catch Lord Nash's eye. At the refreshment table, she procured a glass of ratafia, waiting for Nash to join her.

He strolled up as if he had all the time in the world and didn't hold her entire life in his hands. *Men!*

"Refreshment, my lord?" she asked.

He shook his head. "Too sweet for me." His lips quirked, as if speaking of something other than the drink. Instead, he pulled a slim flask from his inner pocket.

She motioned to a quiet spot at the side of the room. "Shall we move out of the way?"

Once out of earshot of other guests, he said, "Did you have success?"

She kept her voice low and her words vague, lest unexpected ears eavesdrop on their conversation. "Rest assured, sir, you shall have what is your due. May I rely on you to keep your promise?"

"Did I promise something?" His lips quirked, and she wanted to slap the smirk off his smug face.

Why must he make it difficult? "You know very well of which I speak."

He laughed, his black eyes flashing. "Have no fear, Miss Marbry. You shall have your wish by the end of the evening."

"Where shall we meet? There are several possibilities. The small parlor at the end of the hallway, perhaps?"

"I presume you have a library?" he asked.

"Yes, on the left of the stairway landing. But isn't a library a strange place for an arranged tryst?" she asked, although she found the idea somewhat comforting. To be around her beloved books may indeed provide a calming effect.

"I do believe it would be the perfect place for what I have in mind."

She tried to picture a seduction occurring in that particular room, having difficulty imagining how or on what they would position themselves. Heat flooded her cheeks at her next question. "Where would we . . ."

"There is a desk, isn't there?"

Oh, my! "We're not really going to . . ."

He laughed, the sound of it heating her face further. "No." He stepped closer, his gaze dipping to her bosom, the strong smell of whisky on his breath reaching her nose. "Unless you wish me to? You did offer to be my mistress."

"As I've never been seduced before, I'm merely trying to understand how far this farce will go. We must lay out the logistics for it to proceed smoothly." She swallowed. "Am I to . . . undress?"

His eyes raked over her, the pause before answering her near unbearable. "Perhaps if you pull your gown down, off your shoulder enough to suggest I was in the process of removing it."

"Well . . . I . . . is that possible? I've never tried it."

"Oh, it's possible, I assure you. Can you reach the top lace at the back of your gown? Just give it a little tug to loosen it after you enter the library."

"So am I to enter first and you will follow?"

"We must at least appear as if we don't wish to arouse suspicion."

With a nod, Bea prayed he would not let her down.

As Bea waited for the signal that Nash had received the funds for her father's debt, every fiber of her being tingled. The nervous energy coursing through her body heightened her senses. Heat from candle flames seemed to scorch her skin. The music became unbearably loud and grating. Subdued chatter rose in volume until she wished to place her hands over her ears. The acidic taste of bile rose in her throat. Even the muted lavenders and cornflower blue colors of the ladies' gowns assaulted her eyes.

She'd managed to corner Timothy, informing him that upon her signal of a head nod before she left the ballroom, he should wait ten minutes and then lead Lord Middlebury to the library. Her heart beat like a metronome keeping time for an allegrissimo piano piece, and perspiration beaded her brow.

At last Nash, catching her attention, gave a discreet nod, signaling the time had arrived. On shaky legs, Bea wove her way through the crowded ballroom. The sensation that all heads turned toward her—watching, judging—permeated her mind. Her breath caught in her throat as she passed Lord Montgomery, his gaze fixed unwaveringly upon her.

Warmth flooded her cheeks at his stare. Her stomach lurched uncomfortably, tumbling, turning, churning. She allowed herself a long, lingering look into his soft brown eyes one last time, knowing soon any good opinion he held of her would be shattered as easily as glass against a hearth. And although she never truly believed she had any chance of winning his heart, the dream she'd held onto for so long would soon be wiped away by evening's end.

She paused momentarily at the doorway, catching Timothy's attention, and nodded her signal. He returned the nod and pulled out his pocket watch, marking the time.

Out of the ballroom, she quickly made her way to the dimly lit library. A few candles provided enough light to make out the vague shapes of the furniture and rows of books lining the walls. Would they be enough? She quickly lit a few more, maintaining the dreamlike atmosphere but allowing enough detail to eliminate any doubt of what Middlebury would witness.

Her heart hammered so hard she thought it might pop out of her chest. She pulled in three deep breaths, exhaling slowly in a useless attempt to calm herself.

Following Nash's instructions, she pulled at the sleeve of her gown with trembling fingers. It wouldn't budge. Then she remembered the laces at the back. With difficulty, she reached behind her and tugged on the top lace, loosening the gown's bodice. The gown slipped more than she intended, and she held it in place with a shaky hand.

The pendulum of the grandfather clock in the corner moved in arduous motion, as if it too struggled to mark the time as she waited, hoping Nash would arrive soon and this whole business would be over. She'd reached the point of no return, and she closed her eyes to say a silent prayer that her ruination would not be for naught.

Footsteps sounded in the hallway, and she clutched her gown closer to her bosom, preparing for Nash's arrival. The sound of the soft padding stopped at the entrance to the library, and she whispered. "Is it you?"

"Miss Marbry, are you . . . unharmed?" the distinctively male voice asked.

A voice definitely not belonging to Lord Nash.

Bea's eyes shot open, her hand releasing the bodice of her gown as she gazed at her beloved Laurence.

⬨

LAURENCE HAD SEEN NASH SLIP OUT OF THE BALLROOM SHORTLY after Miss Marbry. The blush on her cheeks as she'd darted a glance at him evidenced something was afoot. Surely she had no idea what trouble she'd opened herself to with Nash?

After exiting the ballroom, Laurence had scanned the hallway, but Nash had disappeared. His search of nearby rooms found them empty. Light from a room by the staircase landing spilled from the slightly ajar doorway.

Unsure what he would find, he certainly never expected to discover her half-dressed. Panic shot up his spine like a bolt of lightning.

Miss Marbry's eyes widened, her gasp audible. "Lord Montgomery!" The bodice of her gown dropped, revealing soft, white . . . Laurence swallowed hard, forcing his eyes from her partially revealed breast.

Without thought to propriety, he barged into the room. "Nash, I swear if you've harmed her in any way, you'll pay. If you live to tell about it." Like a man possessed, he frantically surveyed the library, searching behind the sofa, the wingback chairs, any possible hiding place.

Someone grasped his arm, and he spun, staring into the alluring green eyes of Miss Marbry.

"You must leave at once!" she said, her voice rising in pitch.

"Where is he?" Like a magnetic force pulling him, his gaze drew to her exposed bosom. *Look away, man, look away!* Yet he could not.

"Please, sir. There is so little time."

What in the deuce? "It is you who should leave. Nash is on his way, Miss Marbry. Please allow me to help you with your gown." As he reached up to tug the delicate puff sleeve back into place, the touch of her skin, soft as velvet, stopped his fingers as if they too had been fastened to her shoulder by the invisible magnetic force.

The enormity of the situation must have taken its toll on her, for she collapsed against him in a swoon. Quickly, he snaked an arm around her waist to support her. When she gave a soft moan, telling him she was still conscious, he fought the urge to pull her closer to him.

Any further thought about performing such an ungallant action was shattered by a booming male voice. "What is the meaning of this!"

He turned toward the doorway of the library where Timothy and Lord Middlebury had gathered.

"I asked you a question, sir," Middlebury said, raising his voice as if Laurence hadn't heard him the first time.

Timothy stared at Laurence, his mouth agape in disbelief and condemnation in his eyes.

Moments later, Lord Saxton and the cad Lord Nash—who seemed to be smirking in satisfaction—joined them at the entrance.

"Unhand my daughter," Lord Saxton bellowed in outrage.

Miss Marbry tensed in Laurence's arms. "Oh, no. Papa."

As if she were on fire, Laurence tore himself away from Miss Marbry, and indeed he keenly felt the loss of heat from her body. With a quick glance in her direction, his own cheeks flamed as her bodice once again drooped, her delicate skin peeping out and tempting him further.

Middlebury grabbed his chest, his face turning an unnatural shade of purple. His eyes bulged in hideous fashion as he glared at his bride-to-be. "You would cuckold me even before the wedding?" he asked, his voice wheezing. He stumbled against Lord Saxton, who did his utmost to hold Middlebury's corpulent body upright.

"Quick, someone call a servant to fetch Ashton!" Saxton yelled.

Miss Marbry raced toward the bell pull by the bookshelves, giving it a sound tug. Moments later, a footman appeared and Saxton ordered him to find the duke and bring him forthwith to the library.

Laurence reached toward Middlebury in an effort to assist Saxton in settling him on a sofa, but Middlebury batted his hands away. "Don't touch me!" Although his wheezing seemed to lessen, the man's panting, labored breaths did nothing to ease Laurence's worry.

Nash stepped forward in assistance, his mouth still quirking in the sinister way Laurence detested.

"You of all people, Montgomery. A man of honor!" Middlebury barked the words, his glare at Laurence glacial.

Harry rushed into the room, his gaze darting between all parties, stopping momentarily on Miss Marbry and her state of undress, then immediately landed on Nash. "I won't ask," he said as he hurried to Middlebury's side where he reclined on the sofa.

"It wasn't me this time, Ashton. It seems our resident do-gooder, Montgomery, has defiled the young lady." A hint of glee colored Nash's voice.

"Now see here!" Laurence shouted. "I merely came in to offer assistance."

Nash chuckled. "Assistance in removing Miss Marbry's gown. Your hands were all over her when we arrived."

Blast, that did not come out as intended.

Harry called over his shoulder, "Miss Marbry, are you unharmed?"

"Yes." The sound of her voice, so quiet, so timid, grabbed Laurence's attention, and he turned back to her. Tears filled her eyes, a few droplets rolling down her cheeks.

"Have someone grab my medical bag. I left it at the front door with Preston."

Miss Marbry reached for the servant's bell pull, but Laurence stopped her.

"I'll get it." He needed to do *something*.

As he made his way out of the library, Saxton grabbed his arm. "We're not done here, Montgomery. I demand to have a word once we know Middlebury is out of danger."

Laurence gave a curt nod and raced down the staircase, his head swiveling in search of Ashton's bag.

"May I help you, sir?" Preston, the Saxtons' butler, said in his droll, unaffected voice.

"Ashton's medical bag. He has need of it."

After Preston fetched and handed him Harry's bag, Laurence raced back upstairs, relieved to find Middlebury no longer reclining on the sofa, but sitting upright, his cravat untied and waistcoat unbuttoned. Harry grabbed his stethoscope from his bag and listened to Middlebury's heart as everyone in the room held their breath.

Harry gave a satisfied nod. "Rapid, but even and strong. I expect the shock will wear off, and you'll be back to normal shortly."

Everyone issued a collective sigh of relief.

This time, Nash grabbed his arm. Laurence wrenched it from his grasp, meeting the man's black eyes.

"You'll thank me later," Nash said and turned to leave.

"Wait!" Middlebury tried to hoist himself from the sofa, leading Harry to send him a reproachful glare.

"You must remain calm, sir," Harry said, pushing him back in place.

"No! The agreement is off," Middlebury said. "Return my promissory note."

Miss Marbry let out a tortured cry, and everyone turned, having forgotten the poor woman and her ordeal. "You can't. You promised."

The mention of money had the inner cogs of Laurence's mind working at a furious pace. Things began to add up in an odd fashion. His gaze darted between Miss Marbry and Nash, the smugness suddenly wiped from his face.

"I promised no such thing," Middlebury said, interrupting Laurence's process of solving the puzzle. "However, *you* promised you would not break our engagement if I settled the debt before we wed."

Clink. The final piece slid into place.

Miss Marbry lifted her chin in a valiant effort to regain her dignity. "And I did *not* break our engagement. I kept my word."

"The word of a harlot!" Middlebury's face once again flushed red, and Harry grasped his wrist to take his pulse.

"We need a woman in here for your daughter, Saxton. Perhaps send for your wife?" Harry suggested.

"No!" Both Lord Saxton and Miss Marbry uttered the emphatic dissent in unison.

"Perhaps Her Grace?" Laurence said, his voice sounding much too shaky for his own liking.

Harry nodded, lowering the stethoscope he'd held again to Middlebury's chest. "Yes. Excellent idea, Montgomery. Margaret will know what to do."

Laurence tugged the bell pull, then instructed the footman to locate the duchess and request her presence.

Awkward minutes later, the rustling of skirts announced the duchess's arrival. Upon entering, she halted as if her body had encountered a solid wall, her gaze immediately assessing the situation. Laurence had always admired her quick mind and gentle heart.

But at the moment, his primary concern was Miss Marbry. Every instinct compelled him to run to Miss Marbry's side, but considering he had played a pivotal role in the whole debacle, albeit unwittingly, he forced himself to remain where he stood.

Margaret spoke in calming whispers, straightening and refastening Miss Marbry's gown. The women exchanged words in the same hushed tones. When Margaret looked his way, he cringed under her condemning stare.

She wrapped an arm around Miss Marbry's waist. "I'll take her to her room," she said, and led her from the library.

Laurence wished to leave as well, but Saxton fixed him in place with his glare. In a menacing tone, the man who Laurence realized would now become his father-in-law said, "Do you realize what you have done?"

Unable to force down the thick panic in his throat, Laurence merely nodded.

He'd inadvertently found a wife.

CHAPTER 9—CONSEQUENCES

As the duchess steered her upstairs, Bea moved like a walking dead person. Every muscle in her body had become numb, requiring conscious effort to move her legs, each step more torturous than the last.

How had things gone so horribly wrong? The plan had been well-thought out, orchestrated to precision. The only element out of her control was Lord Nash. What had delayed him? And why had Lord Montgomery appeared?

"Which room, Miss Marbry?"

Bea jerked her head at the sound of the soft voice. Concern and compassion shone in the duchess's eyes.

"There." Bea pointed to the room ahead. "On the right."

Once inside her room, Bea allowed her numb body to drop to her bed.

The duchess settled next to her, taking Bea's hands in her own. "Why didn't you ask for your mother?"

Like diving into the icy waters of the lake at their country estate in autumn, Bea gasped for breath. A deluge of tears followed. She thought she had been prepared. After all, her ruination, her disgrace, had always been the end result in her plan. But now, knowing it was for naught, and she wouldn't even have the solace of saving her father from debt, proved one burden too heavy to bear.

A comforting arm wrapped around her shoulders, pulling her into an embrace. She didn't deserve such kindness, especially from a duchess. By rights, the woman should give her the cut direct.

Instead, Bea said the first thing that came to mind. "She will hate me."

"May I call you Beatrix?"

Bea gave a weak nod.

"Oh, no, Beatrix. Your mother could never hate you."

Of course she would believe that. Her Grace was beautiful, elegant, had so many men vying for her hand. Lord Montgomery among them. Her Grace had probably never seen that look in her own mother's eyes that said *you'll never be good enough.*

"Beatrix, please call me Margaret. I feel I must ask you some questions. Anything you say is between us. I won't repeat it unless you give your permission. Will you trust me?"

Bea nodded, her head as dull as if filled with wool.

"Did Lord Montgomery . . . hurt you?"

As if a strong breeze cleared the clouds in her mind, Bea hastened to defend her beloved. "No! It wasn't supposed to be him. But Lord Nash didn't arrive as planned. I believe Lord Montgomery had come to . . . save my reputation."

Even without the confused expression on Margaret's face, Bea realized her words made little sense.

"You were expecting an assignation with Lord Nash?" The disbelief in Margaret's voice stirred the shame already growing in Bea's stomach.

A nasty, sour taste rose in Bea's mouth at her admission. "Yes." Heat rose to her cheeks, no doubt leading Margaret to an incorrect conclusion.

She rushed to clarify, realizing it would do nothing to further Margaret's good opinion. Indeed, her confession would bring about a different kind of shame.

She focused on the hands in her lap, still clasped by the duchess. "It was only to be so Lord Middlebury would find us and break the engagement." She struggled to lift her gaze and meet Margaret's condemning stare.

Instead, she found relief—compassion—understanding. "I don't blame you for your reluctance to marry Middlebury. But why would Nash agree to such a scheme?" Color rose to Margaret's cheeks. "Certainly he would realize he'd be honor bound to marry you. Are you confident he understood it was only to be an act?"

Bea opened her mouth to answer, but snapped it shut. Was she? Perhaps Lord Montgomery had information she did not. She forced out the admission. "I don't know. But I chose Lord Nash specifically, knowing he wouldn't offer to marry me."

The color that had risen drained from Margaret's face. "I see. And your gown? What happened? Did Lord Montgomery . . .?"

Bea shook her head. "No. Lord Nash instructed me to loosen it and pull it down before he arrived." The enormity of the situation settled on her. "Please, Your Grace. Lord Montgomery is innocent."

"Margaret, Beatrix. Remember? I won't deny I'm relieved to know he didn't accost you, but the fact remains, there were witnesses. People will believe what they wish, and so often, what they wish is of an ugly nature."

Of course Margaret would understand. The similarity of Bea's situation and what the duke and duchess had faced with Miss Pratt was almost too shameful to bear. But in Bea's case, she was the guilty party who had orchestrated the compromise. She didn't deserve the duchess's kindness.

"If I know anything about Laurence Townsend, I know this much—he will do the right thing, regardless of his innocence or guilt. He would never allow a woman to be ruined because of him." Margaret squeezed Bea's hand, the caress comforting. Yet the underlying meaning of her words stirred an unease in Bea's stomach.

Oh, dear.

"The question remaining, Beatrix, is do you wish to become his wife?"

Bea swallowed, her throat tighter than the wrappings she'd used to bind her bosom in order to dress in men's clothing and accompany Timothy to lectures at the Royal Society.

She had never wanted anything more.

But not like this.

⚶

LAURENCE REMAINED STATIONARY, LIKE A SCHOOLBOY WAITING TO BE chastised by the schoolmaster. He would have preferred a paddling to what lay in wait. The air in the library had become stifling, and he resisted the urge to tug at his neckcloth. With the women out of the room, the words exchanged became more heated, adding to the already suffocating feeling.

Once Harry had become convinced Middlebury was not about to transpire from a heart attack, he moved to the side of the room, but his presence alone rebuked Laurence.

Middlebury glowered at Bea's father. "I repeat, Saxton, your daughter's actions invalidate our agreement. I demand you return the promise of funds to me forthwith."

Nash straightened. "Too late, Middlebury." He waved a piece of paper like a trophy flag.

"Don't be so certain, Nash," Middlebury said. "If you examine that note clearly, it has a condition."

Nash stared down at the note in his hands, his brow furrowed in concentration. His gaze wandered across the paper, then he pinched his nose with his thumb and forefinger.

"What does it say?" Timothy asked.

Nash thrust the note toward him. "You read it. I'm too angry."

A funereal hush settled on the room. Timothy cleared his throat. "The note is post-dated four weeks from now. The addendum reads, 'Payable after the marriage has been consummated. In the event any circumstances should prevent such from happening, this note shall be declared null and void.'"

Like a man crushed under a heavy weight, Saxton fell into an empty wingback, his eyes pleading. "Middlebury, have mercy. Montgomery seduced the girl. If we keep things quiet, no one will know. The marriage can take place as planned, with no one the wiser."

"Are you mad?" Middlebury gave an indignant huff. "Why, the news will be all over the gossip sheets before dawn." He held out his hand. "Now return that note to me at once!"

Hoisting himself from the sofa, Middlebury waddled over to Timothy, snatching the note from his hand and ripping it into tiny shreds. Pieces fell to the floor like confetti, and Middlebury stomped from the room, yelling at a servant to fetch his carriage.

A vein in his head bulging, Saxton turned his scowl on Laurence. "Sir, I ask you again. Do you realize the enormity of what you have done?"

Laurence swallowed, finally finding his voice. "You have completely misinterpreted the situation, Saxton. I assure you, nothing untoward occurred between your daughter and myself."

The man snorted in disbelief. Laurence could hardly blame him. "A likely story. And I suppose she pulled down her own gown, exposing herself in such an indecent manner?"

Actually. Laurence suspected the very thing. Yet he held his tongue and mustered his courage to accept the man's vitriol with a shred of dignity. The last thing he wished was to cast aspersions on Miss Marbry. Better he was viewed as the villain. It was the gentlemanly thing to do, was it not?

"Your behavior has placed me in a dire situation, sir. I'll give you the courtesy to ponder your decision and return to me in the morning. I expect you to do what is right, Montgomery. For all involved. Now, if you'll excuse me, I have the onerous task of informing my wife."

Timothy cast an accusatory glare toward Laurence as he escorted his father from the room. With a final glance toward Laurence, Harry shook his head and followed them, leaving Laurence alone with Nash.

When Nash moved to leave, Laurence grabbed his arm. "Nash, you owe me a word."

"I owe you nothing." Nash wrenched his arm away. "You should owe me. That was my money Middlebury ripped to shreds."

"This entire fiasco has the foul odor of your involvement. Any loss of funds is on your own head."

Nash's jaw pulsed, his brows drawn down and face darkening as he stared at Laurence. "You can't prove a thing, and it doesn't change the fact that Saxton still owes me. I intend to get what's coming to me."

"How quickly you forget your own debt. Remember, I hold your vowels in the sum of three thousand pounds."

"I can't pay what I don't have. Give me time."

"I'll be happy to do so if you extend the same courtesy to Lord Saxton."

"Very well." Nash glanced around the room. "There should be a few things he can sell to come up with the blunt." He pointed a finger, saying, "But I won't wait long." Then he strode from the room.

Laurence breathed a heavy sigh. Better belongings than his own daughter.

He steeled himself to face his parents with the news that, come morning, he would be making an offer for Miss Marbry.

⚶

IF ANYONE EXPECTED BEA WOULD BE ABLE TO SLEEP, THEY WOULD BE sorely mistaken, especially after the confrontation with her mother. The duchess—Bea struggled to think of her as Margaret—had left, reassuring Bea things would work out. The compassion and kindness Margaret had shown would stay with Bea forever.

When Bea's mother appeared in the doorway with fire in her eyes, steam veritably pouring from her ears, Margaret had politely excused herself, leaving Bea to face the dragon alone. After her mother closed the door, Bea prepared for the tirade to follow.

"What have you to say for yourself?"

Nothing. She had no reasonable defense. Had her father confessed his gambling debt to Lord Nash?

Before she could open her mouth to apologize, her mother paced before her, continuing her assault. "To disgrace us like this.

To insult the man providing the one offer of marriage you had *finally* received."

"I'm sorry." The apology fell lackluster from her lips. Although truly sorry her plan had failed on one account, part of her was not sorry in the least she would *not* be marrying Lord Middlebury.

"Sorry? You're sorry?" Her mother waved a furious hand in front of her as if batting away pesky flies. "That's the best you can do? The girl so enamored with fancy words, books, and things that a *normal* woman should not be concerned about."

Bea recoiled from the escalating volume of her mother's words.

The pacing ceased, and her mother faced her. "You have ruined us. Your father confessed about his debt and that Lord Middlebury would have been our salvation. But I suppose that doesn't matter to you since you'll be in the lap of luxury married to Lord Montgomery, leaving us to live in penury and die in ignominy." She collapsed on the bed in tears.

"Mama, we'll find a solution. Perhaps if we sell our jewelry and some of the gallery paintings, it will raise enough funds to buy some time. And I won't leave you. Lord Montgomery may not even offer for me. He did nothing wrong. I won't hold him responsible."

As if her mother had flipped a magical switch, the tears ceased as she stared at Bea. "But of course you will. You must!" Dabbing her tear-stained face with her handkerchief, a frightening glint appeared in her eyes, much like Bea imagined Victor Frankenstein's as his creature shuddered to life.

"Why had I not thought this through!? Bea, it's marvelous. With Montgomery in line to inherit, you will one day be a countess. Surely he will feel obligated to assist his acquired family. Lord Montgomery will be the salvation of us all!" She gathered Bea in her arms, the embrace so tight, Bea struggled to breathe.

The abrupt change in her mother's demeanor shook Bea to her core, and she tried to scoot out of her mother's grasp.

"Oh my clever, clever girl!" She patted Bea's cheek, kissing her forehead. "Now, I will leave you. You must get some sleep and look your best before Montgomery arrives tomorrow to make his offer."

She practically danced from Bea's bedroom in such an about

face Bea's head swam from the abruptness of the change. Like Mary Wollstonecraft Shelly, Bea had created a monster. But like Frankenstein's creature, did it only appear horrific when inside there was goodness to be found? Of that, she was uncertain.

She'd always longed for her mother's approval.

But not like this.

CHAPTER 10—THE OFFER

"Miss Marbry?! What were you thinking?" Laurence's mother's words still echoed in his head, bouncing about like a perpetual motion machine.

She'd literally shuddered at the news. "Mind you, I have nothing against the poor dear. Even if she is on the shelf. But to compromise a young woman—at her own engagement ball no less. I'm appalled."

To say Laurence's carriage ride home from the Saxtons' residence had been uncomfortable would have been the grossest of understatements.

His father appeared unperturbed. A hint of a smile traced his lips as he muttered, "Well, you did say you wanted him to find a bride, Clara."

In response, his father received an icy glare from his wife, quelling any further contributions he might have added to the conversation.

Miranda eyed Laurence suspiciously, no doubt saving her own line of questioning for a more private moment.

He'd tried to explain, but it mattered little. The die was cast and couldn't be undone. He would either offer for Miss Marbry to save her reputation or be branded a cad. The prospect of the latter left a decidedly unpleasant taste in his mouth. It went against everything he believed in, everything he held to be true and right.

After a fitful night's sleep, if one could call it sleep at all, he rose, threw on his banyan and stared out the window of his bedroom, waiting for Stevens to arrive. A heavy mist hung low to the ground, the sun not yet fully risen to burn it off. It reflected his thoughts perfectly—muddled and indistinct.

He raked a hand through his hair without care. Stevens would straighten it well enough during his morning toilette. Was the situation as dire as it appeared? His parents had an arranged marriage, and they—tolerated each other well enough. At least enough to produce two children.

Contrary to his even-tempered nature, he pounded his fist against the wall next to the window with such force it shook the glass panes. *Blast it all!* He wanted more than a *tolerable* marriage. Why else had he waited all these years to find the perfect woman? He wanted passion, an element sorely lacking in his well-structured, organized, *controlled* life.

The irony of the situation was not lost on him. He liked Miss Marbry—well, truthfully, he wasn't certain, as he didn't really know her. Yet, hadn't he wished to find the lady in green in hopes of an attachment?

But he'd wanted to court her as the rules of etiquette dictated, to provide an opportunity for feelings of affection to develop in a natural course. Not be forced into a marriage she may not desire.

He recalled the panic in her face when he'd discovered her in the library, her urgent plea for him to leave.

But they'd connected on an intellectual level at Ashton's masquerade, had they not? Perhaps given time . . .

"Sir?" Stevens' voice jolted him from his speculation. "Do we have any special plans today?"

Damn the staff! Apparently, word had already spread about his situation. He simply nodded, fully aware his valet would proceed by selecting the appropriate wardrobe, but not willing to open conversation to further probing.

Once dressed, he made his way to the breakfast room. After a light meal of tea and toast—all his jittery stomach could handle—he checked his pocket watch and called for his curricle to be brought around.

The short ride to the Saxtons' townhouse seemed interminable. Like the waves of the sea, Laurence's mind tossed to and fro, searching for the appropriate words with which to make his offer. Would Miss Marbry expect him to fall to one knee? Express undying love? He'd prepared perfect words years ago when he'd planned to offer for Miss Margaret Farnsworth before the former —and dastardly—Duke of Ashton stole her out from under his nose.

He sighed, pushing the duchess from his mind. Hadn't he sworn to all around him he no longer carried a torch for her? He wasn't jealous of Harry, the new duke, who had won Margaret's affections, but he *was* envious of the love he and Margaret shared.

As if the horses had intuited his destination, he barely needed to pull back on the ribbons when he arrived at Miss Marbry's. A groom, who slumped against the outside wall, jumped to attention and raced over to take the vehicle.

Laurence inhaled a deep, hopefully calming breath and lifted his hand to reach for the brass knocker. The door opened before he even had the looping, hinged ring in his fingers.

Preston, the butler who'd handed him Harry's medical bag the night before, greeted him with a bow. "My lord. I believe they are expecting you."

Of course they are. He forced a smile and followed the man to a small upstairs parlor.

As he waited, he focused on the positives, ticking off the list of Miss Marbry's qualities in his mind.

Intelligent.

Well-read.

Lovely green eyes.

Soft, supple, white . . .

He pushed that last from his mind. Thinking about her exposed bosom would result in an embarrassing physical condition.

Unsure what he expected, he listened for sounds of joy or distress. Would his offer of marriage please or dismay Miss Marbry?

Soft footfalls and the rustle of skirts informed him he wouldn't have to wait long to find out.

He straightened, pulling gently on the edges of his coat, smoothing it, and prepared to face his future bride.

No matter how strong the temptation, Bea resisted the urge to dip her quill into the inkpot and put words on the parchment. It would not do to have her gown dotted with black spots when Lord Montgomery came to call.

And call, he would. Of that, she had no doubt. It was who he was. She knew that much about him. Years of blending into the crowds, as any good wallflower was wont to do, had made her privy to many bits of gossip, whether the wagging tongues had realized it or not. She would have a made an excellent spy for the Crown—if they allowed women.

Instead, after consuming half a slice of toast and a few sips of lukewarm tea, she waited patiently in her room, dressed in her favorite light green day gown, her hands folded neatly on her lap. However, the stillness of her posture belied the activity in her mind. As she had most of her sleepless night, she worked through various scenarios of what she anticipated would follow, coming to one foregone conclusion.

As much as she loved her family, wanted to save them from poverty and disgrace, she would not sacrifice the happiness of the man she loved to save her own skin—or theirs. Much sooner than she expected, her mother knocked on her door, announcing Lord Montgomery had arrived.

"Take Fanny with you."

Bea resisted rolling her eyes—barely. "Is that necessary, Mother? All things considered."

"Not for propriety, girl. For a witness. I'll not have him make an offer and later say you refused him."

"He wouldn't do that unless . . ."

Her mother narrowed her eyes. "You *will* accept him, Beatrix."

Was there no end to this nightmare?

"Now go. He's waiting, and for goodness' sake, close the door so that horrid cat doesn't escape." She practically pushed Bea from the room, accompanied by a protesting hiss from Catpurrnicus.

The closer Bea got to the parlor where Lord Montgomery waited, the more furiously her heart pounded against her ribcage. She inhaled a deep breath, trying to stop her legs from trembling beneath her. *Don't stumble. Remain upright.*

But when she stepped into the room, as if on cue, her knees weakened at the sight of the man she loved. Her feet only faltered slightly, but enough that he took a tentative step toward her, his hand outstretched as if to catch her if she would fall, only retreating when Fanny grasped Bea's arm, supporting her momentarily before taking a position at the side of the room.

He executed an elegant bow. "Miss Marbry." His eyes didn't reflect the smile on his lips, and a stab of pain constricted her chest.

How could she do this to him?

She returned a somewhat clumsy curtsy. "Lord Montgomery."

His gaze moved about the room, landing on everything except her. When their eyes finally met, he looked tired, as if he'd slept less than she had. "I expect you know why I've come. Due to the unfortunate incident of last night, I'm here to ask if you would do me the honor of becoming my wife."

So many nights she'd dreamed of him saying those words. But at the moment, it seemed so—wrong. She swallowed the selfishness rising in her throat, the taste of it bitter.

"My lord, you are blameless in what happened. I release you from any perceived responsibility."

From the side of the room, Fanny gasped, and Bea sent her a pleading look.

His mouth agape, Lord Montgomery stared at her wide-eyed. "You don't wish to marry me?" Something tinged the disbelief in his voice. Was it disappointment or relief?

More importantly, how could she answer truthfully? Because of course, the answer was a resounding *Yes. I wish to marry you more than I've ever wanted anything.*

She settled for another, less desperate sounding truth. "I wish for you to be happy. To marry because it is your choice, not because you feel obligated or trapped."

He continued staring at her as if he had unearthed fossilized bones of a yet undiscovered and uncategorized animal. "You're concerned about *my* happiness?"

Now *that* she could answer honestly. "Yes."

"What of your reputation?"

She cast a quick glance toward Fanny, then motioned for her to move toward the far end of the room. "I fully expected my reputation to be in tatters even before your ill-timed appearance," she said, keeping her voice low.

He, too, darted a look toward her maid. "May I speak frankly, Miss Marbry? Perhaps we might sit?"

Why had she not suggested it? She nodded and took a seat on the settee. He positioned himself at the other end. Yet even at the respectable distance, they were able to converse without Fanny overhearing. The arrangement offered an added advantage of Bea being close to him without the fear of her legs buckling.

"Do you wish to marry Lord Middlebury?"

"Good Galileo, no!"

His lips twitched as if fighting a smile. "I see. Forgive me for what I'm about to ask." Color rose to his face, the effect most attractive. "Were you truly expecting Lord Nash to meet you in the library last evening?"

The words tumbled out like a great purge. "It wasn't a true assignation. I only wanted Middlebury to see us and break the engagement." Hot tears blurred her vision, and she blinked them back.

"So you had no wish to marry Lord Nash?"

She shook her head, the words of her confession clogging her throat and making it difficult to speak. "I thought I had it planned perfectly. Middlebury agreed to settle the debt before the wedding, and I promised not to break our engagement. I foolishly thought if he saw me with Nash, he would be outraged and end our betrothal himself, allowing me to keep my promise."

"And on that much, you succeeded. He was indeed outraged."

"But I had no idea he would refuse to honor the promissory note. My father informed me of the addendum."

"Men like Middlebury don't part with their money easily. However, I can't fault you for not wishing to marry the man. Even if I hadn't interrupted your plan, I'm afraid the end result would have remained unchanged." Concern and sympathy shone in his eyes.

"Not entirely."

"Pardon?" The tilt of his head drew her eyes to his strong jawline.

Unable to look him in the eye, she hung her head in shame, the tears breaking free and trickling down her cheeks. "You would have remained uninvolved. I'm so sorry to have embroiled you in this nightmare."

"I'm not."

Her head snapped up at his unexpected words. What was he saying?

His brown eyes, so soft, so kind, so serious, met hers. "I know Nash, Miss Marbry. Although you believed the assignation was merely an act, I'm unconvinced Nash would not have . . . taken advantage." Pink rose again to his cheeks. "At least your innocence has been preserved."

The fleeting spark of hope sputtered out. He'd only been speaking about her virtue—yet there was something endearing about his concern.

He removed a handkerchief from inside his coat and handed it to her.

As she dabbed the wetness from her cheeks, he asked, "Do you find the idea of marriage in general distasteful, or merely marriage to Lord Middlebury?"

Her confusion at his question must have shown on her face.

"Allow me to rephrase. Are there any circumstances in which you would welcome a marriage proposal?"

"I'm not opposed to marriage . . . to the right person. However,

I'm quite certain Lord Middlebury and I would not have been a suitable match."

He chuckled, the sound pleasant and something she would like to hear frequently. "I've held a firm belief that the best matches are between those who are of like minds. People who hold similar values and interests, supporting and encouraging each other. Would you agree?"

Was it any wonder she loved him? "I do. Wholeheartedly."

He shifted slightly, giving a tug to the edge of his coat. "I have my own confession. You may not recall, but I believe you and I had an interesting encounter in Ashton's library during the masquerade ball over a year ago."

When had he sussed out that bit of information? "You recognized me?"

A pained expression passed over his face. "Not until recently, I'm afraid, and by that time, I'd heard about your engagement to Middlebury. However, had I known sooner, I would have called upon you so we could explore our mutual love of science."

Oh, dear. Dizzy from his confession, she could only stare in disbelief, unsure the words she'd longed to hear for so long were not conjured from her own mind.

"I would ask you to reconsider my offer, Miss Marbry. Not only would it salvage both of our reputations, but we might discover we are indeed a good match."

Shame twisted her insides. She hadn't even considered how her actions had inadvertently damaged his own reputation. She opened her mouth, ready to apologize and give him a resounding *yes*, when he held up his hand.

"Before you answer, I'm aware you have no romantic feelings for me. We hardly know each other. However, given time, perhaps we might develop an affection for each other based on our common interests."

Her stomach dropped to her toes. If he truly knew the depth of her feelings and how well she *did* know him. Yet, she had to admit, from his perspective, they were virtual strangers.

She swallowed a lump the size of Catpurrnicus's favorite ball of yarn. "My actions were not only foolish, but selfish. I hadn't considered how they have sullied your own good name."

A sad smile tilted his lips, and she yearned to kiss them and transform them to happiness. "Ah, but it wasn't your intent. My own impetuous actions led to my disgrace."

"You acted as a gentleman, trying to rescue me, and yet you were condemned. It's so unfair."

"And yet . . . here we are," he said, holding out his hands. "Two innocent victims trying to make the best of an unfortunate situation."

He gave another tug on his coat. "Let me propose this. Accept my offer, and I shall speak with your father. It will, at the least, quell some of the gossiping tongues. We have time as the banns are read, and if you permit, I shall call on you so we may get to know each other. If before the wedding you choose not to proceed, you may break the engagement. It will allow you to save face."

"But what of your choice, my lord? If you decide we do not suit?"

He shook his head. "No. The choice should be completely yours. I will not rescind my offer."

She would have expected no less. Everything she had learned about him over the course of the last eight years was summed up in that moment. He was a gentleman to the end, and he owned her heart completely.

CHAPTER 11—THE COURTSHIP

L aurence studied the face of the woman before him. The woman who would most likely become his wife. His skill of reading people, of predicting their actions, failed him. Perhaps his ability only worked at the card table—or with men. Women, on the other hand, were an entirely different matter.

The freckles dotting her cheeks and the bridge of her nose captured his full attention. Through her smudged glasses, the forest green eyes—which had captivated him over a year ago—squinted, as if she too were evaluating him.

He hoped to prevail upon her as a woman of logic by providing a sound argument in favor of their union. There would be time to talk of love and affection after he had won her heart. But first, he needed to convince her to give him a chance.

In truth, her refusal had touched him. Not the refusal itself, although it had indeed surprised him, but her concern over his happiness. The fact a woman would take into consideration what *he* wanted when it was her reputation at stake spoke to her character, and his admiration for her grew.

Her strategy to thwart Middlebury, although faulty, had some merit. It would have worked had it not been for Middlebury's cunning when it came to his money. She expected him to hold to his word—in short—to act like a gentleman.

A naïve expectation at best, and at worst it had been the greatest flaw, leading to the unraveling of her plan.

He reiterated his proposal. "So, Miss Marbry, shall we see if a match between us has merit? Will you accept my offer of marriage with those conditions?"

"Yes. I accept."

At her answer, he released the breath he hadn't even realized he'd been holding. "Excellent. I shall take my leave to go speak with your father. If it is agreeable, I shall call upon you tomorrow."

Pink colored her cheeks, the affect most becoming, and she gave him a tiny nod.

As he rose and bowed, a brief question flitted through his mind. Now that they were engaged, would she permit him to kiss her?

Laurence chastised himself for even entertaining the thought of taking liberties so soon. He would proceed slowly, allowing her to get used to his presence. But a warm, comforting sensation flooded his chest at the idea of having her in his arms and kissing her lips.

He strode from the room to seek out her father. Perhaps things weren't as bleak as he imagined.

The moment Laurence entered Lord Saxton's study, one look at his future father-in-law's face wiped the optimistic thought from his mind. The man's grim expression mirrored the dark, somber colors of the room.

"Sir," Laurence said, nodding in greeting. "Your daughter has agreed to my proposal of marriage."

Saxton slumped back in his chair. "Thank goodness. At least her reputation will be salvaged, and she'll be provided for even if the rest of us are living hand to mouth."

Laurence tamped down the urge to point out the responsibility for the man's debt rested squarely upon his own shoulders. However, as his future son-in-law, Laurence owed him a modicum of respect.

Instead, he sought to reassure him. "I promise you, as unseemly as the situation appeared, nothing untoward happened between your daughter and myself. But I willingly take responsibility for my actions, as unwitting as they may have been."

Saxton held an empty glass in his fingers, and he twisted it back and forth. "Well, I must admit, she'll have a much better chance at happiness with you than with Middlebury. If you think I didn't have qualms about the whole thing, you'd be sadly mistaken. It pains me to think about the depths to which I sank."

Relieved that the man felt some remorse, Laurence said, "Sir, perhaps I might be able to offer assistance."

Saxton's eyes widened with interest.

"I hold Nash's vowels in the amount of three thousand, and I reminded him of the fact last evening. He asked for more time, which I gave, providing he extend the same courtesy to you."

Saxton ran a shaky hand down his face. "I appreciate it, Montgomery, but it doesn't solve my initial problem of where to get the blunt."

"Allow me to work on a solution agreeable to all parties."

"If you can find a solution to this mess, then you're a better man than I and a true godsend to our family." Saxton rose and offered his hand, his expression more hopeful than when Laurence had entered. "Welcome to the family."

The following day as Laurence went through his morning ablutions, he occupied his mind with things he and Miss Marbry could do. What did she enjoy? What did she detest? Would they have topics to discuss or would there be long stretches of uncomfortable silence between them as there had been with other young ladies such as Miss Pratt or Miss Weatherby?

When he arrived again at the Saxtons' townhouse, Lady Saxton met him in the parlor while he waited for Miss Marbry. "Lord Montgomery," she said, an overeager smile spreading across her face. "I beg you to be patient with our dear Beatrix. I've advised her to keep her foolish notions to herself, but I fear she often speaks without first thinking. Admonish her if necessary, and I'm confident she will become a biddable and submissive wife."

Laurence found himself blinking in disbelief at the way the woman disparaged her own daughter. A strange camaraderie with his future bride swelled in his chest, and he remembered the times his own mother had advised him not to spend all his time talking about science to young ladies.

"Young ladies don't give a fig about such things, Laurence," his mother had said. "Talk to them about fashion, about the arts, for goodness' sake, even the weather is a better topic."

Was it any wonder he had difficulty finding a bride?

Before he could rush to Miss Marbry's defense, she entered the parlor, and he rose to greet her.

"I apologize for the wait, sir," she said, her cheeks pinkening in a lovely way. "I had some difficulty constraining my cat."

Lady Saxton coughed, the censure in her gaze clear to Laurence. "I shall sit in the corner with my embroidery while you become better acquainted. Beatrix, I asked Preston to bring tea."

Beatrix took a seat on the settee, her hands clasped tightly in her lap.

"You have a cat?" he asked.

Her face brightened. She clearly loved her pet. "I do. His name is Catpurrnicus."

Lady Saxton gave an audible sigh from her seat in the corner.

"A most interesting name for a cat. Very . . . creative. I take it you have admiration for Copernicus?"

"Indeed. I find astronomy fascinating. Wouldn't it be marvelous to travel into space and visit the planets? To look out and witness how our own appears from the heavens?"

A long-suffering sigh echoed across the room from where Lady Saxton sat. Although Laurence refused to acknowledge the woman's obvious intent to chastise her daughter, Beatrix blushed and lowered her gaze to her hands still clasped in her lap.

"Forgive me, my lord. I do get carried away sometimes," Beatrix said.

Compelled to come to her rescue, he said, "Nothing to forgive. I, too, have wondered about such things. In fact, I was reading a superb article in *The Times* the other day—"

An earsplitting shriek followed by frenzied footsteps sounded somewhere deep in the house. "Catch him!" someone yelled.

When the unmistakable howl of a cat grew closer, Lady Saxton dropped her embroidery. "Close the door!"

Laurence rose, but before he could reach the parlor entrance, a black cat bounded inside, its feet slipping and sliding under him, then came to an abrupt halt.

With intense yellow eyes, the cat stared Laurence down, and although he fully believed Lady Saxton had collapsed in a faint behind him, he couldn't take his eyes off the creature before him.

⚜

MORTIFIED—THE ONE WORD ACCURATELY SUMMING UP BEA'S current emotional state. It had been one thing when Catpurrnicus attacked Lord Middlebury. But to have her one beloved assault the other—and no offense to Catpurrnicus—even more beloved Laurence was quite another.

Breath trapped in her lungs as she waited for Catpurrnicus to thrust himself at her brand new fiancé. Would Laurence be as intolerant of her pet as Middlebury? Ask her to find him another home? Or worse, would he bolt from the house rescinding his offer of marriage?

As if facing each other in a duel, Catpurrnicus and Laurence stood motionless, and the challenged party reacted first.

"Hello, kitty," Laurence said, his voice calm and assured.

Bea forced herself not to follow her mother's example and fall to the settee in a dead faint. She must remain alert to protect her beloved!

Catpurrnicus advanced, taking slow, measured steps toward his prey. Laurence, like the unsuspecting victim he was soon to be, crouched down, extending his hand.

Bea pressed her hand to her chest, hoping to confirm her heart remained beating. Icy chills raced up her spine, although the sunny, late May day promised to be a warm one. She squeezed her eyes shut, unwilling to witness the horror about to unfold.

"That's a good kitty," Laurence said.

At the absence of hissing from Catpurrnicus and screaming

from Laurence, she tentatively peeked through one eye. To her amazement, Catpurrnicus thread himself around and between Laurence's legs, rubbing his furry little body against the man's boots.

Picking the cat up, Laurence snuggled Catpurrnicus against his chest and returned to the settee.

Although it seemed impossible, Bea fell in love with him even more. "He . . . he likes you." Still not quite believing them, the words fell from her lips.

Laurence stroked Catpurrnicus's soft fur, and the cat purred contentedly. "One of my interests is animal behavior. I've always had a way with them. I believe animals have an intrinsic instinct about people. They can sense fear, it would appear, and seem to be an excellent judge of character. Isn't that right, Catpurrnicus?"

The cat's pink tongue darted out, licking Laurence's hand.

"He didn't like Lord Fa—Lord Middlebury," Bea said.

Laurence chuckled, and Bea decided it was the most pleasant sound she'd ever heard. He leaned in closer to whisper, "Proves my theory, wouldn't you say?"

Catpurrnicus purred his agreement.

Good Galileo, she loved him. They both had forgotten her mother entirely. A rustling behind them reminded Bea of her presence. "It's a miracle," her mother said, awe evident in her voice. "A sign from the heavens above. Lord Montgomery, you have a gift."

With the crisis averted, Bea attempted to return the conversation to before Catpurrnicus's escape. "You were about to mention an article you read, my lord."

"Ah yes," he said, his voice as soothing as a warm blanket on a chilly, rainy day. "A fascinating treatise on—ah—ah—ah-CHOO."

Catpurrnicus wiggled his way out of Laurence's gentle grasp and jumped to the floor, apparently startled by the explosive sneeze.

"I beg your pa—ah-choo." A string of successive sneezes followed. Laurence's eyes began to water.

Of course, Preston took that precise, inopportune moment to bring in the tea, but thankfully Laurence's sneezing had abated.

Bea said a silent prayer of thanks to Hippocrates and tacked on a special request to keep her hands from shaking as she poured.

That particular prayer went unanswered. Tea sloshed out of the cup onto the saucer beneath it. She'd keep that one for herself. Mercifully, her hands steadied, and she poured the next neatly, not spilling a drop.

However, her hand trembled as she handed the tea to Laurence, and his fingers brushed against hers. Like a bolt of lightning, energy passed up her arm, making her head spin.

At the moment Laurence began sipping his tea, Catpurrnicus jumped back on the settee and rubbed his head against Laurence's side. Another bout of fitful sneezes ensued, with Laurence's tea being flung from his cup onto his waistcoat.

"Oh, dear," Bea said, rushing to grab a tea towel. As she blotted the damp spot over Laurence's chest, their eyes locked, and a vise-like grip squeezed her chest. *Oh, my!*

He wrapped his hand over hers, his lips curling in a gentle smile. "It's quite all right, Miss Marbry. No harm done. However, it seems I ha-ha-ha—ah-choo—have contracted a cold. Perhaps it would be best if I bid you farewell for today. I have no wish to expose you."

Bea's heart flipped, then plummeted to her toes, wishing he would stay a little longer. "Will you return tomorrow?" She cringed at the hopefulness in her voice.

"If I'm able. I shall send word if my symptoms worsen." He reached down and scratched Catpurrnicus behind an ear, eliciting a contented purr from the black beast. "Goodbye, young Catpurrnicu-cu-cu—choo." Wetness rimmed his eyes as he extended his hand to her. "Miss Marbry."

Gooseflesh rose up her arms as she slipped her hand into his, and he bowed over it, kissing her fingertips. He turned toward her mother. "Lady Saxton. A pleasure. I bid you farewell."

A soft meow came from the settee as Lord Montgomery strode from the room. Bea glanced down at her furry pet. Pleased seemed too inadequate of a word to describe her reaction to his restrained behavior. She hoped fish would be on the menu that evening, for she would save a large portion for Catpurrnicus to reward him.

Then she began counting the minutes until Laurence would, hopefully, return the next day.

GRATEFUL HE HAD RIDDEN TO MISS MARBRY'S RESIDENCE IN HIS curricle, Laurence hoped the fresh air would remedy the odd sensations he'd experienced during his call. In addition to the sneezing episodes, he'd become unusually warm and a strange dizziness had overcome him, especially when Miss Marbry placed her hand on his chest to blot away the spilled tea. And when he'd gazed into her eyes as she hovered over him, his heart lurched, giving a rather hard thump against his ribs.

Seated in his curricle, he placed a wrist against his forehead as his mother often did during his childhood. His skin didn't feel warm. Tiny black hairs lingered on the sleeve of his dove gray coat, and as he brushed them off, one flew up toward his nose, triggering another sneeze. The connection of cause and effect formulating in his mind, he decided to gather more evidence. He snapped the ribbons, urging the matched set of bays forward toward The Hope Clinic.

To say his vehicle and fine horses would be out of place in front of the Duke of Ashton's clinic on the East Side was a gross understatement. However, considering Ashton himself arrived there in his own ducal carriage, only a few eyebrows lifted at Laurence's arrival. He pulled the horses to a stop and called out to a young boy playing with a stick and a ball in the street.

"I say there, young fellow. Two pence is yours if you can find someone to watch my horses for a short time."

The boy's eyes grew as large as the holes in his short trousers. "I'll do it, guvn'r."

"Are you certain you can manage? Not allow anyone to take the horses and curricle away from you?"

"I'll help him," an older boy of about twelve said.

"Very well," Laurence said, reaching into his pocket. "Two pence for each of you, but I'm a friend of the du—doctor's, so any funny business and he'll hear about it." He breathed a sigh of relief he'd caught himself before referring to Ashton as the duke. The man preferred to keep a low profile while at the clinic, but Laurence knew how respected he was among the locals there.

He hopped down from the curricle and strode inside the clinic. A tiny bell announced his arrival, and multiple pairs of eyes turned in his direction.

"Another of the doctor's fancy friends, I'll wager," one man muttered to a woman waiting beside him.

"Shush, Henry. He'll hear you."

Laurence nodded in greeting, then took an empty seat. Luckily, it didn't appear too busy. Only one other man besides himself and the couple waited for treatment. He craned his neck, looking out the window to make sure his curricle remained in front.

After several minutes, Ashton appeared from the back, accompanied by an adolescent boy. Harry's eyes widened, and he nodded, acknowledging Laurence's presence.

Henry and the woman Laurence presumed was Henry's wife stood. "What is it, doctor?" the woman asked, her face drawn with worry.

The boy's face turned a bright red, and he darted a glance at Ashton.

Harry patted the boy on the shoulder. "Nothing life-threatening, I assure you," he said. "I've provided some suggestions to Freddie which should help the situation."

With his cap in his hands, Freddie joined his parents with plodding steps, his shoulders hunched, and his head bowed. Whatever the boy's affliction was, Laurence watched him with empathy as he exited the clinic.

"Why are you here, Montgomery?" Harry's question jolted him back, the cutting edge to his words tingeing Laurence's ears with heat. No doubt the memory of Laurence's embarrassing situation with Miss Marbry from the other night was singed into the duke's mind.

"I've come for a diagnosis."

Harry's eyebrows raised. "Don't you have a personal physician? I have other patients."

Was that the man's way of politely dismissing him? The

remaining man in the waiting area watched with interest, his gaze traveling back and forth between Harry and Laurence.

"I prefer to speak with you. It shouldn't take long. I'm happy to wait as I don't mean to intrude upon your time with your other patients."

"That's a'right, doctor," the remaining man said. "'E looks like a paying customer, and it's only my lumbago what's acting up. It'll take me a while just to get outta this chair."

"Very well. Dr. Mason should be out shortly to see you, Mr. Smith." Harry lifted a hand, motioning for Laurence to follow and leading him to a small room down the hallway.

In an awkward attempt to make small talk, Laurence said, "How is Dr. Mason working out? I would imagine he's been a big help with Dr. Somersby away due to the new baby. Are they doing well?"

Harry looked over his shoulder from where he dipped his hands into a bowl with an odd smelling solution. "Yes. Little Eva is thriving. However, I believe Oliver is anxious to return to the clinic. He says he'll get more rest here than at home."

Laurence wasn't certain if Harry's slight smile indicated he'd forgiven Laurence's transgression with Miss Marbry, or he simply found humor in his colleague's predicament. However, Laurence used the shift to his advantage. "What's in the bowl?" He tipped his head toward the strange liquid.

Harry wiped his hands on a towel. "Chlorinated lime. Not to disparage my patients, but their bathing habits can be lax at best. I've found the solution assists with the odor that can linger after an examination, especially from particular parts of their bodies or open sores."

Laurence thought of the embarrassed young man who had left Harry's care. "Ah, I see."

"I've also discovered, quite by coincidence, it seems to have an added benefit. It's all conjecture on my part, but since I've been washing my hands between patients, I've seen a decrease in the same illness from patient to patient."

"Fascinating." Laurence's respect for Harry grew.

"And since you asked about Dr. Mason, it's been a contentious point between us. I'm concerned I may have to dismiss him if he continues to refuse my direction. As if to support my theory, patients under his care do seem to contract similar sicknesses."

Harry's smile disappeared. "Now, what are your symptoms?"

"A recent bout of sneezing and watery eyes."

"Anyone in your family suffering from similar symptoms?"

Laurence shook his head.

After taking out his pocket watch, Harry lifted Laurence's hand by the wrist to take his pulse. "Other symptoms? Fever, sore throat, lethargy?"

"A tickle in my throat, and I did feel warm during my call with Miss Marbry."

"Your pulse is strong and normal." Harry touched Laurence's forehead. "You don't feel warm now."

"The ride in my open curricle seemed to help. Perhaps it was overly warm at the Saxtons' residence."

Harry's lips pressed in a thin line as if restraining himself from asking the question that lingered in the air between them.

"I've offered for her, Ashton," Laurence blurted, not willing to bear the man's censorious look further. "She nearly refused me, but I convinced her we should see if a match between us has merit."

"As you should, all things considered," Harry muttered. His chest rose, and he heaved a sigh. "I would have never expected such behavior from you of all people. Nash on the other hand . . ."

Laurence bit back the desire to explain everything to Harry. He'd be less of a gentleman if he'd divulged Miss Marbry's plan in an effort to clear his own good name only to sully hers, so he remained silent.

The harsh lines around Harry's mouth disappeared, softening his expression. "I like Miss Marbry. She deserves to be treated with respect and affection. I wish you both joy, and I hope you'll be a good husband to her."

"I'll do my best."

"Now back to your malady, I—"

"I believe it's an allergic reaction," Laurence offered.

Harry's eyebrows rose. "You're diagnosing yourself? Why come to me?"

Heat rushed up Laurence's neck, making him wonder if he actually did have a fever. "I experienced one symptom that doesn't quite fit."

"Which is?"

"A tightness in my chest, not exactly painful, but uncomfortable."

Harry reached for his stethoscope. "Unbutton your waistcoat." After listening to Laurence's heart, Harry shook his head. "Your heart is strong and doesn't seem to be beating in an unnatural rhythm. Have you experienced these sensations before?"

Laurence shook his head.

"I agree that an allergic reaction seems likely, but as you deduced, chest discomfort isn't typically associated with it. What do you believe to be the source?"

Strands of the tiny black hair still clung to his coat. He lifted his sleeve to his nose and subsequently sneezed on Harry. "Miss Marbry's cat."

"Ah, Catpurrnicus. I had my own encounter with the feline. Did he attack you?"

"No. I think he rather likes me. However, I would imagine Miss Marbry will want to bring him with her after we're married."

"I see your point. The most logical remedy for an allergic reaction is to avoid the source of irritation, but I'll investigate other potential remedies. In the meantime, let me know if the chest pain continues or worsens. Make note of when it happens. It could be something as simple as indigestion."

"Thank you, Ashton."

"Harry, Montgomery. And I apologize if I came off as rude. Margaret did her best to assure me you were innocent, but she failed to elaborate in order to keep Miss Marbry's confidence. Having been in a similar situation, I should be more understanding. But unlike Miss Pratt, I cannot imagine Miss Marbry purposely compromising anyone. I consider her a friend and find the whole situation distressing."

"No more than I, Harry. And call me Laurence." He held out his hand, and Harry grasped it, giving it a firm shake. "Now, I should be off and allow you to tend to your other patients. I'll be sure to make a generous contribution when Her Grace makes her rounds."

He buttoned his waistcoat and straightened his cravat, then made his way outside, grateful his curricle still waited.

After tossing another pence each to the two boys, he climbed into the seat, and snapped the ribbons, his mind working on a solution to appease his future bride yet live allergen free of her cuddly cat.

CHAPTER 12—FRIENDS?

The following morning, Bea had a serious discussion with Catpurrnicus before Laurence's arrival. At least she hoped he would arrive for another call. She hadn't received word conveying his regrets. Hopefully, he'd recovered from the sudden onslaught of sneezing he'd experienced the day before.

As for Catpurrnicus, he responded to her lecture by regally lifting his hind leg and licking his bottom. Bea wondered if he intended his actions as a commentary to her request to behave himself.

After securing him in her room—with instructions to the staff not to open the door under any circumstances—Bea tripped down the hallway toward the staircase. Not a happy, light-as-air tripping. Actual tripping as her foot caught on the edge of the hall runner when she drifted too close to the wall, her mind too focused on Laurence to pay attention to her direction. Her hands splayed against the patterned wallpaper, attempting to right herself the same moment her mother peeked out from her bedchamber.

"What on earth are you doing, Beatrix? It sounds like horses galloping across the floor."

"I stumbled on the rug."

"Good heavens. Try to remain upright in Lord Montgomery's presence. If he returns, that is. Request Fanny to remain as chaperone. I'm occupied taking inventory of my jewelry, deciding which pieces I can bear to sell. It's an onerous task." Redness rimmed her mother's eyes.

Bea's stomach knotted with guilt. She kept her eyes on the floor beneath her and nodded, then continued—more carefully—down the hall. *All your fault*, the accusing voices in her head shouted. She imagined the phantoms pointing bony fingers at her, their eyes full of menace and condemnation.

If she'd only accepted her fate and married Lord Middlebury, her family would have been saved. Why had she not considered that the needs of the many outweighed the needs of one unmarriageable bluestocking? Would she even be able to look upon Laurence without sickly bile rising to her throat at the price her family paid for her selfishness?

The euphoria she had just experienced anticipating Laurence's call evaporated like the morning dew. In addition to her family, Laurence, too, was an unsuspecting victim in her plot to free herself from an undesirable marriage. Every derogatory thing her mother had enumerated over the course of Bea's girlhood came into blinding clarity, the truth almost too much to bear. Worthless. Embarrassment. Disgrace. Peculiar.

Trudging into the parlor, she tugged the bell pull for the servants to send for Fanny before taking a seat on the settee and waiting for Laurence. Dampness covered her palms, and she wiped them on the skirt of her gown, grateful no unsightly ink blotches marred the cream-colored muslin. Truth be told, she'd been unable to write a single word since Laurence's proposal. Had he truly jumbled her mind so effectively?

Precisely at ten, Preston appeared, announcing Lord Montgomery's arrival. As Bea rose to greet him, Laurence scanned the room before making a graceful bow.

"No Catpurrnicus, this morning, Miss Marbry?" His tone seemed relieved.

She shook her head, fearful if she opened her mouth, it would be enough to conjure the demon cat out of thin air. And the air did seem thin, as if the moment Laurence entered, oxygen levels had diminished. She pulled the little remaining into her lungs and motioned for him to take a seat.

Thank goodness he had the presence of mind to begin the conversation. "I thought we might stroll in the park today, if that meets with your approval? The sun is out, and it would be a shame not to take advantage."

His gaze drifted around the room, landing on Fanny. "I see not only is Catpurrnicus absent, but your mother as well." From the smile tugging at his lips, his statement seemed to please him.

"Yes, Fanny is my lady's maid. She can accompany us as chaperone."

Bea requested Fanny fetch their bonnets and parasols, and informed Preston of their destination on their way out of the townhouse.

As any gentleman would, Laurence offered his arm. A shiver of excitement raced through Bea's body as she wrapped her hand around his forearm. The magnitude of actually touching him weakened her knees, and she found herself clutching his arm perhaps a little too tightly. However, Laurence appeared unaffected, or if her grip was painful, he ignored it. She forced herself to relax her fingers, focusing instead on the muscle beneath the sleeve of his coat.

They strolled in silence toward Hyde Park. A light breeze blew the sweet, heady scent of a nearby magnolia tree, mixed with something much different. With care not to stumble into him, Bea leaned closer, inhaling deeply and recognizing her favorite scent of parchment mixed with the clean fragrance of shaving soap.

Curious stares accompanied murmured greetings from people passing by. Ladies whispered behind gloved hands as they cast quick glances toward Bea and sad smiles toward Laurence.

Laurence nodded or tipped his hat in reciprocation. As for Bea, her small stature straightened with pride to be seen on Lord Montgomery's arm—as his fiancée no less.

The scandal sheets had wasted no time spreading the gossip of their unfortunate discovery at her own engagement ball and touting the praise of Montgomery for his honor in offering for her. With words such as "questionable" and "desperate," the author's thinly veiled speculation that Bea had coerced him into the compromising situation was obvious.

At the moment, she couldn't care less. Let them talk, say she wasn't worthy of him. She vowed she would do her utmost to become a respectable wife, to make him proud of her and perhaps even happy with his decision to salvage her reputation.

He turned slightly, darting a quick glance toward Fanny walking a few steps behind. When he leaned closer, she breathed in his marvelous clean scent. *Good Galileo, he smells so wonderful.*

His voice, a whisper, sent gooseflesh up her arms. "I have a question, Miss Marbry. It may appear forward, even scandalous, so I apologize in advance if it offends you."

It was as if the electric energy of Victor Frankenstein's reanimation technique jolted every fiber of her being to life. Laurence's careful observation of Fanny stirred hopeful ideas in Bea's mind. Would he try to whisk her away and ask to kiss her? She held her breath, waiting for him to continue.

Red tinged the tips of his ears, and she decided she loved that about him as well. His innocent embarrassment. So unlike men like Lord Nash. Was Laurence as unsure of himself in the situation as she was about herself?

"I know it's unusual, but I wondered if we might follow the duke and duchess's example and call each other by our Christian names?"

Oh. Her heart tumbled. Not that his suggestion wasn't appealing, but her hopes of receiving a kiss vanished.

He must have read the disappointment on her face, for his blanched. "I beg your forgiveness. It's much too early in our association for such familiarities. You must think me much too forward."

Her heart clenched at the pain on his face, and she rushed to salvage the situation. "Not at all, Laurence." His name spoken out loud produced the sweetest sound she'd ever heard. "It simply took me by surprise. I expected another question." *Oh, dear, that slipped out.*

"Oh? What question was that . . . Beatrix?"

Bea amended her earlier thought. Hearing him speak her name surpassed everything.

He waited, the smile on his face tentative and expectant.

Heat flamed her cheeks, and she shook her head vehemently.

His eyes widened, and his own cheeks colored as if he deduced the exact path her mind had taken. Confusion seemed to replace his embarrassment as his brows knit together and his head tilted jauntily to one side. "Yes, well . . ." He gave an awkward cough. "Have you read about the attempts to improve upon Faraday's electric motor?"

She blinked, her mind adjusting to the sudden change in topic. "I have. It seems Barlow's wheel has garnered more interest in pursuing improvements and practical applications."

His eyes lit with interest. "Indeed." He leaned closer. "May I share a confession?"

The enticing aroma uniquely his flooded her nostrils, and she resisted the urge to pull in several deep breaths. Instead, she gathered enough of her wits to nod.

"I'm attempting to build a motor of my own," he whispered.

Even more than his revelation alone—which granted was monumental—the fact he shared it with her, trusted her enough, pleased her more than she could say. Other women may be swayed by compliments of their beauty, their grace, their accomplishments at the pianoforte, or skill in embroidery, but for Bea, these few words meant more than gold.

"That is extraordinary." She struggled to tamp down her building excitement, only slightly less than the thrill she'd experienced thinking he might kiss her. "May I see it?"

A mischievous grin spread across his face, reminding her of Timothy when they were children and he'd done something naughty without getting caught.

"Truly?" he asked, his tone a wee bit dubious.

She nodded vigorously. "Please."

"I've only begun, and I'd prefer to keep it confidential." He turned briefly toward Fanny. "Perhaps after we're married, I'll be further along, and we'll break no rules of propriety by being alone."

Although Bea was not one to giggle, the thought seemed ludicrous, all things considered. Without warning, a girlish giggle burst from her lips, surprising even her. "I believe we've already broken the rules. Hence our engagement."

"Ah, yes." His lips curled up in a most attractive fashion.

Bea's mind returned to the hope of a kiss from that delectable mouth. However, it seemed highly unlikely.

"Still, it would be preferable not to provide any more fodder for the scandal sheets," he said. "If you haven't noticed, people are observing our every movement."

"There is still time to rescind your proposal, my lord." Had she lost her mind?

"Laurence, remember? We agreed." He patted her hand resting on his coat sleeve. "I'm a man of my word, Beatrix. If anyone decides against the marriage, it must be you." His footsteps halted, and he turned toward her.

She drew in a breath, trapping it in her lungs. Her eyes locked with his, then for a brief moment, his flitted down toward her lips. The bit of air whooshed out.

"I do hope you don't," he said.

Discombobulated. That's what he did to her typically sharp mind. "Don't what?"

"Call off our engagement. I've enjoyed this time with you, our conversations. I think we shall make a good match and become friends."

Not at all what she'd hope for. But Laurence apparently failed to recognize her disappointment as he forged ahead. "Currently, after I've attended a lecture at the Royal Society, no one in my family is keen to listen to my excited ramblings. With you, I feel a kindred spirit, and it will be so rewarding to come home and share what I've heard with someone who understands."

"I do wish I could attend those lectures." She silently added *as myself,* for she indeed had attended dressed as a lad.

He waved it off. "It's men only. Especially after that scandalous experiment allowing the Duchess of Newcastle to attend."

No need to remind Bea, but she felt compelled to ask. "Do *you* oppose women in attendance?"

Those kissable lips pressed together in a hard line as he frowned again. "I can't say since I've never been witness to such an occurrence. However, I would imagine women would find it frightfully dull. My mother and sister disappear in hiding for days after I've attended."

Irritation itched at Bea's skin. Could her perfect man be— flawed? Unthinkable—and yet . . .

He'd apparently continued speaking. ". . . interest in hearing what I have to say. Why, a few short weeks ago, I read a most interesting article in *The Times* by a fellow O.B. regarding the advancement of motors. It's where I acquired the idea to build my own."

The mention of O.B. grabbed her attention. "You enjoyed the article?"

"Oh, decidedly. Most enlightening. A brilliant man. I've enquired about his identity in hopes of meeting him, but alas, to no avail. *The Times* is most guarded with their sources."

"Perhaps even they don't know."

He seemed to consider it. "Do you think he might submit the articles anonymously? Then why the initials?"

"Well, to identify it was the same person I would imagine. They would hardly accept multiple articles by an untested source using the nomenclature of anonymous."

"Excellent point."

She pressed on. "What makes you believe O.B. is a man?"

As if his body had encountered an immovable barrier, he stopped in his tracks and turned toward her, his eyes rapidly blinking. "Pardon?"

"A man. What if O.B. is a woman?"

Oh, the look he gave her turned her stomach. The same condescending expression she'd seen countless times from her parents, even at times from Timothy. As if she must be completely mad to believe such *nonsense*.

"My dear, have you read the article?"

"I have."

"Then you must see that the clarity and, shall I say, genius with which O.B. expresses his ideas must come from a male mind. There is simply no other explanation."

She pulled her hand from his arm, no longer desiring to touch him. In one simple sentence, he had both flattered and insulted her. With feet of clay, he promptly stepped down from the pedestal upon which she'd held him for so long, proving himself to be merely human after all. Her legs became considerably less wobbly with the knowledge.

"Have I offended?" Contrition mixed with confusion painted his face.

How could she blame him for such beliefs? The supposed superiority of men had been practically beaten into her at a young age. Would it be any less for him?

"I merely suggest until the identity of O.B. is revealed, it would be prudent to keep an open mind as to the author's sex."

For a moment, Bea questioned her hearing as Laurence's mouth opened and closed several times without producing an audible word.

He looked—aghast.

Oh, Bea, you've done it again. Her mother's words rang in her ears, reminding Bea of her unnerving habit of speaking her mind, especially when her mind and the mind of the person with whom she was conversing did not mesh. She should have followed her mother's advice and agreed with everything Laurence had said.

And yet—she could not. It was the principle of the thing. She stood her ground and waited. Even though he assured her he wouldn't, she fully expected him to change his mind and rescind his proposal.

After a throat clearing cough—thankfully nothing as disgusting as Lord Middlebury—he said, "How is your cat?"

Her mind hiccupped at the non sequitur and she blinked. "My cat?"

CHAPTER 13—TO BE SEEN

D*olt!* What on earth had he been thinking? Asking about her cat? He'd obviously offended her, but for the life of him, he didn't understand how. Then he'd only made matters worse by attempting to right his blunder. In his struggle to find a safe topic of conversation, he'd made an utter fool of himself. No wonder he had trouble finding a bride. His neck heated. Had the sun suddenly become more intense?

"Yes, well . . ." He could imagine the sheepish expression most likely crossing his face. "I thought perhaps Catpurrnicus would be a subject we could agree upon."

The air around him stilled, each tiny sound and scent magnified as if using that particular moment to bombard his senses. Half expecting people's curious stares, he gazed around him, relieved no one had taken notice of his utter lack of tact.

He fully expected her to turn on her heel and return home, telling him to go to the devil. Unbidden, he held his breath and waited.

The trapped air in his lungs whooshed out at her laugh.

Tears formed in the corner of her eyes, and she wiped them away. "I must say, I will have to remember that strategy the next time I've stuck my foot in it. Although I doubt I would be able to use poor Catpurrnicus. Not many people have my fondness for him."

"I can't imagine why. He's a sweet creature."

She laughed again, that time even harder.

What had he said?

He offered his handkerchief, and she took it, dabbing at the moisture around her eyes.

"Am I forgiven?" he asked, still unsure of his offense.

She nodded, gaining control over her fit of hysterics. "Affection for Catpurrnicus covers a multitude of sins."

Warmth flooded his chest. "I shall remember that sage advice for any future missteps in our marriage." He held out his arm. "Shall we continue our walk?"

He'd missed the warmth of her hand on his arm, and he'd been surprised how much he enjoyed it. "Although speaking of your cat, I'm a bit concerned."

Her fingers tightened on his arm. He prayed he would not offend her yet again.

"It appears I might be allergic. The sneezing episode I had abated greatly after I left you yesterday. I called upon Ashton at his clinic, and he concurs Catpurrnicus may be the source. I had my valet thoroughly air and beat my clothing to remove any remaining cat hair."

"Are you requesting I get rid of him?"

He darted a glance at her. Her green eyes no longer danced with amusement, and the sadness he found in their depths touched him. "Oh, no." He placed his other hand over hers, squeezing her fingers. "I would never ask that of you. However, we may need to experiment with ways to reduce the irritation once we are living together."

A light blush covered her cheeks.

"After we are married," he clarified. "We'll work on finding a solution together. Perhaps some experimentation is in order?"

"I shall begin researching immediately," she said.

He found the idea of a woman performing research rather endearing. "If you like. In the interim, during our courtship, it may be best to limit how much I'm around him. Although I'll admit, I will miss seeing him."

"Perhaps if we meet on the terrace when you call?"

"It can be our first experiment." Relief flooded him that they appeared to be back on the right foot following his—still unknown —offense.

They continued their walk without further incident, each taking turns commenting on the various species of flora and fauna they encountered. He appreciated her sharp mind and interesting turn of phrase as she gave her opinions.

Perhaps their marriage would be successful after all.

When he returned her home, Preston, the Saxtons' butler, informed them Timothy had arrived and could be found on the terrace with Lady Saxton.

Trepidation knotted Laurence's stomach. He hadn't faced his friend since the fiasco at the ball. The withering glare Timothy had directed toward him still burned in his mind. "Perhaps I should go and leave you to enjoy the company of your brother." Internally, he cringed at his cowardice.

"But you and Timothy are friends. Surely you wish to at least say hello? We could begin our experimentation with Catpurrnicus." Beatrix's green eyes pleaded, and he conceded to please her.

"Very well, but I shan't stay long." He handed his hat to Preston.

She tugged on his arm, pulling him forward. His feet moved as if he had stepped in spilled honey. One thing Laurence dreaded above all else was losing the good opinion of those he admired, and Timothy being one of his oldest and dearest friends topped the list.

Angry voices exploded from the terrace as they approached. Laurence exchanged a worried look with Beatrix before stepping outside. Apparently, Lady Saxton had been in a heated discussion with her son. Two pairs of eyes turned toward Laurence and Beatrix, the conversation coming to an abrupt halt.

Lady Saxton fanned herself excitedly and rose to greet them. "Lord Montgomery. I trust you and Beatrix had a lovely walk?"

"We did, madam." Laurence turned his gaze toward Timothy, whose ire seemed to have dissipated. Laurence nodded. "Marbry."

His friend rose and approached with heavy steps, his focus never leaving Laurence's face. Timothy paused momentarily before them, then embraced his sister, kissing her on the cheek. "I trust this reprobate is treating you well."

Unsure what to make of Timothy's stern expression, Laurence held his breath. Apparently, all was still not forgiven.

Timothy swung his arm forward, slapping Laurence on the back. "Relax, old man." He leaned in and whispered. "Bea told me everything, but I do appreciate you stepping up and doing the right thing."

Bea. Interesting. He'd have to call her that. Laurence choked out a weak reply. "Of course."

"Besides, I owe you. You've just saved me from another lecture by Mother."

Laurence darted a glance at Lady Saxton, his future mother-in-law. The woman did appear to be a force of nature, not unlike his own mother. The thought of the two of them conspiring together regarding his and Beatrix's future life soured his stomach. No doubt they'd expect a grandchild within the year. The notion of the necessary intimacy to produce a child had him swallowing hard in anticipation.

He cast a quick glance at Beatrix. Had she considered that? They barely knew each other. He shifted uncomfortably.

"Timothy," Beatrix said, "entertain Laurence while I fetch Catpurrnicus."

A groan came from Lady Saxton's direction.

Laurence was unsure if the use of his Christian name or the mention of the cat had caused the woman's distress.

Beatrix raced off, leaving him at the mercy of her family.

"She's calling you Laurence?" Timothy asked, an auburn eyebrow lifting.

Laurence straightened his shoulders. "It *is* my name, and we are to be married."

His friend leaned in and whispered, "Don't misunderstand. I approve, but perhaps you should refrain in front of my mother. And why is Bea fetching Catpurrnicus? Do you enjoy taking your life in your hands? A scandalous compromise not enough excitement for you?" Timothy punctuated the last with a burst of laughter.

Tension in his shoulders eased, and Laurence found himself smiling at the thought. Quite a surprise considering his devotion to a well-ordered and even-keel lifestyle. "Perhaps I've decided to change."

Timothy scrutinized him as if Laurence were a specimen to be examined. "Bea might be good for you."

"In truth, I believe I'm allergic to her pet. We thought to try an experiment and see if the symptoms lessen outdoors."

"You mean to tell me you've already survived an encounter with the beast? I must witness this myself."

Lady Saxton joined them. "Since you have Timothy here, I will leave you. I can't abide that animal." She turned toward her son. "We haven't finished our conversation." The glare she sent Timothy sent a chill up Laurence's spine. He hoped never to incur her wrath.

Timothy watched her leave, then exhaled a heavy sigh. "She's disappointed in me. Now I know how Bea feels. I've always been Mother's favorite, but she does not approve of my decision."

"Which is?"

"To pursue medicine. I have a talent for it, Montgomery, and it gives me a sense of fulfillment. Plus with our financial situation, having an occupation seems prudent."

"I've negotiated some time with Nash on your father's debt. I feel responsible, all things considered."

Timothy shook his head. "Don't. If anyone is to blame, it's my father. I'll admit when I saw you with Bea, I could hardly believe my eyes. You of all people. But Bea was desperate, and it was unfair of my father to put her in the situation to begin with."

He scrubbed a hand down his face. "I love my sister, Montgomery." His eyes searched Laurence's. "Promise me you'll try to make her happy."

"I'll make it my priority." Having a goal had always served Laurence well, and defeat was never an option.

BEA CUDDLED CATPURRNICUS TO HER CHEST. "BE A GOOD BOY around Laurence, Purrny." She stroked his soft fur, the gentle purring against her hand a reminder of how sweet and loving he could be.

When he wanted to.

"Try not to rub against him too much and make him sneeze."

Catpurrnicus opened his jaws in a wide yawn, his little pink tongue curling. She'd awoken him from one of his many naps on the sunny window seat of her room. The trip to her bedroom to retrieve her cat provided time to gather her thoughts about Laurence's comments during their stroll in the park.

Admittedly, his failure to consider that a woman may have written the article in *The Times* had rankled her. As if a woman was incapable of thinking with logic and clarity. She'd had the urge to stomp on his booted foot. Were all men so thick-skulled as to not see past their own noses?

The realization that even her dear Laurence was less than perfect had hit her hard, but perhaps the discovery had its advantages. She'd become considerably less nervous around him, and more importantly, perhaps his own shortcoming—albeit singular—would make him more tolerant of her own shortcomings —which were legion.

And of course there was Catpurrnicus. The smile found its way to her lips without effort. The fact that he had turned the uncomfortable situation around by asking about her cat had redeemed him almost to the point of landing him back on the pedestal.

Almost.

She hadn't forgiven him entirely.

On her way to the terrace, she passed her mother. Catpurrnicus wiggled in her arms, stretching out a paw, claws extended, and hissed.

"Good heavens, Beatrix. Why you insist on inflicting that wretched creature upon your suitors is beyond me."

"Lau—Lord Montgomery likes him, but unfortunately, he believes he might be allergic. We need to conduct an experiment."

Her mother gave the unholy roll of the eyes which she'd mastered to perfection. "I beg of you to suppress those silly ideas of yours, at least in front of Lord Montgomery. Do you want to run him off and lose the second—and possibly your last—suitor in less than a week?"

Bea lifted her chin. "It was Lord Montgomery's idea."

Her mother exhaled a deep sigh, shook her head, and left, muttering in her wake something about the curse of daughters.

When she reached the terrace, Bea stopped short, catching Timothy and Laurence in an apparently serious conversation. Sunlight brushed Laurence's chestnut hair, enhancing the reddish hue at the crown like an auburn halo.

Her heart warmed at her brother's words. "Promise me you'll try to make her happy."

And yet, not as much as the heat generated by Laurence's response. "I'll make it my priority."

Magically, as if angels' wings formed on his back, Laurence resumed his place on the pedestal. However, it did wobble slightly.

Drawing in a breath to calm her racing heart, she announced her arrival. "I have the subject of our experimentation, my lord."

Timothy took several long strides back as she approached, leaving Laurence the sole target in range of Catpurrnicus's attention. "You're on your own here, Montgomery," he murmured. "The cat tolerates me—but barely."

"Stop being a coward, Timothy," Bea said.

"It's self-defense, Bea. Catpurrnicus glares at me as if I'm a succulent mouse."

Laurence laughed and crouched down. "Put him down, Miss Marbry. Let's see if the fresh air helps."

With a prayer to the gods of medicine, she leaned down to place Catpurrnicus on the stones of the terrace. Not waiting, the cat squirmed out of her grasp and scurried toward Laurence. No sooner had he begun weaving his way through Laurence's legs, purring loudly, than the sneezing commenced.

"It would appear—ah-choo—merely being ou . . . ou . . . ah-choo . . . side is not enou . . . nou . . . ah-choo . . . enough."

Bea raced over, scooped Catpurrnicus in her arms, and set him down on the soft grass in the garden. "Go find something to chase, Purrny."

The cat stared up at her, his yellow eyes narrowed as if in protest. Luckily, a butterfly flitted past, diverting Catpurrnicus's miniscule attention span successfully.

As Bea turned back to the men, Laurence tucked his handkerchief back into his pocket. "It appears our experiment is a failure, Miss Marbry."

Timothy resumed his position by Laurence's side. "Or a success, depending on how you look at it."

"Fair point, Marbry. I hate to say it, but perhaps it would have been better if he weren't so fond of me."

"I'm not so sure he is." Timothy guffawed, slapping Laurence on the back. "That cat is devious in finding the perfect torture to inflict upon his unsuspecting victims."

Granted, truth lay in Timothy's words, but Bea rose to her pet's defense. "How could he know Lau—Lord Montgomery is allergic?"

"Relax, Bea. I'm not Mother. If you and Montgomery wish to use each other's Christian names, who am I to judge? But to answer your question, I suspect your cat has unnatural powers from being a minion of the devil." Timothy laughed again.

Bea was not so amused. "Don't be ridiculous. You of all people with your interest in medicine can't believe such superstitious nonsense."

"Timothy told me about his plans to pursue medicine," Laurence said, directing his comment to Bea, then turned toward her brother. "Do you plan to open a private practice?"

"It would be the most logical choice, considering our financial situation. However, before this . . . all . . . transpired, I'd hoped to work with Ashton at his clinic. The idea of assisting the poor appeals to me."

"Your timing might be perfect," Laurence said. "When I saw Ashton the other day, he mentioned difficulty with Dr. Mason. It would appear Ashton's progressive views on cleanliness are not well-received by the good doctor."

"How can one not agree with cleanliness?" Bea asked, horrified that a physician would be unconcerned with such important matters.

Laurence shrugged. "I believe it's more about Ashton's techniques, which, by the way, are most interesting. I should like to meet with him again and discuss the scientific applications and assist in gathering data to support his theory."

"First, I would have to complete my studies and take my exams, but I'll speak to Ashton about the possibility of securing a position once I'm certified. That is if Dr. Mason has left Ashton's employ."

"Perhaps you could also take on a few private patients," Bea suggested. "To supplement your wages from the clinic."

Timothy held out his hands. "Slow down, you two. You both act as if it's been settled. I may fail miserably at the remainder of my studies and my exams. And even if I don't, it doesn't guarantee a position at the clinic. Dr. Mason may remain."

An idea surfaced in Bea's mind. "Perhaps you can assist us in finding a remedy for Laurence's allergies with Catpurrnicus? That would definitely prove your worth to His Grace."

Timothy's face brightened. "That's a brilliant idea, Bea. And it would not only help to convince Ashton, but I may be able to use the findings as a paper for my studies." Timothy held out his hand, palm down. "As we did as boys, 'eh? We shall tackle the problem like companions in arms."

Laurence placed his hand on top of Timothy's, then nodded toward Bea. When she placed hers on top of Laurence's, the warmth of being included was almost as pleasant as the touch of Laurence's hand under hers. He locked eyes with her, and a gentle smile rose to his lips.

"Huzzah!" Timothy shouted, throwing their hands into the air.

For a moment, the camaraderie of the two men she loved most in the world threatened to overwhelm her. The sheer joy of being included was nothing short of heaven.

"Perhaps I'll go off in search of Catpurrnicus," Timothy said, his gaze darting between Bea and Laurence. "Give you two some time alone." He winked at Laurence and strode off down the steps of the terrace to the garden.

"I've always considered Timothy like a brother," Laurence said, watching Timothy's retreating back. He turned toward Bea. "And when we're married, he truly will be."

"I'm grateful that you like at least one of my family members. Although Papa is a fine man—when he's not gambling."

"About that, Beatrix. I told Timothy I'm formulating some ideas that might help. I've bought some time with Nash, but I don't know how long I can hold him off."

"It's good of you to try, especially since it's not your responsibility. And if anything, it's affected you negatively." The joy of the day dimmed as she remembered how her own impetuous actions had precipitated their situation. "I apologize again."

He motioned to a stone bench on the side of the terrace. "May we sit?"

They settled themselves next to each other on the narrow bench, so close together that when she shifted to a more comfortable position, Laurence's shoulder brushed against hers.

"I thought we might go to Scotland on our wedding trip, if that meets with your approval," he said. "I have a cousin on my father's side with an estate in the Lowlands but on the edge of the Highlands. With the heat of the summer, the temperature there is much cooler, and his estate is particularly beautiful that time of year."

With mention of their honeymoon, a strange sensation like birds fluttered in her stomach. She smoothed some imaginary wrinkles in her gown, afraid if she met his gaze, her face would burst into flame at his nearness. "It sounds wonderful."

As she gazed at her folded hands in her lap, he reached over, taking one of her hands in his. "Bea," he said, his voice soft as a whisper. "I know this is difficult for you. I promise I won't rush anything, and I shall do my best to make you a good husband."

She nodded, still terrified to meet his gaze. "I heard you tell Timothy."

The sigh he emitted broke through her resistance, the sound

almost mournful, and she raised her head. "I know you feel obligated to do the right thing." She bit back the rest bubbling on her tongue. *It's one reason I love you.*

An odd flicker flashed in his eyes. If she had to put a name on it, she would say it was akin to having someone actually *see* you—really *see* you for who you were.

Something which she yearned for herself.

CHAPTER 14—THE WEDDING

Bea ran her hands down the front of the lovely pale green gown, sighing with gratitude that—thanks to Laurence's generosity—she was able to wear it. It had turned out more beautiful than she'd imagined. Bright, cheerful daisies embroidered along the neckline and edges of the sleeves would turn anyone's frown into a smile, and the sunny, yellow ribbon encircling her midriff complemented the mint green perfectly.

Her mother had lamented to Laurence—relaying with dramatic effect—the fact that Lord Middlebury had cancelled the commission for the gown upon breaking his engagement with Beatrix. A week before the wedding, a note had arrived from Madame Tredwell, the modiste, stating the gown was ready for fitting, Lord Montgomery having made payment in full.

An additional note had accompanied Madame Tredwell's. Written in a strong masculine hand, the note became a treasure which Bea had tucked away in her escritoire.

Miss Marbry, please accept this gown as a token of my affection on our wedding day. ~Montgomery

She retrieved it and deposited it in her reticule, not willing to leave it behind with her other belongings to be transferred to her husband's home after the wedding.

"Beatrix!" her mother's shrill voice pierced the haze of Bea's daydreaming. "You will be late for your own wedding!"

Her mother bustled into the room amid flounces of lace and swirls of rose water. The fragrance—applied much too liberally—overpowered the subtle scent of vanilla and orange blossom Bea had frugally applied.

Furious swishing of her mother's fan only prompted the dominating scent to travel farther, assaulting Bea's senses. Bea fought the urge to gag. It would not do to evacuate her stomach's contents on her wedding day, especially not on her own mother. Besides, it would ruin her lovely gown.

With a deep, calming breath, Bea forced a smile and willed her hands to stop shaking. Unlike nerves of uncertainty or fear, her insides quivered with anticipation and excitement. Each time her mind wandered to the coming evening, her cheeks warmed. Visions of her first night as Lady Montgomery, wrapped in her husband's arms, consumed all rational thought.

She tied the matching bonnet, decorated with fresh daisies, on her head and descended the stairs to the carriage, waiting to take her to the church.

Polite chatter in her family's carriage barely registered in her mind, the journey to St. George's chapel a blur as she gazed with unfocused eyes at the passing scenery. Vaguely aware the carriage had ceased movement, she turned from the window to find each pair of eyes from her family staring at her.

Her father's gaze appeared proud, and a hint of forgiveness shone in their depths. Timothy's eyes lit with amusement at Bea's muddled state. She turned last to her mother. Searching for the pride and love she'd witnessed in her father's and brother's gaze, or even acceptance, she only found irritation and impatience.

"Matilda," her father said, a note of chastisement coloring his address to her mother. "Wish our daughter well as she leaves our home for her husband's."

"I'll wish her well when the curate has made the pronouncement. Until then, I'm not counting anything as final. She does have a peculiar talent for upending things."

"Mother, really," Timothy admonished, then snapped his mouth shut when he received her glare.

After Timothy assisted their mother from the carriage, her father exited, holding out his hand to Bea. "You look lovely, my dear. If Laurence doesn't know yet what a gem he's getting, I trust he will shortly. Be happy." He leaned in and kissed her on the cheek.

She closed her eyes, saying a silent prayer to Sir Isaac Newton that she would not—again—demonstrate his laws of motion as she made her way to her groom.

◈

LAURENCE HAD TAKEN CARE WITH HIS TOILETTE THAT MORNING, rising earlier than normal and bathing. Stevens had dressed him meticulously, the new superfine bottle-green coat and tan trousers perfectly tailored to fit snugly but allow ease of movement. Laurence had made a special request to Abernathy, the old tailor who did impeccable work. The result of the man's craftsmanship was displayed on the mint green waistcoat decorated with daisies on the points.

Abernathy had raised one gray eyebrow when Laurence requested the flowers be added, instead suggesting a geometric shape. Normally, Laurence would have preferred such a design, but he'd explained he wanted to match his bride's dress.

"You've been speaking to His Grace, I would imagine," the old tailor had said with a grin. "The fellow does have . . . unconventional ideas. Perhaps next we shall see gentlemen sporting skirts like the Scots." He laughed at his own joke.

Unfortunately, Laurence found little amusement in the dig, having Scottish ancestors from the Montgomery line.

Ambient morning light streamed in from the church's stained glass windows, painting the interior with rays of colors. Laurence took a moment to drink it in, savoring the loveliness of the effect.

He breathed a sigh of relief when Timothy entered and took his place by Laurence's side. Had he really thought Bea might change her mind?

Why did that idea seem to vex him?

Expectant faces gazed at him from the pews. Harry and Margaret had come. Margaret smiled fondly at him from her seat next to her husband. He waited for the familiar twinge of regret, surprised when it didn't appear.

Timothy chuckled next to him. "Relax, old boy, it will be over before you know it."

Laurence lifted a brow at his friend. "And you would know how?"

Timothy answered him with a sheepish grin.

About to press his friend further, the thought flew from his head at the sight of Bea making her way down the aisle on the arm of her father. An odd pressure squeezed his chest. Although not uncomfortable, he committed the scene to memory to report it to Ashton at a later time.

A vision in her gown, she darted a quick glance his way, the daisies in her bonnet providing a whimsical touch to the solemn occasion. The pressure in his chest grew stronger.

As she arrived at his side, her gaze lifted to his, then dipped to his waistcoat. The blush on her cheeks which followed informed him she had made the connection regarding the design of their clothing.

Throughout the brief ceremony, he found himself casting quick glances her way, each time reveling in her loveliness. A strange emotion raced through him when she slid her hand into his at the exchange of vows.

Love, comfort, honor.

Always a man of his word, the latter vows would prove to be no issue. But the first? Could he grow to love her? During their short, three week courtship as the banns were read, he'd realized he liked her, admired her intelligence, was physically attracted to her. But love? He never imagined he'd be standing in front a woman he barely knew on his wedding day.

Yet here he was.

Before he knew it, the ceremony had ended. They entered their marriage lines in the parish registry and departed the church, Bea's hand in the crook of his arm—this time as his wife. Cheers greeted them as they exited and boarded his carriage.

Settled inside the compartment, he wanted to kiss her, knew he should kiss her, but what did *she* want? He removed his hat, placing it on the seat beside him. His heart pounded, anticipating the sweetness of her lips.

"I hope to make you happy, Bea." As he leaned forward to kiss her, the blush darkened her face, accentuating her freckles along the bridge of her nose. Careful not to frighten her, he brushed her lips lightly in a chaste kiss.

He pulled back, his stomach clenching at the worry on her face. Had even that paltry attempt at affection upset her? He struggled to redeem himself. "We should arrive shortly for our wedding breakfast. We shall spend the night at my townhouse, then leave for our wedding trip within the week. Does that suit you, my dear?"

She nodded, the crease between her brows lessening.

Perhaps he should pull a married gentleman aside and ask for advice. He considered his options. Not his father. Definitely not Bea's father. Ashton? Weatherby? Both of their wives seemed content. However, asking Ashton for advice on making his bride comfortable in the marriage bed stirred some unwelcome feelings, imagining how the duke had accomplished that with Margaret. Weatherby it would be.

When they arrived at his parents' townhouse, he escorted Bea from the carriage, relieved to see her frown had completely disappeared. After greeting their well-wishers, they took their seats at the table.

Bea remained quiet throughout the meal, pushing food around with her fork. Was she really so unhappy about their arrangement? With him? Precious little time remained until they would depart for his townhouse and be truly alone for the first time.

When she excused herself from the table, he seized the opportunity and flagged down Andrew Weatherby.

"Felicitations, again, Montgomery. I've known Beatrix for many years, I'm sure she'll make you very happy."

He nodded absently. "But will I make her happy?"

Andrew's smile vanished. "Is something amiss?"

"I'm not sure how to put this delicately. Bea and I barely know each other. I don't want to appear . . . overeager about beginning our life together. I'm concerned I will frighten her." He hoped Andrew would understand the hidden meaning of his words.

"Ah," Andrew said, nodding.

"I've no experience with a"—he gulped—"gently bred woman." He met Andrew's knowing gaze. "Might you have some words of advice?"

Andrew darted a look in his wife's direction, his smile reappearing. "I trust you have *some* experience in general. It works the same, but perhaps allow her to take the lead. Be patient and considerate. It all comes naturally."

Somehow, the words provided little consolation.

Andrew slapped him on the back. "You'll be fine and before you know it, you'll be bouncing a chubby infant on your knee."

Mention of a child automatically caused Laurence's head to turn in his mother's direction. The woman's eagle eye trained on him as if not only her sight was magnified but her hearing as well. No doubt she would expect a grandchild within a year.

Pressure swelled within him. So many people to appease, to please. But the one person he desired to please the most strode toward him on dainty feet.

❦

BEA TRIED HER BEST TO REIN IN HER DISAPPOINTMENT. OF COURSE, never having been kissed before, other than Lord Middlebury's slobbery attempt, she didn't know exactly what to expect. However, Laurence's chaste kiss had been less than earth-shattering. She enjoyed it, no doubt, but its brevity and lack of passion stirred the sleeping demons lurking in the depths of her psyche.

They reared in full force, shouting their ugly taunts.

Unwanted.

Undesirable.

Odd.

Laurence had done the gentlemanly thing and married her, but he didn't *want* her. When he'd gazed on her during the wedding ceremony, hope had sparked from the affection shining in his eyes. But if the kiss was any indication of his true feelings, any love he felt was of a philia nature.

I think we shall make a good match and become friends.

The forced smiles and expected exchanged pleasantries during the wedding breakfast had exhausted Bea. Nothing was as trying as pretending. After she'd excused herself from the table, she wandered out into the hall for a moment's solitude. Thank goodness they wouldn't live here with Laurence's parents. She was grateful for that much. The fewer eyes watching her every movement, the better.

"Lady Montgomery, are you quite well?" The gentle voice echoed behind her, but until someone touched her arm, she didn't register that the woman had been addressing her.

Turning, she found the compassionate eyes of the Duchess of Ashton. "I'm sorry, Your Grace. I'm still adjusting to my new title."

"Then perhaps we might make it simpler and call each other by our Christian names."

Muscles in Bea's neck eased. "Margaret, may I ask a rather personal question?"

The duchess's violet eyes brightened. "I suppose that depends."

Heat slipped up Bea's neck and warmed her cheeks, and she lowered her voice to a whisper. "My mother said very little about"— she swallowed the lump down—"the wedding night. She made it sound somewhat unpleasant, but I doubt that's the case."

Margaret gave Bea's hand a squeeze. "Oh, my dear, trust your instincts and your husband. Allow him to take the lead. I have no doubt Laurence will do his utmost to please you and make the experience not only memorable but enjoyable."

Bea thanked her and re-entered the dining room.

Laurence looked up from his conversation with Andrew Weatherby and smiled. His warm brown eyes met hers, and her knees buckled. Thankfully, she'd righted herself before making a fool of herself on her wedding day. She'd made it thus far without an egregious faux pas. Surely she could manage the rest of the day —and the night.

Trust your husband. Bea's heart fluttered. My husband.

She'd never believed she would utter those words, having resigned herself to spinsterhood, and especially not in reference to Laurence. After whispering a silent prayer that Margaret was correct, she joined him.

Once they bade goodbye to their family and friends, they left for their new home. Laurence owned a smaller townhouse not far from his parents. A steady breeze cooled the June air, and they decided to walk home rather than take the brief carriage ride. Grateful for a bit more time to prepare herself, Bea clung to Laurence's arm.

"I hope the servants on staff meet your satisfaction," he said. "However, should any of them fail to meet expectations, alert me and I shall dismiss them and seek a replacement forthwith. The house is yours to run as you see fit."

If only she'd paid more attention to her mother's instruction and example when dealing with servants. She'd always turned a deaf ear during her mother's long-suffering accounts of the servants' many faults. She began a mental list of things to ask one of her married friends.

The notion stopped her short. What friends? Failure to participate in the usual feminine circles had left that resource sorely lacking as well. Perhaps the duchess—Margaret, she reminded herself. Or Mrs. Weatherby. Both had shown concern for her in the recent chain of events. She would make a point to invite them for tea before she and Laurence left on their wedding trip.

Another pang of worry mixed with anticipation of the impending trip, and more importantly, the night to come. Would she disappoint him? Would he turn away in disgust and seek fulfillment with a mistress?

Bea had never given consideration to such matters before, believing they were beyond her concern. But now, grasping Laurence's muscled arm, feeling his warmth through his coat sleeve, an ugly horned demon reared its head at the image of him in the arms of another woman. A sour taste filled her mouth, and she resisted the urge to spit on the pavement before her.

She pushed the unpleasant vision away, relieved when they arrived at Laurence's home—her home. The door opened without having to knock, and a man with thinning hair bowed in greeting.

"Lady Montgomery, this is Carter, our butler," Laurence said.

Servants lined the hall of the brightly lit foyer, ready to meet their employer's new wife. Laurence introduced them one by one, and Bea tried not to cringe under their appraising eyes. One ready smile lifted her spirits as Fanny had joined their ranks in line.

"Of course we brought Fanny." Laurence patted Bea's arm. "I do hope her presence makes you feel at home."

Laurence showed her around the various rooms of the house, telling her she could redecorate at her discretion. "I'll admit, it's obvious a bachelor has occupied it, and it sorely needs a feminine touch."

Bea ran a hand over the collection of books in the library, the familiar smell of parchment and leather soothing her nerves. Sedate but warm colors provided the room with an inviting atmosphere conducive to spending long hours curled up with one of the many offerings. She loved everything about the house. "It's perfect as it is."

Her words seemed to please him. His eyes crinkled at the corners, and she swore he exhaled a little sigh.

Memory of an early conversation during their courtship prompted her to ask, "Now that we're married, may I see it?"

He blinked, his face blanching. "Pardon?"

"May I see it?"

The cravat around his neck moved outward briefly. "What?"

"Your motor. The one you're building. You suggested we wait until after we were married to show me."

His whole body seemed to relax, and color returned to his face. "Oh, of course. First, you may want to change your gown as to not soil it. The motor is up on the roof."

He escorted her to her room, called for Fanny, and left her.

When she joined him again, he'd changed as well, having removed his coat and donned a worn pair of trousers and a plain waistcoat. He looked dashing in his shirtsleeves, which he'd rolled up to his elbows.

"I apologize for my state of undress, but I've found it's best to have as little fabric as possible in the way while I work."

He led her up two more flights of stairs to a narrow passageway. A rope hung from a small square in the ceiling, and he pulled at it, lowering a set of wooden steps.

Proceeding her, he climbed two steps, then turned and held out his hand. A bubble of excitement rippled in her chest at not only seeing his motor, but taking part in such unladylike actions.

The stairs led to an attic space. A hodgepodge of items littered the area, many of which Bea wished to examine further. But Laurence gestured toward a small doorway. As she joined him and stepped outside, she gazed around the roof.

The machine sat in the middle, and Laurence strode over to it, his steps sure and precise.

"Is the roof safe?" she asked, a bit embarrassed by the shakiness in her voice.

"Perfectly," he said. "There is an underlay of copper for support. I'll admit, I was exceptionally pleased to find that particular feature when I purchased the house." He held out his hand, motioning her to join him.

He pulled aside a tarp of material, revealing the motor. Not large, the device sat on a tabled platform in the middle of the roof. He explained his design, a variation of Barlow's wheel. "The challenge I'm facing," he said, "is to find a better source of electricity. The voltaic pile has some flaws. Electrolytes can leak and cause a short circuit, and the battery life is minimal. If I could find a stronger power source, I envision a much larger and more complicated device producing longer periods of motion and more practical applications."

"It's marvelous," she said, her voice breathy to her own ears. She reached out a tentative hand, but glanced up at him for permission. "May I touch it?"

His shoulders squared, drawing her attention to his broad chest. "If you wish. Careful of the wires here." He pointed toward two thin wires attached to rods at the end of the small block of wood.

She'd seen grainy drawings of Barlow's wheel in the journal published by the Royal Society, but her blood raced as she touched a finger to the wheel, and with a push propelled it.

"That's not necessary to begin the motion," he said. His words contained no sting of condemnation or insult, but were tinged with pride. "Allow me to show you." He attached the other ends of the wires to the voltaic pile. The wheel began spinning of its own accord.

Like a child watching acrobats in Vauxhall Gardens, she clapped her hands with delight. Quite automatically, she reached out and grasped his arm. "It's wonderful."

"It's a model for a larger plan once I find a solution for the power."

Emboldened, she asked, "May I assist?"

"If it pleases you, but perhaps this isn't the time. It's our wedding day after all. Would you like to rest? You must be exhausted from the excitement of the day."

Does he mean . . . ? Her face warmed.

"Oh." His gaze darted from her face, focusing on the roof beneath his feet. "I . . . uh . . . thought you might enjoy some tea in your room while I work on something in the library."

Her heart slid to her stomach. Did her disappointment show on her face?

"Unless you prefer to join me in the library? We could take tea together?"

She agreed, hoping to find some books that would assist in the next article she'd been writing. They adjourned to the library, still in their worn clothes, and Carter brought tea.

Hours passed in companionable silence as Bea scoured various books on scientific topics, thrilled Laurence had acquired so many. Laurence sat at the large walnut desk, sketching plans for a larger motor. Occasionally, she'd walk behind him, peeking over his shoulder, impressed with his talent as an artist.

After marking several places in a dozen books, she drew up a chair at a nearby table. "May I have some paper, pens, and ink?"

A thick brown lock of hair had fallen over Laurence's forehead as he worked, and when he looked up at her, her heart gave a sound thump at his adorable appearance.

He retrieved her requested supplies, then returned to his sketching. More than once, she had the distinct impression of being watched, but each time she'd looked up, Laurence remained focused on his own work. She attempted another tactic, and keeping her head low, she slid her gaze toward him, catching him watching her.

Slivers of satisfaction sparked in her chest. The power it gave her—could it be harnessed—would surely be enough to supply a large motor.

Before she realized it, the afternoon had slipped away. They enjoyed a quiet dinner, and she had a suspicion Laurence had enquired about her preferences from her mother, or perhaps Timothy.

His gaze, open and earnest, met hers. "Is everything to your liking?"

"How did you know these were my favorites?"

The tilt of his head jostled the wayward forelock of hair, the casual appearance of it a juxtaposition to his formal dinner wear. "I didn't, but they're my favorites. The cook must have prepared them to commemorate our day." He dipped his fork in his lemon ice. "It's good to know we have more in common than the love of science."

Cool tangy sweetness coated her tongue as she followed suit, wondering if his kisses would take the chill off her lips from the ices.

In a few scant hours, she would find out.

CHAPTER 15—THE WEDDING NIGHT

After dinner, Bea retired to her room. Fanny had prepared a bath for her, and Bea luxuriated in the warm, scented water. Small rivulets of water rolled down her skin, the droplets sensual, and she imagined Laurence's fingers following the trail.

After drying off, Bea applied a few more precious drops of the orange blossom fragrance she'd used to scent the bath water, dabbing her neck below her earlobes and the hollow between her breasts. *Scandalous.* She giggled, hoping her efforts would be worth it.

Fanny assisted her into her new nightrail, a lovely gauzy silk trimmed with delicate lace. She'd used part of her funds to secretly purchase it, and the modiste assured her it was the perfect thing for her wedding night.

Once Fanny left, Bea perched on the edge of the bed, twisting her hands nervously as she waited for Laurence to enter her bedchamber. Her heart pounded furiously in her chest in anticipation of what would come. At last he would hold her in his arms, kiss her lips with more than a chaste peck—finally love her as she had dreamed of for years. She wiped her palms against the silk fabric. It would not do to have wet hands—hands that would soon run down his body.

She practically swooned at the thought. Rising, she checked the candles, ensuring each remained lengthy enough to retain light for some time. She wanted to gaze upon him in all his manly glory. Heat crept up her neck at her brazen thoughts. Her breath hitched at the light tap on the door separating his room from hers.

"Enter," she said, her voice a strangled whisper. The door cracked open, and Laurence peered around the corner, his eyes questioning. She gathered her courage and said more firmly, "Enter."

He took a halting step in, then another. His gaze met hers and quickly traveled up and down her body. Then he searched the room, as if avoiding looking at her directly. He looked magnificent in his banyan—broad shoulders stretched the brocade fabric when he moved, the garment drawn to his narrow waist with a sash.

"I wanted to make certain you were comfortable and had everything you need," he said, his eyes focusing on a spot above her head.

Why wouldn't he look at her? Didn't he like her nightgown?

She swallowed down her disappointment. "Yes. Thank you." *What a stupid thing to say, Bea. Tell him he looks wonderful. Tell him you're looking forward to making him happy. Just tell him something!* "Um, that's a lovely banyan." She blushed at her idiocy. Would the man always befuddle her so, causing every coherent thought to escape her brain?

Laurence ran a hand down the front of his dressing gown. "Oh, yes. Thank you." His eyes returned to her figure. "That's"—he pointed to her negligee and coughed—"lovely, too."

Be a woman of action, Bea. With legs as wobbly as pudding, she stumbled back and sat on the bed. "I'm ready, my lord."

His ears turned a stunning shade of red, and his face flushed a moment later. "Beatrix . . . I know this is a difficult situation. I'm sure with time, we'll overcome it. There is no need to put up a brave front. I shall not force myself upon you. I'm aware you did not want this marriage. Goodnight."

With that, he turned and left, closing the door with a soft snick behind him.

Bea threw herself back on the bed in frustration.

If only he knew how wrong he was.

LAURENCE PRESSED HIS BACK AGAINST THE DOOR AND RELEASED THE breath trapped in his lungs. With no time to spare, he'd managed to extricate himself from temptation. Lord help him. It took every ounce of willpower to keep his eyes from feasting on her, from rushing over and pulling her into his arms and kissing her senseless. The sheer fabric of her nightgown barely concealed the pink buds of her nipples and the triangle of color between her legs.

Desire pulsed through him, and he gazed down at his arousal lifting the front of his dressing gown. *Did she notice?*

Her eyes had widened with terror as she clasped her trembling hands in her lap. Thank God Andrew Weatherby's advice echoed in his memory, bringing him to his senses. *Allow her to take the lead.* It would not do to begin his marriage by forcing himself on his wife, no matter how much he wanted her.

He'd felt them growing closer as the day had moved along. Her interest in his motor seemed sincere, and they worked together in the library amiably, a quiet camaraderie of sorts. However, he'd not expected the intensity of the lust shooting through him as he entered her bedchamber.

His strategy to approach her slowly, kiss her tenderly, and, per Andrew's suggestion, allow her to set the pace, vanished the moment he'd laid eyes on her. The magnitude of desire coursing through him would have made such measured control difficult at best. Much better for her that he remove himself entirely from her presence.

He scrubbed a hand down his face. Now what was he to do? He stared at his empty bed, expecting a long, restless night.

Those expectations were fully met. He had no recollection of when he'd finally drifted off to a fitful sleep.

Sunlight streaming in from the windows warmed his face, and he peeked one bleary eye open. Stevens glared down at him, his hands on his hips. Laurence pulled the pillow over his head, doing his best to ignore the man's accusatory stare.

"Go away," Laurence said, his barked order muffled from the down-filled pillow.

"Your bride rose hours ago and is enjoying breakfast. Don't you wish to join her? It would be most rude, all things considered."

What? A slow groan escaped as he dragged himself from the warmth of the bed.

"I dare say, I expected you to appear more relaxed this morning, sir." Stevens delivered the statement in his usual emotionless tone, but a glint of droll amusement shone in his valet's eyes.

Laurence refused to dignify the veiled attempt to elicit personal information with an answer, instead performing his morning ablutions in silence. Once shaved and dressed, he joined Bea for breakfast.

Unlike himself, she appeared bright and rested. Apparently, their lack of intimacy hadn't affected her negatively as it had him. In fact, a lovely blush covered her cheeks as she met his gaze.

"Good morning," he said, moving to the sideboard to serve himself. "Did you sleep well?"

"I . . . it takes me a while to adjust to new surroundings. I'm such a creature of habit, it would seem."

Was that a no? Perhaps he'd been mistaken. He added a few items to his plate, although he had little appetite, and took a seat across from her. As he studied her more closely, faint half circles darkened the underside of her eyes. Why did that . . . please him?

"Is there anything I can do to assist your adjustment?"

"I do miss Catpurrnicus, he usually snuggles next to me."

Oily guilt swirled in his empty stomach, mixing with resentment that the cat typically shared her bed and he did not. "Should we send for him? I simply thought it would be difficult for him to be uprooted, only to have us leave him when we depart for our trip. I doubt he'd tolerate the long journey to Scotland."

She gave a little sniffle, wetness rimming her eyes. "No. You're right. It would be selfish of me to put him through that."

A tweak of pain twinged in Laurence's chest.

"Besides," she said, "we still haven't found a solution to your allergy. And after all, this is your home."

The twinge pinged again, this time harder. He reached across the table and laid a hand on top of hers. "It's your home, too."

When she lifted her gaze from the plate before her, a tear broke free and trickled down her cheek. Gad, he was a monster. The poor thing had been uprooted from her family, married to a man she hardly knew, and now had been denied her pet. He vowed to correct what he could immediately.

She slid her hand from his and dropped her gaze back to her plate. "I've invited Mrs. Weatherby for tea. I do hope that meets with your approval."

And the twinge turned into a knife, digging further into his chest. "As I said, it's your home. Of course you may invite whom you wish."

Carter entered, carrying the silver salver with Laurence's freshly pressed newspaper. When the man passed by and strode over to Bea, Laurence lowered the sausage-laden fork in his hand.

"My lady, you have mail."

The surprised expression on Bea's face, eyes wide and mouth forming an erotic little O, told Laurence she'd not expected it.

With his first task complete, Carter proceeded to offer Laurence the expected newspaper. However, interest in his wife's correspondence replaced Laurence's usual excitement over reading the latest in *The Times*. He laid the folded paper on the table next to his plate.

"Well wishers?" Laurence asked, curious as to whom might be writing to his wife so soon after their wedding.

Her fingers worked the seal, and her eyes moved rapidly, scanning the contents of the missive. "Mrs. Weatherby. I didn't expect a response so quickly. I just wrote to her this morning. She says she will arrive around one."

Laurence darted a quick glance at the clock on the mantle. *Ten fifteen.* He *had* slept late. Normally, he rose around seven and completed several tasks before stopping for breakfast. Which was precisely what Bea had done.

"Then I shall leave you ladies in peace. I have one errand to complete first. Afterward I think I'll go to White's for a bit." If Mrs. Weatherby came there, perhaps Andrew would be at the club, allowing Laurence to discuss Andrew's previous advice.

Beatrix nodded, her demeanor reserved, but she refused to meet his gaze.

Guilt transformed into genuine worry. "Beatrix," he said, keeping his voice low. "Have I done something to upset you?"

She shook her head, still staring at her empty plate. "It isn't you. It's me. I'm sorry I've trapped you in this marriage. I know you don't want it."

Yes, he most definitely needed advice from an experienced yet happily married man. He decided to postpone his errand and head straight to White's. Unsure what to say to lighten her sorrow, he picked at his breakfast in silence, the cold sausage lying heavily on his stomach.

When she rose, he struggled for comforting words to lift her mood, but before he could come up with anything, she'd darted from the room, practically at a trot.

He hung his head. So far, he was an utter failure at marriage.

BEA HADN'T SLEPT A WINK, WHICH LEFT HER EMOTIONS RAW. ONE peek at Laurence told her he was no more successful in courting Hypnos, the god of slumber, than she, however different his reasons might be. His handsome face appeared drawn, his eyes bleary. Pain pricked at her heart that she had made him so miserable.

She knew him well enough to know he would never leave her. He would perform his *duties* as husband to secure an heir, but the prospect of seeing him so wretched day in and day out pushed her over the breaking point.

And it was all her stupid, selfish fault.

Would he grow to resent her? Keep a mistress to whom he would shower his affection and whisper words of love? Although innocent in the ways of love, Bea wasn't completely ignorant of such matters. Her attendance at lectures at the Royal Society, albeit disguised, had made her privy to casual comments exchanged by some of the men.

Timothy assured her not all men kept mistresses, but it became crystal clear why some would. Arranged or "forced" marriages were more than common, whereas love matches like the Duke and Duchess of Ashton, Mr. and Mrs. Weatherby, and Dr. and Mrs. Somersby were the oddity, especially among the peerage.

She had prepared herself for a cold reception upon seeing Laurence that morning, would have even welcomed it. She deserved the punishment. However, nothing had prepared her for his kindness and concern. Her previously planned request of Mrs. Weatherby changed trajectory.

Throughout the remainder of the morning, servants popped in, checking on her, asking if she needed anything. She finally closed the door to her room, focusing on writing her latest article for *The Times* and hoping the staff would go about their duties without further need for instruction. She added a mental note about running a household to her list of questions for Mrs. Weatherby.

Absorbed in her thoughts, she startled at the soft knock on her door and set the pen down with ink-stained fingers. "Enter." She tried to sound commanding but failed miserably, her voice wavering.

Fanny poked her head around the edge of the door. "My lady, Mrs. Weatherby has come to call. She's waiting in the small parlor."

Bea nodded and darted a glance at her writing hand. Quickly gazing down, she exhaled a relieved sigh, pleased no ink dotted her gown. She wiped her fingers on a used cloth she'd kept for precisely that purpose, then tossed it onto the escritoire before seeking out her caller.

As Bea entered the parlor, Mrs. Weatherby rose in greeting and executed a graceful curtsy. Although her smile was genuine, concern glimmered in her eyes. "Lady Montgomery. I must admit, I didn't expect to hear from you so soon after your wedding. Your note has me . . . concerned. Is all well?"

One thing Bea liked about both Andrew and Alice Weatherby— they came straight to the heart of the matter. No dancing around things to maintain propriety. Her bluntness would make Bea's questions all the more easy to ask.

"First, thank you for coming so quickly. And do call me Bea. I'm struggling with Lady Montgomery."

"Then you must call me Alice. I hope we will become fast friends. Andrew has a great fondness for you, and I've found my husband to be an excellent judge of character. As for your title, I'm sure you will adjust. You've just been married after all."

Bea shook her head. "It's not only that. I have no right to the title, to be Laurence's wife. He's suffering because of my poor choices, and I don't know what to do about it."

Bea expected Alice to bolt from the room, and although her complexion did pale slightly, she remained in her seat and met Bea's gaze directly. "What can I do to help? Your note said you requested my counsel."

"May I be blunt?"

Alice's lips curved in a little smile. "I believe you already have been, but of course, yes."

"How do I seduce my husband?"

Although most likely preparing herself, it appeared Alice had not expected quite so blunt a question. Her lips parted, her eyes widened, and pink covered her cheeks.

Yet she remained firmly in her seat.

Bea plunged forward, the words spilling forth uncontrolled. "Last night, Laurence took one look at me and returned to his room. How am I to be a good wife if he won't touch me? I fear he finds me repulsive."

"I'm certain that's not true. You're very lovely, Bea."

Bea's face warmed at the compliment. If only Laurence thought as much. "I don't wish him to seek comfort . . . elsewhere."

"Of course not. I don't mean to pry, but did you request he . . . stay with you?"

Bea shook her head. "I asked the duchess what I should do, and she advised me to allow him to take the lead, that he would know what to do."

Alice coughed, the blush remaining. "I see. Did your mother . . . prepare you? Explain things?"

"Not really, but I understand the . . . basic principles. I read a book once describing the act."

"What type of book?"

"A medical book. I found it in His Grace's library."

The tiny smile returned to Alice's lips. "Perhaps a medical book explaining the . . . process . . . is a bit too clinical. I have another book that may help. Shall I send it over?"

"Oh, yes, please." Bea's instincts had been spot on. Alice Weatherby knew exactly what she needed.

"My other suggestion would be to talk to him. Tell him you're open to . . . affection. Spend time with him, share small things like touches."

Bea held up a hand, her index finger pointing upward. "One moment." She rose and rummaged through a small table in the parlor. Finally finding what she sought, she dipped a pen into an inkwell and poised the pen over the paper. "Would you mind repeating that? I wish to make a list."

Alice chuckled but complied, also providing additional suggestions.

Bea wrote down every word, confident her new course of action would be the solution.

CHAPTER 16—THE BET

H ushed voices drifted into the hallway from the inner rooms at White's as Laurence handed his hat to the doorman. He loved the sedate and controlled environment of the club. Not usually one for crowds, other than lectures at the Royal Society, it was one of the few places he didn't mind going for interaction with his fellow man.

First, he scanned the reading room for Andrew Weatherby. Lord Harcourt glanced up from his conversation with Lord Trentwith, Laurence presumed exchanging mutual admiration over their new granddaughter. He nodded in greeting and proceeded to one of the gaming rooms.

He stopped short at the sight of his new father-in-law, Lord Saxton, at one of the tables. Would the man ever learn? Laurence took a seat in the empty chair next to him. "Sir," he said, tamping down the annoyance building in his chest.

Saxton darted a glance up, then threw his markers into the center of the table. "What are you doing here? Shouldn't you be at home with my daughter?"

The nerve! However, the accusation had a ring of truth. He was newly wed after all. "Bea expected a caller, and I wished to give them some privacy."

Saxton gave a short bark of a laugh. "I presume you have more than one room in your home." His gaze darted sideways, briefly catching Laurence's. "It seems a bit early in your marriage to be avoiding your wife. I think it took me at least a week." Another bark of laughter followed.

Laurence's shoulders involuntarily straightened. "I'm not avoiding her. As I said, I wished to give her—"

"Privacy. Yes. Yes. I heard you. No need to defend yourself to me. But she is my daughter after all, and I'm concerned for her happiness, even under the circumstances."

Laurence bit back the words he wanted to say, swallowing the taste of bile in his mouth. Wasn't that the reason he was there? Yet Saxton had no way of knowing what happened—or *didn't* happen between Bea and himself. And besides, if he had truly been concerned over his daughter's happiness, he would have refused Middlebury's offer to expunge his debt in exchange for Bea's hand.

Which speaking of . . . Laurence pointed at the bet the man placed. "Are you certain that's a good idea? All things considered."

"Are you my keeper now in addition to my son-in-law? I'll have you know, I'm up fifty pounds."

"Then perhaps it's best to quit while you're ahead. It's the first rule of gambling." Laurence had always respected his elders, but his lack of sleep and frustration regarding his marriage apparently had made him remiss in his manners.

Saxton threw his cards down and stomped from the table, taking his winnings with him.

Laurence raked a hand down his face. Hopefully, the encounter wouldn't get back to Bea. It would only serve to strain their relationship further. She'd made it clear she doted on her father, regardless of the pain his gambling had caused her.

"Well played, Montgomery," Lord Cartwright said. "I advised him as much myself. It's common knowledge what happened." He puffed on a cheroot. "Felicitations on your marriage. But like

Saxton, I wonder why you're here instead of at home getting an heir on your wife."

"I'm looking for Weatherby. Have you seen him?"

Cartwright shook his head. "Not today."

Laurence cringed as Lord Nash entered the card room, another accuser to point the finger at Laurence's failure as a husband. The smirk on Nash's face was surely a precursor of what would follow.

"Well, well. What are you doing here?"

Cartwright barked a laugh, but otherwise remained silent.

"My *wife* has a caller," Laurence spit out the words. "And I don't need to answer to *you* of all people."

Nash held up his hands in defense. "No need to go on the attack. It was a simple question." He took a seat next to Laurence and placed his markers on the table before him. "However, if you need any pointers on pleasing your wife, do ask."

Laurence bit back the retort begging to escape. It would serve no purpose to egg him on, but it galled him Nash had said *your wife* instead of *a woman*. As if Bea would sully herself with such a scoundrel.

"Why don't we change the subject?" Cartwright suggested. "How's that contraption of yours coming along, Montgomery?"

Laurence's mood lightened at the mere thought of discussing his machine. "I'm redesigning it, but I need to discover a better power source."

Nash snorted. "Considering you're here instead of at home, you'll have as much success with that ridiculous machine of yours as you will getting an heir on your wife."

A beat of silence passed, and then Nash added, "Which is to say —none."

Nash had gone a step too far, and Laurence straightened in his seat. "Would you care to wager on it?"

"Which one, the machine or your inability to bed your own wife?"

Laurence tamped down the urge to plant the man a facer in the middle of White's. He opened his mouth, prepared to say he had no such inability, but snapped it shut. He had, after all, left her alone on their wedding night.

Which reminded him of the reason he came to White's in the first place.

The smirk on Nash's face grew. "I thought so. Are you rescinding your offer of a wager already?"

"No. I'll wager I'll have both my machine functioning and my wife with child by the end of the year." Lord, what was he doing?

Nash's eyebrows raised. "Confident, are you? How much?"

Laurence swallowed. It was a huge risk, but his manhood and intelligence had been insulted. "The amount of Lord Saxton's debt."

Cartwright's cheroot fell from his fingers, singeing the felt covering of the card table. After quickly brushing the embers from the cloth, he said, "Good God, man. Are you mad?"

Nash's dark eyes bored into him. "Bring the book," he said to a footman standing at attention, gaze still locked with Laurence. "I want it in writing. No gentleman's agreement."

It was Laurence's turn to snort. "Unlikely, as I'm not wagering with a gentleman. If I succeed, you will cancel your debt with Lord Saxton. In the interim, you will refrain from demanding any payment."

Nash slammed his hands on the table. "Now, wait a minute. I didn't agree to postponing collection on a debt that's not even yours."

Like a cat with a mouse, which oddly reminded him about Catpurrnicus, Laurence sat back in his chair, enjoying the scowl on Nash's face. He pulled gently on the ruffled cuff of his sleeve as if he had all the time in the world. "Your choice. Take it or leave it. If you're so certain I'll lose, you'll double the amount owed you. If I win, you will cancel Saxton's debt."

The footman approached with the betting book, his nervous gaze darting between Nash and Laurence. "My lords?"

"Very well," Nash grumbled, the sound like music to Laurence's ears. He motioned for the footman to lay the book in front of Laurence.

After the footman fetched pen and ink, Laurence entered the bet into the book, witnessed by Lord Cartwright.

With exaggerated movement, Nash rose and stretched. "I think I shall go find a willing wench. Celebration of my future winnings is in order." He cast one final glance at Laurence. "My offer of advice still stands, Montgomery. All in the name of fair play, of course." He exited the card room with a raucous laugh.

Silence filled the room, and with certainty, Laurence knew what would appear in the scandal sheets by next morning. Cartwright stared at him, giving an almost imperceptible shake of his head.

"I hope you know what you're doing, Montgomery."

So did Laurence.

Angry voices boomed from outside. One of them Laurence recognized as Timothy's.

"Excuse me," Laurence said, rising and leaving Cartwright at the table. With hurried footsteps, Laurence made his way out of the card room.

Timothy stood, chest to chest with his father, their faces red, an unsightly vein bulging in Lord Saxton's forehead. "Remember who is the parent here, *boy*," Saxton bellowed.

"I haven't been a boy for over fourteen years. And one of us needs to be responsible. You can't climb out of a hole if you continue to dig deeper." Timothy paused in his castigation of his father, catching sight of Laurence.

He turned his anger on a new victim. "Why aren't you home with Bea?" The words delivered like a slap from a glove.

Holding his hands up in supplication, Laurence took a step backward. "Why don't you calm down, and we can go somewhere quiet to discuss this?" He nodded toward one of the smaller rooms of the club, hoping it would be unoccupied.

Timothy reached for Saxton's arm, but the man jerked out of Timothy's grasp. "You don't have to lead me like a pup," he growled, undermining his assertion.

Thankfully, only a footman stood at attention in the room, waiting to be of service.

Laurence jerked his chin toward the servant. "Leave us."

Once they were alone, he motioned to the chairs. As Saxton and Timothy each took a seat, Laurence moved to the sideboard and poured three glasses of brandy. "Now," he said, handing them each a glass then directing his gaze toward Timothy as he took his own seat, "allow me to begin the conversation. As I explained to your father, Bea expected a caller this afternoon, and I simply left to give them some time alone."

"And I told him he could have easily gone to another room in the house." Saxton took a large gulp of his brandy.

"He has a point, Montgomery," Timothy said, taking a sip from his own glass. "My concern is for my sister's welfare. Is she upset about something that you felt the need to make yourself scarce?"

Laurence grappled for a viable explanation, clutching at all possibilities but landing on a solid choice. "She misses her cat. I planned to call on your household, Lord Saxton, to retrieve Catpurrnicus for her."

Saxton snorted a disbelieving laugh. "That demon creature is hardly here at White's."

"True," Laurence said, "but while I was out, I needed to speak with Weatherby about another matter. My next stop was to be your home. Perhaps you could save me a trip and have a footman bring Catpurrnicus to Bea?"

"Aren't you still allergic to the beast?" Timothy asked.

"I am, but I wish to make Bea happy." The answer seemed to appease both his brother-in-law and father-in-law, and Laurence breathed a sigh of relief to have the attention off of his and Bea's marriage.

With Saxton and Timothy's anger subdued, Laurence pressed forward. "Sir, I understand your need to right your own situation, but risking more blunt isn't the answer. As I've said, I've put off Nash for the time being. I'm working on a solution, but you must give me time. I can't devote myself to your daughter and your problems with equal fervor if I'm to succeed at either one."

Saxton's body closed in on itself, appearing much smaller than its actual size. He scrubbed a hand down his face, drawing attention to its haggard appearance.

A twinge of pity flickered in Laurence's chest at the man's predicament. To be responsible for his family's ruination had to be a heavy weight to bear. "Sir, Timothy and I only wish to help, desiring what's best for you and your family. If you choose to stay here, perhaps avoid the card room?"

Saxton gave a weary nod, his mood resigned. "I'll return home and have Bea's cat sent over. It's the least I can do for all the damage I've done. I apologize, Montgomery. It's clear you have my daughter's best interests at heart." He quit the room with lumbering steps.

Timothy watched his father leave, concern etched on his face, then turned his gaze on Laurence. "Father's gone. What's the real reason you're here?"

Laurence bristled at the accusation that he had prevaricated. "I've given it, and I'm insulted you doubt my veracity."

As he slumped back against the seat, Timothy seemed to have aged ten years in a matter of minutes. "Sorry. I'm on edge about everything. Mother is on a rampage about my decision to pursue medicine, and my whole family is headed toward ruin"—he darted a quick look toward Laurence—"except for Bea, of course. But I'm worried about her as well. Seeing you here the day after your wedding doesn't bode well for her happiness."

"Ah, on that account, allow me to ease your mind. I'm here precisely because I wish to ensure her happiness."

"You said you came here looking for Weatherby. I don't see a connection to my sister's happiness."

Laurence scrambled again for a reasonable response. "They were friends, were they not? I wanted to ask about things I could do for her to assist her adjustment to married life." *There. Not a lie.*

However, Timothy did not appear convinced, the lines between his drawn brows indicative of his disbelief. He opened his mouth, presumably to question Laurence further at the exact moment Andrew Weatherby strode into the small room from the hallway.

"I understand you were looking for me, Montgomery."

Laurence released the breath he didn't realize he'd been holding.

"No offense, Marbry, but I prefer to speak with Weatherby in private."

Timothy crossed his arms over his chest. "If it's about my sister, I'd prefer to stay."

Although Laurence admired Timothy's protective nature, at the moment it proved most inconvenient. He shifted uncomfortably. "I certainly wouldn't appreciate hearing a conversation about *my* sister's married life once she manages to leg-shackle someone, and I doubt you would either."

"Assure me Bea is well, and I'll leave," Timothy said, appearing to accept the fact he wasn't welcome.

"I give you my word. And once Catpurrnicus joins us, she'll be even better."

With a nod, Timothy left, promising, or perhaps threatening, to call upon Laurence and Bea when they returned from their honeymoon.

Andrew watched him exit the room. "What's he so on edge about?"

"Primarily about his father. Saxton was at the card table again, but it didn't help when he saw me here as well."

"Ah," Andrew said. "Saxton's presence I understand, even if it's ill-advised. Yours, however, I question. Alice informed me she received a request from your wife to call at her earliest convenience. She didn't tell me what the message said, but my wife seemed concerned. Is all well?"

Laurence shook his head, his body falling against the leather wingback. "No. I followed your advice, but I fear I've made a horrible start to my marriage."

"Good God, man, what did you do?"

"Nothing. And that's precisely the problem. When I approached her, she seemed terrified. The poor thing was trembling, her eyes the size of saucers when she looked at me. I bade her goodnight and returned to my room."

"Hmm, I'll admit my own experience was much . . . different. What I meant by allowing her to lead was simply to allow her to set the pace . . . direct how things . . . proceed, what you do, and all that. That doesn't mean you do *nothing*."

"Then what *do* you suggest? How can I make her comfortable with the idea of . . .?" He waved his hand, embarrassed to give voice to the rest.

Andrew rolled his eyes. "Good God, man, you woo her. Speak little nothings, compliment her beauty, give her flowers. Dog violets were ours." Andrew's face took on a besotted expression Laurence found most unusual, as if his mind had traveled to a far away land. Andrew shook himself. "Kiss her, touch her, play with her hair. She isn't a courtesan with whom you can simply lower your fall and have at her."

Laurence straightened. "I *know* that."

"You must make her feel wanted, like she's the only woman in the world for you. Listen to her, understand her dreams. Allow her to be herself with you. My point is, you must take some sort of action. Slow at first. Learn how she needs to be touched by how she responds."

Laurence hung on every word, committing it to his razor sharp memory.

"You do that, my friend, and before you know it, you'll be lying in her arms, helpless and completely hers."

"That sounds . . . unnerving."

Andrew laughed and swatted him on the back.

Laurence needed to start with the practical side of things first. "Do you know what Bea's favorite flowers are?" A prick of guilt poked at his mind that he wasn't even privy to this small bit of information about his new wife. He brushed it aside, reminding himself theirs was not a love match.

"No. Sorry. Think of a flower that reminds you of her, has some type of meaning. If you do that, if it's not her favorite, it will soon become so."

Armed with his arsenal of ideas, Laurence said his goodbyes and strode with purpose from White's. He waved his carriage driver off, saying he wanted to walk for a while.

A visit to a flower peddler first on his agenda, he enquired about the different meanings of the flowers. He left with a bouquet of English daisies symbolizing hope and innocence. It helped that when he saw them, they reminded him of Bea—bright, sunny, and unpretentious. Plus, the simple flower had adorned their wedding garments.

He hoped the bouquet would lift her spirits. When he explained his purpose to the flower peddler, she insisted he purchase another flower as well, which he tucked within the bunch of daisies.

Next step, to put his plan into action.

CHAPTER 17—WOOING YOUR WIFE

S trands of lovely music from the pianoforte greeted him as Laurence entered his home. Carter took his hat, informing him Lady Montgomery was in the music room. As if Laurence couldn't deduce that himself.

He recognized the dulcet tones of Schubert, but the passion in the interpretation stunned him. Transfixed, he leaned against the doorway of the room, allowing the music to wash over him in waves.

He'd heard Bea play before at musicales held by her family, and her talent had impressed him then. But nothing compared to what poured from her long, gifted fingers at that precise moment. Her intense concentration at the keyboard remained unbroken by his arrival. It was as if she came alive in the piece. The sadness evoked in the last remaining notes tugged at his heart, and he sighed heavily.

She glanced up from the instrument, her eyes widening as she realized he'd been listening. Rising from the bench, she blushed. "I beg your pardon. I didn't hear you approach."

With a shake of his head, he tried to reassure her. "I didn't wish to disturb you. I'd almost forgotten your skill at the keyboard. It's practically hypnotic." He closed the door and entered the room fully, holding out the bouquet of flowers. "They seem inadequate after that performance, but I hope you like them."

Her eyes widened in surprise. "For me?" The long fingers which had recently stroked the keys of the pianoforte caressed the daisies' blossoms.

"Do you like them?"

His heart stuttered at the smile she gave him—genuine and appreciative. "I recalled the embroidery on your gown for our wedding. They remind me of you."

"Daisies?"

Drat. He scrambled to redeem himself. "In their simple beauty." Lord, he was making a muck of this sweet nothings business. "Unpretentious," he added, hoping to soften what she must have interpreted as a slight to her attractiveness.

Tension in his chest eased at her laughter.

"I am that, my lord. It would appear you know me better than you imagined. They're beautiful. And *I* recall the embroidery on your waistcoat points." As she admired the simple bouquet, her gaze landed on the one odd addition the flower peddler insisted upon. "What's this doing in here?"

"Ah. Purple hyacinth. I believe their meaning is *please forgive me.*"

"Precisely what am I to forgive?"

"My . . . lack of attention last evening."

Like the sun on a wintry day, her smile disappeared in an instant. "You have no need to apologize. You cannot help if you find me repulsive."

What? "How on earth can you believe that?" If she only knew how much he desired her.

Wetness rimmed her eyes, but she didn't answer. The bouquet in her hand dropped to her side. "If you will excuse me, my lord. I'm suddenly exhausted."

When she moved to walk around him and exit, he grasped her arm. "Bea, wait. Allow me to explain."

A single tear broke free and rolled down her cheek. She brushed it away with the back of her free hand. "You explained adequately, my lord. This marriage was forced upon you—*I* was forced upon you. What else is there to say?"

Not relinquishing his hold, he turned her to face him fully. "You appeared terrified of me last evening. I had no wish to force you into relations. But that doesn't mean I don't wish for it to happen eventually. The flowers are my peace offering, a beginning to an unconventional courtship. One taking place after the wedding rather than before."

He waited, holding his breath. When she remained silent, he pressed on. "What do you say? Shall we start over? Give this marriage a try?"

ALL THE NOTES BEA HAD TAKEN OF ALICE'S EXCELLENT SUGGESTIONS flew out of her head the moment she saw the flowers. She did love them. But as perfect as they were, the comparison of daisies to more elegant flowers only brought to the forefront how she would never measure up to the duchess, the woman Laurence had pined for so long.

Yet, here he was, trying his best to make things work. Why was she making this difficult? She gazed into his pleading brown eyes, her knees giving way. "Yes. I would like that."

The wobbling in her limbs worsened as he smiled, lighting up her day more than the sunlight streaming in from the window. He nodded toward the piano. "Would you continue? And if I'm not intruding, may I join you?"

She nodded, then moved to resume her place on the bench, making room for him to sit next to her. The heat of his thigh as it pressed against hers radiated even through the fabric of her gown and his trousers. "Perhaps a piano four hands piece?" she asked.

"As you wish, although my skills do not match yours."

She sent him a shy smile. "I will slow the tempo." She searched through the music, finding the perfect piece. "Mozart's Sonata for piano four hands in D major?"

"Very well."

They switched places on the bench, with Bea positioned at the higher register keys and Laurence at the lower. "Ready?"

He nodded, and they began—his assertion regarding his skills underestimated. Although she slowed the tempo as promised, he kept up with her note for note, only fumbling twice when their fingers brushed slightly.

When they finished, he wrapped his pinkie finger around hers, keeping their hands joined on the keyboard. Waves of pleasure raced up her arms, gooseflesh forming in its wake.

"Bea," he whispered her name with gentle reverence.

She met his gaze directly, grateful they were seated upon the bench, for surely, had she been standing, her legs would have given away fully.

"You're wrong, you know," he said. "I find you most attractive. So attractive I feared how I might behave if I'd have stayed last night. I'm sorry it made you feel unwanted."

Oh, my heart. She had an urge to pinch herself, but her hand was joined firmly to his.

He broke eye contact with her, his gaze dipping to her lips as his tongue darted out to wet his own. Her racing heart stuttered to a full stop as he began to lower his head.

"With your permission," he said, his words puffing against her lips, the scent of his breath sweet and clean. "I should very much like to kiss you."

"Yes," she squeaked out the response.

Warm pressure from his lips sent a jolt of energy through her body, muddling her mind. Her heart pounded so hard it thumped in her ears. Much more than the chaste peck he'd given her on their wedding day, she still wished to deepen it further. Her free hand reached up, encircling his head, her fingers threading through his hair. So soft—

Blood-curdling screams came from outside the music room, as if someone were being brutally hacked to pieces. Racing footsteps pounded, accompanied by shouts of, "Catch it!"

Laurence jerked away as if pulled by an unseen magnetic force, his face darkening, brows drawn down so close together they nearly joined.

Nothing could disguise the howling sound echoing throughout the house. Bea sprang from the piano bench. "Catpurrnicus? He's here?" She raced to the entrance, throwing open the doors. "Purrny!" she called. Claws skittered against the floorboards, growing closer.

The black ball of fur darted ahead of a frantic footman and maid, Timothy bringing up the rear, albeit none too urgently. She scooped her cat into her arms, cuddling him to her chest.

"I'm happy to see you." She stroked his soft fur. "But I would have preferred you had waited a tiny bit longer to make your appearance."

"I tried to warn them," Timothy said as he joined the rest of the entourage. "They insisted on taking the beast to you directly."

Red welts from scratches covered the footman's face and hands. The maid's cap was askew, her face flushed. Timothy, on the other hand, was completely unscathed, being one of the few people Catpurrnicus tolerated.

Still cradling the now calm cat in her arms, Bea turned toward Laurence, certain her puzzlement appeared on her face.

"I requested he be brought here, hoping it would ease your adjustment," Laurence said. He glared at Timothy. "Although I hadn't expected him quite so soon."

"Once my mother heard you wished to relieve her household of the beast, she was all too eager to accommodate you," Timothy said.

Bea threw herself into Laurence's arms, the cat squirming while caught between their bodies. "Thank you."

TAKEN ABACK BY BEA'S SUDDEN DISPLAY OF AFFECTION IN FRONT OF the staff and a guest—albeit her brother, Laurence wrapped his arms loosely around her back, patting it gently. If pressed, he'd have to admit he found her lack of propriety, although disconcerting, rather pleasing. "You're wel—wel—ah-choo! Welcome."

"Oh, dear, your allergies. Perhaps we should remove him." Bea turned toward the footman, holding out Catpurrnicus.

The man backed away, hands outstretched and eyes darting toward Timothy in pathetic pleas.

"Allow me," the maid said, stepping forward. "I like cats."

"Careful," Bea said. "He's a bit finicky about whom he trusts."

Timothy snorted a laugh, his eyebrow arching dubiously.

With slow steps, the maid approached, speaking in soothing tones. Catpurrnicus allowed her to pet him, most likely swayed by the promise of fish in the kitchen. The transfer came off without any further incident, and Bea watched him carted off by her—now—favorite maid.

"Thank goodness for Essie," Laurence said, punctuating his appreciation with another sneeze.

"Quite a sacrifice, it would seem, to request him here," Timothy said. "How do you expect to manage with him roaming about?"

"Perhaps if we keep him confined to certain rooms and outdoors," Bea suggested.

Laurence had his doubts, but the hopeful look on his wife's face had him agreeing—that and the memory of his lips on hers. Lord, the kiss had tilted his world on its axis. He took solace in the fact they would be leaving for Scotland soon and Catpurrnicus would not be joining them.

Always the proper host, he motioned to a chair in the music room. "Please sit, Marbry. Bea and I just finished a four hands piece on the piano."

Timothy waved him off. "Thank you, but no. I didn't mean to intrude." With two long steps, he moved to Bea's side, kissing her on the cheek. "Write when you have an opportunity. Mother will be anxious to hear how the marriage is faring." He strode toward Laurence, grasping his hand and pulling him close enough to whisper. "Did you tell her about Father at the club?"

Laurence shook his head. Truth be told, it had been the furthest thing from his mind the moment he saw Bea at the piano.

"Good. It would only upset her." Timothy pulled back, saying a little more forcefully, "Remember our conversation, Montgomery." Without fanfare, Timothy left.

Bea tilted her head, reminding him how she'd so recently discombobulated his own sense of balance. "What conversation?"

"We spoke briefly at White's. As any good brother, he's concerned for your happiness."

Her eyes widened. "Did he threaten you? For if he did, I shall have words with him."

Heat, like a small burst of energy, formed in his chest, expanding outward and tingling his skin. A surge of satisfaction followed that she would defend him against her own brother. "Nothing like that, I assure you. Your family loves and misses you."

She snorted an unladylike laugh, then darted a glance toward him, her cheeks pinkening. "More likely, my family is relieved to be rid of me. One less mouth to feed and body to clothe." Her expression darkened, brows drawing together. "Did he ask for money on behalf of Father?"

"No, Beatrix. Cease your worry. Your brother and I are on good terms. Instead of fretting over a private conversation, I'd rather we spend time getting to know each other." He shot her a sheepish look. "Perhaps resume where we left off before Catpurrnicus's ill-timed arrival?"

He dropped his gaze to her mouth, imagining his lips on hers again. They'd formed a delightful little round shape, matching her widening eyes. Desire stirred, and he shifted uncomfortably, remembering how she'd threaded her fingers through his hair. There was no mistaking her own enjoyment of the kiss in the heat of the moment, but did she regret it once it had ended? "Unless I proceeded too quickly. Perhaps I should leave you to——"

Before he could finish his statement, she had traversed the distance between them, wrapped her arms around his shoulders, and pressed her mouth to his.

His eyes closed in bliss, relishing the sweet softness of her lips. Heedless of his need to adhere to propriety, he gave in to desire, pulled her close, and deepened the kiss. The soft moan she uttered into his mouth only fueled his passion.

With reluctance, he broke the kiss and leaned his forehead on hers. If he didn't slow down, he would begin removing her clothing and ravish her in the middle of the music room. Lord, the door had even been left open. Why, the servants could have walked in at any moment. The thought mortified him.

What had possessed him?

"Perhaps it would be best if we approach this slowly. Allow you time to adjust?"

From the disappointment etched on her face, he realized his poor excuse had fallen flat. He nodded toward the open doors. "It's the middle of the day, and the servants are bustling about."

Color rose to her face, and she lowered her gaze to the floor. But a sly smile curled her lips. "Oh."

He moved toward the entrance of the room and gave the bell pull a sound tug. Turning toward Bea, he said, "Perhaps request a vase and water for your flowers. I shall be in my study working on the design for my machine if you require me."

She opened her mouth as if to say something, but closed it as if deciding it was best left unsaid. Sadness returned to her expression, and guilt buzzed in his chest, pushing out the wonderful warmth that had occupied the space minutes before.

Although he preferred to work alone in silence, hoping to appease her, he said, "Once you request the vase, you may join me if you like."

When her face brightened, he surrendered to the idea of making concessions in order to make his marriage succeed. He turned to leave, but stopped and looked back. "Next time, we shall close and lock the door."

CHAPTER 18—SEDUCING YOUR HUSBAND

B ea brought her fingertips to her still tingling lips, admiring the view of her husband's retreating backside. The kisses they'd shared, much improved over the chaste peck he'd given her on their wedding day, more than exceeded her hopes. Indeed, her knees had grown wobbly, and her toes curled in her slippers. Finally, they had made some progress.

She picked up the bouquet of daisies, admiring their sunny faces. The sensation like tiny birds flitted in her stomach that he'd remembered the flowers embroidered on her gown and had thought of her when he procured them. She must continue with the momentum, perhaps even increasing the velocity toward her objective.

Tucked away in the pages of her favorite book, the list of ideas she'd compiled during Alice's visit was the logical place to start. Once she had requested the vase from the servant for the flowers, she strode with purposeful steps into the library and pulled the tiny volume from the shelf. She would need to plan and prioritize her actions. A few of the ideas would be more difficult to accomplish than others, requiring practice of skills she, admittedly, lacked.

She scanned the list.

Gently run your hand up your husband's sleeve while gazing at him through half-lowered lids.

Yes, that would indeed take practice. She scoured the list for an item more easily accomplished with her meager skills at seduction.

Compliment him often on his best qualities.

Next to that idea, she'd written *intelligence, honor, loyalty.*

She pursed her lips, wondering if those particular qualities were ones most women found useful to mention during seduction tactics.

Ah, wait. When she'd pressed Alice for additional suggestions regarding that particular item, her new friend had suggested complimenting her husband on his masculine physique.

He did have a well-formed backside. She added that feature to her list as well as *excellent at kissing.* The last thought reminded her of his parting words. Perhaps if she joined him in his study, they could practice—with the door closed.

"My lady," a footman said, jolting her from her plan of attack. "A package arrived for you." He held out a rectangular item wrapped in brown paper. A letter rested on top.

She thanked the footman, and sat down to read the letter and open the package, most likely the promised book from Alice Weatherby.

After opening the letter first, she read:

My dear Lady Montgomery,

I enjoyed our visit this morning, and I do hope I was able to assist in your endeavors. Enclosed is the book which I mentioned. Hopefully you will read this letter first, as I wish to prepare you.

I discovered this book during my time in India, and although you may find some of the illustrations shocking, they have proven most helpful and instructive for my married life.

I have several pages marked which I recommend specifically for your newly married life. Although the text is written in Sanskrit, I have added some notes in the margins that help translate.

Wishing you the very best of luck.

Regards,

Alice Weatherby

Shocking?

Bea was most definitely intrigued. Quickly removing the brown paper, she stared at the strange writing on the cover. When she opened it to the first marked page, her face flamed. She quickly peeked up, confirming no servant had entered unannounced. Illustrations depicted men and women in various intimate embraces, many unclothed. Bea read the notes in the margin on a page Alice had marked.

An excellent choice for a new bride.

The woman appeared to be straddling the man who lay under her. Both seemed quite pleased.

She flipped through several more marked pages, and even some unmarked ones, skimming Alice's notes in the margins. Unlike the medical books she'd perused, this stirred unfamiliar, yet pleasant, sensations in her. Feeling a bit overwhelmed by it all, she closed the book and secured the brown paper around it, tying it with the twine. After reviewing the list of notes she'd taken during Alice's visit and depositing the book safely in her room, she made her way to Laurence's study.

On a mission to seduce her husband.

LAURENCE TRIED IN VAIN TO CONCENTRATE ON HIS DRAWING. WITH the wager against Nash, it became even more imperative he succeed in his attempts. Yet his mind continued to return to the kisses he and Bea shared in the music room. He consoled himself that at least he had made progress in the secondary part of his wager.

His well-ordered life seemed to be crashing around him. Had taking a wife reduced him to a mindless idiot? Although he'd promised Timothy he wouldn't mention her father's presence at the gaming tables at White's, he wouldn't be able to keep the news of the wager with Nash from Bea for long.

The gossip sheets would see to that.

Would she think him a beast to brag about getting her with child before year's end? Perhaps he could keep that part to himself. His mind whirled with possibilities. Would she be grateful for his impetuous attempt to erase her father's debt, however foolish it might be? Or would she be furious that he would put their own financial security at risk, thereby categorically thwarting his efforts to woo her into his bed and get her with child?

Lord, what a mess.

After numerous false starts, he finally managed to concentrate his attention on the sketch before him. Excitement sparked within him at an idea that might indeed solve his problem of maintaining power.

Intense focus had always been both a blessing and a curse, allowing him to ignore outside distractions, but becoming so immersed he'd often failed to recognize when someone had entered a room or spoken to him. Pressure on his shoulders alerted him that he was no longer alone in the room. He tensed, setting the pen down on the desk blotter.

"Bea?" he asked, his voice tentative. At least he hoped the hands caressing him belonged to his wife, but even that thought seemed unlikely.

"Am I disturbing you?" she asked.

Yes. He bit back the honest answer, relaxing a bit that no one else had touched him so intimately. "Of course not." He swiveled the chair toward her. A light blush of color covered her cheeks. Yet she seemed to have something in her eye as she blinked erratically.

"May I be of assistance with anything?" he asked stupidly.

Her attempt to clear the foreign object must have succeeded, as the odd blinking ceased. "No. Yes. I mean, you said I could join you."

He did say that, he reminded himself. "Would you like to read? Do you need paper and pen to write?"

She shook her head, suddenly seeming unsure of herself. The strange eye blinking, batting movement began again as she reached up and mussed his hair.

"Are you feeling unwell?" he asked—again completely at a loss as to what she was about.

"No. I'm quite well, thank you." She stopped making a mess of his hair and placed her hands on his shoulders again, then proceeded to climb onto his lap.

"Bea, what's the meaning of—"

She pressed her lips to his. Instinctively, he closed his eyes and wrapped his arms around her waist, holding her securely on his lap.

His sketch and motor completely forgotten, he lost himself in the soft sweetness of her mouth. Before he realized it, she had untied his cravat. Her hands moved back to his head, but this time, the movements didn't seem so awkward as she raked through his hair, lightly scratching his scalp.

Like a fool, he grabbed her hands at the wrists and pulled them from his body. "Bea, what are you doing? The servants could come in."

She continued to press little kisses to his lips. "I closed and locked the door." She began tugging at his coat, her mouth still pressed to his, garbling her words. "This chair is a problem."

"It is?" His mind continued to try to make sense out of her strange statement.

"Yes. I'm unable to get my legs around you in it. We should move somewhere else."

"Your"—he forced down the lump in his throat—"limbs? Why do you want to get your . . ."

The realization slammed him in the chest, making it even more difficult to breathe. "Beatrix, are you trying to seduce me?"

"Yes. Am I doing it incorrectly? The book showed the woman astride the man, but I can't in this chair."

Book? What book?

Did his head spin from her kisses or her strange statement? "It's the middle of the day." Each utterance from his mouth became more and more ludicrous and absurd.

"Is it not permissible to have relations in the middle of the day?" The serious tone of her voice stopped him short.

He wanted to laugh at the innocent expression on her face, but thank goodness, he restrained himself. It would not do to offend her by laughing at her attempts to lure him to her bed. In reality, many men found sexual fulfillment in the middle of the day. Hadn't Nash implied as much when he left White's?

However, Laurence had not expected it from his bride. In truth, he presumed most married couples performed their marital duties at night upon retiring. Perhaps he was wrong. An odd—and somewhat unsettling—thought.

Could they?

Why not?

It would certainly move him in the direction of securing one portion of his wager with Nash.

Bea continued to gaze at him with expectant eyes.

"It's just not . . . common," he said. "But certainly not prohibited."

"Good." She resumed her kisses along his jaw, edging down his now exposed neck. "Perhaps the settee?" Her warm breath tickled against his throat, and he began to lose what little control he fought to maintain. The spark of desire ignited into a full blaze as she moved her hands down his chest toward his fall.

He pushed her gently from his lap, relieving the pressure of her body against his arousal, but making it that much more urgent to move to a more suitable location.

As she stood before him, her shoulders sagged, a sad little pout adorning her very kissable lips.

"Upstairs," he said, his voice becoming gravelly with need. He grasped her hand and led her to the door. Furiously tugging at the handle, he'd forgotten she said she'd locked it. A new urgency set in as he spun in a circle, searching for the key.

"On the table," she said.

His gaze darted to the small, half-moon table at the side of the doorway. He quickly plucked the key and inserted it into the lock, his hand shaking.

Finally opening the door, he pulled her from the room toward the staircase. Essie stopped, duster poised in mid-air, to stare wide-eyed, no doubt at his state of undress and, more embarrassingly, his obvious arousal.

A giggle followed in their wake as he raced past the amused maid.

When they reached the staircase, with Bea's hand firmly clasped in his, she tripped and stumbled against him. He turned toward her, finding her face flushed and her breath coming in short, quick pants.

Not willing to waste any more time, he simply picked her up and raced up the stairs with her in his arms. He found himself breathing heavier as he reached the top of the staircase, but not from exertion. As light as a feather, he felt he could carry her forever and not tire.

Sheer desire drove him, coursing through every fiber of his being and affecting his physiology as he'd never experienced before. He burst through the door to his chamber.

And came to a dead stop.

Stevens glanced up from where he'd been placing clean shirts into the clothes press.

"Out," Laurence barked. "Now."

Stevens scurried from the room as if he were a mouse chased by Catpurrnicus, the remaining linen shirts left carelessly on top of the clothes press.

Laurence cringed at his behavior. It would seem that married life had turned him into a complete arse. He would apologize to Stevens later. At the moment, he had more urgent matters to attend to.

⊗⊱⊗

BEA CLUNG TO LAURENCE'S NECK FOR DEAR LIFE. THE CRAZED LOOK in his eyes both surprised and excited her. When she'd fantasized about this moment, she'd envisioned slow, long kisses and soft, gentle caresses. Admittedly, she didn't know exactly what to expect when she entered Laurence's study. But this frenzied, panicked man wasn't it. He'd always been so controlled, so sedate.

However, she had no complaints about this side of her husband. In fact, she rather liked it.

Her husband. And from what she could gather, they were about to consummate their marriage.

Finally.

He lowered her feet to the floor, but kept his arms around her. "Bea, are you certain?" he asked, his voice gentled from the gruff order he'd just issued Stevens.

Her voice, on the other hand, had completely left her, and she could only nod.

"You're trembling." His pupils had expanded so much, his already dark brown eyes appeared black, but concern shone in their depths. "Have I frightened you?"

"No," she managed to squeak out.

"You're certain? We don't have to—"

She ended the tiresome debate by pulling down his head and covering his mouth with hers. His arms wrapped around her waist, drawing her close to his body, the hard planes of his chest pressing against her breasts and the ridge of his arousal teasing her abdomen.

A quick tug on the laces of her gown reminded her of the evening which precipitated everything. However, this time, Laurence was a willing and active participant rather than an unwitting victim.

She groaned with disappointment when he broke the kiss, leaning his forehead against hers, but took heart as he started trailing kisses down her neck and across her shoulder.

"Tell me if I do anything you don't like," he said, his hot breath oddly sending gooseflesh up her spine and arms.

"I think I shall like everything you do."

Air from his soft chuckle brushed against her skin.

He lifted his head, gazing into her eyes. "I certainly hope so."

His lips pressed against hers, the kiss soft at first, then building in intensity as his hand gradually moved from her waist up her side, brushing against the underside of her breast.

As he nibbled on her ear, she asked, "Should I tell you if you do something that I especially like?"

His lips widened in a smile against her skin. "An excellent idea. Or if there's something you want me to do."

"And you? Will you tell me what you like and want as well?"

He met her gaze again, the fire in his eyes heating her from the tip of her head to her toes. "At the moment, I'd prefer we limit our discussion and continue with action."

Although already warm, more heat flooded her cheeks. She opened her mouth to provide an apology, but he quickly covered it with his, his tongue probing inside, playfully nudging hers.

It was quite enjoyable.

Following his lead, she tentatively brushed her own tongue against his, and he deepened the kiss, moaning into her mouth.

His hands wrapped in her hair. Pins dropped haphazardly to the floor, red strands spilling free from the coiffure Fanny had so meticulously fashioned.

Good Galileo. Tension built low in her, a throbbing between her legs she found not unpleasant, but producing an urgent need for pressure.

Before she knew it, Laurence had tugged her gown from her shoulders, exposing the tops of her breasts above her stays. Like the tension between her legs, her breasts now tightened, with the same need to be touched. "Touch me," she whispered, moving his hand upward. "Here."

With one hand threaded in her hair, he teased the exposed skin above her stays with the other, then hurriedly unlaced the contraption, tossing it to the floor and freeing her. Through her chemise, his fingers toyed with the tingling area of her nipple, sending waves of pleasure through her.

Someone moaned.

Laurence broke his kiss and rubbed his nose against hers. "You like that?"

The moan must have come from her. "Hmm," she said. He had her so befuddled, she struggled to remember her list and the notations in the margins of the book. If it felt so good to have him touch her, would he like it as well?

Perhaps . . .

Slowly moving her hand down his chest, she reached the hard

ridge pressing against her. At first, as she ran her fingers down its length, he tensed, then groaned.

Did he like it, or had she hurt him?

"Um, does that . . . hurt?"

The soft chuckle he emitted mixed with a moan as he pressed her hand more firmly against him. "No. It feels wonderful. Your boldness just . . . surprised me. Pleasantly," he added.

Encouraged, she stroked him through his trousers, enjoying the power surging through her when he continued uttering nonsensical words.

He released her breast and tugged upward at her chemise, pulling it over her head and tossing it to the floor next to her stays and gown. Prickles of sparks shot up her spine as his hand traced the skin of her leg, up to her thigh, and her knees gave out from under her. With one smooth motion, Laurence scooped her up and carried her to the bed, laying her down gently in the center.

For a moment, he stood over her, and his heated gaze, full of lust, raked over her as she lay exposed before him. She knew she should be embarrassed about her nakedness, but the desire in his eyes wiped all thought of modesty from her mind.

"It might be easier without these," he said, removing her spectacles and placing them gently on a table nearby.

With a fluid motion, he sat upon the bed and yanked off his boots and stockings, scattering them carelessly on the floor. He shrugged out of his coat and ripped the untied cravat from where it hung loosely around his neck.

"What about *my* stockings?" Bea asked, for indeed they were all that remained on her body, tied with delicate blue ribbons above her knees.

His lips quirked in a playful smile. "Leave them. I quite like the look."

Try as she might not to blush, heat rushed up her neck to her cheeks.

The urgency he exhibited moments ago seemed to pass, and he slowed his movements as he continued to disrobe. Bea's anticipation grew with each pop of a button from his waistcoat. Once removed, he pulled the linen shirt over his head, depositing it on the floor along with the rest of his discarded clothing.

Bea's breath caught in her throat at the sight of him. A dusting of dark hair covered his chest, and she longed to run her fingers through it to see if it was as soft as it appeared. The quick peek she'd had the night before as he stood before her in his banyan only hinted at his full masculine beauty. Her gaze dropped to his trousers and the enticing bulge pressing against his fall.

For a moment, she wished he'd left her spectacles on longer. Images from Alice's book flashed through Bea's mind. Would Laurence's sex appear similar? She'd only seen pictures, and she shivered in anticipation she would soon experience the real thing.

"Are you cold?" he asked, concern laced in his voice, and his eyebrows drawing down.

"No," she said, the word coming out in a little squeak.

"If you are, I'll warm you up." As if to prove his point, he stretched out next to her and began stroking her skin while he nuzzled her neck, leaving a trail of gooseflesh from her fingers to her toes.

Indeed, his body was like a roaring fire, the heat emanating off of him glorious. Remembering Margaret's initial advice to follow Laurence's lead, she mimicked his movements, and placed soft kisses against his neck. The scent of shaving soap mixed with bergamot and the slightly salty taste of his skin teased her senses. His light stubble of a beard scratched against her lips, but the effect was quite pleasant. She wondered what it would feel like against other delicate parts of her body.

With the urge to duplicate the overwhelming pleasure when he caressed her breast, she traced the hard planes of his chest, her fingers confirming the softness of the hair covering it. An odd thought seized her, and she bent to lick one of his nipples. His chest muscles contracted, and he emitted a low, sensual moan.

"Yes?" she asked.

His hand threaded through her hair at the back, holding her to his chest. "Yes. Definitely yes. In fact . . ."

With gentle hands, he pushed her away and on her back, then

lowered his head to her breast. Rather than simply lick, he suckled, and she swore her toes curled. "Yes. Definitely yes," she echoed. Dampness formed between her legs, and the building pressure became almost uncomfortable.

As he continued to suckle, he trailed a hand down her abdomen, toward the source of her discomfort. He teased the flesh hidden under the soft curls between her legs, the sensation both wonderful and frustrating. She squirmed under his ministrations.

To her dismay, he stopped his attention to her breast and met her gaze. "You're wet." As if to answer her unspoken question, he smiled and clarified. "That's good. It will help."

Finally, as if reading her hopeful thoughts, he unbuttoned his fall and slipped his trousers off his body, throwing them to join their companions on the bedroom floor.

"I'll have you know, I'm not usually this careless with my clothing. But you have entirely made me forgo my usual fastidious tidiness."

"I'm sorry?" she said, not quite sure if she should apologize.

"Don't be." He reassured her with another searing kiss, then resumed his torturous teasing between her legs.

Again, remembering the advice to follow his lead, she ran her hand down his chest and abdomen toward the heat of him. "May I touch you?"

He peered up, his eyes half-lidded and dusky. "I would enjoy that immensely."

Tentatively, she ran a fingertip across the head, intrigued with the contrast of its velvety softness and the hardness of the shaft. "Amazing."

"Indeed," he uttered with a moan, then placed his hand over hers, wrapping her fingers around him and moving them up and down along its length.

Good Galileo!

More visions of the book flashed in her mind. One in particular showed a man kissing a woman in that most private place. If Laurence's attention to her breast had been so wonderful, what would it be like if he were to kiss her *there?*

He did say she could tell him what she wanted. But how could she put it into words? She pushed his shoulders, indicating he should move down her body then managed to croak out a simple command. "Your mouth. There."

His low laugh alone sent tingles up her arms, but when he obeyed her request, energy surged through her as if she'd been hit by a bolt of lightning. The sheer delight from the sensation convinced her nothing else would ever feel so marvelous. She writhed under him, but thankfully, he persisted, slowly driving her mad.

Pressure continued to build, and she felt she would come apart. Sparks danced in her mind as her body convulsed—the experience more pleasurable than anything she'd ever known. Perhaps this was what it would be like to travel to the stars?

When she finally came back down to Earth, he rose above her and kissed her lips. She tasted herself. Not unpleasant, and mixed with his alluring scent, it became quite heady.

He stroked her hair, gazing into her eyes. "Yes?" He grinned, as if knowing full well what her answer would be.

"Definitely."

His expression grew serious. "Are you ready?"

She nodded, but right before he began to position himself, she remembered Alice's suggestion. "Wait."

He tensed, fear etching his face. "Should I leave you?" His voice cracked with such emotion she thought her own heart would break.

She rushed to ease his concern. "No. But I should like to try the suggestion from the book."

His low delicious chuckle sent gooseflesh up her arms. "I would very much like to know about this book of yours. What would you like me to do?"

"Lie on your back."

"Ah," he said and rolled off of her.

"I'm not quite certain how to accomplish this, but it appeared something like this in the book." She climbed over him, straddling his hips as she sat on her knees. How would she get it in? "I'm not sure how to . . ."

"Allow me to assist." He grasped her hip with one hand, positioning himself with the other. "Lower yourself when you're ready. You will be in control. A most excellent idea for a new bride."

Bea laughed aloud that Laurence had stated nearly verbatim what Alice had written in the margin notes.

She moved slowly, unsure and a little nervous, but as she eased down onto him, the urgent need resumed, building inside her and propelling her. Something stopped her progress and, grasping her hips, with a quick thrust upward, Laurence breeched the barrier.

A little burst of pain shot through her, and she gasped.

With a gentle motion, he stroked her thigh and hip. "Forgive me. I thought it best to get it done quickly." Little lines formed between his eyebrows, and his voice sounded strained, as if saying the words through gritted teeth.

"Did it hurt you, too?" she asked. "Is this your first time as well?" He certainly appeared to know what he was doing, but she wasn't one to presume.

The lines disappeared as he muffled a soft laugh. "No. I'm trying not to move while you adjust."

Once the twinge of pain subsided, she resumed, her movements still tentative but more pleasurable.

Laurence groaned under her, his eyes closed tight, as if he concentrated on a difficult mathematical problem. Slowly, he moved his hands from where they grasped her hips, one cupping her breast and the other coming to rest on the back of her head. He pulled her down toward him for a passionate kiss, their tongues once again playing against each other in a frantic dance.

As he teased her nipple, she drank deeply from his mouth, the pressure building once again to a crescendo. And though Laurence assured her she would be in control, he began to move faster within her, the rhythm of their movements matching those of their tongue play.

With both her and Laurence's movements picking up the pace, Bea edged close to that euphoric sensation of shooting stars. Laurence nudged her over the precipice when he shifted his ministrations from her breast to between her legs, finding the sensitive area throbbing with need.

The burst of pleasure shot through her again, then her body became limp in Laurence's arms, collapsing on his chest.

He, on the other hand, moved even more vigorously, both hands firmly grasping her hips as he thrust inside. His brow furrowed deeply, and she pressed her lips to the lines, hoping to smooth them, then moved down to capture his mouth in another searing kiss.

He convulsed under her, his body jerking and nails digging into her hips.

Good Galileo, it was glorious.

Without warning, a feline cry cut through the haze of Bea's passion. Footsteps pounded outside the door, followed by voices both screaming in terror and coaxing with gentleness.

"Get him off me!" came a male voice, the words laced with pain.

"There, there, Catpurrnicus. Your mistress is busy at the moment." That had to be Essie.

Both Laurence and Bea stilled, but Laurence pressed his lips together as if stifling a laugh. He stroked her hair. "Busy indeed. I shall have to increase Essie's wages."

At the absurdity of the situation, Bea giggled, tucking her head against Laurence's chest and feeling safe, secure, and—for the first time in her life—wanted.

They both erupted in laughter, heat rising in Laurence's gaze once again.

CHAPTER 19—KEEPING SECRETS

Years ago, while in Naples on his grand tour of Europe, tremors from an earthquake near Mount Vesuvius had rocked Laurence off his feet. At the time, he believed it was the most powerful force he'd ever experienced. That was no longer the case.

Propped up on one forearm, he gazed in wonder at his wife, overcome with what they'd just shared. Lips, red and swollen from his kisses, beckoned him to drink from them again. A flush from their heated encounter covered her skin, and her eyes still bore the haze of desire. Her hair spread over the pillow like flames surrounding her head. He traced over the fine strands, relishing the silkiness against his fingertips.

"You're so beautiful," he whispered.

The sight so enraptured him, he felt compelled to capture it. Not that he would forget so readily. When he made the effort, his memory was precise, unwavering. But the wish—no, the urgent need—to have a tangible reminder overpowered him.

"Don't move," he said, forcing himself from the bed and the soft warmth of her body. Thankful he'd chosen his bedchamber, for he didn't want to waste a moment, he threw open the drawers of his desk and retrieved a sketch pad and charcoals.

When he sat back on the bed, perching the sketch pad across one bare leg, her eyebrows arched in question.

"What are you doing?"

"I want to draw you," he said, realizing the grin spreading across his face resembled that of a naughty schoolboy.

Pink blossomed on her cheeks, and she tugged at the rumpled sheets in an attempt to cover herself.

After a quick glance to sear the attractive image of her embarrassment in his mind, he stilled her hand. Once he had repositioned the sheet, draping it seductively across one breast, while exposing the other, and snaking down the lower portion of her body, revealing her midriff, left leg, and a tiny fraction of the auburn hair between her thighs, he picked up the pencil and began sketching. The task proved more difficult than he'd intended—not drawing itself, but the concentration he needed to muster in order to resist throwing the sketchpad aside and ravishing her again.

He drew like a man possessed. A fitting description, for it was how he felt. As if something gripped him in its power—something he couldn't name. Something foreign and all consuming. The sensation simultaneously exhilarated him and frightened him.

He abhorred losing control—over anything. Even his liaisons with courtesans had been restrained to some extent. Often a physical, even mechanical experience to meet a need, they'd been devoid of real emotion. How had Bea unleashed such a powerful force?

Initially, he'd half expected to fall into a comfortable pattern of nightly visits once they'd managed to get past the first awkwardness. Similar to, he supposed, most married couples of the *ton*. He did *not* expect such passion from his scholarly bride.

Most surprising of all—it pleased him.

The blush on her cheeks began fading, so he ran a hand up her thigh close to the peek of hair, and the blush returned. Soft light from the window cast a shadow under the curve of her breast, and he shaded the sketch accordingly. When he finished, he took a moment to study her, fixing the colors, the mood in his mind. He would paint it later.

"May I see?" She blushed again at her own question.

When he turned the pad over to show her, she gasped.

"You don't like it?" Pain sliced through him that he'd disappointed her.

"It's . . . beautiful. Is that really how you see me?"

Too overcome with emotion to speak, he nodded. Then, laying the sketch and the charcoals aside, he prepared to show her how truly beautiful he believed she was.

IN THE MIDDLE OF A LINGERING KISS, LAURENCE ABRUPTLY FROZE AT the raised voices outside the door.

"Contain that beast. I don't want it anywhere near me," a woman's high-pitched voice joined in, the strangely familiar sound cutting through his fog of lust.

"Laurence, I know you're home. Come out here at once and speak with me!"

Laurence's eyes shot open. "My mother!"

Bea jerked out of Laurence's grasp and pulled at the sheets to cover her nakedness.

He bolted from the bed and grabbed his trousers. In his haste to dress, his foot slipped, and he fell against the side of the bed, bumping his head. He muttered an expletive and managed to finish pulling his trousers up his body.

When he haphazardly slipped on his shirt, he failed to notice it was inside out. The seams, although carefully stitched, brushed against his fingertips as he attempted to smooth it. *No time to waste changing it.* Like the wheel on his motor, Laurence spun around, searching the floor. "Where is my neckcloth?"

A sharp rap came at the door. "Laurence! I insist on speaking with you this moment!"

Giving up the hunt for his cravat, he threw open the door. He sent a quick glance over his shoulder, catching Bea pulling the counterpane closer to her chin, no doubt in an attempt to hide from his mother. He could hardly blame her. If only he could hide under the covers with her. Instead, he stood in the opening of the doorway, closing it enough to prevent his mother from peering in farther.

"Good heavens, Laurence. Are you ill? Why are you not dressed at this . . ."

Her eyes bulged as her gaze raked over him, her hand raising to her throat, and her censorious brows drew downward.

The sight of it brought back the memory of the time she had lectured him soundly for misbehaving at Eton. His one and only indiscretion in boyhood had set the bar for his upright and moral compass. He vowed never to endure that particular look on his mother's face again.

Yet, he was no longer a boy. He could do as he pleased, could he not? Still, he raked a rather shaky hand through his unkempt hair. Bea had certainly made a mess of it.

"Might I remind you I'm newly wed, Mother? We didn't expect callers."

A giggle sounded behind him, and he glanced back again. Bea had pulled the counterpane over her head, but the bump underneath shook with amused laughter.

His mother's mouth opened and closed soundlessly several times, apparently at a loss for words—an event of outstanding proportions.

No doubt she prepared to give him a dressing down regarding the appropriate time of day for performing one's marital duties. The thought of what he'd just shared with Bea as a *duty* had him pressing his lips together to restrain an outburst of laughter.

Finally finding her voice, his mother said, "It's the middle of the day."

Her statement pushed him over the edge, recalling his own initial objection to Bea's seduction, and he joined Bea's amusement with a rather undignified guffaw. He'd never enjoyed a middle of the day activity more.

His mother stared indignantly. "And precisely what do you find so humorous?"

After swiping a hand over his eyes to remove the tears forming at the corners, he shook his head. "It's *my* home and I have the right to do what I wish in it, Mother. I suggest you return to yours."

"You will *not* speak to me in that manner, Laurence. What has become of your manners?" The disappointed expression on her face had him reeling, and a sour taste rose to his mouth from his churning stomach.

"I apologize, Mother. But as you can surely see, your impromptu arrival has taken me off guard. What is of such importance you demand to speak with me?"

Tension in his stomach eased as his mother's eyebrows rose on a more upward trajectory. "I've come about this outrageous wager you've made with Lord Nash. What possessed you to risk your fortune on such an unreliable outcome?"

How in the world had she found out so quickly? The bitter taste intensified, but he swallowed it down. After another glance over his shoulder, he moved out into the hallway, closing the door behind him. He had no desire to unravel the tenuous progress he'd made with Bea—or rather that she'd made with him—if she found out about his wager with Nash, especially the condition regarding an heir.

Even though the door was closed, he lowered his voice to a whisper. "Exactly what have you heard and from whom?"

Unfortunately, his mother failed to follow his lead and lower her own voice. "Miranda informed me. I assured her she must be mistaken. Wagering on that ridiculous machine of yours can't compare to a game of cards."

The insult to his motor proved sufficient to detract him from inquiring not only how Miranda had come across the information, but when. For the second time in a single day, he rose to its defense. "It's not a *ridiculous* machine. If you had an iota of faith in me, Mother, you would understand its importance."

"But the amount, Laurence," her voice escalated further.

He prayed Bea hadn't heard. At least his mother seemed oblivious to the second part of the wager. Awareness of that particular portion would surely put distance between him and Beatrix—an idea he found most troublesome. In fairness, the amount was exorbitant, the wager reckless. But he refused to admit as much to his mother. And if he could pull it off—addendum, *when* he pulled it off, he would be a hero in Bea's estimation, saving her family from penury and ignominy.

He thought about the soft, luscious body of his wife waiting for him and straightened his shoulders. "I assure you, Mother. I know what I'm doing. Don't fret. Go home." Gently grasping his mother's shoulders, he turned her toward the staircase and gave her a tiny push.

She exhaled a vocal, "Harrumph," and proceeded toward the staircase, muttering about ungrateful and ill-mannered sons.

He wondered if they should leave for Scotland as soon as possible to remove Bea from any further exposure to his folly.

⚜

BEA CEASED GIGGLING THE MOMENT LADY EASTON MENTIONED A wager with Lord Nash risking Laurence's fortune. What had he done? Once he closed the door, she pulled the counterpane from her head and crawled to the edge of the bed, straining to hear the conversation. Only able to pick up isolated words uttered by Lady Easton, such as ridiculous machine and amount, Bea's frustration level grew while she waited for Laurence to return.

At the sight of the door opening, she flung herself back up the bed and threw the counterpane over herself. The expression on Laurence's face did nothing to ease her concern. Eyebrows drawn down—this time not from concentration—face flushed, a muscle along his jaw twitching, had her stomach churning uncomfortably. She pulled the counterpane up to her chin.

He darted a glance her way, his features softening. "I apologize for the interruption. My mother's unexpected arrival leads me to believe we should leave for our wedding trip posthaste. Away from London, we might find the peace we need to get to know each other."

He sat next to her on the edge of the bed. "You appear

frightened. How much did you overhear?" Although gentle, his voice held a note of worry.

Should she lie? Tell the truth? Her list from Alice contained no advice regarding dealing with such matters. Involuntarily she sucked in her bottom lip and chewed, a habit her mother had soundly reprimanded.

"You can tell me, Bea."

Secrets and the damage they had wrought upon her own family flashed through her mind. Her father's debt, Timothy's study of medicine, her own deceit regarding O.B. and her disguises, the last directly bearing on her future with Laurence if and when he found out.

Perhaps truth was the better path.

"Something regarding a wager with Lord Nash involving your motor." She swallowed hard, adding, "And a large amount."

Laurence hung his head, diverting his gaze while his hand traced an invisible image on the bed linens. "You will find out soon enough. Even ushering you hastily out of London won't shield you forever." He took a deep breath and locked his gaze with hers. "I've done something rash."

"The wager?"

"Yes. I allowed my pride to overcome my reason." He shook his head. "It's a rare occurrence for me, I admit. I'm not sure what came over me. Nevertheless, the wager involves the successful completion and operation of my newly designed motor by year's end. If I succeed, Nash will forgive your father's debt. If I fail . . ."

An uncomfortable plummeting sensation occurred in her chest, as if leaving the normally occupied space hollow. "You would owe Nash the same amount."

"Yes. And your father's debt would remain."

No wonder his mother was angry. Although Bea had no idea of Laurence's financial assets, the amount exceeded the yearly income of even the most wealthy of aristocrats. They might be bankrupt if he failed, and her father would be no better off.

She steeled herself and took his hand that traced the design against the linens. "You won't fail. I believe in you. We'll make it work—together. Allow me to assist."

Laurence's eyes widened, staring at her for what seemed an eternity. He uttered a soft, "Thank you, Bea," then leaned his forehead against hers. "Now, where were we when we were so rudely interrupted?"

"Right here," she said before capturing his mouth in an earthshaking kiss.

CHAPTER 20—... AS THOSE WHO CANNOT SEE

After spending most of the remaining afternoon in bed, Laurence rose and gathered his clothing while Bea napped. He gazed down at his bride, no longer feeling trapped. Instead, he counted his good fortune at finding a woman who not only supported him in his endeavors but exhibited such passion in the marital bed.

When he confessed about the wager, he'd been unable to bring himself to tell her about the second condition. Guilt weighed heavily on him, especially considering her support of the first condition. He should tell her. It was the moral thing to do, but fear pricked at him she would misunderstand and attribute what they'd shared as a means to an end.

In Scotland, away from wagging tongues and scandal sheets, he could devote equal attention to both conditions of the wager in relative peace. He chuckled at Bea's offer to assist with the motor. What in the world could she offer to achieve a successful outcome? Yet, the offer was genuine, given in faith that he would succeed.

Whistling while he sketched out a new idea for his plans, he found his mood greatly improved from his dour state that morning. Bea had turned his day around, giving him hope. Absorbed in his work, he startled when hands pressed against his shoulders for the second time that day. The alluring scent of orange blossom and vanilla confirmed her presence, and he placed his hand over hers and squeezed.

She leaned in closer, her lovely fragrance tickling his nostrils. "Are these your plans?"

"Yes," he answered, keeping his attention on his sketch. "It's the power source that puzzles me. My challenge is to find something that would power it for longer periods of time."

"It's the interaction between the electric current and the magnetic field that makes it run, is it not?"

Her words pulled his attention away from his drawing to her face. "Precisely."

"And the electric current is conducted through the wire from the energy storage of the voltaic pile."

He nodded, amazed she had remembered and understood the process. "But the problem is the battery life is so short."

"So what's necessary is a larger power source, a way to store it more efficiently, or a combination of both."

Their exchange stirred something inside of him, another type of energy—sexual and raw in nature. "Yes, exactly. The major flaw with the voltaic pile is that the current produced electrolyzes the brine solution, causing hydrogen bubbles to form on the copper, which then diminishes its power and longevity."

"Hence the search for a new power source," she said, almost as if speaking to herself. Her eyes lit up as if such a source had sparked in her mind. "What if you could harness lightning?"

At the expression on her face, he bit back the laugh. "You're serious? Beatrix, that's dangerous. Where in the world would you get such an idea?"

She straightened before him, stretching her diminutive stature to its full height. "I've done extensive reading myself, and I'm not ill-versed in scientific matters. I'll have you know I've even—"

At her incensed reaction, he held up his hand, stopping her. "I don't mean to disparage your intelligence, Bea. It's clear you have a better understanding than even most men, but lightning?"

"Benjamin Franklin demonstrated that lightning contains an electrical charge."

"An interesting experiment, true, but one serving no true practical purpose."

"But the charge contained in one bolt of lightning might be large enough to run the motor for extremely long periods if it could be contained."

"Very well. Assuming it's feasible"—he sent her a dubious look—"what type of condenser would you use to capture and contain it? The force of the lightning alone would shatter anything."

Her hands dropped to her sides, his heart squeezing at the dejection on her face. "Franklin used a Leyden jar."

"From what I understand, what he captured wasn't lightning itself, but much smaller atmospheric sparks from the storm. An attempt to attract a bolt of lightning would be folly. And the Leyden jar is outdated. It simply doesn't hold the charge long enough. Even the voltaic pile produces a more stable and continuous source of electricity."

"What if there was a way to weaken the power of the lightning? A diffuser of sorts, so it didn't destroy the containment vessels? Perhaps if we improved upon the concept of the Leyden jar? Either a larger Leyden jar or a number of them, attached in a series." She pointed to his sketch. "You already have a large metal pole. It would attract the lightning and lead into a containment area holding the Leyden jars."

Although reluctant to discourage her enthusiasm, he couldn't countenance such a wild and dangerous leap. He shook his head, and much like her suggestion of diffusing the power of the lightning, she deflated before him.

Hoping to recover the closeness they'd achieved earlier, he placed his hand on hers, giving it a gentle pat. "We'll continue exploring options—safer options."

A weak smile crossed her lips, which didn't quite meet her eyes, and she slid her hand out from under his. "Very well. Since I don't seem to be offering anything of use, I'll leave you."

As she turned, he opened his mouth, ready to encourage her to stay, but he delayed too long and before he could force the words, she slipped out of the room, closing the door behind her with a soft snick.

He ran a hand down his face. *Women.* Did any man truly understand them? With a sigh, he turned back to his drawing, scribbling a note next to the place he'd left blank for the condenser.

Multiple containment vessels?

Perhaps at least part of Bea's idea was worth pursuing.

BEA TAMPED DOWN THE ANNOYANCE BUBBLING IN HER CHEST FROM her discussion with Laurence. The lack of confidence in her ideas had been written all over his face.

She'd believed he was different—wanted to believe it—needed to believe it. Why, she'd almost confessed the identity of O.B. to him. Thank goodness he'd interrupted her. Their fledgling relationship had barely sprouted feathers, much less developed wings to allow her to soar above the typical expectations for a good wife.

Wisdom advised her to proceed with caution. She left him to work on his plans in the solitude he apparently desired, while she began a design—although not unlike his—incorporating her ideas. Once again, she found herself working in the secrecy of her room. Heaviness weighed her down at the knowledge. She'd hoped she would have abandoned working behind locked doors when she finally left her parents' home.

Immersed in her work, she hadn't even registered the time until a sharp rap at her door grabbed her attention. Catpurrnicus gave a soft mew and stretched his legs, lengthening his body in a long line as he roused from his nap.

Laurence's voice traveled from behind the door. "Bea?"

Catpurrnicus's ears pricked forward to catch Laurence's dulcet tones. He rose from the window and arched his back, his tail curling, then flicking.

"Stay, Purrny." Bea doubted he would heed her command, but she had to try.

When she rose to open the door, she gazed down and sighed in dismay. Another gown ruined by ink-stained fingers. With care to open the door but a fraction, she poked her head around. The effort to restrain Catpurrnicus proved fruitless as he easily slipped through the gap and wound himself around Laurence's legs, rubbing his little body contentedly against his new favorite person. Bea could hardly blame him. Admitting defeat, she threw the door open wider.

Laurence's gaze fixed squarely on her face. Amusement sparkled in his eyes, and his lips twitched as if fighting a smile. "It's late. I've come to alert you about supper." He shifted his weight from one booted foot to the other. His eyes darted to the side, then down to Catpurrnicus. "I know I could have sent Essie, but I wanted to come myself." He lifted his gaze to hers once again. "I worry I've offended you."

Any remnants of irritation blew away at his contrite expression. How could she stay angry with him? The words she'd used so often to reassure other parties who apologized for offending her formed on her lips, but she refused to say them. Because it *did matter.* Instead, she opted for honesty. "I will admit, it pained me that you dismissed my ideas so quickly. Although I should be accustomed to it." She waited for his response, her stomach clenching in readiness for his rebuke of her openness.

"I beg your forgiveness. I promise I shall do my utmost to consider your suggestions with the degree they deserve."

A kernel of something in his answer niggled at her, poking her brain with warning, but she held her tongue.

"Now," he said, touching a fingertip to her nose, "shall we prepare for supper? Fanny should be along shortly. I requested a few moments alone with you before she arrived to assist you in dressing." He leaned in and kissed her cheek, lingering for a moment before moving to her lips.

The sweetness of the kiss, although not as passionate as the ones they'd shared earlier in the day, held a promise of more to follow.

When he pulled away, he rested his forehead on hers, his smile returning. "I should leave you or we may miss supper."

He turned and strode from her doorway. The loud sneeze reminded her about Catpurrnicus, and she raced to retrieve him from where he followed Laurence to his room. She stooped to pick up the cat. At the precise moment she rose with Catpurrnicus in her arms, Laurence turned. She stopped her ascent, her face eye level with his fall. Memories of what they'd shared and especially what lay behind that flap of material heated her face.

He sneezed again, propelling his body forward into hers. Catpurrnicus yowled and squirmed from her arms, racing back toward her room and sending her completely off balance. She swayed, windmilling her arms to keep upright, then grabbed the nearest stationary object—Laurence's hips. The momentum sent her tumbling backward, pulling Laurence on top of her. Arms and legs tangled together in a heap on the floor.

Unable to resist joining what he most likely presumed an enjoyable game, Catpurrnicus returned, hopped onto Laurence's back, and began licking his face. Laurence's face contorted, his eyes squinting, his chest hitching. Quickly bringing an arm up to block himself from sneezing in Bea's face, he inadvertently bumped her chin.

Pain shot up her jaw, traveling to her ear. She blinked back the tears.

"Forgive me," Laurence said, his sorrowful expression melting Bea's heart. He kissed along her jawline, Bea supposed as an attempt to soothe the pain.

Fanny chose that precise moment to appear. She stopped short, no doubt embarrassed by the sight of her employers in such an unusual arrangement on the hallway floor. "Oh dear. I beg pardon. I shall return . . . later."

"Wait," Laurence called after her, scrambling to remove himself from Bea's person and regain his footing. He reached a hand toward Bea to assist her up. "We had a minor fall. There is nothing untoward happening, Fanny."

While his words were true, the red tint appearing at the tips of his ears informed Bea that, much like her, their *mishap* had incited less than pure thoughts in his mind. He gave her a tiny smile and ducked into his room, closing the door.

Fanny turned her attention back to Bea, her eyes widening. She lifted a hand to cover her mouth, her eyes crinkling at the corners.

Bea squared her shoulders, doing her best to appear dignified. "As my husband said, it was merely a slight tumble."

Fanny shook her head, no longer able to control her laughter. "It's not that, my lady. You have a . . ." She pointed her finger at Bea's face.

"What?" Bea asked, perplexed as to what would cause her lady's maid such amusement. She reentered her room, Catpurrnicus at her feet, and walked toward the mirror on her dressing table. A black dot of ink decorated the tip of her nose, giving her an almost feline appearance.

Good Galileo!

Even scrubbing with the brine mixture Bea had procured on a summer's trip to Lyme, Fanny only partially removed the unsightly black dot from Bea's nose. Bea conceded the futility of the attempt and allowed Fanny to finish dressing her for supper.

Laurence rose to greet her when she entered the parlor, his lips quirking slightly as he held his arm to escort her to the dining room.

Between sips of broth, he said, "What were you writing?"

Blink. Her own spoon poised mid-air. "Pardon?"

"The ink. I presumed you were writing something. Correspondence to your parents already?" His eyes twinkled. "I hope not to tell them of our . . . unusual afternoon . . . encounter. One set of parents with such knowledge is sufficient, I should think. Although, my mother may take it upon herself to convey the news to yours. No doubt they will already have chosen names for our offspring."

Her spoon clanked to the bowl. Mention of babies diverted her from formulating a response to his question about her writing. *Children.* Why hadn't she thought of that? It was a natural enough outcome from what they had done, but nothing had been further from her mind when she'd set out to Laurence's study. Unlike her aversion to the image of a squalling infant sired by Lord Middlebury, she found a chubby, pink-cheeked cherub with Laurence's brown eyes much more agreeable.

She returned to his question at hand. "No correspondence. Simply jotting down some ideas."

"Ah." He nodded. "Miranda journals. She finds it an excellent way to clear her head. I've often wondered what she finds to write in it, but she's made it abundantly clear it isn't meant for my eyes." He chuckled, returning to his broth.

Bea had nothing against women who wrote idle thoughts into journals, but if Laurence presumed she spent her afternoon with such trivialities rather than working on a solution to his problem, so be it. However, the fact he'd already forgotten her suggestions for improvements to his motor and his promise to consider them more carefully stung. Would she forever be ignored?

Bea remained silent during the remainder of their meal as Laurence conveyed information about his cousin and their destination in Scotland. Bits and pieces of the one-sided conversation registered in Bea's mind—beautiful, tranquil, jovial— but Laurence's failure to consider her ideas stood like an immovable force, blocking out the pleasant images.

When they retired for the evening, Laurence tapped on her door, peeking around the corner. Unlike their wedding night, he seemed relaxed, confident. His eyes darted to Catpurrnicus, lying on Bea's bed.

"Perhaps my bedroom?" he asked, wariness lacing his voice.

The internal struggle between the allure of spending the night wrapped in his embrace and her annoyance at his easy dismissal of her ideas lasted for more than she cared to admit.

The latter won the battle. "I'm tired and a bit . . . sore," she said, the last part truer than the first.

His crestfallen expression nearly had her rethinking her vow to remain angry with him. "Of course. How thoughtless of me." He took one step inside her room, then halted as Catpurrnicus rose to attention. "Might I have a goodnight kiss before leaving? Please?" He held out his hand, inviting her closer.

All her defenses crumbled. He *wanted* to kiss her—not an obligatory gesture, but genuine desire.

"Stay, Purrny."

Miraculously, the cat obeyed, stretching out on the soft counterpane and purring gently.

When she reached Laurence, he slid an arm around her waist, pulling her tight against him. His eyes searched hers as if seeking something. "I enjoyed our afternoon together. But I feel that sometime during the day, I misstepped. If so, I apologize. I will make blunders, Bea, but you must tell me what they are so I may correct them."

Hadn't she already told him and he'd so quickly forgotten? Before she could huff in frustration, he lowered his head, his lips brushing lightly, teasing and tasting, driving every reason why she should remain angry with him from her mind. An urgent need to rescind her excuses of exhaustion and tenderness rose dangerously close to the surface.

When he broke the delicious kiss, he placed a lighter one on the tip of her nose. "Goodnight, Bea. Rest well."

Before she could protest, he returned to his room, closing the door behind him.

"Goodnight," she whispered to the heavy panel of English oak.

It seemed impossible to stay angry with him.

CHAPTER 21—JOURNEY TO SCOTLAND

Servants bustled down the corridors the following morning as Bea made her way to the breakfast room. Maids carried dust sheets to cover furniture during their absence while footmen lugged heavy trunks down the long staircase.

Each of them greeted her with a polite, "Good morning, Lady Montgomery," accompanied by bows and curtsies, their lips tugging in restrained smiles as she passed by. Bea swore one of the maids actually giggled.

As Essie hurried past, her arms laden with clean linens, Bea asked, "What is going on? Everyone seems in a hurry."

Essie dropped in a quick curtsy. "Yes, my lady. In preparation for your journey."

So soon? Laurence had spoken of Scotland at supper the night before, but had he mentioned when they would depart? She couldn't remember. Her anger with him had blurred bits of their conversation.

As she entered the breakfast room, Laurence rose in greeting. He remained standing as she prepared a light plate of toast and kippers, then held her chair when she took her seat.

"I trust you slept well," he said.

She studied his face for signs of annoyance that she had put him off the night before, but she found none. She nodded the affirmative.

He leaned closer. "Your decision to . . . sleep . . . alone was wise. The servants have packed everything in record time. We leave for Scotland later this morning. It's beneficial we're both well-rested. It can be an arduous journey as we near the border."

This morning? "Are you certain we can't bring Catpurrnicus?" The thought of leaving him behind tugged at her heart.

"Well, I suppose he could travel in the carriage with the servants. But being confined in the close quarters of our carriage with him for hours on end, I'm not certain I would manage."

The twinge in her heart deepened. Could she really inflict such suffering upon Laurence? "Of course, you're right. It was selfish of me to ask. And I doubt Purrny would tolerate the carriage ride for that distance." She pushed the kippers around on her plate. "But I shall miss him."

Laurence placed his hand over hers, squeezing gently. "I know you will, and he shall miss *you*. It's not selfish at all to want him with you. Perhaps we'll leave Essie here to care for him? Would that please you?"

She nodded, staring at her suddenly unappealing breakfast.

"You'll love Scotland and my cousin's estate. I can't wait to show you the surprise."

When his lips quirked up, her anger abated, and she had an overwhelming desire to kiss them.

And so she did.

❦

IF FORCED, LAURENCE WOULD HAVE TO ADMIT—AS MUCH AS HE liked Catpurrnicus, as well as his desire to please Beatrix—he looked forward to having her alone without her allergy-producing cat to interrupt private moments.

Moments like the current one.

The kiss, although unexpected, tilted his world on its axis.

A kiss—at the breakfast table.

With servants present.

Such scandal.

As if remembering the servants' presence, she pulled back, breaking the kiss. Her cheeks darkened with the enchanting pink color he loved.

Her impetuosity both surprised him, naturally—and even more shockingly, pleased him. Up until their marriage, he'd found surprises distasteful and disconcerting. Especially when they pertained to matters of proper behavior.

His thoughts heated, remembering their afternoon interlude the day before. Catpurrnicus might not be the only living thing who would find the lengthy carriage ride difficult.

However, there *were* curtains on the carriage windows.

Never in his thirty years would he have predicted experiencing such fanciful notions. The idea of making love in a closed carriage, curtains or not, made him question his own sanity. What on earth had Bea done to him? He fluctuated between amusement and annoyance at the change.

However, the idea of making good use of the carriage ride remained rooted in his mind, prodding at his unwavering belief in propriety.

Yes, a long ride indeed. One he eagerly anticipated more with each passing moment. Unable to restrain himself, he grinned, feeling much like a naughty schoolboy who had planned a sneak attack on his tutor.

Blinking, Bea cocked her head. "What is it? Is the ink stain still visible on my nose?" She reached a hand up and rubbed at the faded spot.

"No," he said, kissing said nose. "I was just thinking about our journey."

She blinked again. "You said it was arduous, but you're smiling."

"It is. However, I may have found a way to make it more pleasurable."

"Oh? What?"

A pang of guilt twisted his insides at her innocent expression with those wide, inquisitive eyes. He chided himself for entertaining such scandalous ideas. His bride would think him a libidinous rake.

And yet . . .

"A fanciful notion, probably not worth pursuing." He placed his napkin on his plate and rose. "I'll give instruction to Essie regarding Catpurrnicus. Feel free to take anything here with you. Although my cousin Fergus should have everything we need, you may wish to bring some items for the journey. Perhaps some books?"

"While in the library the other day, I did see several I'd love to read again."

"Excellent. If you'll excuse me, I'm going to oversee the transport of my machine to the carriage. I'm planning on devoting time to it during our stay."

For a moment, he considered kissing her again before taking his leave, but quickly dismissed it. It would be prudent to restrain himself.

Yet the carriage curtains whispered their seductive call.

⌘

WITH THEIR TRUNKS LOADED, CORRESPONDENCE TO FAMILY AND friends written and posted, and servants gathered, Bea cuddled Catpurrnicus as Laurence waited by the side of the carriage.

"Be good for Essie and perhaps she'll let you mouse out in the gardens." She kissed the white dot on the top of his head that disrupted the solid sheet of black fur covering his little body.

"Don't you worry, my lady. Purrny and I have become good friends," Essie said as she gently lifted the cat from Bea's arms.

Oh, how she would miss him. She sniffled back the tears threatening to break free and turned toward her husband.

Once Laurence had assisted her into the carriage, he joined her, taking his seat by her side. The carriage gave a lurch forward, and Bea craned her neck out the small window and waved goodbye.

The heat of London receded as they made their way out of the city. Laurence provided more detail about his cousin Fergus's family and estate.

"He's a jovial fellow, Bea. I'm sure you'll like him. Although his language can be a bit colorful, he means no offense. His wife is a saint to put up with him, or so she insists and he doesn't argue. They have a young daughter named Catriona who holds her father in the palm of her hand."

The lovely picture he painted both tugged at Bea's heart and worried her. How could she ever live up to such paragons of familial bliss? "Do you think they'll like me?"

"I have no doubt."

The confidence in his words shone in his eyes, and Bea's spirit soared, much like the starlings dancing in the sky.

He moved to the opposite seat and grew contemplative, as if studying her.

Sweet scents of honeysuckle and sweet pea from surrounding countryside gardens spilled into the carriage windows, the cooler breeze refreshing the compartment.

Laurence startled her when he said, "I love the smell of the country. However, I prefer the scent of orange blossom. Along with vanilla, I find their scents very pleasing." His gaze locked on her.

Lips curving in a sensuous smile conveyed that he knew he'd named the very fragrances she wore.

Suddenly, the breeze drifting in through the windows no longer cooled the carriage compartment.

He leaned toward her, the knees on his long legs bumping hers. "How are you feeling? Still . . . tender?"

The blush she'd been fighting won the battle, and her cheeks warmed. *Is he implying . . .?*

"Well, I . . ." Memories of their lovemaking the day before flooded her mind. Even angry at him for dismissing her ideas, she'd spent the evening studying the book Alice had sent for additional ideas to tempt him. Perhaps unnecessarily it would seem—at least the tempting part.

If she understood him, he was attempting his own seduction.

In a carriage?

He continued to watch her, waiting for her answer.

"I'm somewhat recovered," she admitted.

After drawing the curtains on the windows closed, he pulled her to him, settling her on his lap. With a single tug, he untied the ribbon on her bonnet, and tossed it on the opposite seat she had just vacated. "I've thought of a way to pass the time, if you're amenable?"

It turned out she was most amenable.

By the time they approached their first stop on the journey, Bea found herself as relaxed as Catpurrnicus when he lay on the window seat, enjoying the golden beams of sunlight. She snuggled on Laurence's lap, her head nestled against his chest as he stroked her cheek and played with a loose tendril of her hair.

"Your hair reminds me of flames, and I'm the moth drawn to them. You consume me, Bea."

It was one of the most beautiful things she'd ever heard.

He helped straighten her gown and tidy her hair. She in turn fussed with his cravat, although not able to duplicate the complicated folds Stevens had no doubt worked on tirelessly that morning.

After their second stop for a brief rest to change horses and refresh themselves, Bea retrieved several books from a valise, while Laurence secured a sketchpad and pencils with which to occupy himself before re-boarding and proceeding onward.

Bea found her attention wavering from the pages of her book, glancing up occasionally to find Laurence immersed in his sketching.

"More plans for the motor?" she asked.

A smile ghosted his lips, and he shook his head, attention still on the drawing. "Not quite. However, it is something that moves me." He turned the sketch toward her.

She gasped at the image on the paper, not entirely unlike the one he'd drawn the day before, for it, too, was beautiful. Yet this image showed her not in the afterglow of lovemaking, but reading, her hand playing carelessly with a lock of hair that had drifted down her neck. Instead of eyes dusky with desire, in this drawing, they appeared intense and studious.

How could he capture her so proficiently? Even the artist commissioned to paint her portrait on her eighteenth birthday hadn't captured the essence of her so perfectly.

"You like it?" Worry painted his words.

"No," she answered truthfully, and his mouth dipped. "I love it."

With that, his smile returned. "I brought the other as well. Perhaps I'll find time to paint while we're there. Fergus has a spot at the end of his gardens with perfect lighting."

He nodded toward her hands. "How is your book?"

"More interesting than my mind appears to believe at the moment." Her fingers traced over another book lying on the seat by her side. Re-wrapped in the brown paper and tied with twine, she'd boldly retrieved it from her valise along with Copernicus's *On the Revolution of Heavenly Spheres*. Try as she might, the only heavenly body holding her attention was seated across from her.

His gaze followed the slow movement of her fingers against the concealed book. "What is that?"

Heat rushed to her cheeks. "Oh." She chided herself for her embarrassment. Why else had she retrieved it if not to show Laurence. He had requested to see it the other day, had he not?

"Alice Weatherby sent this the other day. It's the book I mentioned. She obtained it in India."

With wide eyes, he stretched out his hand, motioning for her to hand it to him. "*The* book? With the suggestions?"

She nodded, handing the book to him.

His eyes never left her face as he unwrapped the paper from the book. She swallowed, hoping he wouldn't think her brazen.

When he opened the book and thumbed through the pages, the tips of his ears reddened, and for a moment she prepared herself for a lecture on the proper comportment of English wives. "Mrs. Weatherby gave you this?"

She nodded.

A smile spread across his lips as he muttered, "That explains quite a lot." He continued to peruse the book, then stopped on a page and glanced up at her. "What do you say we try this one?"

Bea tilted her head, studying the image. "Do you think it's possible in this small space?"

Not only possible, it proved a most wonderful way to spend time on their journey.

CHAPTER 22—THE KINCAIDS

Laurence gazed out the carriage window at the purple heather dotting the lush green hills of the Scottish lowlands. Uncertain if the earthy fragrance drifting throughout the compartment was due to the abundance of flowers or from his and Bea's latest amorous activity, he smiled at how quickly the time had passed.

They had occupied themselves in much the same way as they had the first day of their journey, alternating between reading, working on sketches for his motor as well as of Bea, and finding new ways to please each other in the small confines of the carriage before retiring at a coaching inn for the nights.

When they reached the end of their four-day journey, he sighed. It would be good to stretch his long legs and walk the scenic paths on his cousin Fergus's estate.

Bea had badgered him for information about the surprise he'd mentioned, and during one of their lovemaking sessions, he'd almost given in.

If the sky stayed as clear as it was at the moment, he would be able to show her that very evening.

"Look, Bea." He pointed out the window from his position next to her. "There's Glenhame."

She followed his finger with her gaze. "Oh, Laurence, it's magnificent."

"Aye, it is," he said, slipping into the comfortable Scots he used as a lad when visiting.

Laurence had always loved Fergus's home and lands. As a boy when he'd visited with his family, the home's unconventional design had delighted him. He and Fergus had made a game of hiding in the labyrinth of wings spreading out from the main section of the house like a giant sea monster. The tradition of each successive heir adding or modifying a wing had ended with Fergus.

"I dinnae want tae get lost in ma own home," Fergus had said, chuckling good-naturedly.

The seclusive nature of the home's design ensured that Laurence and Bea would have plenty of privacy from Fergus and his family.

"We will have one of the wings entirely to ourselves." He grinned at her, hoping she understood his meaning. From her blush, she apparently did.

"Beyond the gardens there are lochs, teaming with fish, and the wildlife, Bea, is incredible."

"Is that a tower?" Bea pointed to the crenelated structure rising from the middle of the house.

"Yes. And it holds the surprise."

Nervous energy filled Laurence at the sight of his cousin waiting in front of the line of servants. He hadn't seen Fergus in four years.

The carriage slowed to a stop in front of the massive home, and Laurence bounded from the compartment before Nelson, his driver, could lower the steps. In reward, Laurence promptly received a rather disgruntled glare from the man. With the steps properly lowered, Laurence extended his hand to assist Bea out.

He linked her arm in his and led her to his cousin.

A giant of a man, Fergus stood with hands on his hips and a scowl on his face. His thick head of russet-colored hair, bushy eyebrows, and matching bristly beard added to the image of a man not to be trifled with.

Nothing could be further from the truth.

Bea leaned in and whispered. "He's so large. And frightening."

Laurence patted her hand as it tightened on his arm. "He's all bluster."

He glared back at his cousin. "Are you trying to frighten my bride, Fergus?"

A wide grin broke across Fergus's face. "Is it no working? Damnation if I've lost ma touch."

"Never ye mind ma husband, lamb," Fiona said. "He forgets who wears the breeks in this family."

"Och, how could I when ye remind me daily?" Fergus turned his gaze on Beatrix. "Och, Monty, ye've married yerself a redhead. Good on ye, laddie. Good on ye! Why she's so tiny, she looks verra like a wee Elven princess." He opened his arms. "Come here, lassie, and give yer cousin Fergus a hug."

Bea turned a worried glance toward Laurence.

"Go ahead, Bea. Just don't let him squeeze too hard."

BEA TOOK A TENTATIVE STEP TOWARD THE HULK OF A MAN, HOPING her knees wouldn't give out. She'd finally overcome her clumsiness around Laurence. Mostly. She didn't need another man to be stumbling around.

She curtsied before him. "Pleased to meet you, Laird Kincaid."

He gave a dismissive wave of his hand. "None of those fancy manners and titles here, lass. Call me Fergus." He turned toward the woman next to him. Pride shone in Fergus's eyes as he gazed upon the stocky woman. "And this is ma wife, Fiona."

A broad smile covered the woman's ruddy complexion. The knot of dark blond hair fastened at the top of her head wobbled as she nodded toward Bea. Considering how Fiona had put her husband in his place, Bea knew she and Fiona would get along famously. Yet adherence to propriety mattered to Laurence, so she still curtsied. "Pleased to meet you, Fiona."

Fergus opened his arms again. "Now where's ma hug?"

Bea stepped forward and into the man's large arms. Like a boa constrictor she'd read about, his arms wrapped around her body and squeezed, lifting her off her feet and swinging her around in a circle.

"Why, she weighs no more'n a pebble. You'll have no trouble at all throwing her over yer shoulder and taking her straight tae yer bed."

Fiona slapped his arm. "Fergus, mind yer tongue. They're newly wed."

Although a stern expression painted Fiona's face, her eyes sparkled with amusement and affection toward her husband. She wrapped her arm around Bea's waist, giving her a quick tug and leading her toward the house. "Come now, lass, let these two eejits talk about old times while you and I get tae ken each other."

Bea's Scots was rusty at best. "Eejits?"

Fiona laughed, the sound hardy and genuine. "What ye English call a nodcock, cabbage-head, dolt, dunderhead—"

Bea held up her hand, bursting with her own laughter. "Stop, stop, I understand. Idiot." No doubt about it, she and Fiona would definitely get along. Bea already felt a kinship with the woman. "How long have you and Fergus been married?"

"Och. Seems like forever." Fiona's gaze darted toward Bea. "A good forever, mind ye. Nigh on seven years this winter. I was no more'n a wee lass myself when Fergus stormed into ma pa's study, telling him he was going tae marry me whether Pa liked it or no."

"Your father didn't like Fergus?" Bea found it hard to believe anyone would dislike the bear of a man—a cuddly bear, that is.

"Pa liked him fine. But he didnae let on, making Fergus work harder tae win me."

"And win you he did," Bea said, as certain of the outcome as she was of Copernicus's heliocentric view of the cosmos.

"Aye. Heart and soul." Fiona stopped at the bottom of the staircase which wound to the upper floors. "From the stars in yer eyes, I can see Monty has won yers."

"Monty?" Bea chuckled, remembering Fergus had also used the nickname.

"Short for Montgomery. Yer man is so keen on the rules he didnae like us calling him Laurie."

Bea filed away the *Laurie* for a more *private* time with Laurence. "He does highly value propriety and society's rules." Unease tightened in her stomach. Too highly to accept a wife who writes scientific articles.

Fiona showed Bea around the grand house, explaining she should make herself at home and she and Fergus weren't ones for formality. Upstairs, giggles drifted from a room down the long hall, and Fiona motioned Bea forward, putting a finger to her lips.

When Bea peeked into the room, a young girl about five gazed up from where she sat at a child-sized table. Vibrant shades of blues, reds, greens, and yellows decorated her face and hands. It appeared more paint had found its way to her body than it did to the small canvas in front of her. Bea restrained a smile of camaraderie. White teeth broke through the streak of blue covering the girl's mouth.

"Ma! Have they come?"

"They have, ma princess. Catriona, meet Cousin Monty's new bride, Beatrix."

The child raced up to Bea and wrapped her paint-covered hands around Bea's legs.

"Och, child! Ye've gone and covered poor Beatrix with yer art."

"It's quite all right, Fiona. I've done as much damage to my gowns with my own ink-stained fingers." Bea squatted before the child. "I'm so pleased to meet you, Catriona. Please call me Bea."

"Like a bumblebee?" Catriona asked, her blue eyes as large as saucers.

"Not nearly as graceful as the insects, I'm afraid. B-e-a."

Catriona released her grip and motioned Bea toward her canvas. "I'm painting fer Cousin Monty. He likes tae paint. Do ye ken he'll like it?"

Bea gazed at the kaleidoscope of colors covering the pint-sized canvas. "I'm sure he'll love it."

Fiona nodded toward Bea. "What he'll no love is the art on Bea's gown. Let's get ye tae yer rooms. Yer trunks should be there by now."

Bea waved goodbye to Catriona, who had returned to her masterpiece.

Fiona led her down a hallway where another passage joined at a forty-five degree angle. "You and Monty will have this whole wing tae yerselves."

"Fiona, may I ask you something?"

"O' course."

"Are you aware of the circumstances of my marriage to Laurence?"

Fiona's gaze shifted, her lips tightening. "We get the gossips sheets here—late, but we get them." She locked eyes with Bea. "But we dinnae believe everything in them, lass."

"In this case, I'm afraid what you read is true. I didn't mean to trap Laurence into marriage. It just . . . happened."

"But ye do love him?"

"So much. But he doesn't love me. What can I do? Is there a way to make him love me?"

Compassion etched Fiona's face and shone in her eyes. "Ah, lass. Love is a strange thing. Sometimes it sneaks up on ye, catching ye unawares, sudden like. Other times it happens so slowly, ye hardly ken how it happened."

She patted Bea's hand. "Give him time, lass. He's a good lad. He'll see what a treasure he's lucked into."

Bea certainly hoped so. And if his affectionate attentiveness was any indicator, the odds were in her favor.

☙❧

LAURENCE EAGERLY WAITED FOR NIGHTFALL, CASTING GLANCES OUT the window every five minutes. Proud he'd held firm and not revealed the surprise, even when at his weakest, his increasing eagerness to share the wonder with Bea grew almost unbearable. Finally, around nine p.m., the last rays of sun sank below the horizon, leaving a burnt orange halo.

"It's time for the surprise," he said, slipping his pocket watch back inside his coat and grasping Bea's hand.

He led her up the stairs and down the hallway, passing the portraits of Fergus's ancestors who scowled down at them through the same bushy eyebrows. When they reached the end of the hall where the west wing jutted off to its own, he stopped at an old wooden door.

When Laurence pulled at the heavy circular ring, the blackened iron hinges—appearing to be as ancient as the home itself—creaked and groaned, as if protesting the intrusion. A winding stone stairway waited beyond, the narrow passage only allowing one person at a time.

"It's a bit like the hidden staircase to my roof. But much sturdier." He held a lantern in front of him. "Shall I lead?"

"Yes," she said, her answer breathy.

His boots slapped against the hard surface of the stairway, Bea's slippers producing a much softer sound behind him. "I loved going up here as a boy. It was as if I were going to defend a castle from an invading army."

"Is that what it was used for?"

"According to Fergus, yes. However, I have my doubts." He chuckled more to himself than to Bea as he remembered Fergus's claims his ancestor had single-handedly fought off the English army.

Reaching the top, they came to another wooden door identical to the one they'd entered at the foot of the stairway. And like its predecessor, it too made protest at being disturbed.

He held his hand out to stop her, blocking her from viewing outside. "Close your eyes."

"I'm not sure that's wise, considering my proclivity for stumbling." A nervous edge to her laughter indicated she truly feared falling.

"Take my hand. I'll protect you."

As he held out his hand to her, both the action and the word stirred something inside him—a desire to always keep her safe from harm.

Her smile wavered slightly, but she obeyed, slipping her hand in his and closing her eyes.

"One more step," he said, guiding her up and out to the cooling summer night.

He watched her face as he led her to the surprise. "No peeking."

At last, reaching his destination, he held the lantern high enough to illuminate what lay ahead. "Open your eyes."

Joy shone on her face, the light dancing across it, and he'd never seen anything so beautiful.

"Marvelous," she said as she gazed at the magnificent telescope.

"Indeed," he said, enraptured by his bride. "Now, shall we explore the heavens together?"

꙳

NERVOUS ENERGY SKITTERED THROUGH BEA AS SHE MOVED TOWARD the astronomical instrument. Even with its enormous size, her hand reached out tentatively, as if it might crumble at her touch. "Is it a reflecting telescope?"

"Yes. It's a Herschelian design. The heavens always fascinated Fergus. When you mentioned an interest—not to mention the name of your cat—I knew you'd wish to see it. Other than the cooler weather here, it was the deciding factor for the location of our wedding trip."

Her fingers stroked the cold metal as if it were a living thing. "I had no idea they were so large." Indeed, it surpassed even Laurence's tall height. A small set of steps led up to a platform from which they would reach the eyepiece.

He climbed up first and held out his hand. "Come."

She expected him to gaze through the eyepiece first. Instead, he moved aside and gestured for her to move forward.

Her spectacles made it a bit difficult, but she still gasped as she viewed the heavens up close for the first time in her life. "Is that constellation Virgo?"

She moved aside, allowing him to take her place. "Yes." He adjusted the position a bit and gazed through the eyepiece again, then moved aside. "Here's Venus."

As she gazed in wonder at the heavens, a burst of light streaked across the sky. More followed in quick succession. They lit up the night like the fireworks in Vauxhall Gardens. "Laurence, can you see it?"

An arm wrapped around her waist. "Yes. It's wonderful. Like fireflies dancing in the sky."

She pulled him over, allowing him a closer view through the telescope. A sense of magic settled around them as they gazed at the meteor shower.

"I know how it feels," she whispered, more to herself than to him.

He raised his head from the telescope. "Pardon?"

"The sensation of shooting stars." Grateful the darkness hid her blush, she said, "When we make love. It's like bursts of light in my body."

He pulled her into his arms and kissed her lightly. "Then shall we return to our room and make our own shooting stars?"

CHAPTER 23—FREEDOM TO BE

Initially, trepidation had filled Bea over meeting Laurence's cousin and his family. Always uncomfortable around people she didn't know, she braced herself for the inevitable moment when they would peer down their noses at her with disdain. Usually after she'd expressed her opinion. Of course, those moments were either preceded or followed by a warning from her mother.

Without her mother present, Bea lowered her defenses—marginally. At first, she still worried about embarrassing Laurence. But as her time with the Kincaids progressed and they directed their good-natured teasing and cajoling more toward her husband, she discovered a blessed freedom in being herself.

Oh, she'd still stumbled a few times, primarily when Laurence directed a heated look her way, catching her unaware. But slowly, she managed to keep herself upright even when her knees weakened at the sight of him.

She enjoyed spending time with Fiona and Catriona when Fergus and Laurence went hunting or fishing, but even during those short periods, an ache formed in her chest at his absence, as she anxiously awaited his return. When the men would appear, guns or tackle tipped lazily against their shoulders, she'd run down the tree-lined, hard-packed path in front of the house to greet her husband, throwing herself into his arms and covering his face with kisses.

Fergus would continue on, muttering something about lovesick females.

After the first week, Laurence limited such outings, telling Bea he'd grown tired of Fergus's teasing. However, Bea suspected it had been no hardship for her husband to spend more time with her.

As the weeks passed, spending time with Laurence as they worked on the design for his motor, or on quiet walks exploring the beautiful countryside around the estate filled her days. At times, Laurence would disappear, promising he wouldn't be gone long, saying he was working on a surprise.

They spent evenings with the Kincaid family, either with Bea entertaining them on the pianoforte or, on clear nights, up on the tower, viewing the heavens through the telescope.

Throughout both days and nights, Bea shared private moments with her husband whenever the mood would strike. The fact those occasions occurred often pleased her.

Yet, something seemed to be missing.

One dreary day, Bea stared out the window at the rolling Scottish hillside and sighed. Soft footfalls announced Laurence's approach even before the clean scent of shaving soap teased her nose. Strong arms circled her waist, pulling her back flush against his firm chest.

"You're sad. What can I do?" he asked, his whispered words gentle.

His simple acknowledgment of her melancholia alone would have been sufficient to unleash the flood of emotion she tried in vain to hold back, but the caring tone of his voice precipitated the tears to break free and trickle down her cheeks. She shook her head, reluctant to meet his gaze and confirm his suspicions.

"Bea," he said, turning her toward him, and lifting her chin with a forefinger. "Have I done something to upset you?"

She sniffled back the sobs and shook her head. "I miss Catpurrnicus."

He held her to his chest, stroking the back of her head. "Do you wish to return to London? Cut our trip short?"

Did she? Everything had been so perfect. The ability to be herself had freed her from the typical constraints, even allowing her ideas to flow more readily upon the page. She'd finished several articles for *The Times* and was working on one she hoped would solve Laurence's issue with the power source for his motor.

Back in London, she would be expected to receive callers and participate in the usual activities with other ladies of the *ton*. Was she ready to become the wife and hostess society expected?

"I just miss his little face." She cringed at her admission. He must think her a child. Had she embarrassed him by her outburst?

"Perhaps there is something I can do about that." He held out his handkerchief. "Here, you never seem to have one of these."

After she had dried her tears and blown her nose, he kissed her, the sweetness of his lips a balm in itself. "Allow me a bit of time. I had come to show you a surprise, but I need to make a slight change. Will you excuse me for a little longer?"

She nodded, and after another lingering kiss, he left her.

While she waited, she worked on her article, doing her best to keep her mind busy. With each strike of the clock announcing another quarter hour had passed, she rose to peer out the window again, willing him to return.

Fiona popped in, asking if Bea wanted to join her in the garden. As Bea instructed a footman to inform Laurence of her whereabouts, a sly smile curled Fiona's lips as if she had some secret knowledge.

Not far down the path amid the field of flowers, Laurence waited in front of an easel.

"I'll leave you two alone," Fiona said, then skirted off back toward the house.

Cloth covered the large canvas upon the easel, and Laurence finished cleaning black paint off a brush, setting it aside.

"I apologize. This took longer than I anticipated. I had to paint him from memory. Are you ready?"

Did he paint a picture of Catpurrnicus in only an hour's time? She nodded, anxious to see his masterpiece.

Nothing could have prepared her. A beautiful woman lay on a bed. From the seductive nature of the linens barely covering her torso and the hooded eyelids, it appeared she'd been thoroughly loved.

She recalled the sketch he'd done after they had made love the first time. She had thought it beautiful then, but this rendering was magnificent. The color of her hair burned like flame. The pink on her cheeks was a strange mix of innocence and carnality. Heat warmed Bea's face as she gazed upon the exposed breast and peek of hair by the juncture of her thighs. Was this truly how he saw her?

"Is that . . . me?"

He chuckled, sending a delicious shiver up her spine. "Who else?" He wiped his hands on a cloth, then wrapped his arms around her, nuzzling her neck. "I hope you don't think I would paint some other woman in this pose. Do you like the addition?"

She reached forward, the image so lifelike she wished to touch it.

"Careful, the paint is still wet."

The black paint. There, curled up next to the woman, lay a cat, its little pink tongue sticking out, its yellow eyes gazing at the viewer as if to say, *Don't you wish you were me?*

She adored it.

Life breathed from the portrait. "There's such passion in it, the vibrancy of the colors, the depth and texture the shading gives." She gazed upon her husband with new admiration.

His cheeks darkened. "I've always loved painting. It's the one way I'm comfortable expressing what's in here." He tapped two fingers against his chest.

As if the admission itself embarrassed him, he turned away and reached for the paintbrush, wiping its already clean bristles. "As a gentleman and heir to a peer, I was reared to rein in my feelings, to appear impassive at all times." He darted a quick glance her way, meeting her eyes before returning to the paint-free bristles. "It does take a toll. After many years of repressing them, it's easy to forget what it's like to experience strong emotions. Painting has helped remind me."

His admission shocked her. She'd presumed men always had the advantage to be true to their nature. "Do the colors chosen reflect your mood?"

Once again, his gaze darted then locked on hers. "Yes. That's most perceptive of you. Not only the colors, but shapes and texture reflect my state of mind. When I'm angry, I paint in sharp edges and slashes of reds and blacks. Blues and purples with softer, undefined edges for melancholia. For joy, yellows and golds with an overall brightness."

Oh, how she understood. "I'm the same at the piano. I have my favorite pieces for when I'm happy and when I'm sad."

She stepped closer to the painting, admiring the bright colors. "You were happy painting this."

"Yes," he answered, stepping behind and wrapping his arms around her again. "Very."

Warmth filled her chest. "We have more in common than I imagined. For years, I felt trapped in my own body, unable to express my thoughts without censure. Forced to fit into an ideal mold of what a woman should be when my mind screamed to rebel. I often regretted being born a woman."

He kissed the sensitive area under her earlobe. "Would it be callous of me to admit I'm very glad you were?"

She giggled, partly in response to his question and partly from the sensations of his lips against her neck. "Under the circumstances, I will allow it."

The breath from his chuckle floated across her neck and tickled her already sensitized nerve endings. He turned her to face him, his expression growing serious. "It's more than physical for me, Bea. I want you to know that. Your mind fascinates me." He gathered her hands in his, engulfing them and lifting them to his lips.

As she stared into his eyes, a lightness filled her chest, and hope surged that he was growing to love her. Love her for exactly who she was. "Perhaps with each other we will find the freedom to be ourselves." The sheer joy of the idea nearly overwhelmed her.

He answered with a passionate kiss, making her glad indeed she'd been born a woman.

⚜

One day as they strolled the outer boundaries of the estate, Bea paused in thought when they stopped at the edge of a loch. Dragonflies flitted across the clear water, dipping down to brush against the surface. On occasion, a fish would rise and snatch one of the unsuspecting insects. Tiny bubbles would form, then pop when met with a gust of wind.

"I've been giving some thought to the problem with your motor," she said.

Laurence rose from where he was chiseling pieces of flint from an outcropping of rocks, his expression curious but not dismissive. "What's made you think of that?"

"The bubbles rising there." She pointed to the surface of the loch. "See how they dissipate in concentric ripples when they pop."

"Interesting," he muttered. "And that led to . . .?"

Emboldened by his interest, she forged ahead. "What if the current causes the corrosion? Indeed exacerbates it? The higher the current, the faster the corrosion."

"I'm listening." He straightened, indicating she indeed had his attention.

"The correlation cannot be ignored. I'm not convinced of Volta's presumption that the current is the result of contact tension between the metals. What if it's a chemical reaction of the zinc, copper, and brine solution?"

His lips pursed, and she braced for his dismissal. Much to her surprise and delight, he nodded. "You may be right. There's been some speculation on that precise idea."

"I'll concede that lightning is perhaps too volatile and unpredictable to pursue as a source. So perhaps, rather than trying to find a completely different power source, why not fix the issue with the current one?"

The piece of rock he'd chiseled from the ground dropped from his fingers. "What did you have in mind?"

"What about a chemical solution to counteract and neutralize the hydrogen bubbles?"

He tilted his head as if considering it. "Even so, introducing another chemical solution would disrupt the chemical reaction, would it not?"

"True, but what if there was a way to achieve the desired result without mixing the solutions?"

"Would that be possible?" he muttered as if asking the air instead of her.

"If it's a chemical reaction, I believe so. Perhaps a way to allow the positive or negative ions from the new solution to travel to the brine solution without the actual solutions mixing?"

Excitement shone in his eyes as he gazed at her, and Bea had never been prouder. "You may be on to something, Bea. We just have to find the precise chemicals necessary and a way to contain the solutions yet allow the reactions."

She tugged him close. "Together, we can do anything."

He dipped his head, whispering against her lips. "I believe you."

Energy bubbled within her from her idea, begging for release. After a quick peck to his lips, she pulled back. "Let's go swimming."

⚜

LAURENCE BLINKED TWICE, STRAINING TO PROCESS BEA'S WORDS. Surely he had misunderstood? "Go swimming? Together?" The scandalous nature of her suggestion tipped his world yet again. It simply wasn't done.

Her head tilted in the alluring way that always drew his eyes to her slender neck. "Don't you know how?"

He squared his shoulders, thrusting his chest at her insult. "Of course I know how. But men and women do *not* swim *together*."

"Why ever not?"

"Do you mean to tell me you have gone swimming with men

before?" A growl formed deep in his chest at the idea of another man seeing her luscious body nude, the thought rankling him.

"Well, not really, although my brother and I used to swim together as children."

"Swimming as children is one thing, but as a grown man and woman . . ." He shook his head.

Her bottom lip protruded, and he wished to kiss her, pulling its plumpness into his mouth and nipping it every so gently.

"Very well," she said. "Be a spoil-sport. I shall go alone."

She tugged off her half boots and removed her stockings, then turned her back to him. "Kindly unlace me."

"No," he said, crossing his arms over his chest. He would stand his ground on this. One could only bend the rules so far before they broke—irreparably.

Her exasperated sigh left him unmoved.

Until she reached behind her and struggled to grasp the top lace of her gown. "Ugh. This is as hard as I remember."

The words teased his own memory of the night twelve short weeks ago when he'd stumbled into the darkened library to find her with her gown partially undone.

The subsequent discovery of their compromising situation.

Their marriage.

His Bea.

He hadn't realized what a gift that well-meaning but ill-timed attempt to rescue her from a seduction attempt had been.

Until that moment.

His resolve weakened. "Well, it *is* quite deserted here. I don't suppose anyone would see us."

With quick work, he tugged the laces of her gown free, and it fell to the ground in a yellow puddle at her feet. After he assisted with her corset, he fully expected her to go into the water in her chemise. Instead, she pulled it over her head and jumped into the loch as natural as the day she had been born.

Transfixed, he watched her for a few moments as she splashed around in the clear water. She ducked underneath the surface. Unease gripped him when she didn't rise back up as expected.

Frantically, he yanked off his boots, stockings, and coat, prepared to dive in still wearing the remainder of his clothing.

Every muscle in his body coiled like a snake ready to strike. He couldn't lose her. The breath trapped in his lungs released with a whoosh as she popped up in the middle of the loch, laughing and spurting the water from her mouth like a fountain.

"Bea, don't ever frighten me like that again!" His voice sounded harsher than he intended.

But she laughed again, waving at him to join her. "It's wonderful in here. What are you waiting for?"

That, indeed, was a good question. He scanned the area around him as if a crowd would materialize from behind the surrounding trees to witness their impropriety. Other than birds and undoubtedly some woodland creatures, no one lurked to point accusing fingers.

He hesitated but a moment before stripping off his waistcoat, shirt, and trousers, then jumped into the lake as quickly as he could.

How many rules had he now broken?

When he reached her, she pulled him toward her, kissing him soundly, wiping the thought completely away.

As they splashed and frolicked like children, exhilarating freedom flowed through him, bringing every cell in his body to life.

Perhaps rules were indeed made to be broken.

❈

LYING BESIDE HER ON THE SOFT GRASS, LAURENCE PLAYED WITH A damp tendril of Bea's hair. Their lovemaking, which began in the water, had been slow and sensual, and as natural as the setting around them. The strange tugging in his chest had occurred both in the water and out, and he cataloged it.

"Are you happy, Bea? Sorry you married me?"

Although she laughed, her forest green eyes remained serious. "How am I supposed to answer with one word? I should contradict myself."

He kissed the tip of her nose. "Then one at a time." He repeated the one plaguing him for the last nine weeks since their wedding, knowing her response would answer the other. "Sorry you married me?"

She reached up and pushed away the lock of hair hanging in his eyes. "Not in the slightest."

"Then you're happy?"

"Hmm. Yes," she said, running her fingertips down the side of his face.

Oh, how he loved her touch. In keeping with the unconventional events of the day, he asked, "Do you think you could ever grow to love me?" He hoped she didn't notice the pleading tone of his voice.

Her laugh unnerved him. He had *not* expected such a strong response to that particular question.

"I already do."

And he had expected her answer even less. "You love me?"

"I've always loved you. Since that first night when you so gallantly came to my rescue. Loved you so completely I believed it would consume me like an uncontrollable fire. From that moment, every time I saw you, it was as if I had become possessed by someone other than myself, tripping and falling over my own feet."

Another piece of the puzzle snapped into place as he recalled a comment from Miranda. *And honestly, I've had numerous conversations with her, and she's remained perfectly upright.*

He chastised himself for criticizing her when *he* had been the cause of her perceived clumsiness.

"I came to your rescue? I don't recall." The admission alone pinged discomfort, not only because he didn't remember, but that he failed to recall something so vitally important to her—and in truth —to them.

"Yes. During my first Season. A ball at Lord and Lady Cartwright's. Apparently, gossip had spread of my . . . oddness. I waited, mortified when no one asked me to dance. Then you appeared, holding out your hand, rescuing me from embarrassment."

Her confession dusted away the cobwebs which held the memory hostage, and it flooded back.

Timothy had been away, serving in the military, or he surely would have rescued his sister from her social disgrace. Even with their pledge as boys still fresh in Laurence's mind, he'd made an exception in the name of gallantry. One dance would not break his promise.

Clarity illuminated the memory like the clouds parting on the summer's night when they'd stood on the tower and viewed the stars through the telescope. She had not worn her spectacles, and her eyes had captivated him. When she'd tripped and fallen against him, the heat generated from her closeness unnerved him. How anyone could call her odd had perplexed him. She was lovely.

He'd fully prepared to ask her for the honor of another set when his vow with Timothy barged forward, reminding him Beatrix was the one woman he could not pursue.

He'd spent the remainder of the evening watching her blend into the walls of the ballroom, with no other gentlemen offering to partner with her. Guilt had assaulted him that night, both for leaving her to face the wagging tongues alone and for his own emotions threatening to throw his friendship aside for the sake of a woman.

Instead, he'd pushed Beatrix deep into the recesses of his mind, sealing her off, away from further examination. He avoided her and focused instead on Margaret Farnsworth, a much safer prospect.

What a fool he'd been.

CHAPTER 24—TROUBLE IN PARADISE

L aurence's cue billiard ball smacked against the red, spinning it into the corner pocket, and he grinned. "Ha! Three more points brings me to our agreed two hundred. I believe you owe me ten pounds, Fergus."

Fergus grumbled and strode to the sideboard, then poured himself a glass of whisky. "I should ken better than tae bet against ye. That mathematical mind of yers has an uncanny way of determining the perfect angles for the shots."

"Double or nothing? I'll give you a ten point lead."

After a long swig of the whisky, Fergus shook his head. "No, thank ye. I ken when I'm bested." He settled in an overstuffed chair, his big body sinking into its soft depths. "Ah."

After placing the cue stick aside, Laurence poured his own drink and joined his cousin, taking a seat in the matching chair opposite him.

"So, cousin," Fergus said, "tell me true. What happened with yer lass?"

Laurence turned the glass in his hand, studying the glow of light reflecting off the crystal that gave the amber liquid within a golden appearance. "Bea was in an untenable situation. Her father accrued a large gambling debt. An offer was made to settle the debt in exchange for Bea's hand in marriage."

Fergus straightened in his chair, his golden eyes widening. "Ye didnae!?"

"No, no. Not me. Another man." Laurence gave a full account of the events leading to his marriage.

"Yet, ye seem happy."

"I am, Fergus. I . . . care for Bea."

With narrowed eyes, Fergus scrutinized Laurence, as if trying to categorize a new species of mammal. "I didnae hear the word *love*."

No, you didn't.

Laurence swallowed the remainder of his whisky in one gulp, trying to drown the guilt swirling in his gut that he hadn't returned Bea's declaration, the burn of the alcohol down his throat a poor punishment. "I don't know what I feel yet. It's all so confusing. Bea is different. She throws me off balance."

Fergus furrowed his brow, and Laurence shot up a hand to silence his cousin. "Not necessarily in a bad way. But she's nothing like I imagined my wife would be."

Fergus snorted a laugh and finished his own drink. "They never are."

"Her mind is extraordinary. I'm torn between being flattered by her interest in my ideas and disconcerted when her own seem to overshadow mine." He shifted in his chair, the mere admission enough to make him uncomfortable.

Fergus grunted and nodded in sympathy. "Fiona makes me feel like an eejit even on ma best days."

"Any advice you care to share?"

"It depends on what ye value more. Peace or holding tae yer need tae be right."

Laurence jerked back, blinking. "Are you saying I should compromise my values and beliefs to maintain peace in my household?" The idea was unappealing at best and unacceptable at worst.

"That, laddie"—Fergus pointed his empty glass at Laurence—"ye must decide fer yerself." He rose and poured more whisky.

Laurence's head reeled. Surely Fergus exaggerated? Bea would never do anything so drastic that would necessitate he bend his beliefs to such an extent as to break them.

Would she?

Hadn't she already? Swimming nude together. Making love in the middle of the day. How far had she already pushed him?

He ignored the unease churning in his gut, hoping to turn the conversation to a less controversial and upsetting topic. "Catriona has grown since I've last seen her."

Fergus chuckled. "Bairns have a way of doing that. Although she's no longer a bairn. Soon I'll be shooing off the laddies who come sniffing about." He shook his head. "I dinnae look forward tae it."

"It took a while to . . . have her. Did it not?"

One of Fergus's bushy eyebrows rose. "It wasnae fer lack of trying."

Heat rose up Laurence's neck. "I didn't mean to imply . . ."

"Are things no good with ye and Beatrix in the bedroom?"

Memories of heated moments in the carriage during their journey, the inns in which they stayed, as well as his own bedchamber, brought a smile to his lips. Even their discussions of scientific subjects stirred a fire within him. Desire wasn't a problem. "They're fine."

"From the look on yer face, I can see that's true. Is there some other reason for yer odd question?"

"I wondered how long until I might expect Bea to conceive."

Fergus batted his thick thigh with his free hand, bellowing a hearty laugh. "However long the good Lord decides." He eyed Laurence over the rim of his whisky. "Is there a reason yer keen to get her with a bairn? Why no enjoy the makin'?"

Laurence grinned. He enjoyed the "makin'" immensely. "I'm afraid I've done something rather foolish."

Whisky sloshed down Fergus's neckcloth as he coughed mid-drink. "What? You? Foolish? I dinnae believe it."

"It's true." Laurence nodded, ashamed to admit to his impetuous wager.

He turned his gaze away, not willing to meet Fergus's knowing stare. "All things considered, Bea and I had a rather difficult start to our marriage. I didn't want to force her, so our wedding night was . . . less than . . . productive. While at the club the next day, someone insulted both my ideas for my motor and my . . . manhood. He goaded me into a wager."

Fergus's eyebrows drew together so tightly they practically joined. "I dinnae like the sound of this," he said, the words more of a low growl.

"I bet him I would both complete my motor satisfactorily and . . ." He paused, struggling to get the foul words out.

"Och, tell me you didnae."

Laurence nodded, his stomach souring. "It's true. I wagered I would get Bea with child by year's end."

A feminine gasp sounded from the open doorway, and Laurence's head snapped toward it, finding Bea at the entrance.

Her hand clutched at her breast, and the pain in her eyes tore at his heart.

Unbidden, his body rose from the chair, lumbering toward her on heavy legs. He had to explain. "How much did you overhear?"

"Enough," she said, her words choked with emotion. "So that's the reason you've been so . . . attentive. You only wish to get me with child to win your bet. How much am I worth, Laurence? A few pounds?"

"It's not like that, Bea. Let me explain."

With her hand held out to stop him, she shook her head. "Stay away from me." She stared at him as if he were a complete stranger. "How could I have been so wrong? I don't even know you."

She spun around, leaving the scent of orange blossom in her wake and taking Laurence's world with her.

⚜

VIOLENT SHAKING OVERTOOK BEA'S BODY AS SHE FORCED HERSELF out of the room away from Laurence's presence. Queasiness followed, and she raced to the small space used as a guest necessary room, barely arriving before her Burns supper left her stomach.

Used.

Deceived.

Unwanted.

Like a fool, she'd believed the intimacy Laurence had shared with her indicated his growing affection.

Lies.

All lies.

She was nothing more than a means to an end.

To win a bet.

A nasty taste filled her mouth, and not only from what sat in the chamber pot. She spat in it again, trying to clear the foulness.

Hot tears flooded her eyes, blurring her vision. She stumbled forward, pulling open the door, desperate to find Fiona.

When Bea had left her after their talk, she'd been giddy with anticipation to find Laurence with her possible news. Her courses had always arrived with precision timing, her last only occurring one week prior to the wedding. In the nine weeks since they'd been at Glenhame, she and Laurence had made love daily. Often more than once.

With the men settled in the billiards room, Bea had taken the opportunity to ask Fiona about the signs of pregnancy. Other than her missed monthly, her breasts had become sensitive, but she'd initially attributed that to Laurence's frequent attention.

She never imagined herself wishing for a child.

Until Laurence. To give him a happy, healthy heir seemed the greatest gift she could offer. A child born of their love.

She huffed, more disgusted with herself for believing he cared than Laurence's deceit.

Fiona remained in the nursery, where Bea had left her before the devastating discovery. Fiona's gaze lifted from one of Catriona's painting masterpieces, her eyes smiling with hope that Bea had delivered her news.

One look at Bea, and Fiona's smile vanished, concern replacing the hope and happiness in her eyes. She rose from Catriona's side with a soft word to her daughter, then rushed to pull Bea into her arms.

"What's wrong, lass? Surely he wasnae upset with yer news?"

Bea blinked, trying to clear her vision. "I didn't tell him." She sniffled, wishing, once again, she had a handkerchief. "I heard him say something . . ."

"What? What did ye hear him say?"

How could she admit to Fiona that Laurence had not only married her under duress and obligation, but had wagered he would get her with child? She could hardly believe it herself.

It was so unlike Laurence.

Not her Laurence.

Not the Laurence who believed in doing what was right. In honor and virtue.

What he had done was despicable.

She opted for a less horrible truth.

"His exact words don't matter. He doesn't love me, Fiona. He only married me because he had to. All I am to him is a means to an end."

Fiona wrapped her sturdy arms around Bea, pulling her close and cradling her against her bosom. "I dinnae believe it. He loves ye, lass. He may no ken it, but he does. I see it on his face when he looks at ye."

Bea shook her head, refusing to accept the words of consolation. "No. Fiona. It's all a front. A way to keep up appearances." She swiped away her tears with the back of her hand. "That's what matters to him—appearances and propriety."

Silence settled around Bea as Fiona stroked her back and hair, making shushing sounds of comfort.

She needed time to clear her head—away from Laurence. "May I stay in a different room?"

"Aye. Come with me."

Fiona led her from the nursery to another wing, shooting off at an odd angle from the main hallway at the opposite end from the wing she and Laurence had occupied. Once settled, Bea sat on the bed, waiting for the servants to bring her belongings and wondering what in the world she would do next.

❧

FERGUS GAVE LAURENCE A SOUND SHOVE TOWARD THE DOOR. "Don't jes stand there, man, go after her."

But what could he say to make things right? What she heard was the truth. It was how she interpreted it that was wrong.

Could he really blame her for coming to those conclusions? Their marriage had not been planned. He had presented his proposal more like a business arrangement than a romantic entreaty promising undying love, suggesting they might become friends.

His own wife had to seduce him into bed.

No wonder Bea's logical mind had so quickly latched on to her mistaken belief. All the evidence pointed the accusing finger directly at him.

"I can't Fergus. You heard her. She needs time, wants me to stay away. I should respect her wishes."

"Eejit," Fergus grumbled, pouring himself another whisky.

Yet Bea loved him. Her declaration earlier that day as they lay on the bank of the loch rang in his ears, the words filling his heart with so much joy and happiness it almost burst. He'd always wanted someone to love him desperately. And Bea had.

For a much longer time than he'd even known.

And what had he done?

Mucked it up.

Completely.

Hopelessly.

But irretrievably?

He would not believe that. Wouldn't her love for him allow her to see reason—to forgive him for his foolishness? He'd grovel if he must.

Laurence scrubbed a hand down his face.

He would fix this mess he'd created.

But first, he needed a plan.

Without another word to Fergus, he strode from the room and bounded up the stairs in long strides. Servants rushed past him in the hall, and although they nodded and muttered a soft, "Excuse me, my laird," they kept their eyes downcast, their faces solemn.

When he reached their room, the door stood ajar. He took a deep breath and pushed it open, preparing to throw himself at Bea's feet and beg her forgiveness.

His heart tumbled. The room was empty except for Fanny, who had gathered some of Bea's gowns in her arms.

As Fanny tried to exit the room, Laurence grasped her arm, stopping her. "What's happening, Fanny? Where are you going with Lady Montgomery's clothing?"

Fanny's face flushed, and like the other servants, she would not meet his gaze. "I'm sorry, my lord. I've been instructed not to say."

Usually in command of his emotions, Laurence bristled at the maid's refusal to answer. Worn thin from the events of the day, he barked at the poor woman. "I am your employer, and you *will* answer me."

When tears filled her widened eyes, remorse slammed into him, and his gut twisted in shame at his outburst. "Forgive me, Fanny. I'm concerned about Lady Montgomery."

She nodded. "My lady is well cared for, sir. That's all I'm permitted to say."

He released her arm, and she scurried off, glancing over her shoulder as if he would race after her and grab her again.

As he entered the room, he cast his gaze around. Bea's hairbrush, her hairpins and the vial of fragrance no longer rested on the dressing table. Only a few of her gowns remained in the wardrobe. It's as if someone tried to remove her very presence.

He spun on his heel and headed back out of the room, determined to find where she had gone. At each room, he poked his head in, hoping to find her, only to discover it too was vacant. As he remembered the remaining gowns, he ducked into an empty room, and peeked around the door, waiting impatiently for Fanny to return.

His legs grew weary as he stood by the partially open door.

Finally footsteps approached, and he breathed a sigh of relief. A few minutes later, the footsteps came back from the opposite direction. He waited a few beats, then slipped back into the hallway and silently followed the unsuspecting maid.

Several times, she paused as if sensing his presence and he darted into another empty room, waited a moment, then proceeded on his quest. For once, he cursed the tangled layout of the home as he wove through the maze of wings. As if hitting a solid wall, he came to a halt when Fiona approached from the opposite direction, the scowl on her face enough to stop even a charging bull.

"And jes what do ye ken yer doing?"

Laurence squared his shoulders. Although not wishing to offend his cousin's wife, he would not be bullied by a woman. "I'm looking for my wife. I wish to explain something."

He should have listened to Fergus. Fiona was not to be trifled with. She strode up to him and poked him in the chest. "Ye've done enough already, ye big beast." How she'd managed it, he'd never know, but Fiona grasped him by the shoulders and spun him around. "Now off with ye! I'll not have ye upsetting the lass any more than she already is."

"Bea!" he cried out, twisting around in hope of seeing her. "I only wish to explain."

Sobbing echoed down the hallway, and Fiona sent him a softer look. "Leave her be, Monty. Give her time."

He trudged back down the winding maze toward his now desolate room. Without Bea, all life seemed to have been drained from it.

The bed they shared mocked him, and he threw himself on it, wondering how in the world he would ever make this right.

CHAPTER 25—TORTURED HEARTS

Tears welled in Bea's eyes as Laurence's tortured voice drifted in from the hallway. "Bea! I only wish to explain."

But there was nothing to explain. He'd made his meaning perfectly clear to Fergus. He'd placed a wager not only on completing his machine, but on getting her with child.

How dare he use her so ill?

Curled up like Catpurrnicus in a tight ball on her bed, she wept so hard her body shook. Little did he realize that he'd already succeeded with one of his wagers, and if her ideas proved fruitful, she'd assisted in achieving the other as well.

Countless scenes ran through her mind like a play, all taking on new meaning. Laurence's enthusiasm during the carriage ride. Sharing the view of the night sky from Fergus's telescope. Their lazy lovemaking by the loch where she professed her love and bared her soul.

And what had he done? Returned her words of love with his own?

No.

He'd taken and used her affection for his own gain.

She punched her pillow, then pressed her face to it before releasing a bloodcurdling scream.

At least Middlebury had been open about his views of women. As unsatisfactory as a match with him would have been, at least there had been no risk to her emotions.

Not only had Laurence fractured her heart, he'd destroyed the hope she had of being a true and equal partner to him.

Argh!

She cried until she believed she had no more tears left. Then she cried some more. Her chest ached as if someone had ripped her organs from her body and stomped on them with glee in her presence, leaving a desolate void.

Eventually, she must have dozed off, but fitful, disjointed images filled her sleep. People pointed fingers, not even bothering to wait until she turned her back but rather laughing in her face. In their midst, Laurence stood, proudly holding their newborn babe.

She jolted awake, her skin clammy from perspiration, her stomach lurching again. Bolting to the chamber pot, she dry retched. No moisture remained in her body to yield to the vessel. Her stomach was as empty as her foolish dreams of Laurence's love.

Rays of the morning sun streamed in from the window. Crumpled on the floor by the chamber pot, she reached up and fumbled for her spectacles on the bedside table, then glanced at the clock on the mantle. Seven twenty-three. Unable to move farther, she lay on the hard floor, listening to the sounds of the outside world. Apparently, life had the audacity to continue on even in the midst of her misfortune.

A soft knock at her door caught her attention.

"Go away," she said, her voice cracked and dry. She crawled toward her bed, her legs wobbly and refusing to support her, but she managed to pull herself upright.

"Bea, please," Laurence called from outside the door. "Please speak with me."

She collapsed half on the bed, her legs dangling over the side. She repeated her command, doing her best to sound forceful. "Go away."

Ignoring her, he cracked the door and peeked around the corner.

A muttered curse sprang from her lips that she'd forgotten to lock it. She squeezed her eyes tight, refusing to allow the sight of him to sway her resolve.

"Bea!" He raced to her side. "What happened?" He lifted her gently and placed her entire body upon the bed. Thank goodness she remained fully dressed, having been too upset to change into her nightclothes, instead sending Fanny away.

After forcing one eyelid open, she chanced a glimpse at him, hoping to keep her feelings at bay, yet knowing full well the gamble was a fool's bet she would lose.

Good Galileo. He looked worse than she felt. His disheveled hair stuck up at odd angles, he wore no cravat and his shirt hung open, exposing his neck and the top of his chest. Stubble from a morning beard still covered his cheeks and chin.

Yet with one look in his eyes, her heart stuttered, reminding her it still beat in her chest.

He appeared positively—haunted.

With gentle movements, he dipped a cloth in a bowl of water and wiped her brow. "Bea. Are you ill? You're so pale." He darted a glance at the chamber pot. "Should I send for a physician?"

She shook her head, her dry mouth unable to form the words.

As if sensing her discomfort, he poured a glass of water, and placing his hand behind her head, lifted it while raising the glass to her lips. "Drink."

After taking a small sip, she pushed the glass away. "Thank you," she said, her voice still cracking.

"Bea, please let me explain."

New tears sprang forth as if the water replenished her reservoir, but she managed to gather her courage. "Explain what? I'm the fool here, believing our marriage could be real, that you . . . cared."

ACTIONS HAVE CONSEQUENCES. THE WORDS HAMMERED IN LAURENCE'S mind as if trying to get through his thick skull. Memories barreled forward of his childhood indiscretion when, at fourteen, he'd sneaked from his dormitory after hours to wreak havoc in town with his friends. Angry fingers pointing, harsh words hurled his way. All culminating in his vow to never break the rules again.

And yet, he had.

Egregiously.

By wagering using his marriage. His own wife.

"I do care, Bea. Truly."

Her eyes flashed with fire. Restrained anger practically bubbled beneath the surface. How could he expect her to believe him after what he'd done? How could he show her how sorry he was for his actions?

He grasped her hand, lifting it to his face. "Strike me."

She blinked, the tears welling in her eyes breaking free and rolling down her cheeks. "Wha . . . what?"

"Strike me. Hard. I deserve it. Slap me. Perhaps it might make you feel better." He braced himself for the impact.

She jerked her hand away, her expression dumbstruck. When she lowered her hand, he relaxed.

Without warning, she drew back and slapped him soundly across the face.

Pain radiated across his cheek, and his eyes watered from the sting. "Again," he said. "Harder."

He closed his eyes to prevent himself from preparing. Better that it be unexpected. He needed the punishment of the pain.

She slapped him soundly again, then her fists beat against his chest as she sobbed uncontrollably. The force of her blows lessened, and he opened his eyes, his own heart breaking at the agony on her face. The blows became mere taps, slowing in rhythm and force until she collapsed against the very chest she had attacked.

He wrapped his arms around her and held her. "I'm so very sorry, Bea. I should have told you immediately and explained. I have no excuse other than being caught up in the wonder of you and not wishing to spoil it."

She hiccuped a mumbled, "Why?"

"Because I'm a stubborn and proud fool." He lifted her chin with his forefinger, needing to meet her gaze when he confessed. "Nash goaded me. I told you the part about the motor, but I stupidly kept the other from you."

He offered a handkerchief he'd pulled from his pocket. "You never seem to have one of these."

She emitted a strangled little sound, somewhat of a mix between a laugh and a cry.

After she had wiped the tears from her face, he continued. "I understand women like to gossip."

At her confused expression, he rushed to clarify. "Not you." He sent her a sad smile. "But I do have a mother and a sister. My point is, men are not unlike women in some respects. However, they have a different way of going about things. When I went to White's the day after our wedding, several other gentlemen expressed . . . surprise that I was not at home with you."

Lines formed on her forehead as her brows drew together.

"To be indelicate, consummating our marriage."

"Oh." The soft utterance of the word accompanied by her blush conveyed her comprehension.

"Nash was among them, and he implied . . . that perhaps I was incapable." Although not wishing to keep anything further from her, he refused to tell her how Nash offered his own services.

"Oh!" she said, this time much louder. "He insulted your . . . manhood?"

"Yes. And I foolishly took the bait, wagering that I would not only complete my machine but get you with child by the end of the year."

He struggled to continue, pathetically hoping to redeem himself. "I regretted it immediately. But . . ." He shook his head, finally breaking eye contact with her.

"It was too late."

"Yes," he answered, still refusing to look at her, to witness the disgust in her eyes. "I didn't mean it the way it appears. And when we . . . when you showed me how wonderful being with you could be, the guilt of my wager ate at me. How could I tell you? I prayed you would never find out. It wouldn't matter if I won or lost. My only concern was you." He finally raised his gaze to hers. "*Is* you."

Her hand drew back again and this time he did brace himself. Yet instead of a strike, she rested her hand gently against his cheek and rubbed the sting away.

Wetness formed in his eyes, not from pain, but from gratitude. "Can you forgive me?" He took her hand and kissed her palm.

"I'll do my best."

It's all he could ask.

꧁꧂

TRY AS SHE MIGHT, BEA COULDN'T STAY ANGRY WITH HIM. HER LOVE for him overrode her own pride and pain. But could she forgive him so easily for what he had done?

Was it foolish? Certainly.

Prideful? Absolutely.

Forgivable? Of that, she wasn't certain.

The dejected expression on his face tugged at her heart. Yet she stood her ground. "It will take me time. Can you be patient?"

She thought of the life possibly growing inside her and how it would fulfill that portion of his wager. As punishment, she held the information back.

Was it spiteful? Perhaps.

Did he deserve more than a few slaps? Possibly.

But Bea had her own pride. For so long, she'd felt unworthy and unwanted. No matter what she did, it hadn't been good enough. Hadn't her mother reminded her on a daily basis?

Beatrix, your embroidery is atrocious. You shall have to pull each stitch out and begin anew.

Beatrix, one must listen attentively to a gentleman's topics of conversation and not interrupt to correct him.

Beatrix, why are your fingers forever marred with ink?

The realization hit her like the bolt of lightning she had proposed for Laurence's machine. Achievements didn't make you worthy. Who you are determines your worth. Simply being who you are—being accepted for who you are.

To give him one of the things he'd gambled on would certainly make her rise in his esteem. But she wanted to do so for who she was, not for what she did.

She remained silent with her news. She only hoped he would declare his love before she grew too large to hide it.

"Very well." He nodded and rose from her bedside. "I'll be out in the garden painting should you need me." As he strode toward the door, his broad shoulders slumped, and the urge to call him back to her bed poked at her pride.

Yet she resisted. Constantly relying on a physical relationship to heal the rift between them did nothing but avoid the actual issue. Besides, she had her own project to occupy her time.

When the door closed with a soft snick behind him, Bea rose and rummaged through the escritoire for paper, determined to channel her energy into something productive.

At first it had been difficult to concede Laurence's point about lightning being both too volatile and unpredictable to use as a power source. But as she contemplated and focused on the issue of the hydrogen bubbles, she grew more confident it was solvable.

What chemical reaction could neutralize the hydrogen produced by the first? And how would she keep them from mixing but allow them to interact? Her mind whirred with possibilities.

With a flash of inspiration, she jotted down her notes, hoping to secure the materials necessary to experiment using various combinations. A warm glow filled her chest as if the very sun illuminated her body. Regardless of the success or failure of her idea, her confidence in herself rose.

She wouldn't solve the problem for him or for his wager.

She would solve it for herself.

CHAPTER 26—O.B.

After spending two days secluded in her bedroom, even to the point of taking all her meals in private, Bea needed a change of scenery and ventured to the downstairs study. Relieved to find it empty, she took a seat at the escritoire.

Rare sunlight streamed in from the open windows overlooking the terraced grounds behind the house. Autumn approached, the crisp scent of the air and sunny cheerfulness tempting her enough to risk the possibility of encountering Laurence. True to his word, he had kept his distance, giving her time.

She still hadn't forgiven him, but she longed for someone with whom to discuss her ideas—someone who would understand and appreciate them. Although Fiona was a charming woman and did her best to feign interest in Bea's long discourses on science, her eyes would soon develop a far-away look Bea knew only too well. With a sigh, Fiona would apologize, stating she needed to tend to Catriona.

Her abrupt departures didn't offend Bea. In fact, Fiona's excuses had the opposite effect, and Bea would place a hand on her abdomen, wondering if she, too, would have to put aside more interesting pursuits to tend to her babe. Such was a woman's lot, she presumed. But by her calculations, she had at least seven months to use wisely before she had to devote herself to motherhood.

Warmth flooded her chest as she finished the article for *The Times* she intended to submit once her experiments proved successful. With her pen poised above the foolscap, she nodded in satisfaction, then added her signature. O.B.

A gentle breeze drifted in, bringing with it the sound of Catriona's excited shriek. Bea rose and rushed toward the window. Catriona darted onto the terrace from the side of the house, giggling furiously and coaxing a smile to Bea's lips. A growling noise followed.

Bea's mind struggled to reconcile the juxtaposition of the threatening sound and the child's laughter. She leaned to the side, trying to obtain a better view, worried that a wayward animal had stumbled onto the grounds from the nearby woods. A protective instinct set Bea's nerves on edge. Was the girl unaware of the potential danger? Surely the child's nanny or one of her parents was nearby to protect her.

Catriona shrieked again, running down the terrace steps onto the grassy area of the gardens. The growling grew louder, and Bea's worry increased, until Laurence appeared from the shadows of the house, crouched down, his hands curled into claws as he raced toward the laughing child. Catriona squealed as she slipped from his grasp. With another fierce growl, he lunged for her again, this time catching her and spinning her around until both fell to the ground in gales of laughter.

Bea's heart melted. Regardless of his feelings for her, Laurence would love their child and be a wonderful father. And if they were blessed with a girl, surely he would accept her for who she was. How could she withhold the news from him?

As if sensing she had witnessed his raucous behavior, he propped himself on one elbow, his gaze rising to meet hers. A wayward lock of hair fell carelessly onto his forehead from his exertions. Although it gave him a decidedly rakish appearance, he brushed it aside, presumably to make himself more presentable.

She lifted a hand in greeting, giving a little wave.

After saying something to Catriona, who nodded in response, he stood, brushing grass from his trousers. For a moment he remained stationary, as if fearing to break the spell, then took a tentative step forward. Apparently encouraged she didn't back away in disgust, he neared the window, stopping a short distance before it.

"Bea? I didn't realize you were there."

On closer inspection, what she presumed had been a ruddy complexion from his rough and tumble play with Catriona, she now understood as embarrassment, the telltale sign of his reddened ears giving him away.

In an attempt to put him at ease, she said, "Your play with Catriona appeared most enjoyable. It's good to hear laughter for a change."

He winced and dropped his gaze to his feet. "I'd almost forgotten how."

Her heart squeezed. He'd misinterpreted her comment. "Children have a way of making us forget our troubles, if only for a while." The words reminded her of the life inside her, and her hand automatically moved to caress her abdomen. Was it fair to keep it from him, regardless of his sins?

"Is something wrong?" he asked, his voice tremulous with genuine concern.

"Nothing . . . additional . . . is wrong. I do, however, wish to speak with you."

"Very well." He took another step closer to the window.

Catriona skipped up to the terrace. Her little eyebrows rose above her widened eyes, and her head shifting with interest between Laurence and Bea.

The words Bea wished to say refused to come. Her gaze darted to Catriona, standing by Laurence's side. Bea couldn't simply blurt out that she was increasing with the child in earshot. "May I speak with you privately?"

His face remained guarded, but he nodded. "Give me but a moment." He bent down to the child and, with gentle words, promised they would continue their game at a later time.

Bea paced the length of the study as she waited for Laurence to arrive. Nervous tension coiled in her stomach as she wondered how he would receive the news. He'd be happy, no doubt, but would the prospect of fulfilling that part of his wager overshadow his happiness at the prospect of an heir?

That much remained in question, and it pained her to consider the possibility. Would the tender shoots of forgiveness just burgeoning in her heart be uprooted so easily?

He would have no idea of the news she planned to convey. Would he? Did he understand enough about a woman's body to wonder why, until recently, she hadn't put him off once during their ten weeks of marriage?

By the time Laurence stepped into the study, her stomach roiled, threatening to reject the meager slice of toast she'd managed to keep down that morning. Desperation filled her to find a private place to succumb to the nausea.

"Bea?" he said, his face etched with worry. "What's wrong?"

"Nothing. Wait here. I'll only be a moment." She raced from the room. Panic seized her as her stomach lurched. Barely making it to the necessary room, she dashed inside, reaching the receptacle in the nick of time.

She placed trembling hands against the wall to steady herself, spitting the remaining foul taste from her mouth. Sweat dotted her brow, and her knees grew weak. On shaky limbs, she made it to a chaise longue in the outer sitting room and rested briefly, trying to recover her composure.

Regaining some strength, she rose and glanced in the mirror on the wall. Oh, how she wanted to be radiant when she gave Laurence the news, not a sickly green or pasty white complexion. Weren't expectant women supposed to glow? Leave it to her. She couldn't even do pregnancy right.

In an attempt to bring color to her face, she pinched her cheeks as her mother had taught her, the action only causing odd red blotches on her pale complexion. She shrugged and turned back toward the study to inform her husband of his impending fatherhood.

When she arrived, Laurence stood facing the escritoire, his back toward her. She took a deep breath and stepped inside the room, the rustling of her skirts announcing her presence.

The smile on her lips vanished as he turned.

❦

BEA'S GAZE DARTED TO THE PARCHMENT LAURENCE HELD BETWEEN his fingers.

Her latest submission.

Signed O.B.

His eyes flashed with something she'd never witnessed from him. He thrust the paper forward, slicing the air. "What's the meaning of this, Bea?"

"I . . . I . . . where did you find that?"

"On the escritoire." He turned, tossing it carelessly back where he'd found it. "Care to tell me how you came to possess an article by the elusive O.B.?"

In her excitement at finding him with Catriona and the prospect of telling him her news, she'd completely forgotten she'd left it on the desk. She swallowed the Catpurrnicus-sized lump in her throat. It would serve no purpose to lie to him any longer. She would face this like a . . . woman.

Pulling herself to her full five-foot-three inch height, she squared her shoulders. "I'm O.B. I've been writing articles for more than two years. If I thought they'd be accepted, I would submit them as myself."

He slumped against the escritoire behind him and ran a hand through his thick hair. "It's simply not done," he muttered. The sadness in his eyes as they lifted to meet hers broke her heart. "What else haven't you told me?"

The time for lies and secrets had ended. "I've attended lectures at the Royal Society. Dressed as a boy."

Color drained from his face. "With Timothy." It wasn't a question. He obviously remembered seeing them together.

"Yes."

He shook his head. "This goes too far. I can't condone it."

245

Icy pain lanced her heart. "You can't . . . *condone* it?" Tears blurred her vision. "I believed you were different. But you're no better than Middlebury with his pompous 'women should be lovely ornaments.' It's fine if I ooh and ahh over your ideas, praise you for your attempts, but I'm to remain silent about my own? To hold the gift inside me like it's an abomination? Do I need your *permission* to do anything outside the purview of what's expected as *proper* behavior for a lady? *Like a child?*"

Pressure built in her head, pounding at her temples as if the very ideas themselves sought to escape from his harsh disapprobation. The anger in his eyes chilled her, and she withheld the one secret that might have softened his heart.

She glared at him, not sure she had ever really known him. "Since you find my true self so distasteful, I shall remove myself from your presence." She spun on her heel, heading for the door.

"Bea, wait. Stay."

She halted but didn't turn.

"Why O.B.? What does it stand for?"

"How everyone views me. Insignificant. Worthless. Only Bea. I intend to prove you wrong." With her head held high, she quit the room, slamming the door behind her.

She would show him. She would show them all!

⚜

STILL SLUMPED AGAINST THE DELICATE PIECE OF FURNITURE, Laurence scrubbed a hand down his face. *Dear God, is that truly how she sees herself? Only?*

Upon finding it, the shock of the signature had prevented him from reading the entire article. All his mind could comprehend were the initials O.B. written in Bea's delicate hand.

All the signs had been there—if he'd chosen to see them. The pair of breeches she'd worn as they worked together on the machine, saying she'd borrowed them from a stable boy. The depth of familiarity with the articles that went beyond what a reader would have remembered. Her knowledge of mechanical and electrical engineering.

Had he purposely ignored them? Afraid to admit to himself that his own *wife* had breached the rules of society, stretched them so far as to rip them into shreds? Surpassed him in intelligence? His well-ordered, structured life had not only been changed. It had been destroyed.

By Bea.

Almost relieved when she ignored his feeble plea to remain, he needed time to process this deluge of information. And, for the time being, he would keep his distance. They both required cool heads before they could discuss how to proceed.

Yes. Time and space would do them both good.

He strode from the room and ordered a horse to be saddled and brought to the front of the house. A brisk ride along the winding paths of Fergus's estate would clear his head.

What started as a peaceful trot quickly turned into a frantic gallop, the passing scenery only reminding him of the joys he'd experienced with Bea.

Late blooming heather in the meadow where they'd frolicked like children and he'd arranged stalks of the flowers in her red hair.

The tree where he'd carved their initials into an old willow.

Their lovemaking by the lake both frenzied and sweet.

The odd squeezing sensation gripped his chest yet again. He reined the horse to a halt, then absentmindedly rubbed the area of discomfort, filing the occasion away for later examination.

He kicked the horse into a flying pace, knowing that no matter how far or fast he went, he'd never outrun Bea.

CHAPTER 27—WHEN RULES BREAK

Hours had passed and night had fallen by the time Laurence returned to the house. Sweat beaded his forehead and dripped down the collar of his shirt. He'd removed his neckcloth and used it to wipe his face, grateful no one witnessed that the moisture he'd removed contained more than perspiration.

He poked his head into the library, hoping to find Bea and praying she had calmed so they could mend the rift between them with a few chosen words, and—perhaps—less loquacious actions.

Fergus lifted his head, moving his gaze from the book he held to meet Laurence's.

"She's no here," Fergus said.

Laurence bit back the retort and remained civil. "Is she in her room?"

"Nae. Packed a bag and left the estate hours ago. Said ye would ken why."

Left? Panic slid up Laurence's spine, edging away the exhaustion. "What? Where? You didn't ask?"

"I didnae want tae pry." A sheepish expression crossed Fergus's face. "Besides, the wee creature looked verra angry. I feared for ma life."

Despite his growing concern, Laurence snorted a laugh at his cousin's expression. "Did she say when she would return?" Unease rooted in Laurence's chest, taking a strong foothold as Fergus shook his head.

"Nothing at all?" Laurence cringed at the pleading tone in his voice. Gentlemen did *not* beg.

Fergus rose and stretched his long legs. "I'm sorry, lad. She was hell bent tae get out of here. I loaned her my carriage tae take her and her maid tae the nearest coaching inn in Edinburgh."

Bitterness rose to Laurence's mouth. To borrow a carriage from Fergus instead of taking one of their own? Did her actions convey a hidden meaning?

Fergus delivered a solid thump to Laurence's back. "Take heart. Women are flighty creatures. She'll most likely return in the morra, all smiles and kisses. Now, I'm off tae bed."

Would she? Laurence wasn't so certain. Bea wasn't any woman, and he would never use flighty to describe her. Determined, focused, independent. But never flighty. His body fell onto the soft cushions of the sofa.

He stared at the ceiling until his eyelids grew heavy and his mind fogged, surrendering to blackness.

Bea patted his cheek, and he couldn't help but smile even though his neck hurt like the devil. She'd returned and forgiven him! He rubbed the sleep from his eyes to find a pair as blue as the summer sky staring at him.

"Why are ye sleeping here?" little Catriona asked, her hand clutching a half-eaten sausage. "Dinnae ye like yer bed?"

Daylight streamed from the large windows. He'd spent the entire night on the sofa. "Have you seen Lady Montgomery this morning?

Catriona shook her head, her yellow curls bobbing. "I like her."

Laurence pulled himself to a sitting position, his body stiff from his awkward position on the sofa. "I do, too."

The child tugged at his arm. "You promised tae pretend tae be the loch monster again."

Memories of the ugly confrontation with Bea cascaded through his mind like a chain reaction.

Moments of laughter playing with Catriona.

The fleeting hope when Bea requested to speak with him before his world collapsed.

Finding the article.

Her confession.

His adamant refusal to accept what she had done.

Without another word to the waiting child before him, he stormed out of the library to search the house for Bea, hoping against hope that she'd returned. Quiet dread filled him with each empty room and each negative response from the servants when he enquired about his wife's whereabouts.

He saved her room for last, knowing its emptiness would confirm the finality of her departure.

Her room. Not *their* room. The sting of it more powerful than her blows to his face and chest.

After drawing a deep breath and saying a brief prayer, he tapped on the half-open door.

There was no response.

A spark of hope ignited in his chest as he cast his gaze about the room, landing on the open doors of the clothes press with Bea's gowns folded neatly inside. Would she leave her gowns if she hadn't planned to return?

The spark sputtered and died when he stepped forward for closer inspection to find her wedding gown and the lovely green gown she'd worn on the nights of the masquerade and their compromise. A strangled cry rose in his throat.

But a gentleman didn't weep.

He swallowed the urge, and his body roared in protest, begging for release.

Every bone in his body seemed to have disappeared, and he dropped to the bed for support.

To taunt him, sunlight streamed in the window, shining happy rays across the room. From the corner of his eye, something glinted, and he turned, seeking the source.

He would have wagered he could not feel any worse. And the mere idea of wagering soured his stomach once again. But there, on

Bea's dressing table, sat her wedding ring. The simple band of gold he'd purchased for her.

Unbidden, he rose from the bed and strode toward the ring as if it beckoned him. As he lifted it, examining its simplicity, Bea's words rang in his ears.

Insignificant. Worthless.

Only Bea.

Hadn't he shown her he cared?

How could she do this to him?

Damnation!

He flung the ring across the room.

LAURENCE'S MOOD CONTINUED TO SOUR WITH EACH PASSING MOMENT that Bea did not return. The crackling fire in the library's hearth did nothing to remove the chill from his heart. He scrutinized the amber liquid in the glass as if it contained the answers. However, he'd been studying it throughout the evening without success. The only result he would obtain from the Scottish whisky, albeit smooth and delicious, would be a rousing headache in the morning.

He met Fergus's concerned gaze. "She lied to me, Fergus. For weeks, she hid the fact that she's been penning scientific articles for *The Times*. Prior to our marriage, she'd even dressed in men's clothing to attend lectures at the Royal Society."

He shook his head as if it would remove the whole untenable situation. "It is unacceptable, breaking every rule."

"Are ye more upset she—as ye say—broke the rules, or she failed tae tell ye?"

Laurence prepared to respond, his mouth opening to deliver a sound refusal that she'd wounded him by keeping it secret. It would be a lie. He was wounded.

Deeply.

Profoundly.

She'd betrayed him.

He raked a shaky hand through his hair. "Both. But I suppose I object more on the principle of the matter. Rules are meant to keep society safe, organized, functioning at the optimum. Rules have been my guiding star my entire life."

A snort came from Fiona's direction where she sat by the window, working on a delicate piece of embroidery. "Mayhap that's yer problem," she muttered.

He'd forgotten she was there. "Rules are not a *problem*, Fiona. You can't go breaking the rules because they don't suit your purpose."

Fergus shot him a cautionary look. Laurence was unsure if it was meant to convey Fergus's displeasure or warn him of Fiona's impending wrath.

With a lift of a shoulder, Fiona continued. "The way I see it, Bea had no choice but tae keep things secret. Tae break the rules. Dae ye no ken she would wish tae be recognized fer such wonderful ideas?"

The embroidery fell to her lap, freeing her hands to gesture wildly. "But no! Men are what's kept her mouth locked." She pointed a finger at Laurence. "Men like ye and yer precious rules!"

He understood why Catriona toed the line—and Fergus's warning.

Ignoring the finger and the glaring look from Fergus, he continued, "But she didn't tell me!"

"Och! Because she couldnae! The wee creature loves ye, wants tae please ye. But ye cannae stop her from being herself. Twould be cruel."

Laurence blinked, processing the truth of Fiona's words. How stifling it would be to have a gift you couldn't use. To pretend to be something other than what you were.

He argued his defense. "But I would have understood."

A chill as brisk as a winter's day settled on him from Fiona's glare. She rose, throwing her embroidery down, her hands planted on her hips. "Would ye now? Like yer understandin' at the moment?"

She stormed from the room, uttering a final, "Eejits, all of ye!" before she slammed the door behind her.

Fergus shook his head. "Now ye done it. Couldnae keep yer trap shut." He stood and stretched. "I'll leave ye to yer thoughts. Ye may consider finding yer wife and doing some groveling."

Loud banging echoed throughout the house, and Fergus raised his gaze to the ceiling. "I best be doing some groveling of ma own." With a last fortifying drink of whisky, he left Laurence alone with his thoughts.

Could he do it, bend the rules and not break them? Would his orderly, well-structured world survive?

Knowing there was only one way to find out, he penned the necessary correspondence he needed to find Bea.

LAURENCE STARED OUT THE WINDOW AT THE IDYLLIC SETTING BEFORE him, but it did not bring him peace. His own soul had been in turmoil. Eight days had passed, and Bea had not returned.

Nor had he received any response to his letters to family and friends, not to mention Bea herself, as to her whereabouts, although he'd barely given it time considering the distance it would take for the post.

Had she returned to London? Would his letter to her reach her there? Perhaps she'd returned to her family's country estate in Wiltshire, leaving him in both presence *and* spirit?

Even Fergus could not elevate his mood, try as he might.

As Laurence's anger cooled, he returned to the article, finally reading it and doing his best to separate the identity of the author from the piece itself. As always, the precision and clarity of the chosen words elevated the article from merely informative to brilliant. Laurence rubbed his chest, the odd tightening sensation not quite painful, but still uncomfortable.

Cataloging the times he'd experienced the pain, they all contained one common factor.

Bea.

Each time he'd either been thinking of her, gazing at her, holding her in his arms, remembering moments he shared with her.

It led to one undeniable conclusion.

He loved her.

The irony of the moment unsettled him, pulling him further from his structured existence. She'd not only destroyed everything he held dear, but she'd taken his heart in the process.

Once again, he stared at the signature. O.B.

Only Bea.

Her assessment of herself haunted him.

Were the ideas presented less brilliant? Less eloquently phrased? Made any less important? Because she was a woman?

Would he have done any differently had he been born a woman instead of a man?

Many questions. One answer.

No.

Worse, her angry words ricocheted in his mind. *You're no better than Middlebury.*

Accusing him.

Condemning him.

He had no defense.

Guilty as charged.

He'd bared his soul to her when he confessed how his painting afforded him the freedom to be himself and not the image he projected to the world.

And she had understood.

Did she deserve any less?

How she must hate him. He hated himself for words he couldn't take back. For pain inflicted in anger.

Why?

Because his fragile manhood had been threatened? Was protecting his carefully constructed view of the world more important than the happiness of the woman he loved?

"Argh!" With one furious swipe, he flung the items on top of the escritoire to the floor. Ink splattered on the Aubusson carpet and papers flew in the air, floating down and landing in uneven piles not unlike his now chaotic life.

He collapsed back against the chair, expecting to find his world falling apart.

It remained solid around him. Unchanged.

No. That wasn't quite true. It had changed. The sun streaming through the windows seemed brighter, more welcoming. The warmth of it on his skin more pleasant. Catriona's bubbling laughter more joyful. Smell of baking bread drifting from the kitchen more comforting. All his senses heightened. The only thing missing was the sweetness of Bea's lips.

"Sir?" A footman stood at the open doorway, his eyes darting to the room's disarray. "I knocked."

Had he truly been so lost in his thoughts?

He motioned the man forward.

The footman held out a silver salver. "Post arrived for ye, sir."

Without even thanking the footman, Laurence ripped open the correspondence with eager fingers. A letter from Miranda.

Dear Laurence,

We were distressed to learn of Beatrix's departure from Scotland. I made some inquiries and discovered Beatrix has requested some odd materials to be delivered to your townhouse in London.

I wrote and received no response.

My own concern rising, I stopped by, but the servants said she was unavailable to take callers. They seemed quite nervous, my dear, as if they had taken an oath of secrecy.

I could have sworn I saw someone on top of your roof.

Laurence, what has happened?

Your devoted sister,

Miranda

In a panic, Laurence searched the jumble of discarded papers that mimicked the morass of his mind. His fingers finally latched onto the article, and he reread it carefully. The idea was still brilliant, no doubt, but with Miranda's message, it took on a completely new meaning. The final piece of the puzzle slid into place with a resounding *click.*

Bea planned on creating the power source herself.

To save his sorry hide and prove her worth to him.

One slight detail had caught his attention at the last read. The substance suggested for the secondary solution could be unstable. Had she realized that?

Dear God, he must stop her!

CHAPTER 28—WHAT MATTERS MOST

Bea's return trip to London had little in common with the
pleasant journey to Scotland. Rather than passing time in her
husband's arms, she spent the majority fighting the never-ending
nausea that rose with every jar and bump along the road—which
were many. When she obtained passage on a mail coach in
Edinburgh, the accompanying passengers gave her as wide a berth
as possible, urging her to sit by the window of the carriage.

Fiona had insisted Bea take the money she offered for lodging
and coach fare, grumbling about the idiocy of men the entire time.
Bea didn't disagree, and she promised to pay Fiona back in full once
she could secure more funds from her articles.

"Bah!" Fiona had said. "We womenfolk need tae stick together.
Fergus can afford tae spare a few pounds."

Unbenown to Fiona, Fergus himself had forced money on Bea
as well, telling her to spend the night in Edinburgh, think things
over, then return.

"He's an eejit, lass, there's no doubt. But he's a good eejit."

As well meaning as Fergus had been, Bea couldn't in good
conscience return to Glenhame. It would take more than one night
at an inn to solve her and Laurence's problems.

She'd taken little with her. Her clothing, personal items, and her few cherished books. Stubborn pride had led her to remove her wedding ring, leaving it behind, along with the two gowns that held special meaning, as a message to her husband. She did, however, relent and tuck the sketch Laurence had drawn during their journey to Scotland into her valise. Each night she pulled it out, wondering how she could have been so mistaken.

By the time she arrived back in London, although still brokenhearted, she had resolved to not be the one who apologized. Laurence would have to admit his error. If he did not, so be it. She would give him one child, then live the remainder of their marriage as she supposed many in the aristocracy did—separately.

Admittedly, it pained her to think Laurence would seek pleasure elsewhere. That part of their marriage had been nearly perfect, and she sighed with the memories. The only thing sullying it was his blasted wager.

When she arrived at the townhouse, Essie's eyes widened. "My lady, we didn't expect you back so soon." She gazed around Fanny. "But where is Lord Montgomery?"

"He decided to remain in Scotland," Bea answered, not willing to provide more information. "Where is Catpurrnicus?"

Familiar sounds of mewing and skittering claws lifted Bea's spirits, as the black ball of fur raced toward her, practically leaping into her arms. She cuddled him to her chest. "I've missed you so much," she said, placing a kiss on the little white dot of his head.

Essie reminded her only a few servants remained to care for the house, asking if Bea would require more to be hired temporarily. Bea informed her it wouldn't be necessary, that her needs were few, but she would require a footman to purchase some items for her.

After settling into her room, Bea organized her plans to begin her experiments. First, she needed to find the exact solution to use. During the journey home, a shadow of doubt had filled her mind that the chemicals she proposed in the portentous article might prove too volatile. Inspiration filled her that zinc sulfate rather than sulfuric acid might prove to be a much more stable solution.

Once the footman had procured her supplies, she began testing the exact combination of solutions necessary to achieve the desired results. With any luck, she would have success before Michaelmas.

She refused to become discouraged when attempt after attempt proved unsuccessful. To further blacken her mood, thoughts of Laurence broke her concentration. A dull ache formed in her chest. It would be an empty victory if he was not there to share it with her.

CLOTHES SCATTERED ACROSS THE BED AND THE FLOOR AS LAURENCE hastily threw items into a valise.

"Sir, allow me," Stevens said, his normally droll voice shaking. He held out his hands, but Laurence pushed him away.

"Time is of the essence. We can't waste any of it for tidy packing." Laurence examined a waistcoat and carelessly tossed it into the valise. A few pairs of trousers, some shirts, and an extra waistcoat would be sufficient. He would continue to wear the same coat he currently had on. If people commented on his lack of wardrobe, so be it.

Not meeting Stevens' disapproving glare, Laurence snapped the valise shut. "You may pack the rest. Have a maid pack up Lady Montgomery's belongings—the few that remain," he mumbled the last, the pain of it still too fresh.

His hand slid absentmindedly over his coat pocket holding Bea's wedding ring. "When finished, gather the rest of my staff and return to London."

Stevens' eyes widened, the horror of the idea clear on his blanched face. "But, sir, I should accompany you."

Laurence shook his head. "There's no time. I must leave now. I'll take my carriage as far as Edinburgh, then send it back for you, you'll need both carriages for the trunks and my motor. I'm putting you in charge to ensure it's secured properly. Once in Edinburgh, I'll obtain a seat on a mail coach for the rest of the journey."

"But . . . but . . . sir," Stevens blustered. "A mail coach?" The man spit out the words as if the taste of them fouled his mouth.

"It was good enough for Lady Montgomery. It will be good

enough for me." Laurence stormed from the room, ignoring Stevens' continued protests.

Fergus, Fiona, and Catriona waited at the bottom of the long staircase.

"Goodbye, cousin," Laurence said, grasping Fergus's meaty hand. "Wish me luck."

"Aye, lad," Fergus said, pulling him into a hug.

Fiona kissed him on the cheek. "I'm glad ye came tae yer senses."

Catriona lifted a parchment. "I made this for ye Cousin Monty."

Vibrant colors of blues, greens, and yellows covered the surface. Laurence squinted, trying to decipher the image.

"It's Cousin Bea. Cannae ye tell? I made it fer ye tae keep ye company."

Ah, yes. A dot of red at the top of the figure wearing a green blob of a dress. Laurence squatted before the child. "It's beautiful. I shall treasure it."

As the Kincaids waved goodbye, Laurence dashed out the door, tossed his valise inside the compartment, and climbed in, saying a final prayer that he wouldn't be too late.

❧

RAIN POURED DOWN IN HEAVY CURTAINS, OBSCURING LAURENCE'S view of the passing countryside from the post chaise window. A jagged flash of lightning split the night sky, striking perilously close to the carriage and illuminating an ominous mountain of clouds overhead. Before he could even count off the seconds, the subsequent crack of thunder followed.

Laurence gripped the seat cushion as the carriage shook violently, his knuckles whitening. The sound of the frenzied horses filled the small compartment, and the pungent odor of mud mixed with the chemical scent of the storm.

Before he could brace himself further, wood cracked. The carriage lurched viciously, tilting at a precarious angle.

Thrown against the side of the compartment, Laurence

struggled to straighten himself, crawling along the seat to grasp at the left door. Pulling himself up, he clambered out of the carriage. Heavy pellets of rain sliced at his face, and he wiped at his eyes, trying to clear his vision.

One of the wheels had broken, the others were mired deep in the muddy ruts of the road. The postilion tried his best to calm the frightened horses and glanced up as Laurence approached. "Best get back inside, guvn'r. The storm won't be stopping any time soon, and you ain't goin' nowhere until I get help."

Once he set upon a course of action, Laurence would not be deterred—certainly not from a broken carriage. He must get to Bea. He'd been on the road for two days, not bothering to rest at a coaching inn. Rather, he'd hired another coach and pressed on. He was almost there. He'd come too far to give up.

The man was correct on one account. The rain showed no sign of ending. As far as not going anywhere, it was obvious the carriage itself would not be their conveyance any time soon.

Holding out a hand, he approached the horses—their eyes so wide they appeared only to be the whites.

"I'd stay back," the postilion said, unharnessing the left horse.

"I have a way with animals. Allow me to try." With another tentative step, he shushed the frightened beasts, brushing the post horse's soft muzzle. Slowly, they began to calm as he whispered assurances to them.

The postilion shook his head, rain flinging from his hat. "Well, I'll be damned."

"Allow me to take him," Laurence said, doing his best to keep the pleading from his voice. "I'll stop at the nearest inn and send help back. I presume that's what you were planning?"

The postilion shook his head, rain sluicing from the brim of his hat. "I'm not sure that's a good idea. I'm used to riding in this weather."

Laurence tried another tactic. "Please . . . what's your name?"

"Bertie."

"Please, Bertie. You've seen how I calmed the horse. I'm an excellent rider." The pleading no longer restrained, Laurence pressed further. "I can't waste time waiting. I'll pay for the horse, the repair for the carriage, whatever you ask. But I must get to London immediately. I'm Viscount Montgomery and my father is the Earl of Easton." He hated using his rank, but even he had his limits.

Several minutes later, after a heated debate with Bertie and providing instructions where to send his valise, Laurence mounted the post horse. Not as comfortable as his custom-made saddle in the stables of Dunbar House, his family's estate in Dorset, but it would have to do. With another soothing word to the horse and a nudge from his boots, he encouraged the mount forward in the pouring rain.

Progress remained slow, and the horse reared several times when the sky brightened with lightning, the claps of thunder reverberating up and down his own spine. How he managed to hold the reins with one hand while wiping the rain from his face and eyes, he would never know. Sheer determination and love propelled him forward, coaxing the horse through each torturous step.

Finally reaching a coaching inn, he handed the poor beast off to the ostler. He gave instructions to send help to the waiting postilion and requested a fresh horse to continue.

"Sir, please, come inside and rest yourself by the fire. You're drenched through," a young serving wench said.

The girl's red hair only reminded him of Bea and how she outshined any other woman. He shook his head, "I must proceed, but a cup of hot tea while a horse is readied would be most appreciated."

She curtsied, leaving him to his thoughts. When she returned with his tea, he asked, "How far to London?"

"About five miles. There must be something very important to make you journey in such nasty weather."

Even amid the challenging situation, Laurence couldn't stop the smile pulling at his lips when he thought of Bea. "Yes. Someone very important."

The girl gave a knowing nod. "A woman, then. You must love her more than the moon."

He laughed at her choice of words. "More than the solar system."

"The wha'?"

"Never mind." He shook his head.

The groom entered, announcing the fresh horse was saddled and waiting. Laurence gulped down his hot tea and headed back out into the storm. With luck, in another hour or two, he'd have Bea back in his arms, telling her what a fool he'd been and how much he loved her.

⚜

MICHAELMAS HAD ARRIVED, AND BEA'S OWN SELF-IMPOSED DEADLINE loomed before her. Confident she'd finally discovered the correct combination of solutions, Bea worked at a frantic pace on the townhouse roof.

Dark clouds filled the sky, threatening foul weather. Yet she remained determined to finish the experiment before the storm hit. So heedless of the weather, she pressed forward, hoping the lantern she'd fortuitously brought up with her would not sputter out.

She'd obtained a plaster of Paris shell from Dr. Somersby, which —if her calculations were correct—would provide a sufficient barrier between solutions but be porous enough to allow the electron exchange necessary to eliminate the issue with the hydrogen bubbles. She assembled everything with utmost care, careful not to spill any of the solutions.

Although larger, her machine followed Laurence's design almost to the letter, except for the newly developed power source. A long, thin metal pole supported the perpendicular arm holding the wheel. Wires from the battery connected to the metal prongs at the base.

A crack of thunder sounded in the distance, and she hurried in her efforts. Storm clouds moved in from the north at a furious pace, and the temperature dropped, sending an icy chill through her. A sense of urgency propelled her. She connected the wires to the metal prongs. After carefully pouring the mercury solution into the contained reservoir on the platform, she quickly covered it with the metal plate she'd obtained.

Fat drops of rain splattered against the roof of the townhouse, producing a metallic pinging. Her rain sodden dress became heavy, and she struggled to pull the skirts from her legs so she could move. If only she had worn the trousers she'd often used as a disguise. Why did men have it so easy?

Lightning flashed less than a mile away, judging from the length of time until the clap of thunder echoed. Another bolt of lightning lit the sky, this time much closer.

"Not yet," she muttered, pleading with the ominous sky.

With everything connected, she backed up away from the machine, seeking shelter by the door to the roof, but the rain slashed at almost a perpendicular angle. She promised herself a warm bath once she'd completed the experiment. She squinted, watching for the beginning of movement.

There! The wheel began turning, slowly at first, then picking up speed. It worked. She pulled out the pocket watch and began timing how long the current would continue to propel the machine.

Sounds of shouting came from the street below. *What fool is out in this weather?* Strong wind fought her as she moved to the edge, climbing on the small wooden step to see who made such a commotion. A rider on horseback peered up, his hand shielding his eyes from the beating rain.

"Bea!"

Streaks of rain coated her spectacles, and she swiped a finger across the lenses in an attempt to clear them.

A deafening crack of thunder immediately followed a flash of light, illuminating and sizzling the air around her. The man dismounted his horse moments before an electric discharge from the nearby bolt of lightning landed on the metal pole and shot across the copper roof to her feet.

CHAPTER 29—A PRICELESS JEWEL

Mercilessly pushing the horse forward, Laurence raised a hand to shield his eyes from the pelting rain and peered up, catching sight of a light moving on the roof of his townhouse. *The motor.* Instinctively, he knew it was Bea testing her theory. When he drew the horse to a stop in front, he called out to her. Her figure appeared at the edge of the roof.

"Bea!" he repeated his frantic cry.

The horse shimmied and jerked its head. Laurence reined in the frightened animal and dismounted. Seconds later, thunder cracked, and a slash of lightning struck the neighboring townhouse. A smaller, spidery vein of the lightning bolt broke off, slicing across the gap between the houses, directly toward his own roof.

Panic gripped his chest like a vise, and he raced up the steps. Had she forgotten about the roof construction?

One of the maids left to attend to the upkeep on the home during his absence startled as he burst into the house. "Sir, we did not expect—"

Wasting no time on pleasantries or manners, he ignored her, taking the stairs two at a time up to the top floor. His heart beat faster than the hooves of the overburdened horse he'd ridden. Icy fear pricked his already soaked skin. Grateful the retractable steps were still down, he scrambled to the top.

At the entrance, he held onto the door frame, his boot hovering but a moment over the copper plated roof. Bea lay crumpled by the edge, and his racing heart stuttered to a stop. Without further regard to his own life or safety, he sprinted toward her.

He gathered her in his arms and patted her face. "Bea! My darling, can you hear me?" He placed his head near her heart, praying to hear the telltale thumping, but the only sounds were the pinging of the rain as it fell upon the roof and a familiar humming sound. His head jerked in the direction of the motor, and his eyes widened in surprise at the whirring wheel.

She'd done it. But at what cost?

A copper pot had tipped over, spilling shattered contents of a material he couldn't place. The moving wheel slowed, then came to a halt.

As gently as possible, he draped her over his shoulder to carry her inside and down the steps. The maid had followed him, no doubt concerned over the urgency in his expression, and waited at the bottom. Thankful he didn't have to summon her with the bell pull, he said, "Have a footman go to the clinic and fetch either His Grace or Dr. Somersby posthaste." He raced forward to take Bea to their bedroom, the maid on his heels.

"Sir, it's late. Surely the clinic is closed."

What had he been thinking? His mind was a morass of confusion and panic. "Of course. Now that I think about it, I believe His Grace returned to his estate in Kent for a few months. Go to Dr. Somersby's home." He laid Bea on the bed and retrieved pen and paper to jot down Dr. Somersby's address. Finished, he handed it to the maid with a final plea. "Tell the footman it's urgent."

"What about Lady Montgomery's wet clothes?"

"I'll take care of that. Now, go!" He practically pushed the poor woman from the room, praying the footman would locate Dr. Somersby quickly.

Time crept, his anxiety increasing as rain beat against the

windowpanes and the clock on the mantle ticked its torturous rhythm, marking the passing, vital seconds. Layers of Bea's sodden clothes lay on the floor by the bed where he'd carelessly tossed them, leaving her body cold to his touch. He toweled her dry and dressed her in a clean nightrail the maid provided.

The steady rise and fall of her chest and the faint thrum at her wrist reassured him she clung to life. Ends of her beautiful hair were singed, the smoky smell lingering. He continually called her name, stroking her hair and face, and cursing himself for being a dunderhead. When her eyelids fluttered, his hope rose, only to sink back when they failed to open.

Wax dripped in fat globs and the flames lowered on the candles by the bedside. *Where is Somersby?* He rose momentarily to stir the fire in the hearth. Even with the additional heat, Bea remained cool to the touch, and he tucked the counterpane around her.

At last, heavy footsteps and muffled voices echoed up the stairs. Dr. Somersby strode in, dripping wet and still wearing his greatcoat. He stripped it off and handed it to the maid before approaching the bed.

"What happened? The footman didn't provide details." Oliver set his medical bag on the bed and reached for Bea's wrist to take her pulse.

Laurence struggled to find the words. "I have a machine on the roof. Bea had an idea for a longer lasting power source. A lightning discharge traveled across the rooftop straight to Bea."

Oliver's eyes widened. "You allowed her to go outside in a lightning storm?"

As if he could stop Bea from doing what she wanted. If not for the seriousness of the situation, Laurence would have laughed at the absurdity. "We had been in Scotland on our honeymoon. There was . . . we argued, and Bea returned here to London. I had no idea what she planned."

The half-truth stuck in his throat.

Dr. Somersby pulled his stethoscope from his bag. "But you're here now."

"I realized I overreacted. I came to apologize."

As he examined Bea, a little smile crossed Dr. Somersby's lips. "A fine thing to learn when you're married. You'll find yourself doing it quite a lot. Good thing to practice early on."

Laurence stared. Was the man trying to be humorous at a time like this? When he opened his mouth to complain, Dr. Somersby held up a hand, effectively shushing him while he listened to Bea's heart.

"I was concerned about an erratic rhythm, but her heart is beating evenly. I'm afraid there's not much I can do until she wakes. Now, we wait."

Bea gained consciousness for a brief period, but was unable to answer any of Dr. Somersby's questions to test her memory and cognition. Then she drifted back into deep slumber.

At morning, when the sun's rays peeked through the slits in the curtains, announcing both the morning and the end to the terrible storm, Bea finally stirred, answering Dr. Somersby's questions to his satisfaction. After she whispered something in Oliver's ear, his eyes widened, and he practically threw Laurence from the room.

Fear gripped Laurence as he pressed his palms and forehead against the closed door. Long minutes passed, and he paced the hallway in front of the room, wondering what had the doctor so concerned. The odd squeezing in his chest turned to an almost unbearable pain. If this was what it meant to love someone, he wasn't certain he wanted it.

When Oliver allowed him to reenter, Laurence raced back to Bea's side. "What's wrong?" he asked, not removing his gaze from Bea's face.

Oliver snapped his medical bag closed, the tiny smile on his lips odd but reassuring. "I expect a full recovery. Don't press her with questions. She needs to rest. Allow her to sleep, but try to rouse her every few hours to make sure she hasn't lapsed back into unconsciousness. She'll be weak for some time. Be patient, make sure she receives some nourishing liquids, food if she'll take it. I'll check on her each day, but send for me immediately if she worsens or doesn't rouse."

After thanking Oliver, Laurence began his vigil, remaining by

Bea's bedside while she regained her strength, gaining consciousness in small stretches, only leaving her side during Oliver's examinations. He fed her broth, wiped her brow, even insisted on bathing her himself, much to Fanny's objection.

On the fifth day, he woke to a hand stroking his hair. He'd dozed off, his head resting on the bed beside her. Opening his eyes, he found her alert and watching him with a smile on her beautiful face.

"You're awake," he said, taking her hand and kissing it. "I'll call for someone to bring you something to eat." As he rose, she grasped his shirtsleeve, keeping him in place.

"That can wait," she said. "How long have you been sitting here?"

He stroked her hair. "Not that long. I'd sit here forever if necessary."

"Perhaps I should ask how long I've been in this bed?"

"Five days."

Her eyes widened. "Have you been here the whole time?"

"It was no hardship."

"Really?" She gave a tiny chuckle and ran a hand across his face, the bristles of his beard rasping against her fingers.

He returned her laugh. "Well, I might need a shave. I've sent Stevens away each time he insisted on seeing to my toilette. I didn't want to be away from you in the event you would awaken."

She turned her gaze away, focusing on her hands folded on top of the counterpane. "I know you're angry that I've deceived you about my articles as Only Bea."

"I never want you to use that signature again."

Her eyes widened, and she scooted away from him.

He'd botched it again. "What I mean is, you are not *only* Bea. Perhaps T.O.A.O.B.?"

"What in the world does that stand for?"

He lifted her hand and kissed her fingers. "The one and only Bea. There's no one like you. No one as brilliant as you." He swallowed, preparing for his apology. "I was wrong to ask you to be anything other than who you are. It's men like me who force women like you to hide behind embroidery hoops and garden parties even if you'd rather be on the floor of the Royal Society, contributing more than most men dream of in their lifetimes."

"I know I'm not what you expected as a wife. I'll never be like the duchess."

He shook his head, everything crystallizing before him. "I wouldn't want you to. I love *you*, Beatrix Marbry Townsend, Lady Montgomery. It's true I was enamored with Margaret for years. I saw her as the perfect wife, adept at all the social graces, of fitting neatly into my well-ordered life. But it's you, Bea, who've brought me *to* life. Who've upset the balance of my controlled existence. Yes, that's what it was, existence. Predictable, orderly, certainly, but boring. I don't only love you, Bea, I need you. You make me a better man."

❧

BEA QUESTIONED IF HER HEARING HAD BEEN AFFECTED BY THE lightning. "Would you mind repeating that?"

The warm, delicious chuckle she had sorely missed rang pleasantly in her ears, and his eyes sparkled. "Which part?"

"All of it, if you can remember, but especially the love part."

"Ah, you forget I have an uncanny memory." He tapped a finger to the side of his head. "Do you remember when I told you of my early memorization of a Shakespeare sonnet?"

She nodded.

"At that time, they were mere words. But now . . ."

He cleared his throat and recited.

> *Let me not to the marriage of true minds*
> *Admit impediments. Love is not love*
> *Which alters when it alteration finds,*
> *Or bends with the remover to remove.*
> *O, no! it is an ever-fixed mark*
> *That looks on tempests and is never shaken;*
> *It is the star to every wandering bark,*
> *Whose worth's unknown, although his height be taken.*

Love's not Time's fool, though rosy lips and cheeks
Within his bending sickle's compass come;
Love alters not with his brief hours and weeks,
But bears it out even to the edge of doom.
If this be error and upon me proved,
I never writ, nor no man ever loved.

"They are no longer only words, now they hold a deeper meaning." He kissed her lightly, then proceeded to repeat everything he'd said, ending with an additional, "I love you. Nothing will change that. Make no mistake, Bea, it will take me time to adjust to the fact my wife is more intelligent and capable than I am. But I will." He kissed her hand again. "And I shall be proud to admit it to all who will listen."

As Bea's mind cleared, she remembered Laurence standing in the rain outside of the townhouse moments before she'd lost consciousness. "The machine." She tried to sit up, but he placed gentle hands on her shoulders, keeping her still.

"Destroyed, I'm afraid. The lightning shattered the vessels with the solutions. Parts may be salvageable. But at the moment, it's useless."

Her heart tumbled. "Oh, no. It worked, Laurence. My idea worked."

"Then we shall rebuild it together." He paused, as if considering his words. "That is, if you will allow me to assist."

Those simple words exploded like a meteor shower in Bea's chest, filling her heart with so much love she believed it would burst from happiness. "Well, after all, it is *your* wager with Lord Nash, so you must take part."

The smile on his face vanished, his expression growing solemn. "Bea, about the wager. I hate to think my insensitive and prideful nature has sullied what we've . . . shared. Our time together has been the most beautiful of my life, and I will cherish each and every time whether or not we conceive a child."

Bea's face warmed. "About that."

"Shush. I'll find a way to pay Nash. I only feel responsible that

I've caused you so much pain. Unfortunately, the loss of the wager means your father's debt still stands."

She shook her head. "You haven't lost. If we can rebuild the machine, you will win the wager . . . on both counts."

Color drained from his face. "Wha . . . what?"

"Dr. Somersby confirmed it. I'm increasing. At first he'd been concerned, but he believes the danger of losing the baby has passed. He said I should expect to deliver sometime in March." Bea studied his face. "Perhaps you should lie down beside me. You appear ready to swoon."

The grin which spread across his face reminded her of Catriona's blue, paint-covered smile. He looked ecstatic.

"I trust this is good news?" she asked, teasing.

"I would say the best, but the best is that you love me. Nothing could be better than that." With care not to disturb her, he lay down next to her, wrapping her in his arms and kissing her soundly.

Her fingers raked across the stubble of his beard. "Perhaps you should allow Stevens to do his job. Your beard is rather scratchy." She sniffed, wrinkling her nose. "And one of us smells."

With a lift of his arm, he placed his nose by his armpit and inhaled. "Ah, that would be me. I've bathed you every day, but neglected my own ablutions." He rose from the bed. "I will see to it at once. In the meantime, someone is anxious to see you. I've selfishly kept him at bay. I do hope you'll forgive me."

As he strode toward the door, she wondered what visitor had been waiting. Once the door opened, Catpurrnicus raced into the room and leapt onto the bed, purring and licking her face. After turning in a circle precisely four times, he curled into a ball next to her.

"I shall leave you two and be back shortly." He exited the room, emitting a resounding sneeze.

"Oh dear, Purrny. We need to find a solution to Laurence's allergies." New confidence surged through her that with Laurence's support, she could do anything.

FOR THE NEXT WEEK, LAURENCE INSISTED BEA STAY IN BED AS HE tended to her every need, suffering countless sneezing spells as Catpurrnicus remained faithfully by her side. He found wearing a kerchief around his nose and mouth reduced the irritants somewhat, but Bea searched countless medical journals she'd borrowed from Harry to find a more effective remedy.

However, he did discover the kerchief provided unexpected side benefits.

"You look like a highwayman," she said in jest one day as he bent over her to adjust her pillow.

He wiggled his eyebrows playfully. "And what of value have you to give me, good lady?"

She threw the back of her hand to her forehead in dramatic fashion. "I have only myself, sir. I beg of you to show mercy."

"There is no *only* when it comes to you. For you are the most priceless of jewels."

Amid giggles and sneezes, the kerchief was discarded, and kissing and other affectionate activities commenced. Laurence permitted her to rise from the bed long enough to set Catpurrnicus outside to Essie's waiting care. A lightness he'd never experienced before filled his chest as he made love to Bea with no secrets between them and no wager to win. No monetary treasure had ever been as sweet.

When Bea had recovered fully, they focused their efforts on rebuilding the machine. On an uncommonly sunny October day, with hands on his hips, Laurence contemplated the genius of using the plaster of Paris inner shell as a barrier between the electrolyte solutions.

"You should do the honors and start it," Bea said, moving to the side, dressed in her own pair of breeches. Laurence had to admit, she filled them out quite nicely, making it difficult for him to concentrate on the task at hand.

"If you're certain." He waited for her confirmation, then attached the wires. "Ready?"

She nodded again, the pocket watch in her hand to mark the time.

They checked on the machine several times during the day, pleased it had well exceeded the amount of time the Voltaic pile had lasted.

Laurence tugged Bea to his side. "You did it!"

Placing her delicate hand on his chest, she shook her head. "*We* did it."

The pride flowing within him had nothing to do with the machine, although the prospect of becoming a father may have contributed slightly. Primarily, he reflected on his good fortune in managing to secure the most brilliant, loving, and wonderful woman in all of London as his wife.

And when his chest gave the—now—familiar squeeze, he welcomed it as confirmation that Bea had brought him to the fullness of life.

EPILOGUE

L aurence cleared his throat, his nerves calming as he gazed at Bea, standing to the side by her family. A brisk late October wind chilled the air, and Bea pulled the shawl closer around her body. At least the weather had cooperated, and other than a few puffy, non-threatening clouds, the day remained perfect for the demonstration.

Titters of excitement, or perhaps doubt, drifted from the crowd gathered on the terrace of his and Bea's townhouse. He had moved the machine to the yard to permit easier access to viewing. In addition to Bea's family, his own had assembled, along with Harry and Margaret, Andrew and Alice Weatherby, and Oliver and Camilla Somersby.

Manny, Harry and Margaret's ward, squatted before the machine, examining the construction. Camilla and Oliver's ward, Pockets—or rather Philip, Laurence couldn't get used to calling the boy by his new name—bent beside him, reaching out a hand to the attached wheel.

Victoria, Oliver's eldest daughter, scowled, her hands resting on her hips and the toe of her half boot tapping against the stone terrace. "Don't touch it, Pockets. You might break it."

"I'm only looking. Besides"—he swiped his hand across his nose—"Manny touched it."

"Manny's older," Victoria said as if that explained everything. She sent a doting look toward Manny.

Unease flitted in Laurence's stomach at the thought of dealing with a daughter in the throes of infatuation. He took solace in the fact he would at least have experienced friends to advise him. He scanned the group before him.

A fitting gathering for the occasion—family and friends.

Well, all except one. Off to the side by himself, Nash frowned, his arms crossed against his chest, most likely hoping to witness a complete failure.

"Thank you for attending, everyone. Bea and I are very proud of what we've accomplished." He held out his hand, beckoning her to join him. She deserved to be by his side. "I couldn't have done this without Bea."

She made him promise to take credit. He'd argued, saying he didn't deserve it, but had finally acquiesced, knowing her father's financial future was at stake.

Nash arched a dark eyebrow, but it didn't deter Laurence. He'd already prepared a way to handle Nash.

Once he connected the wires, power surged through the machine, turning the wheel. Unbeknown to Bea, he'd made a slight modification. Movement of the wheel cranked a gear, which opened a hidden compartment. Then, rising from the hiding place, a parchment appeared, the image of a woman holding a babe in her arms beautifully painted on its surface.

He grinned at Bea's wide-eyed expression. "I hope you don't mind. We did agree to tell everyone."

"Lord Montgomery, what an unconventional way of announcing it." Her smile sparkled with a promise of her appreciation to follow.

His mother shrieked, and his father wrapped an arm around her waist.

Miranda threw a hand to her mouth, her eyes glistening.

"Huzzah!" Timothy yelled.

"Another baby!?" Manny said. He turned toward Pockets, "We're being overrun with 'em."

Bea's mother wiped her eyes with her handkerchief, and her father beamed with renewed pride.

"When?" her mother asked, now clutching the handkerchief to her heart.

"Spring," Bea answered. "Dr. Somersby confirmed it."

Camilla swatted her husband on the arm, as if to chastise him for not sharing the information. Harry and Andrew hugged their respective wives.

And Laurence felt completely a part of them all.

Nash groaned and turned to storm off.

Stopping him, Laurence said, "A word before you leave, Nash. In private."

As everyone gathered around Bea, hugging and congratulating her, Laurence led Nash inside the house to his study.

"I'm surprised you didn't wish to gloat in public," Nash said, his tone as icy as the brisk winds outside. "I suppose I should offer my congratulations as well, but considering it's lost me forty thousand pounds, you'll understand if I withhold them."

Laurence pulled a bank note from his desk drawer. "This is for you. In fairness, Bea worked out most of the details of the power source, so guilt would haunt me if I accepted all the credit."

Nash's gaze darted to the note, his own eyes widening. "Ten thousand?"

"Not enough? I'm also expunging what you owe me. I believe it was three thousand, was it not?"

"It was." He tucked the note into his pocket. "I'm only wondering why."

"In honesty, I should give you more. The night of Bea's engagement ball, when she and I were . . . caught. You said I'd thank you later. It's my feeble attempt to show my appreciation for giving me something so valuable. In truth, no price would be enough."

Nash's lips twitched as if fighting a smile. "Perhaps a promise to lose a little more at the tables?"

"That I can't promise, but I may choose another table other than yours."

Nash held out his hand. "Agreed."

When Laurence grasped Nash's hand, an odd sense of peace settled over him. He pitied Nash and his lonely bachelor life.

When Nash turned to leave, he stopped in his tracks, his gaze traveling to the portrait adorning the wall of Laurence's study. "Well, I'll . . ." He jerked toward Laurence. "Is that her? Who painted that?"

Heat crept up Laurence's neck. How could he have forgotten the painting when he brought Nash into his study? But pride filled him that the beautiful woman gracing the canvas was his and his alone. "It is, and I did. As I said, I am thanking you."

Nash considered the painting a little longer than Laurence appreciated. "You have a gift, Montgomery. You've really captured her." He laughed and slapped Laurence on the back. "But you're right. You owe me more."

After Nash left, Laurence sighed as he gazed at Bea's seductive figure with Catpurrnicus curled by her side.

More than all the world.

⚜

BEA HAD NEVER BEEN COMFORTABLE BEING THE FOCUS OF ATTENTION, usually because some embarrassing incident had precipitated it. Yet, even in a more positive setting, with everyone embracing, congratulating, and praising her, a small part of her yearned to recede into the wallpaper, or—in this case—the shrubbery.

However, she smiled graciously, owing much of the liberating acceptance to Laurence, though he would deny responsibility. She'd grown confident in his love for her over the past weeks, giving her the strength to stand up to anyone—even her mother, who, at that moment, studied her with a serious expression.

"Beatrix, may I have a word in private?"

Bea narrowed her eyes, attempting to gauge the reason for her mother's request. "Very well. But if you intend to give me a lecture about proper comportment, you may wish to save yourself the trouble. I'm married to a man who loves me for who I am, lack of social graces and all."

Grasping Bea's elbow, her mother pulled her to the side. "It's not that . . . Bea. I wish to apologize. I truly believed I was fulfilling my duties as a mother when I . . . . discouraged your interest in science. But the truth of the matter is, I was jealous of you, of your determination to challenge society and follow your own path."

Her mother sighed. "As a girl, I hoped to become an author. Of course, until Miss Austen, it was a completely unacceptable and inappropriate ambition, especially for a girl born into the aristocracy. When I saw the heights you could reach, I had so many regrets. You were a constant reminder of what I left behind. It is a bitter pill for me, Bea, that I may have had potential to be great and wasted it."

Numbness fogged Bea's mind. For once in her life, she struggled to comprehend the meaning. Jealous? Of her? Her mother. An authoress? "It's not too late, Mother. I'm sure there are stories still flourishing in your mind you could put to paper. Why don't you try?"

As if twenty years melted from her mother's face, Bea gazed upon her as she must have appeared as a young girl—full of hope and promise of things yet to be.

Her mother giggled.

Giggled.

Like a debutante.

"Oh, I couldn't." She cast a sideways glance at Bea. "Could I?"

"Mother, you're a woman. Women can do anything."

Bea's spirit soared as if little wings had sprouted. Believing nothing could improve on the already perfect day, she blinked when Laurence emerged from the house with Catpurrnicus snuggled in his arms.

Bea waited for the subsequent sneezing to commence. Much to her surprise, no sternutation followed. Although moisture and slight redness rimmed his eyes, Laurence remained sneeze-free.

"I don't understand," she said, baffled at the improvement.

Timothy joined them. "It worked?"

"It would appear so," Laurence answered.

"Would someone explain what is happening?" Bea's mother asked, affronted not to be privy to the information.

"Timothy suggested a tea made from stinging nettles to treat my allergic reaction to Catpurrnicus," Laurence said. "My nose does still itch a bit, but it's much better than it was. And the tea doesn't taste half bad."

Harry patted Timothy on the back. "Excellent idea, Marbry. We could use a man like you at the clinic."

"I concur," Oliver said, exchanging a look with Harry.

Her mother threw up her hands. "I see I'm outnumbered once again. I suppose if a duke can be a physician, a viscount certainly can."

Bea's father chuckled. "Matilda, I'm still alive. He's not a viscount yet."

"I'll have to finish my studies and take the exams," Timothy said.

Harry held out his hand. "Then do that. But hurry. Dr. Mason grows more difficult by the day. Once you're finished, you'll have a position waiting for you at Hope Clinic."

Timothy held out his hand, palm down. "As we did as lads?"

Laurence shifted Catpurrnicus to one arm, then placed his hand on top of Timothy's. "You, too, Bea. You're part of this."

Bea placed her hand on top of her husband's, a sense of rightness and completion filling her.

They threw their hands in the air. "Huzzah!"

A perfect day indeed.

With the excitement of the day behind them, Bea and Laurence retired to their bedchamber. Although the tea had reduced Laurence's reactions to Catpurrnicus, he requested Essie keep him for the night.

At her dressing table brushing her hair, Bea glanced up, catching Laurence's reflection in the mirror. Dressed in the same banyan he'd worn on their wedding night, he removed the brush from her hand and proceeded to complete the task himself.

"I love your hair," he whispered, leaning down to kiss her throat. "I love *you.*"

She turned to face him and moved to stand, but he kept her in place. His expression grew serious, and her heart gave an erratic thump.

"Bea, when you left Glenhame, I found your wedding ring on the dressing table in your bedroom. It broke my heart. But when I looked at that plain gold band, it gave me pause."

He knelt before her, taking her hands in his. "The ring was as lackluster and unromantic as my proposal. You deserve so much more. Being the perfectionist I am, I would appreciate another crack at it." He pulled out a ring from the pocket of his banyan.

Emeralds and diamonds glittered around the gold band. "Beatrix Marbry Townsend, you are by far the most wonderfully unusual woman I know. You pushed me beyond the bounds of my comfort, and in doing so, you made me open my eyes to all the glorious possibilities life has to offer. Will you marry me?"

She laughed. "We're already married."

As he slipped the ring on her finger, he chuckled, the deep, sensual sound sending gooseflesh up her arms. "Which makes it ever so convenient because it means we can skip right to the wedding night."

He pulled her into his arms, sending all rational thought from her mind, save but one.

She was very, very grateful to have been born a woman.

Saving her reputation, he lost his heart

Scan the QR code below to continue the journey of the Hope Clinic with *Saving Miss Pratt*.

Saving Miss Pratt

I hope you enjoyed Laurence and Bea's story. Would you like to have a peek into their future? Sign up for my newsletter to keep apprised of new releases and to receive a free bonus scene (as well as other freebies).

Simply scan the following QR code.

Healing the Viscount's Heart Extended Epilogue

If you've jumped into the series mid-way, find out how it all started with *The Reluctant Duke's Dilemma.*

You can find it on Amazon, or scan the QR code below:

The Reluctant Duke's Dilemma

Lastly, if you enjoyed Bea and Laurence's story, why not let other readers know by leaving an honest review. Scan the code below to take you to the review page. Easy peasy.

Healing the Viscount's Heart

AUTHOR NOTES

❦

I won't lie. When I started writing *The Reluctant Duke's Dilemma*, Beatrix Marbry was only supposed to be an incidental character, designed to illustrate how many women poor Harry had to deal with as he navigated the rough waters of the Marriage Mart. She wasn't even shown in the book, only mentioned. (I'm so sorry, Bea).

However, by the time I finished *The Reluctant Duke's Dilemma*, my critique group started asking me if I had books planned for the other characters. So with their encouragement, I sat down and planned out a five book series (plus the prequel novella with Andrew and Alice—so six total). I use "planned" in the loosest sense possible. I am <u>not</u> a plotter. I'm a discovery writer, and my characters will often direct how the story goes. Sometimes they misbehave badly.

As I thought about the subsequent books, various parts of *TRDD* sparked my imagination, making Bea come to life.

Harry and Margaret discuss her during their carriage ride home right before their fateful night together. (Sigh, I loved that part. Harry is so romantic). Margaret mentions that if Bea's mother would allow her to wear her spectacles perhaps she wouldn't fall so much. Later, as Margaret and Camilla are discussing the latest gossip, Camilla mentions Bea's fall into the rose bushes.

So I began to wonder. What makes Bea fall all the time? Is it really because she can't see well? And why doesn't her mother want her to wear her spectacles. Margaret mentions she overhears Laurence's grandmother (the Dowager Countess Easton) mention that Bea's mother doesn't want people to think her daughter is a bluestocking, and Harry states he doesn't understand the belief that men don't find intelligent women attractive.

Bea began to take shape, coming to life in my mind.

Then there was poor Laurence. A good guy who always seemed to lose out (when it came to Margaret, that is). When I began writing *No Ordinary Love*, it hit me like the proverbial Mack truck. Bea is in love with Laurence—and she stumbles whenever he's around. So in the first chapter of *No Ordinary Love* there is a not so subtle hint about Bea and Laurence, as well as Bea's interest in all things scientific.

Bea simmered in my mind while I wrote *A Doctor For Lady Denby*, and the more she simmered, the richer she became. I developed a deep kinship with her and her struggle to be accepted in a man's world. Which led me to be completely confident that the perfect man for her (or perhaps she is more the perfect woman for him) was Laurence Townsend, with all his rules and stringent adherence to propriety. What better conflict than a man who lives by rules and a woman who breaks them. She does indeed make him a better man by the end of the book.

I loved these two characters so much, and I hope you did, too. I'm sure you'll see them make guest appearances in the upcoming books. Like Harry, Margaret, and Manny (and Pockets—gosh, I love that child) they always remind me to include them.

Another quick word about characters. I realize some of my readers may be very angry with Lord Saxton and his selfishness of using Bea to get out of a situation of his own making. I don't disagree with these readers. We should be outraged. I know it might be particularly hard because other fatherly characters have been painted in a much more favorable light—I'm thinking of Camilla's father, Lord Harcourt.

However, when creating characters, I try to take into consideration not only their personalities, which include not only their strengths *and* their flaws, but also remain mindful of the time in which they lived and the pressures they may have had due to their social standing.

Being of the peerage, neither Lord Saxton nor his family could be thrown into debtor's prison (I had to do some digging on this), but being financially ruined would not only affect him and his family, but all those he employed, and indirectly his tenants as most peers were landowners. So as harsh as Saxton's actions were with regard to Bea, he truly would have been desperate because not only his life and well-being hanged in the balance, but the lives of those who depended upon him. Bea would have realized this as well.

But take heart, dear reader, Lord Saxton's arc is not complete. We shall see more of him in the next book, and hopefully you'll derive a little satisfaction as he comes to truly understand the consequences of his actions.

On another note, I can't tell you the amount of time I spent researching women in science during the early 1800s and scientific articles, especially those of early motors and batteries. What Bea "invents" is kind of a combination of the Daniell Cell and the Porous Pot batteries, both of which were right around the time period of the story—so her solution is quite feasible. I did play around a bit with the idea of Bea coming up with something similar to the Tesla coil, but the time necessary for her to build it and test it before Laurence arrived to her "rescue" wasn't plausible. But it sure would have made my insistence on involving lightning a whole lot easier. (smiley face here).

I tried to keep things realistic, but I did take some creative license.

Thank you again for reading and for sharing what was, for me, a rather personal exposition.

DISCUSSION QUESTIONS

1. Bea struggles through the story to win the approval from those she loves: Laurence, her mother, her father, Timothy, her friends. Discuss what it means to you to be worthy. Things to consider: Is it based on accomplishments, or something more intrinsic and intangible?
2. Have you ever struggled to be worthy?
3. As Bea struggles with her own self-worth, do you think her view on what makes her worthy changes in the course of the story? If so, what do you think was the precipitating factor?
4. Have you ever been in a situation where you felt you had to hide who you were? How did you handle it?
5. Laurence finds security in structure and rules. When, if ever, do you feel it's acceptable to bend or break the rules?
6. As a man of his times, Laurence struggles with Bea's identity as O.B. Do you think things have improved in

the last almost two hundred years or are women still disparaged and dismissed? What can we do as a society to make things better?

7. Bea feels guilty when she decides to sabotage her engagement to Lord Middlebury. Do you think her guilt is justified? Would you have done the same thing?

ALSO BY TRISHA MESSMER

<u>The Hope Clinic Series</u>

No Ordinary Love (Prequel Novella)

The Reluctant Duke's Dilemma

A Doctor For Lady Denby

Healing The Viscount's Heart

Saving Miss Pratt

Redeeming Lord Nash

Coming Soon

<u>The London Ladies' League</u>

A Duke In The Rough

<u>Different World Series (Contemporary Romance):</u>

The Bottom Line

The Eyre Liszt

Look With Your Heart

ABOUT THE AUTHOR

Trisha Messmer had a million stories rattling around in her brain. (Well, maybe a million is an exaggeration but there were a lot). Always loving the written word, she enjoyed any chance she had to compose something, whether it be for a college paper or just a plain old email. One day as she was speaking with her daughter about the latest adventure going on in her mind, her daughter said, "Mom, why don't you write them down." And so it began. Several stories later, she finally allowed someone, other than her daughter, to read them.

After that brave (and very scary) step, she decided not to keep them to herself any longer, so here we are.

She hopes you enjoy her musings as much as she enjoyed writing them. If they make you smile, sigh, hope, and chuckle or even cry at times, it was worth it.

Born in St. Louis, Missouri, Trisha graduated from the University of Missouri – St. Louis with a degree in Psychology. Trisha's day job as a product instructor for a software company allowed her to travel all over the country meeting interesting people and seeing interesting places, some of which inspired ideas for her stories. A hopeless (or hopeful) romantic, Trisha currently resides in the great Northwest.

Made in United States
Troutdale, OR
04/30/2024

19557238R00169